"Look," Dylan said, coming to a halt before her, "I have no idea what's going on here. But for some reason things are going very, very well."

"They are," Penny agreed.

"I don't want that to stop. We have no business being in the FA Cup fifth round, none at all. We've had an extraordinary run of luck, but we've been playing really well, too."

Dylan paced another lap, his muttering growing louder.

"Maybe I'm being greedy but fuck it, I'm not in the habit of looking a gift horse in the mouth. The fifth round is in three weeks and we will absolutely get our arses kicked because no top tier club is going to make the mistake Nicholas Reef made today. But until then we need our playing ground."

"What do you want to do?" Penny asked.

Dylan stared down at her, his gaze dancing with mischief. "I want to keep playing. What do you want to do?"

Penny picked up the golden torc, stretching the ancient necklace between her fingers. "I want to keep digging."

CUP-TIED

Kingsbury Town Football Club Romance
— Book Three —

Marina Reznor

Cup-Tied

Kingsbury Town Football Club Romance Series, Book 3

ISBN: 979-8-9850984-0-2 (eBook)

ISBN: 978-0-9994297-9-2 (Paperback)

Editor: David Ballheimer

Cover design: UpdateDiva Design

Back cover photo credit: DBeechPhotography, used by kind permission

Published by Kingsbury Town Press LLC

Birmingham, Alabama

Kingsburytownpress.com

For Moose

Chapter One

Penny Adams crouched on the hill that overlooked London from the north. Her stomach growled—it was still on Central Daylight Time and demanding breakfast. She reached into the duffle bag she'd dropped on the grass next to her and unwrapped a granola bar and nibbled on it. There were three left, and they'd have to hold her for four days.

Her watch said it was after four-thirty in the afternoon, but the setting sun made it seem later. She freed her long hair from the braid keeping the thick curls tamed and massaged her scalp.

Further down the hill, a Saturday afternoon soccer match was being played by Icelton Football Club in a shabby stadium called Mortager Park. Concrete stands with rusted roofs lined three sides of the field and a cinder block clubhouse ran along the fourth. Lights around the perimeter attempted to illuminate the field but only half were working. An occasional blast from the referee's whistle was followed by moans from the sparse crowd.

The gravel parking lot beside the stadium was half-empty, and even from this distance Penny could see it was badly rutted.

Excellent.

Penny yawned. She'd been traveling for over thirty-six hours and had only gotten fragmented sleep. Her stomach rumbled again, but she ignored it and drew her sweatshirt around her, wishing she'd brought a warm coat. Who knew London in late October would be so cold? At home it was still warm, almost an Indian summer. The kids trick-or-treating wouldn't need jackets.

Next to the stadium was a dilapidated foundry surrounded by a sagging chain-link fence. It enclosed several one-story brick buildings and a weed-filled scrap yard. The north sides of the buildings were moss covered, and several windows were broken and boarded up. Penny noted the garbage strewn everywhere and was offended. A faded sign over the locked gate read: 'Icelton Aeronautics Foundry & Casting Works, Ltd'.

She knew there was a stream lined with scrubby overgrowth beyond the foundry. You probably couldn't see it unless you were on top of it, but aerial digital imagery saw it. The stream was called the Silk, and it had been much larger a long time ago. A very, very long time ago.

Behind Penny was the castle on the hill, silhouetted against dark clouds. The turrets were made of white marble, and banners even fluttered from the tops like a real fairy-tale castle. When the sun managed to break through, the gold roundels at the top glistened.

It was exactly the way she said it would be.

———◆———

Another burst of booing erupted from the soccer match below.

Icelton Aeronautics Foundry, Penny's research had revealed, had been established in 1915 to service the Royal Air Force station just to the east, in Hendon. The foundry had prospered during the two wars and in between, at its peak running three shifts a day and employing over five hundred workers, many of whom probably lived in the rows of neat townhouses across the road. The British called them terraces. Penny had no idea why—they looked perfectly level to her.

The little village of Icelton had grown along with the foundry until it was now part of the urban sprawl that radiated out from London. The land the foundry sat on sloped to the Welsh Harp Reservoir, which two thousand years ago had been swamp. The land had been drained in the Dark Ages by local Anglo-Saxons who had moved into the area abandoned by the Romans.

Remarkably, Penny had been able to travel there from the airport easily by train and subway, notwithstanding having to hunt for the Northern Line at Leicester Square Station. The network of underground trains that crisscrossed the huge city was marvelous, easily dwarfing the L in Chicago, which Penny had ridden once when her high school debate team had gone to the city for a competition. To be able to go so far so fast without having to drive your car was incredible.

Penny consulted the map she had drawn. It all fit—the stream to the left ran northeast to southwest, the ancient Roman road was a half-mile to the east, and the gap in the hills that everyone had ignored was five miles directly north.

The knoll she was sitting on was at the southern tip of the Edgware plain, and clearly matched the description in Tacitus of the wide, flat area where the last battle took place. It really wasn't much of a plain, she decided, but

Tacitus was relating the story second-hand, probably from his father-in-law Agricola, who was present at the battle. The Romans had hidden in the gap between Barnet Gate hill and Highwood Hill, watering their horses in the pokey little Dollis Brook stream and waiting for her to return to London after burning St Albans to the ground.

Which, in Penny's opinion, St Albans had coming.

Professor Jain, along with all the other First Century AD Romano-British scholars, had overlooked this part of England. Instead, they were focusing on Mancetter as the site of the last battle, a hundred miles northwest and in Penny's opinion, obviously incorrect. The Corieltauvi tribe, who had occupied that area, didn't have a good relationship with the Iceni tribe, who were from Norfolk. The Iceni, in turn, only had a tenuous relationship with the Romans, who had moved onto their lands and were making pests of themselves. The Corieltauvi had welcomed the Romans in 44 AD and the 14th Gemina legion was garrisoned in Mancetter, for heaven's sake. There was nothing for her and her people to the north. She was heading back to London when she encountered the Romans.

If the Rhea family had built that foundry only two hundred yards to the west in 1915, they would have found the burial site. Instead they had built the playing field and stadium, and sometime after World War II dumped several tons of gravel to make the parking lot.

She was close.

Penny checked her watch and re-braided her hair while she listened for the long whistle blast that signaled the end of the match. When it finally came, she stood and brushed the grass off herself and swung the duffle bag over her shoulder, taking care to avoid the sharp end of the pick-axe wrapped inside. She headed down the hill, tucking her long braid into the hood of her sweatshirt and pulling it up around her face.

In the pocket of her jeans were four small stones, each painted with bright yellow nail polish.

Chapter Two

"*AH, THE BRAVEST SIGHT in the world is to see a great man struggling against adversity,*" Len Case quoted, clapping Dylan Rhea on the back with a bit more force than was necessary.

Dylan sat at a table in the Icelton clubhouse and stared straight ahead, watching the football club supporters mob the bar after the loss to visiting Thurrock FC. They didn't bother to mask their dark grumbling about the team's performance and the obvious unfitness of the current manager.

Which would be himself.

They were also loudly voicing their displeasure with the team's owner, noting his poor choice of players and lack of organizational skills.

Which would also be himself.

He was, Dylan knew, responsible for the entire mess. Which was the least of his problems.

"How about a pint then, lad?" Len said, helping himself to the seat next to Dylan. "You've certainly earned it. I don't think Icelton has had as bad a home defeat since before your dad and I played."

Dylan shook his head and nodded at the energy drink he clasped in his hand. "I don't drink while I'm training."

Len chuckled and sipped his beer. "Yes, but it might have helped your tactics. Today was a disgrace."

Dylan let that pass. What Dad had seen in Len was lost on him.

"Dylan, lad, it's time you got on with your life. You know your dad would have wanted that," Len continued. "*While we are postponing, life speeds by.*"

The dull ache behind Dylan's eyes began to pound. The asshole had a Seneca quote for every occasion. "Dad left me the club. I have to do right by it."

"So he did, God rest his soul. But you're making a hash of it."

"We've qualified for the first round proper of the FA Cup next week. That should count for something."

"Icelton has qualified three times in the last ten years. And bowed out just as fast," Len countered, warming to the subject.

Dylan shifted in his chair. "We're a Tier Seven club. Our players have day jobs. It's not as ordinary as you make it out to be."

Len nodded. "You're right. But Dylan, look at the toll it's taking. You look like you haven't been to the barber in ages, nor eaten a decent meal. You can't be owner and manager, it's too much. At least look for a new manager."

Dylan knew they couldn't afford it. The last manager, a very decent bloke, had waited weeks to be paid before finally getting a better offer at a Tier Eight club in Essex. The team physio had gone with him, with apologies, and two assistant coaches. Dylan couldn't blame them.

"Or sell up," Len continued. "The club would fetch good money. I've told you, I know a very generous buyer. He's ready to take everything off your hands—the ground, the foundry, the club, everything."

"It's not for sale."

"He'll give you top money. In cash."

"I said, it's not for sale."

Len sipped his beer while the muted big screen television on the wall played the evening's sports recaps. "I feel terrible having to press you to repay the loan."

Dylan forced himself to relax his jaw, shifting it side to side to try to break his unconscious habit of grinding his teeth. "You will be paid."

"Yes, of course. It's just, I'm a bit pinched myself. I owe others. And your dad, he was sure he'd have me repaid within a year," Len Case paused. "A quarter of a million pounds is a lot of money, Dylan. Even for you. Especially now, since you've quit Kingsbury Town."

"Retired."

"Yes, retired. Of course. But still, you've not got a tremendous Premier League paycheck coming in every week."

As if Dylan needed to be reminded. And contrary to rumor, it hadn't been a staggering figure. Sir Frank Poleski, Kingsbury Town Football Club's owner, liked you to show a bit of what you got before ramping up the salary. But by Icelton standards, he had lived like a king.

A gaggle of young women approached the table holding a plastic bucket decorated with "Snowball Fund" in jolly script. They were dressed in matching green and grey tracksuits that informed everyone they were from the Icelton Girls' Under 18 team, with their names embroidered under the crest—*Chloe, Kristie, Charvi, Kiva,* and *Cassie*—and their hair pulled back into identical ponytails. "Come on, gents, cough up for the Snowball!"

"Yes, time for the Snowball!" they chorused. "Dig deep!"

Oh, Jesus. Dylan did the calculations in his head. By club rules, the team owner—himself—had to donate fifteen quid for every goal the opponents scored, regardless of the result. That was doubled if Icelton lost and quadrupled if they failed to score. The final score had been four-nil, so he had to plunk in two hundred and forty pounds.

Dylan pushed his chair back and went to Dad's office, now his office. It was more of a cubbyhole in the pass-through to the boiler room behind it, but it did feature a tiny private bathroom which Dylan's bladder demanded he visit. Again. He was tempted to brush his teeth, but the jar of tooth powder in the medicine cabinet was empty and he had left the vial he carried with him in his jacket back at the table.

The petty cash box in the bottom desk drawer was almost empty, as was his wallet. Dylan took the remaining notes and added them to what he had in his pocket, the total exceeding what he owed the Snowball Fund by exactly £2.07. His billfold yawned back at him and he was struck by the realization he'd left tips bigger than this when he and Sue had been out on the town.

Now the club was broke, and he was right behind.

"What's the total?" Len Case asked the girls as Dylan returned and deposited the roll of bank notes in the bucket.

They turned to their team captain, Chloe, who took out her mobile phone and tapped some numbers.

"Just short of five thousand quid. We get half at the final drawing Tuesday night, and if the guys keep losing like this, we'll be touring the States in style next summer," she announced with satisfaction.

"Luck is what happens when preparation meets opportunity!" Len quipped. "And if the rest of the season continues to be the disaster we had today, you young ladies will be able to afford to hire a limousine to drive you around."

A player passed by, heading for the clubhouse exit. "Tamba! A quick word, please." Dylan's tone made clear the invitation was non-negotiable.

"Yeah, boss?"

"You ended up an auxiliary full-back today."

"Sorry, boss."

"Thurrock saw you coming a million miles away—you telegraphed every move. And why did you get so jammed up in the box? Monday at practice, we need to work on the right side in attack and defense."

"Can't do Monday, Boss," the player apologized. "I've got an audition in Ealing after I'm done with the bakery deliveries."

"Somebody making a movie about a striker who can't win crosses?" Len asked.

"No," Tamba replied, oblivious to Len's sarcasm, "It's the next James Bond movie, they're casting hundreds. My agent said I might even get to read lines for a proper role, like a waiter or a policeman."

Dylan rolled his eyes and took a deep pull on the straw of his energy drink, grimacing as the dull green liquid ran down his throat. Funny thing, it actually did give him energy, but in a strange, artificial way. Sue drank lots of it herself, but it had never seemed to make her run to the loo every twenty minutes.

"You know, Dylan, when your dad and I played, there was a striker from Corinthian-Casuals, used to get our number every time. Every bloody time!" Len hooted. "There was a match, right before you were born if I'm remembering, where..."

As Len droned on, Dylan saw the clubhouse door open and a girl slip in. The hood of her sweatshirt was pulled up so he couldn't see her face, but he could see she was tall, taller than any of the players on the girl's team. When she pushed the hood back, her hair looked blonde in the dimly lit doorway, but as she walked into the club the overhead lights showed it was more ginger. No, copper actually.

Len drifted off to chat with friends, and Dylan watched the girl with mild curiosity. He'd never seen her before. This in itself was a novelty—he'd known everyone in the clubhouse practically his entire life. She wasn't from Thurrock—they'd gotten changed, had a friendly drink, and left an hour ago. She was too young to be one of the mums, and he knew all the players' wives and girlfriends.

There was still a crowd at the bar and she approached Harry Goodnaught, the club kitman. He smiled and sized her up, the daft old bugger—she was young enough to be his granddaughter. They chatted for a moment, and Harry turned and nodded towards Dylan. The girl followed his indication and looked Dylan straight in the eye.

A strange chord plucked Dylan's heart, a feeling he would remember for the rest of his life. It was a pleasant sensation, and for someone who'd been feeling like shit for so long, it wasn't unwelcome.

She made her way towards him, walking with an economy of movement that was alien to him. It was more of an amble, like the way people moved in western movies, when they needed to be somewhere but had all day to get there.

"Dylan Rhea?" The girl was before him, and he realized he had stood to meet her. "I'm Penny Adams."

She came to his shoulder, and he was a tall man. Up close he could see her hair was many shades of copper and ginger, and the word tawny popped into his head. Yes, that was it. Her eyes seemed to match the color of her hair. Remarkable.

He glanced down and saw her hand had been extended for some moments. "Yes, pleased to meet you. Penny." He engulfed her hand in his, her fingers fine and slim. "What can I do for you?"

"I'm from Princeton College," she said. Her voice was soft, her American accent flat. "Where I'm a doctoral candidate in Histeogeography. We're doing a soil survey of north London, and I've been assigned this quadrant. With your permission, I'd like to make four small test bores in your parking lot, sixteen inches in diameter by three feet deep, and take samples."

She set a large bag on the floor with a clank and pulled out a rolled-up piece of paper.

"My field of research is Roman and post-Roman Britain," she continued, unrolling a map on the table, "With the advent of high definition satellite imagery, we've concluded that this area, here, might contain very important evidence of Roman occupation in what is now north London."

Dylan struggled to focus on the map before him. "That's the car park for my football club."

"Yes, indeedy! This corner, here, the northeast one, is of the interest. You're a very busy man, so I won't go into boring details, but if you permit me to take the samples, I can cross it off my list and move on to the next site."

The girl tilted her head so that Dylan got the full effect of the twinkle in her eyes and the pleasant curve of her full lips. He realized his mouth was very dry.

"To sites that are of more interest to us," the girl added when he didn't answer. "Of much more interest."

Dylan forced his attention back to the black and white aerial map. It was outdated by at least twenty years, but the fifteen acres the stadium and foundry sat on had barely changed. Dylan's mobile rang and he ignored it.

"As you can see," Penny continued, drawing a finger across a wide swath of Hendon, Icelton, and Wembley, "this area is the Harwich Formation, which is clay from the Paleogene era. As I'm sure you know, the soil here is composed of glauconitic sandy clay and pebble beds of black flint, calcareous and ferruginous cement—"

His stomach began to clench. Was it just him, or was she talking faster?

"—which is fairly homogeneous, but we've detected a unique outcropping of Bracklesham Group characterized by a finer-grained quartz sand containing zircon and tourmaline."

Dylan fought back rising nausea as he struggled to untangle the jumble of words spewing from her. "This part here, over by Hendon Park," he interrupted. "You've circled that as well. And there."

"Yes. Originally it was thought that the Bracklesham sub-group was pre-Anglian clay and that flint deposits were only in the northeast of this region because it's a heterogeneous, unbedded residual deposit formed by the solifluctions of the original Paleogene deposits."

How the hell did she say that without drawing breath?

"—but aerial surveillance has revealed an exciting vein of Triassic sandstone with evidence of a fluvial deposition."

Jesus, her words were beating against his head like a drum. The technical gobbledy-gook continued to pour out of her mouth at an alarming rate.

"Luckily, the Quaternary layer is very thin in this region. At the base there is a layer of manganese precipitated by groundwater with a green glauconitic cortex that we think was subjected to several periods of periglacial activity." She paused and smiled. "I just need to dig a small sample to confirm it didn't come this far west, and I can be on my way."

The girl stood there expectantly, the tip of her index finger pressed on the image of his car park. His brain refused to function. "I need to brush my teeth."

Chapter Three

DYLAN RHEA GRABBED HIS jacket and disappeared down a corridor. Penny stood by the table, afraid to breathe.

Please, please, please.

Had her well-rehearsed babble of geological jargon convinced him she was a doctoral candidate at a prestigious university? Which was the furthest thing from the truth that existed.

Dylan returned several minutes later, focused and alert. His eyes, she had noted when she met him, were bloodshot and red rimmed. So, a druggie. She had read rumors in the online British tabloids. That might be a help.

He pointed at the map. "You want to dig some holes in my car park to see about some mud layers."

Amen. "Yes."

"Are you here with a team?"

"I'm the send-first girl. The rest will come after me. I'll do a quick evaluation of your site and cross it off the list."

Dylan looked at the map again, his dark eyes darting around the random circles Penny had drawn. He pointed to one.

"That site is of much greater importance than yours," Penny lied. "With your permission, I'll dig four holes, sixteen inches in diameter and a yard deep, here," she pointed, "here, here, and here. It won't take more than a few hours, and I will fill the holes in and then be off."

"You'll dig the holes? There's nothing but stones and gravel out there, love." Dylan surveyed her critically from head to foot. "It would take you a week."

"I'm stronger than I look. And I brought my own pick-axe."

He rubbed his hand over the stubble of beard on his jaw. "Shouldn't you have some kind of letter of introduction?"

Reaching into her jacket, Penny extracted an envelope and flourished it before him, revealing a letter with the words 'Princeton' and 'College' before she tucked it back into the envelope and slipped it in her pocket. "We're doing over fifty sites, and I have a long list."

"You're not the first one who's come here wanting to dig in my car park, you know."

Penny's jaw dropped in astonishment.

"Ever since they dug up King Richard III in that car park in Leicester," Dylan continued, "I've had every loony in England thinking they'll find another king."

Penny didn't flinch. "I'm not a loony."

"You're a lot more persistent than the rest, I'll give you that. Look, I appreciate you coming all this way to dig a few holes, but the answer is no. The lads play twice a week—"

—*lose twice a week*, Penny thought to herself.

"—and I can't have the car park torn up. So the answer is no."

"I can do it in two hours. Three, tops."

"When did you want to do this?"

Penny rolled the map up and stashed it in her bag. "Now."

"The car park is as hard as cement."

"And as holey as Swiss cheese!" A rotund man with a red face snorted, appearing at Dylan's elbow. "Pleased to meet you, I'm Len Case. Who's our new friend, Dylan?"

━━◆━━

Screeching feedback filled the clubhouse as Ned, the goalkeeper, broke out the karaoke machine and was warming up to "Bohemian Rhapsody" by Queen, with the Icelton midfielders as his backup singers.

Dylan grabbed Penny's bag and steered her by the arm through the clubhouse to the back door stoop off the kitchen. It was quieter there and out of ear-shot of nosy supporters.

A small awning shielded them from the drizzle that was turning into a steady rain in the early evening darkness.

"Now tell me again, what do you want to do?" Dylan demanded now that his head was clearer.

"Over there," the girl pointed to the car park, "we need four soil samples. With your permission. Look, I've brought my digging tools," she pointed to the duffle bag. "And I'll refill the holes as soon as I'm done."

"But it's pouring with rain."

She flashed him a teasing smile that seemed rehearsed. "I don't melt."

Something was very, very wrong. "No."

"Excuse me, but why? This is, this is part of an important geologic survey," she was saying, her voice speeding up, "and absolutely no damage will be done to your lot. The data we obtain will be entered into a matrix of hundreds of sites all across the greater north London area, and correlated with—"

"Passport." Dylan snapped, cutting her off before she could begin that incessant technobabble again.

It took her a moment to retrieve it from the depths of her bag. Feeling hyper alert, Dylan noted that Penny seemed to be moving slower. When she finally produced the passport, he snatched it out of her hand and examined it closely.

"You just got this passport."

She didn't reply to that.

"Let me see that letter again."

He scrutinized the paper she handed him. "Penny Adams, from Princeton College," he read, pointing at the letterhead. "Princeton is in Indiana?"

Penny nodded.

"I thought it was near... New York City or somewhere."

"It's easy to get mixed up. America is a big place. Indiana is quite close to New York."

To whom it may concern... please permit Miss Adams to sample the geographic area... you are entitled to be notified of the results... our utmost gratitude for your cooperation... the signature was a scribble across the name of some dean.

Dylan pocketed the letter, noting that the rain had picked up. "It's too wet. Come back Monday."

"I'll be digging elsewhere on Monday. I have a lot of sites to sample. It's best if you let me do it now."

The girl stood before him, meeting his gaze straight on with silent intent. Her eyes, the color of topaz, held his own and Dylan felt like she was looking straight into his soul.

Sue had never looked at him the way this girl was. Sue's gaze twinkled blue, darting everywhere, noticing every-thing, always two steps ahead. This was different.

In the forced confines of the tiny porch, Dylan felt a stirring within him, like a cobra that had been sleeping for a long time suddenly awakening and uncoiling as he stood over her.

"No. And that's final." Dylan had no idea why he was being such a hard ass. In reality, the girl wasn't asking for anything that would cause a fuss. But something just wasn't right.

He knew he should just walk away, go back in the clubhouse, close the door behind him and leave her to her business. But he stood rooted to the ground, standing over her, a volley of sensations ricocheting through him, disjointed and confusing and damnably pleasurable.

The fresh scent of the rain mixed with the warmth of her skin and the feel of her breath against his cheek. A miraculous flush of pure desire overwhelmed him, and before he knew it, he snatched the girl to him and kissed her.

Dylan felt the intake of her breath as his lips closed over hers. Caught off-guard, her hands went to his chest. He steadied her, pulling her against him. The taste of her was fresh and sweet, and for an instant, he lost himself in her. God, it had been so long.

Penny pushed him away, hard. He released her immediately, shocked at his reaction.

Her eyes blazed. "I haven't come four thousand miles for a make-out session on a back porch."

"I'm, I'm so sorry," Dylan attempted to apologize. "I don't know what came over me."

Without a word, she grabbed her bag, spun on her heel, and disappeared into the night.

Chapter Four

It wasn't just luck that there was no moon out that night. Penny had specifically planned the trip around a new moon and the heavy cloud cover was an added bonus, although the rain was a nuisance. As she walked away from the Icelton clubhouse, she also noted there were no lights around the parking lot, an unexpected bonus, and that it was lined by a mature twenty foot hedge.

Penny spat the metallic peppermint taste of Dylan Rhea into the hedge, wiped her lips, and began walking a broad zigzag pattern through the parking lot. Counting her steps, she dropped the yellow painted stones at exact intervals, carefully skirting the few remaining cars, until she ended up in the southwest corner.

She rejected the idea of stashing the duffle bag filled with digging equipment under a thick part of the hedge to save herself the effort of lugging it back to Hendon and back out later that night. Instead, she shouldered the load, her back aching after carrying it with her on the fifteen-hour bus ride from Evansville, through two transfers, before ending up at the airport in Chicago.

At the end of the long lane, she turned left and continued on her mile-long walk back to Hendon. Penny meant what she had told Dylan—she hadn't come four thousand miles to be put off. She hadn't expected him to come on to her, and interestingly, he seemed just as shocked as she had been. But junkies, she knew from experience, did a lot of impulsive things. And he was, or until recently had been, a Premier League soccer player and they seemed to have a large sense of entitlement.

He was tall but very thin and looked a mess. He had that haunted, struggling look she'd seen in other patients at the hospital. When he'd returned from the men's room he'd been sharper and more focused, so he'd probably done a hit. No wonder he wasn't a professional soccer player any-more—the guy was a wreck.

Turning left again, Penny stuck to the side of the narrow Cool Oak Lane. The occasional car passed her on the wrong side, adding to the Alice in Wonderland feeling. She crossed the one lane bridge over the Silk Stream that opened into the Welsh Harp Reservoir and began the trudge up the hill. She switched the duffle bag to her other shoulder, the pick-axe digging into her back.

There'd been recovering addicts at the hospital in Cincin-nati, including her roommate. Penny had asked her what the drugs felt like. "Great, at first. Then horrible. The problem is you keep remembering how great it was. But you can never get that back."

She hadn't expected Dylan to kiss her, though. Wonder what his girlfriend, the short blonde, would think. Penny didn't expect to be around long enough to find out.

If anything, his refusal to let her dig only fueled her re-solve. To be honest, she probably wouldn't have known what she would have done if Dylan Rhea had invited her into his office, offered her tea, listened attentively to what she had to say, and then offered to dig the holes himself.

Nothing about this had been easy, and she didn't expect it to start now.

———◆◦◆———

At the top of the hill, Penny turned onto the busy Watling Street, with its traffic either fleeing or attacking London, depending on the direction you looked. In two thousand years it had been expanded to four lanes, was paved, and labeled the A5. Through the working-class section of Hendon it was lined with three-story late-Victorian brick buildings with shops on the ground floor. Most had steel security doors rolled down for the night, but a kebab shop was still open and wonderful smells wafted onto the sidewalk. Penny paused to look at the menu in the window, doing rapid calculations of the prices charged versus the money in her pocket.

It'd be no good if she was too hungry to work tonight. She needed energy, so she pushed open the door to Ye Olde Kebab Shoppe and waited her turn in line to order.

Loud opera music blared in the narrow restaurant and patrons at the counter had to yell to make their orders heard. As she inched closer, Penny felt an absurd jolt of happiness to see a few brands of soda she recognized, even if the rest were alien.

A robust man at the counter wiped his forehead with a paper towel. "What'll it be, love?"

Penny pointed to a two foot tall ceramic statue of Luciano Pavarotti, arms extended in dramatic supplication, holding a chalkboard menu. "I'll have the special, and a cola, for here."

Penny offered a pretty piece of money with the Queen's picture on it and got a handful of change back.

"Order chicken kebab special, Scott!" the counter man called, handing her a lukewarm can of soda. "Right, next—"

"May I have some ice? In a cup?" Penny inquired.

"Oh right, Yank. Next!"

Penny found a spot at a narrow table, and five minutes later a heaping plate was brought over. She began to eat hungrily. The chicken was tender and flavorful, piled next to buttery rice that had a slight tang of lemon. Wedges of pita bread accompanied a fresh salad with a light vinegar dressing. There were two sauces Penny had never tasted before and she experimented with dipping the chicken in them. The food was spicier than she was used to and reminded her of a Middle Eastern food truck at the Indiana State Fair that she had tried once and liked.

More customers came in and the line to order now stretched to the door. A tenor sang passages of a song in Italian, drowned out at points by a much louder chorus, and the man at the grill cursed as flames flared to the top of the grease hood. Penny finished her last pita bread wedge and washed it down with a sip of cola. A muted television on the wall above her showed an American detective show she remembered having seen a few years before.

"Oi, what's this Scott? What's the matter with me soda?" a customer yelled from a table near the door.

"Stuff it, Gerhart!" the grill man yelled over his shoulder.

The customer pushed his way to the counter, grabbed a takeout carton, and proceeded to pour the contents of his can of Lemon Fanta into it for all to see. The soda was blood red.

The counter man paused and dipped a finger into the liquid. "Tastes right."

The grill man took another can from the shelf. "Here, have this one."

"Give me a Sprite instead."

The grill man handed him the new can and returned to his work. The customer opened the can and frowned. "It's red as well."

By this time, the entire restaurant was watching the exchange. Penny tilted a few drops of her half-finished can of cola onto her napkin. It too was bright red.

Several other diners did the same. "You trying to poison us, Jeff?"

The grill man and counter man pushed their way into the dining area, grabbing cans and pouring the contents into a bowl. Everything was red, regardless of the product. They stared at each other for several moments.

"Right!" the grill man clapped his hands while the counter man opened the register and took out a wad of bills. "Everybody out. We're closed. Sorry for the inconvenience."

"Yes, sorry," the counter man said, hustling people to the door and shoving money in their hands as they left, "dinner's on us. Have a lovely evening."

"But I haven't finished—" Penny complained. The grill man grabbed a takeout container and dumped what was left on her plate into it and pushed it into Penny's hands, along with several pieces of change.

"Thanks for coming in, lovely to have you." He handed her the duffle bag and with a firm push Penny found herself on the street. The door was locked behind her, the sign flipped to 'Closed'. The steel security gate lowered and crashed to the ground with a resounding clang.

Penny followed Watling Street two blocks north and stopped at a door beside a tiny betting shop called Billy Dale. She read the security code from the email printout the rental site had sent her and pushed buttons until the door buzzed and she could turn the knob.

Inside, Penny lugged the duffle bag up two flights of stairs to the room she had rented for four nights. It was spartan—just a bed, a chair, a dresser with a mirror, and two lamps. But it was clean, and the shared bathroom was next door. The rest of the floor seemed deserted.

She unpacked the few things she had brought along; an extra pair of jeans, a change of underwear, a flannel shirt, and two t-shirts. The one bit of frivolity was a travel bag her older sister Ruth had given her, which she had gotten as a contestant gift in the Miss Indiana pageant a few years before. The bright pink glitter fabric contrasted starkly with the plain room, but made Penny feel a bit more at home. Inside were her toothbrush, toothpaste, sunscreen, travel alarm clock, and a prescription bottle with the five tablets of Leahzapine.

Feeling very full, Penny took off her hiking boots and socks and reclined on the narrow bed. She unbraided her hair, watching the bright lights from the busy street below through the single window. It would be best if she napped; her body was exhausted from being on the road for almost two days. But her mind refused to turn off.

She should feel proud of her accomplishments. She'd gotten herself to England, to Icelton, found the parking lot, figured out where to dig, and was prepared to dig that night. The insistent urging that had been a part of her life for the last five years had disappeared as soon as she'd boarded the bus in Evansville, and her tattoo hadn't itched once. Everything was the way she'd said it would be.

There was some work to be done tonight, she'd find Boudica, and that would be that. She could get on the plane home Wednesday and get on with her life, the trials of the past five years behind her.

Chapter Five

THE TRAVEL ALARM CLOCK woke Penny at midnight. She had slept for five hours and felt refreshed. Tugging on her socks and hiking boots, she shrugged into the still damp sweatshirt, braided her hair, shouldered the heavy duffle bag and headed back down the stairs and into the night.

The rain had stopped, replaced by a dense fog that shrouded everything. It was stupid to walk around a major city at night undefended, Penny realized, and paused in a deserted doorway to take the cold chisel from her bag and slip it up her left sweatshirt sleeve, gripping the end in her hand. It looked inconspicuous and was better than nothing.

She started the walk back to Mortager Park. The streets were deserted and she relaxed a bit, grateful for the cloaking fog. On the next block she cursed under her breath as she passed a perfectly adequate building supply store. It hadn't occurred to her that the English might have stores where she could have bought the hammer, cold chisel, and pick-axe instead of lugging them all the way from home and paying the excess baggage fee. The plan had been to take the bag as carry-on, but the airline lady had been adamant it had to go in checked luggage. It was an unexpected expense, but she only had to pay it one way. No matter what happened, the tools would not be returning to Indiana.

She crossed back over the Silk Stream and headed up the hill to Mortager Park without encountering another person.

The grounds were a different place in the inky darkness. There was a dull glow from a security light at the foundry a distance away, behind the fence. Penny walked to the closest corner of the parking lot and began searching for the first marker stone. Pulling a tiny LED pen light from her pocket she trained it at her feet, sweeping the beam in small arcs, the fog enveloping anything beyond. There were no yellow stones.

She set her bag on the ground and shook the chisel out of her sleeve. Taking the map out of the bag she reoriented herself and walked to the corner of the lot and started over, moving across the rutted surface in what she hoped was a systematic path, looking for any of the four yellow marker stones.

The stones were gone. Damn.

The choice of digging in the parking lot had been a matter of elimination. The local paper had followed the construction of Icelton's new playing field with interest, and Penny knew they had dug two meters deep and found nothing. This part of London had had been heavily bombed by the Germans during World War II and several anti-aircraft bunkers had been built in the field behind the foundry.

The dirt beneath the gravel parking lot was the only large space that had remained untouched for two millennia.

A first century Britannic tomb could be anywhere from a small hole under a half-yard in diameter to covering a vast area. But the graves were shallow and she would only have to go down two feet, three at the most. It would take some luck but this was the best and fastest way to discover what lay beneath.

Boudica said she was here, close to the Silk and below the white castle.

The clubhouse building was to her right so she was facing south, and the holes she hoped to dig were spaced twenty yards apart. There was no other choice but to eyeball the distances. Penny retraced her steps, paced off the distance, raised the pick-axe, and swung with all her might.

The sharp tip bounced off the hard-packed gravel, throwing Penny backward with the force of the recoil. The ground was like granite.

Penny swung again and was rewarded with a dislodged chip the size of an ice cube. Ten minutes later she had stripped to her long-sleeved black t-shirt, and after twenty minutes she was breathing hard and took a break.

An emergency car with a siren passed the lane that led to Mortager Park, helping to cover the sound of her digging. More wailing cars passed, heading elsewhere, their flashing lights muted by the thick fog.

Penny worked her way through nine inches of hard-packed gravel until she reached looser soil and the digging got easier. Within forty-five minutes she had a hole two feet deep and two feet wide. She held her flashlight to the sides of the hole but saw no disturbance in the soil.

There was no time for disappointment. Quickly refilling the hole and tamping the gravel back in place she paced off the distance to the next spot twenty yards away and began digging. Her wristwatch said it was 3:30 a.m.

Penny worked steadily, switching to the cold chisel and wrapping the hammer with her sweatshirt to muffle the sound of the strikes. The results of the next two holes were exactly like the first, and Penny even dug an extra ten inches deeper in the third hole to be sure. There was nothing.

A breeze picked up, lifting the fog and scattering some leaves across the lot. Penny was fifteen inches down the fourth hole and considering digging a fifth when a strong light shone in her face, temporarily blinding her. She straightened and let the shovel fall from her hands.

Dylan emerged from the darkness. "Thought I'd find you here."

He walked towards her in no great hurry, the blazing flashlight marking his path, and held out his hand. "Looking for these?"

In his palm were the four yellow stones.

Penny stood over the last hole, breathing hard. There was no use apologizing, she had been caught. The hole showed exactly the same sediment striations as the last three. This soil had not been disturbed in millennia.

Dylan looked in the hole, and then at Penny, seeming more amused than anything. "You're lucky the neighbor called me instead of the police. What have you found?"

Her lips formed the word but her pride refused. But it had to be said. "Nothing."

"You've been at this for over three hours."

Penny nodded, wiping her arm over the mixture of sweat and dirt on her face.

"What are you looking for?"

"Whom," Penny said, "Your question should be, whom are you looking for?"

"Oh, hell. You *are* one of those nutters looking for Richard III under my car park."

Penny flinched. "No. There was only one King Richard III, and he's now buried in Leicester Cathedral."

Dylan crossed his arms over his chest. "Alright, whom then?"

Penny went back to her duffle bag, Dylan following her. She pulled out a picture and handed it to him. "I'm looking for her."

Dylan trained the flashlight on the photograph. "I've seen this statue. It's in front of Parliament. It's, what's her name, Queen Boadicea. The one that chased the Romans out of Britain. She drove a chariot."

"Her name was Boudica. Boadicea was a Renaissance translation mistake."

"Why are you looking for her here?" Dylan looked genuinely perplexed, as well he should.

Penny swallowed. "Because she told me this is where she is."

Dylan stiffened. "That's bonkers."

Penny couldn't disagree with him.

"You came all the way from America to dig around my car park looking for her?"

Penny nodded, feeling the energy drain from of her.

"You're not going to find anything under here, lass." His tone was stern now, lecturing. "This whole area has been dug up for over a hundred years, since before the First War. My foundry, the pitch, the clubhouse, the lots, it's all been here for ages. If there's anyone been buried here they'd have been found long ago. Shove off."

"No. This area was grazing land for centuries, and then farms. Your foundry was built in 1915, during the First World War, and expanded twice before the Second. That building there," she pointed to one of the long brick buildings, "the old warehouse, had a dirt floor until 1967. This car park has only been stone for the last few decades. It's all just slap-dash. She's here."

Dylan raised a wry eyebrow. "You know a lot about my property."

An awkward silence stretched between them. "I've been studying it for a while."

"You're not really from Princeton, are you?"

Penny shifted. "I am. But this has nothing to do with them."

"So what was the plan? Come and dig holes in my car park until you found a body?"

"I'm not sure what I'm supposed to find. And I doubt it would be a body. Her tribe, the Iceni, usually cremated the dead and buried their remains in ceramic pots."

"Oh, so you're looking for treasure. Gold and such. Well I'll tell you straight up it would belong to me because this is my property."

"I don't care about the gold, or the jewels. I'm just supposed to find her."

Dylan looked at her in disbelief, and then at the hole at their feet.

"Bloody Americans," he muttered, dislodging a chunk of rock with his shoe. "Come back later this morning. Eleven, sharpish."

"Why?"

"Because we're going to do this properly."

Chapter Six

In the morning, Dylan had a shave because he couldn't remember the last time he had. The dark circles under his eyes were nothing new—he'd been awake when the neighbor had called at three a.m. to tell him there was someone causing mischief in the car park. When he'd gotten home he had tried to go back to sleep but instead spent the rest of the night staring at the ceiling.

In the kitchen he opened the powdered drink jar and dumped a scoop into a tall glass and added water, then on second thought added another scoop. He would need the extra energy today. Dylan squeezed his eyes shut and gulped down the familiar bitter concoction.

Noticing his jeans sagging on his hips, he made a mental promise to order himself a stonking big pizza for dinner—his weight loss had been getting worse and Kingsbury Town wouldn't take him back if he was underweight. There was a box of cereal flakes in the cupboard but he had no appetite at the moment. It was a good thing his godmother Gwen was on another of her holidays and hadn't been at the match yesterday. He'd been avoiding her—she was also his doctor and asked far too many questions. That he didn't have answers for.

Back in the bathroom he dipped a wet toothbrush in the tooth powder from the special chemist and leisurely brushed his teeth, enjoying the sensation of the soft brush massaging his gums. He noted with alarm he was almost out. In fact, he'd run out several times and had to go a day or two before the delivery driver had shown up with a refill. He tried to ration himself but wasn't always successful. There was this bottle, plus the bottle he kept at Dad's office at the clubhouse, and a small vial Sue had given him that he kept in his jacket that came with a little toothbrush. She'd always kept one stashed in her pocketbook.

Pulling the front door shut behind him, he armed the security system and locked the deadbolts. He'd grown up on Elthorne Road and knew everyone, but you couldn't be too careful these days. Mum and Dad had only had the one deadbolt and usually forgot to even lock that, but after Sue had thrown him out and he'd had to move back home, he'd had everything re-keyed and a security system installed. It was only temporary, of course, until he moved back to his and Sue's flat in Chelsea.

Dylan walked the few blocks to the foundry. As he got closer, he could see Penny waiting for him. She was a peculiar bird, this Penny. Seemed as normal as the girl next door—no indications at all that she was as daft as a box of frogs. Dylan sighed. Sue wouldn't like her.

At the foundry he unlocked the gate and went to the old garage. Dad had let a local construction company keep some of their heavy equipment in the empty bays with the agreement that Alan, the Icelton club secretary and along with his younger brother Ned the last employee of the foundry, could use them for odd jobs around the property. Dylan grabbed the backhoe keys from a concealed spot behind a post and swung into the cab. The machine sputtered to life and he let it warm up for several minutes. When the engine settled into a steady growl, he put it in reverse, backed out, and headed towards his car park.

Penny looked up as he approached. Dylan noted she looked as exhausted as he felt.

He idled the engine and hopped down next to her. "Tell me where to start digging."

"But that will destroy your parking lot."

"I can put it back. Where do we start?"

She referred to a map, which he was surprised to see was a detailed satellite image of the entire fifteen acres of the foundry and Mortager Park.

"I'm not digging up my pitch," Dylan stabbed the map with his finger. "That's a 4G pitch, state-of-the-art, cost Dad a bloody fortune."

"You don't have to, she's not there. I watched while they excavated the pitch, and they dug very deep. They would have found her."

"How did you watch?"

"Satellite telemetry, aerial images detailed to one yard."

Dylan's jaw dropped. "You mean like spy satellites?"

But Penny had turned away and was pointing back to the car park. "This entire area is really the only flat spot that corresponds to the description Cassius Dio gave, once I discovered the other markers, like the river."

"There's no river here. There's just that piddling little stream."

"Yes, the Silk Stream. It was much larger two thousand years ago and was a major tributary to the Brent River. There was a bridge across it to Watling Street up there. Based on

Tacitus's description of the last battle, we know it took place very close to Watling Street."

"You mean the A5? That goes all the way to Shrewsbury."

"Yes. It was a main road in Roman Britain. But Cassius Dio and Herodian point to a lost source who said she was buried by the Silk, which is that stream over there, but it was mistranslated as 'buried in silk'. Which is incorrect because silk wasn't introduced to Britain until five hundred years later."

"That's it? Why haven't I been overrun by people digging for her before?"

Penny's topaz colored eyes seemed intent on not meeting his. "I've done a lot more research than most."

"What do you expect to find?"

"I have no idea. Tacitus doesn't mention a burial, but Cassius Dio does and says it was lavish. But he's not always a reliable source."

Dylan had no idea who these blokes were, but Penny was talking about them like they were her best mates. He sighed and swung into the seat of the backhoe and followed her to the car park.

⸻◆⸻

They started digging in the northwest quadrant, opposite the first hole Penny had dug last night that had produced nothing. The clawed shovel made a terrible noise as Dylan maneuvered it to break through the gravel surface, and it took several tries before he could get a good bite on the footing and begin to remove material.

Penny held her breath as Dylan worked, exhaling when each scoop revealed nothing but clay-like dirt. Penny jumped into the shallow trench, carefully measuring the striations in the soil and noting their uniformity. Dylan dug deeper than a yard but there was nothing but clay.

By three o'clock Penny had stripped off her sweatshirt and was working in her flannel shirt with the sleeves rolled up, and Dylan was digging the last of a series of trenches that crisscrossed the parking lot. In four hours they had uncovered an old pipe, two broken bottles, a long piece of rusted fender, and several rotting tires. Dark clouds stacked up over the white castle behind them and it began to drizzle.

Dylan shut down the engine and hopped off, wiping his face with a handkerchief. "There's nothing."

It couldn't be possible. She had to be here. Penny could not let herself believe otherwise. Because otherwise she was insane.

Penny walked the narrow trenches, knowing Dylan was watching her. There were no clues, no dark spots, no unevenness in the clay soil. Her fingers traced the ridges of crumbling shale as she walked, hot tears spilling from her eyes.

Having Dylan dig these trenches was an undreamed of boon because her calculations might have been off slightly. But now there was no doubt. She wasn't here.

Penny's legs wobbled and she sat down hard on the edge of a trench. It became difficult to breathe, and she doubled-over with soul-wrenching sobs. There was no stopping them, and Penny didn't even try. She had spent years fighting the voice, trying to live a normal life while being tormented by an unseen force demanding to be obeyed. And when she had given in and dedicated her life to doing what she was being asked, it was wrong.

There was no first century burial ground here, there were no ceramic pots filled with ashes, there was no dead queen talking to her. It was all manifestations of a psychosis.

They were right. I really am schizophrenic.

Strong arms wrapped around her, pulling her against a hard chest. Dylan crouched next to her and lifted her onto his lap as her cries became wails. She couldn't fight the tears. Misery poured forth in a torrent as all hope vanished.

She had no idea how long they sat there amongst the piles of gravel in the rutted park. His body sheltered her from the drizzle that turned into a steadier rain, her face buried against his rough wool sweater that smelled of sweat and soap, his rain jacket wrapped around them both. Dylan smoothed her hair back, crooning meaningless words, but didn't question, pausing to dab her eyes with his handkerchief.

Behind them on the hill, the white castle towered over them, majestic in the dampness.

"I'm sorry for messing up your parking lot," Penny sobbed.

"No one's going to notice much difference," Dylan said against her ear. "How did this all start, then?"

"My grandfather gave me a book about Boudica when I was seven, because she had red hair, like me. I always loved that book," Penny replied, numb. "When I was eighteen, I was in my first year of college at Indiana University. Everyone at school was sick with the flu, and I got a very bad case. My fever got very high and my roommate took me to the campus medical clinic. They kept me overnight. I was delirious, but I remember it exactly. Boudica came to me and told me she was here, and that it was time for her to be found."

Dylan nodded. "What else did she tell you?"

"That I was to look for the Silk Stream, and that it was near the large city of the Romans that she had burned to the ground," Penny said, pausing to blow her nose in the handkerchief. "And that a large, white castle had been built on the hill above her."

"I guess I can see about the stream, and the city is London, but there's no—" Dylan began but looked to the castle on the hill behind them. "Bloody hell. The Mandir."

"Is it a castle?"

"No, it's a Hindu temple, the Shree Swaminarayan Mandir. It's actually kind of small compared to the one they built over in Neasden. Nice folks."

Penny sat, shoulders slumped, looking at the network of trenches they had dug.

"Where are you from? Really from?" Dylan asked.

"I'm from Indiana. It's very far from New York City."

"So you're not from Princeton."

"Princeton Community College in Princeton, Indiana. I got a job as a custodian there so I could have access to the research library at night."

"How long have you been planning this?"

"Five years."

"All that gobbledy-gook you were spewing last night, about the soil and rocks—"

Penny absently rubbed the tattoo on her chest. "I memorized the geology of north London from a copy of the British Geological Survey in the library at the college."

Dylan shook his head, a wry grin spreading across his face. "And you hauled that bloody pick-axe all the way across the pond to do this job?"

"Yes."

Dylan nodded. "I guess I've heard stranger things. Where is she then?"

"I have no idea."

Chapter Seven

THE RAIN BEGAN IN earnest. Dylan helped Penny up and walked her back to the old watchmen's hut, a building attached to the tooling shop that the long ago security guards had used as an office and place to keep warm. It had been deserted for years but had a knocked-together kitchen Alan used occasionally. Inside Dylan found a few pieces of wood to throw in the old stove and lit it.

The small room quickly warmed, the bright light of the fire cheerful amidst the gloom outside.

Penny took off her soaking wet flannel shirt and Dylan hung it on a nail behind the stove. Underneath she wore a white t-shirt, which gapped at the V-neck to show part of a tattoo in her cleavage.

Dylan pulled the only chair in the room next to the fire and helped Penny sit. At the stained porcelain sink he turned the tap on and the pipe coughed to life, spitting out a trickle of brown water that eventually turned clear. He filled the electric kettle and set it to boil.

Penny sat, lost in her own thoughts.

"What's your tat of?" Dylan asked. "There, on your chest."

"This?" Penny blinked and drew the fabric aside to reveal the design. "I think it's supposed to be a horse."

The water boiled and Dylan made her a cup of strong tea, dumped in three sugar cubes and pushed it towards her. "You think? They didn't tell you when you got it?"

"She told me to get it. I saw it in a dream. I had to draw it when I woke up, so I wouldn't forget."

"That's—"

"I know. Insane." Penny agreed. "The thing is, I hate needles. I hated getting it. It hurt, and it itches a lot. I'm afraid it will get infected."

Dylan nodded at the mug. "Drink up, you'll feel better."

Penny took several sips of the strong brew, and he could see it reviving her a bit. With nowhere else to sit, Dylan settled on the edge of the narrow cot frame, the springs protesting loudly under his weight. Outside the rain pelted the small room, leaving streaks in the dirty window.

"I played with a guy once, that had some issues," Dylan said. "They gave him medications that helped him. He was pretty normal after that."

"I have a prescription, it's for a new drug called Leahzapine. It's my last hope—drugs like Clozapine and Haldol, that helped everyone else, only made me feel tired and killed my appetite. Leahzapine is supposed to work for cases that all the other drugs don't work. It's very powerful."

"Sounds like a godsend."

Penny nodded and drank more of her tea. "It's addictive, though. They told me that upfront. My family didn't want me to come here, they thought it was too dangerous. So I agreed to bring five tablets with me, just in case."

"I guess this is the 'just in case.'" Dylan said.

"I don't want to take them, but now I have to."

"It's best to let it sink in, and not try and figure things out straight away. You've had a terrible shock, and it's no good trying to figure out what happened."

They sat for a while in companionable silence, enjoying the warmth of the stove.

"What is this place?" Penny asked, gesturing around the room.

"It's the old watchmen's hut. When Granddad was running things, there were three shifts a day and full security. That door there leads to the tooling shop which is where the machinists and die makers worked. It used to be full of metal lathes, vertical milling machines, forges, benches, you name it."

"What happened to all of it?"

Dylan stretched his long legs out in front of him, the squeak of the cot springs punctuating his movement. "The industry automated, but Dad couldn't bear to do things differently. Orders dropped off, workers retired, a lot of the equipment got sold for scrap. The tooling shop is empty now. Alan and his younger brother Ned are the only ones left working here—they've got their own shop over in the main building, doing custom aluminum work. Real craftsman they are. Their family has worked here for over a hundred years."

Penny finished her tea and stood to look out the window. "It's gotten dark. I should be getting back."

"Where are you staying?"

"In Hendon. On West Hendon Broadway."

"I'll give you a ride."

Her t-shirt had dried but the flannel shirt was still damp. Dylan noticed a rain jacket hanging on a hook in a corner—the colors were bright and the pattern garish but it looked like it would fit her.

"Here you go, a memento of Icelton Football Club," he said helping her into it.

"Whose is it?"

"Don't know. It's been here for ages. Probably one of the players left it. We've been through so many it's hard to tell."

Dylan went to fetch the keys to the old delivery van Alan and Ned used. His Porsche was still with Sue—she'd picked it out, and it was red, her favorite color. The monthly lease bills were staggering.

Penny waited for him outside the watchmen's hut, her shoulders slumped in exhaustion. He helped her into the front seat.

"We could stop and get you something to eat," he offered. "There's a Chinese food place near where you're staying, and a pizza place, and a kebab shop…"

"No. Thank you. I'm not hungry."

"What about your tools?"

"I never want to see them again."

Penny was silent on the short trip back to Hendon. Dylan pulled up to the flat where she was staying and parked. "How long are you here for, then?"

"Till Wednesday. I thought that would be plenty of time," she said, struggling to take off the coat. "Thank you again."

"No, keep it," Dylan said. "Good luck, Penny."

"You too. Sorry for the bother."

"Penny, look—" Dylan reached for her hand as she began to get out of the van. "I'm sorry for kissing you last night. I don't know what I was thinking."

This brought a small smile to her lips. "Not a problem."

"I mean, you're not my type."

"Oh." The smile evaporated. "Okay."

"I just didn't want you to get the wrong impression."

"Yeah, not a problem, I didn't. Goodbye, Dylan."

Dylan waited until Penny had gotten safety inside the door and drove away. Behind him a thin bolt of lightning illuminated the skyline over London, vanishing as fast as it had appeared.

Chapter Eight

Back at his house, Dylan methodically worked the locks on the front door and disabled the security system. The wind had picked up and trees on the road were swaying towards the southwest.

The house was generous by north London standards; three bedrooms upstairs, a little first floor suite Dad had added for Grandpa, and a tidy garden in the back. Mum hadn't taken any furniture with her when she'd moved to the Costa del Sol after Dad died, which was convenient because Sue was still in their flat in Chelsea. That was costing him a king's ransom in rent each month. But he'd be moving back there soon. When Sue was ready.

In the kitchen, Dylan opened empty cabinets, exhausted and hungry. His stomach revolted against the thought of another glass of energy drink and he was too tired to order the pizza he had promised himself. He grabbed the cereal box from the counter and didn't bother looking in the fridge for milk—of course there was none. Flopping on the couch, he clicked the television to life and began shoving fistfuls of the crunchy flakes in his mouth, indifferent to where the crumbs landed.

Arsenal were in the 79th minute of having their way with the South Quay Road Potters, which was fine by him. He had no love for either team. Not particularly interested in live action, he downloaded a recording of the Kingsbury Town match from the Wednesday before and began watching that. The boys looked good and played very well against Burnley.

His replacement, the new boy Will Currie, scored one goal and had two assists. One of Giles's mysterious network of scouts had found him in a Tier Six club around Hull, Hensfield Tuesday, and he was a genius. Still young, Currie had missed one glorious chance, set up by Fernando Garcia Lopez, the sort of opportunity that he himself would have taken almost every time. Dylan knew he was the type of central midfielder who could burst forward and change the game... until he retired.

Retired. The word left a bitter taste in Dylan's mouth.

After the game ended, Dylan channel-surfed until he found a recent episode of *Fraud War*.

Sue was standing in the plaza of a tidy Scandinavian city, a scenic fjord behind her. She was bundled up in a tailored overcoat with brass buttons, her posture ramrod straight. "Tonight we are in Oslo, Norway, where we've uncovered a clan of charlatans posing as a sailor's charity," she announced, her tone brisk. "So far they've raked in millions of pounds from unsuspecting donors in the UK. But they are in our target sights and we're ready to shut them down. Because we're *Fraud War*, and it's our job to fight fraudsters."

She'd had her hair cut, Dylan noted. It was blonde and fell straight around her face, like a helmet. The trendy glasses were new and almost indistinguishable from the last pair. They were just an accessory anyway—Sue's eyesight was perfect. But she thought they gave her legitimacy.

The camera panned back, but not so far back that you could see her platform shoes. She was petite and had to remain stock still in shots, terrified of another disastrous fall on camera like the one early in her career that could still be found on the internet.

"Our intrepid team of investigators have interviewed dozens of people and tracked down the perpetrators. Let's go to the studio and find out what's happening."

The show cut to a studio control room where Sue was mic'd and pointing to camera displays. This was her idea—that she was a general at headquarters issuing commands and planning the battle. She was killing it in the ratings.

Dylan was in love with Sue. She was his first love—before her he'd honestly never had the time for a girlfriend. They'd met shortly after he'd joined Kingsbury Town, at a fancy-dress party thrown by her boss, Reno Tedesco. Sue had come dressed as a Roman centurion in a cute little red dress and cape, and wore a metal helmet with a big red brush on the crest. She'd caught his eye and they'd chatted for hours. When they bumped into each other again a week later, he'd asked her out and she'd accepted. After a whirlwind romance she suggested they get a place together and Dylan had heartily agreed.

Dylan tried to focus on their year together but the memories were blurry—there were happy bits and funny bits, but mostly he remembered the raw emotions of true love, the kind that one minute made his heart race and the next made it plunge. And it wasn't just the sex. In fact, Sue had assured him that his erectile dysfunction problem that began a few months after they moved in together didn't matter and she loved him just the same.

Sue had missed Dad's funeral. She'd been on a *Fraud War* shoot in Dublin and said she couldn't get back in time.

Everything had blown up when she'd returned and he told her he'd just retired from Kingsbury Town. Her reaction had been one of genuine shock, and she had pleaded with him to change his mind. It hadn't been announced, she reasoned, so why not just take a week or two off and then get back to it? It would have been what his father wanted.

When Dylan wouldn't budge, the tears had started. It had lasted for hours. She had begged, but he couldn't tell her the reason. How could he?

His refusal had infuriated her. She'd thrown him out of their home and he'd come here. The house was empty—Mum, grieving for Dad, had gone to their house on the Costa del Sol.

The next day Sue had texted him and asked to meet. Relieved, Dylan agreed.

GOOD COME OUTSIDE was the reply text.

Startled, Dylan had pulled on his shoes and ran to the street, where a luxury chauffeured car idled in the cold. Sue was sitting in the back, tapping on her other mobile phone.

She had rolled the window down. "Look, Dylan, I'm on my way to the airport. The Dublin shoot is a mess and I have to sort it."

"Okay, not a problem," he'd said, his breath coming out in puffs. "We'll talk when you get back."

"No, Dylan. I need time to process all this. It's all so, so, sudden. Promise me you'll give me time." It sounded more like an order than a request, but that was Sue.

She had made him swear, and he had. Without another word the window had rolled back up and the car had driven away. He'd gone back inside and broken down, the tears pouring out of him. Within five days he'd lost his father, his career, and the woman he loved.

This bird, Penny. When she'd cried this afternoon, he knew exactly what she was feeling. The awful, soul-shaking sense of loss. The loneliness, the desolation, the feeling that everything in your life had dissolved.

It had been going on nine months now and all he'd heard from Sue were brief text messages. She said she still loved him and was working through things, but she still needed time. He had promised to give her that time, she reminded him, and she needed him to be true to his promise.

Dylan sighed. He was trying to be a man of his word, but he was getting tired.

The clatter of a trash bin being blown down the road woke Dylan. Startled, he sat up and rubbed his eyes. He must have drifted off because the television was showing the late night Sunday sports chat show featuring an interview with the noted sports journalist, Joe Lyons.

"Right!" The presenter, a former winger Dylan had played against many times, rubbed his hands together. "The world's greatest knock-out competition, the Football Association Cup, began in August with 748 clubs playing in front of crowds counted in dozens, and by the end of that month more than 340 of them had been knocked out. These were clubs in Tiers Eight through Ten, filled with semi-pros in the beautiful game, all dreaming of FA Cup glory."

A diagram on the screen showed the impressive whittling down of teams since August.

"After the two preliminary rounds in August, there were four more rounds of qualifiers in September and October.

It's now November and the last **124** clubs have reached the first round proper—don't forget, those 44 in the top tier Premier League and Championship enter the competition in January. The first round proper games will be played next weekend, starting on Friday. Any matches you fancy, Joe?"

The journalist chortled. "Well, there are 40 across three days, but I'll be keeping my eye on a few."

The screen flicked to show footage of a small club playing before a few hundred spectators, a herd of sheep grazing on the hill behind the pitch. "Down in Brighton, Whitehawk will be playing Maidstone. They've been having a good season and soundly beat Enfield Town in the last qualifying round. That should be a good match."

"But how will they do when the top clubs enter the third round in the New Year?" the presenter asked.

"A handful of small clubs will probably make it through to that stage and they will be hoping for the glory of playing one of the big Premier League clubs. For the players it will be the chance to shine against their heroes and, who knows, perhaps get an opportunity to sign for a full-time club."

More matches were highlighted and Dylan watched with cursory interest. He knew what would be coming next.

"And last but not least, Icelton has made it to the first round again, but this time with former Kingsbury Town midfielder Dylan Rhea at the helm. What do you rate their chances, Joe?"

Both men shared a laugh as Dylan's face covered the screen. "Poor Rhea, his first steps in management haven't gone well," Joe Lyons said. "When he was playing for Kings-bury Town, he was wildly unpredictable—brilliant one mo-ment, a disaster the next. I know their manager Giles Roberts was pulling his hair out. But his retirement in the middle of their FA Cup run last year left Kingsbury Town woefully thin in midfield and they were knocked out in the semifinal by South Quay Road."

"Rhea's retirement was very sudden, and with no explanation given. Any clues, Joe?"

"Not a peep. But Sir Frank is notoriously discreet, and Dylan's father had just died. It's not a secret he'd been struggling."

A new slide popped up and Joe Lyons pointed out Icelton's path to the first round proper. "Icelton were fortunate in the second qualifying round when they got a walkover when Collingwood Park were expelled after fielding an ineligible player. Dewsbury, who they are playing Saturday, have been doing very well in the Pennine Premier League this season. Icelton are coming in with almost as many wins as losses and sit comfortably in mid-table in the Atlas League. Icelton have some talent, but I think Dewsbury will get the win."

The presenter nodded. "Now, don't you think if Rhea would only concentrate on a more forward attacking formation, he might—"

Dylan clicked off the set and closed his eyes for a moment, his lids heavy. Bloody pundits, like to see one of them playing with a groin injury screaming up their spine. It was all so easy from the comfy chairs.

He wanted to get up and brush his teeth, as was his routine, but his limbs felt like lead. Outside in the darkness, the wind was making a branch of Mum's cherry tree in the front garden scrape against the window.

Penny. Pretty girl, shame she was a nutter. Not his type at all, although his body would argue that point. Bit on the lean side, but truth be told he'd been more ogling her generous breasts than her tattoo in the watchmen's hut.

When Penny had cried, her pain had been his pain.

Chapter Nine

THE DEAFENING CHONG OF the doorbell startled Dylan from a deep sleep. His bedside clock said, astoundingly, ten o'clock in the morning. He had no memory of going to bed but the insomnia, blessedly, had taken the night off. He hadn't slept so long in ages. For the first time in a long while he felt good.

Dylan pulled on a pair of jeans and a t-shirt and padded to the front door. Alan stood on his front stoop.

"Morning, Alan. To what do I owe the pleasure?"

"Morning, Dylan. Thought you'd want a damage report."

Dylan blinked, but the way his memory had been working lately he didn't trust it. "Of course. Cup of tea?"

"Thanks." Alan followed him back to the kitchen and stood looking out the back window as Dylan filled the electric kettle. "Your garden wall as well. That's a shame. I remember when your dad put in those rose bushes."

Dylan followed him to the window and stared, dumbfounded. An entire section of brick wall had collapsed, burying Dad's rose bushes.

"What the hell?"

"And the wooden fence at number eighteen," Alan, a gangling six foot four, stood on tiptoe to get a better look at the destruction, "and, oh, that nice deck the Bartletts put on at number forty-two."

Dylan's mouth gaped open. The entire back alley looked like a war zone. "What happened?"

"D'ya mean besides the wind storm?"

Dylan shut his mouth before anything more stupid came out. He reached into the cupboard and pulled out the jar of his energy drink and dumped the last two heaping spoonfuls in the blender along with a fistful of ice cubes and some tap water. "What does Mortager Park look like?"

The jar was now empty.

"Two sections of tin roof over the north stands, that sign, and the awning over the players' tunnel," Alan said over the whirr of the blender.

"And the foundry?"

Alan shook his head. "Part of the east side of the tooling shop just collapsed. They say it was a straight line wind but damned if it doesn't look like a tornado hit. Tree limbs everywhere, two windows broken in the main shop." Alan blew on his tea and took a sip. "And for some reason the car park's torn to shreds."

"That was me, I was prepping to do the re-grading," Dylan lied. The old tooling shop was on its last legs anyway, no surprise there. "What about the rest of London?"

"That's the bugger of it. It was only the Icelton area, right here. It blew in from the North Sea and set down in the area, hitting us like a laser beam. It's all over the news—there's a picture of one of them delicate flower pots they've got out in Harrow on the Hill three miles away that weren't touched."

Dylan drank the energy drink in three gulps, the watery green mix leaving the usual bitter taste in his mouth. But it did the trick, he felt his pulse leap and his attention focus. Time to start the day.

Alan hadn't understated the situation. The foundry and playing ground were a huge mess. Several large trees had been toppled and debris was strewn everywhere, yet the sun was shining and birds were singing. It was as if they could have had a picnic amongst the wreckage.

They walked to the tooling shop, which was the furthest back and mostly hidden by the other buildings. Through the entrance door they saw where the windows had blown in, shattering glass along the empty interior. The skylights in the metal roof had stayed intact but a front section of the brick wall had collapsed, bringing down part of the roof with it.

"Is it a complete loss?" Dylan asked.

"I'm surprised it lasted this long," Alan said, kicking at the rubble. "Granddad said it went up in three days, just before the Blitz."

"Looks like they didn't even bother to prepare a proper foundation, just leveled some ground and poured the concrete pad," Dylan noted, pointing to where a support column had been dislodged, revealing nothing but dirt beneath.

"Ned's calling around to ask for some clean up help, lads will be arriving in an hour," Alan said. "There's insurance, I suppose?"

Dylan hoped so. "I'll go down the bank and get some cash to pay the lads, just make sure you put it through the payroll as day labor. What about your area?"

Alan ran a small shop in the main building making custom aluminum purge valve canisters, the last work being done at the foundry. "Untouched. Ned and I will be able to get the orders done this week."

"Glad to hear it."

Alan nodded. "We'll start with the stadium."

"I'll be out in a minute to help," Dylan said.

Dylan hurried to Dad's office in the clubhouse and checked the bathroom for tooth powder. The jar was empty, as was the one in his pocket. The chemist might deliver at any time; he never knew, and they didn't send alerts. Since he had moved home, he had run out several times.

Dylan took the keys to the backhoe and went to help Alan and the lads sort out the damage. By noon he had cleared the lane and put the car park back to rights, and scheduled a builder to go to the house and repair the back wall. He checked his watch frequently—the chemist's delivery car could show up at any time of day and was never the same driver twice. But they always knew where to find him.

That wasn't difficult, he didn't stray far from Mortager Park or his house. He didn't have a phone number for the chemist, nor was one listed on their label. It had been Sue's idea to start using them. In reality they weren't a proper chemist but a private shop, Sue called them 'naturopaths' whatever that meant. She said they used a lot of herbs and such. It was damned expensive, but their custom concoctions were amazing.

Dylan had been wary of them sneaking in anything that would come up on a drug screening. In theory football clubs were supposed to drug test the players randomly but in reality it was next to impossible with everyone's schedule. Sue had insisted he give the ingredient list to Duncan, the Kingsbury Town physio, who had checked it and declared everything fine.

"It's your money to waste, my good man," Duncan had advised, "but I'll tell you, you're just as well off eating healthy, keeping hydrated, and getting your sleep."

There was no mistaking the energy boost the concoction provided. Sue had shared the tooth powder she swore by, and he'd gotten his own supply. And now couldn't live without the stuff.

⸻◆⸻

It was three o'clock and the chemist's shop still hadn't delivered.

Dylan sat in Dad's office in the clubhouse, supposedly looking at the lineup for tomorrow's Atlas League match against Hoxton Borough but in fact keeping one eye out the window. He hadn't brushed his teeth all day, and his jaw was sore from clenching it. He toyed with the idea of taking the foundry delivery van down to Chelsea and visiting the chemist himself, but he might miss them if the delivery driver came while he was out. He decided to sit tight.

Despite appearances the wind storm destruction had been limited to some roof panels over the stands, two uprooted trees near the goal-line that had fallen on the security fence, and a lot of debris the lads had cleaned up. The FA was sending out a grounds inspector tomorrow but things would be tidied up by then and there wouldn't be any problems. The tooling shop, however, was a complete loss.

Alan had balked at tearing down the entire structure, arguing that the damage was only at one end of the building. But when the insurance adjuster had seen the pictures, he'd told them to scrap it as a total loss. The value paid out just covered the men's wages for the cleanup job.

"Dylan, come in here and give me a hand with this fitting on the water heater," Alan called from the boiler room adjacent to the office. "The old girl doesn't have much life left in her, but if I can replace this fitting, we should have a bit more hot water for the changing room showers."

Dylan blotted the beads of sweat that had formed on his forehead and clenched his jaw to cut off a sharp reply. What was he, the bloody boot boy? Instead he got up and walked into the small utility room.

"Grab that pipe wrench in the tool kit, there," Alan directed from where he stood behind the mammoth water tank, "and hold it on that feeder line, here, so I can loosen the connection."

Dylan picked up the wrench. It took him a moment to settle it on the pipe, the tool clanking against the copper pipe as his hands shook.

"The bloody thing keeps slipping," Dylan cursed.

"Here, let me give you a hand," Alan said diplomatically.

"I can do it."

Dylan finally anchored the wrench against the pipe and Alan unscrewed the coupling, revealing heavy corrosion. Dylan was disgusted. The heater was older than he was.

"Hey guys," Chloe called from the doorway, "we need the keys for the trophy cabinet."

"–again," Cassie chimed in.

"Fourth time this year!" Carlie added.

The three girls stood at the door giggling, holding a large silver trophy.

"Well done, girls, we'll be needing a new cabinet," Dylan managed to laugh.

Chloe blinked. "You said you'd already ordered one."

"I did?"

"Yeah, last week. We picked it out of the catalog and you said it would be here next month."

Jesus, another thing he'd forgotten.

As he reached in the top drawer of the desk to get the keys, he saw an unmarked white car speeding down the lane to the clubhouse.

"Here you go," Dylan tossed the keys to Chloe and bolted out the door.

A woman driver rolled down the car window and thrust a small bottle in his hand.

Dylan grabbed it. It was the tooth powder, praise the Lord. "What about the energy drink—" he began, but the woman had rolled up the window and put her foot on the accelerator, driving away fast without reply. There was no bill of sale, although his credit card showed a large deduction after each delivery.

The label on the bottle was blank except for two lines at the bottom that read Malnutria Homoeopathy Laboratory, 749 Danvers Street, Chelsea, London.

⸻ ◆ ⸻

Cleanup continued into the next morning. Dylan was brushing his teeth in the bathroom in Dad's office when Alan ran in.

"Dylan, you might want to get down here. The boys have found something."

Dylan followed Alan to the tooling shop. A pile of bricks was stacked on one side, next to thin slabs of concrete the small bulldozer had pushed back.

"There, we were removing that bit of flooring. It's really thin and came up easily, which explains all the cracks."

Dylan glanced at the poles supporting the beams that in turn supported the shallow roof.

"It's all sound," Alan assured him. "The posts are supporting the trusses and roof beams. Turns out the walls are the flimsiest part."

The bulldozer had scraped back the thin cement and clay soil beneath, exposing a definite change in soil color, this time to an unusual dark brown, with flecks of colors.

As Dylan got closer the colors resolved into shards of broken pottery. The dozer blade had pushed for over twenty feet, revealing a bed of things that looked very old.

"What d'ya think, Dylan? Some sort of old trash heap?"

Dylan crouched down and pushed aside the soil, careful not to disturb the bits and pieces where they lay. The pottery was thick clay, with curved walls, like bowls. Swirls were incised on the unglazed surface.

Dylan pushed the loose soil further until a large piece emerged, causing his heart to stutter. It was a horse—primitive, but still a horse. The legs were long and the body stretched in a gallop, the horse's head thrust high in defiance.

He'd seen that horse before. It was the tattoo on Penny's chest.

A low buzzing started in his ears. "Send the lads home, Alan."

Chapter Ten

It wasn't unusual for Penny to awaken to a pounding in her head. She squeezed her eyes shut. She was thirsty, and had to use the bathroom, but willed herself to sink back into the drugged oblivion the Leahzapine tablet must have delivered.

The tempo of the pounding increased.

She cracked her eyes and focused on the travel alarm clock on the stand next to her bed. It read 10:05 a.m. The sunlight streaming through the blinds confirmed it was morning.

It took her a moment to realize the pounding was coming from the door to her room.

Beneath the covers she was wearing a t-shirt that she didn't remember putting on when she'd gotten home last night. She stumbled for the door, her heart thudding for real now.

"Who is it?"

"It's Dylan. Open the door."

Penny opened the door a crack, rubbing her eyes. "Dylan?"

He stood in the hall, his expression frantic. "Penny, I think you need to come see something."

"See what?"

Dylan glanced at her t-shirt and bare legs. "Just get dressed and come with me. I'll wait downstairs."

Penny dressed quickly in her jeans and flannel shirt. In the bathroom she brushed her hair and clubbed it into a braid and grabbed her bag. Her sweatshirt was still wet, so she put on the colorful jacket Dylan had given her and met him at the bottom of the stairs.

"Where are we going?" she asked, following him onto the street, where she stopped dead in her tracks.

Storefront signs hung off-kilter and debris was strewn across the street and sidewalk. The grill man and counter man stood in front of Ye Olde Kebab Shoppe looking at the sign which had flipped completely upside down.

"What happened?"

"You mean the storm damage?" Dylan asked.

"What storm?"

"The storm Sunday night," Dylan replied, helping her into the delivery van. "Did you sleep through it?"

"I must have," Penny said, seeing more destruction as they drove the mile to Mortager Park, taking several detours as roads were closed. "Is it like this everywhere?"

"No. That's the damnedest thing. It just hit northwest London. We spent most of yesterday cleaning up the playing ground."

A familiar tingle started at the base of Penny's neck. "What day is it?"

"Tuesday, of course."

Good Lord, the Leahzapine had knocked her out for an entire day. The thought made Penny feel sick.

The lane back to Mortager Park had been cleared, with piles of brush stacked along the side. The parking lot had been restored and a crew with chainsaws were linking a downed tree in a neighbor's backyard.

Dylan drove through the gates of the foundry and Penny could see the damage here was much worse. He parked around the back and pointed to the long brick building that he called the tooling shop, which connected to the watchmen's hut. Part of its wall had collapsed and a blue plastic tarp covered a section of the roof.

"Did the wind do this?" Penny asked, getting out of the van and following Dylan to the entrance of the building.

"Yeah, blew out the windows, brought down that bit of roof there," Dylan said, holding the old door for her. "I had Alan bring out the 'dozer to knock it down. The place is ancient and wasn't built properly in the first place. They were digging up the cement floor when this was found."

Inside the empty building Dylan jumped down into the shallow trench the bulldozer had scratched and turned to grab Penny by the waist. His big hands easily lifted her and set her down beside him, then he reached down and picked up something from the soft dirt at their feet. "Is this what you're looking for?"

Dylan placed a large shard of pottery in Penny's palm. The breath began to burn in Penny's lungs as she struggled to understand what she was seeing. The background was grey, the color of the clay. Drawn on it in sharp, bold strokes was clearly a horse.

"That piece," he said, "it looks like what's drawn on your chest."

Penny turned the shard over.

"Looks old," Dylan said, watching her.

"Are there more pieces like this?"

"Those bits on the ground, there," Dylan motioned to the dirt track left by the bulldozer.

Penny's fingers trembled as she unbuttoned her flannel shirt. Dylan's eyes widened as she pulled the fabric away, revealing the tattoo on the mound of her left breast. The horse on the shard matched exactly.

Dylan's eyes darted between her pale flesh and the crude ceramic drawing. "Your tat. And this pot piece. How's that?"

Penny barely heard him. The joy in her heart was swelling to bursting. "It's her," Penny's voice was a whisper. "It's her, it's her, it's her." It was impossible to draw breath.

Penny leapt into Dylan's arms.

"Don't cry again," Dylan warned.

"I'm not! Do you understand? She's here!"

"Where?" Dylan asked.

"Under here, somewhere under here." Falling to her knees in the trench, Penny began to brush dirt aside with her hands.

"Are you saying there's someone buried under all this?"

"Iron Age Britannic tribes like the Iceni didn't do burials, they usually cremated their dead and buried the remains in urns," Penny said, immediately finding three more pieces.

Dylan stood next to her. "What does this all mean?"

"Well," Penny swept the hair away from her face and gestured to the debris before them, "it means I get to go home and start living my life."

Dylan's eyes narrowed. "I don't understand."

"I found her! I did what I was supposed to do. Now she'll leave me alone and I don't have to be obsessed with this anymore. I'm not insane!" A giddy sob erupted from Penny's mouth. "I'm going to go back to the university. I'm going to have friends again. I'm going to be, I'm going to be—" Penny gasped at the enormity of her emotion as tears and laughter and pure joy battled to express themselves. "I'm going to be *normal.*"

"And what the hell am I supposed to do?" Dylan demanded.

"About what?"

"About a dead queen being buried under my bloody tooling shop!"

"Oh, yes. Right," Penny looked around. "Your government says that any treasure found needs to be reported. I guess you should get in touch with HARP, the Historical Antiquities Recovery Program. They're coordinated by the British Museum, and they'll want to know all about this."

Dylan paled. "Is this place going to be crawling with archaeologists?"

"Oh, yes. This site is now immensely important." Penny waved her hand around, grinning. "All of it."

"I don't like the sound of that. I'd have to find another playing ground for the club. We can't afford it."

"I'm sure they'll work it out with you," Penny assured him. "You've got a mint on your hands."

"Right now I have a huge security risk."

"I would think they could help you with that as well."

"So what do I do? Call them?"

Penny thought for a moment. "We should go see them in person and take some of the fragments with us. That would probably be the fastest way."

"Is this treasure?"

"They say treasure is anything metal, and by that they mean gold. But this is very important."

With Dylan's help, Penny unearthed more large fragments and Dylan found a box to put them in.

"I think it's a cup," Penny said, looking with delight at the large fragments she arranged on the ground. "See, there's part of the base, and that piece is the short stem. Those three that fit with the horse piece are part of the rim."

She put some newspaper in the bottom of the box and carefully wrapped the pieces in toilet paper from the primitive bathroom in the watchmen's hut.

"Was she buried in this?" Dylan asked.

"Maybe. Professor Padma Jain, she's the director of HARP at the British Museum, has a theory that the Iceni would have buried her instead of cremating her. Cassius Dio says that after the last battle the Iceni had an elaborate burial for her. Tacitus says nothing, but that's to be expected. And Herodian references two sources we've lost who say it was a burial and not a cremation."

"We just can't knock on the door of the British Museum."

"Oh, she'll want to see this." Penny assured him. "She's the world's leading authority on first century Britain. Trust me, she'll want to see this."

Chapter Eleven

"You'd like to see Professor Jain?" The receptionist at the British Museum information desk didn't bother looking up from her mobile phone. "I suppose you've found Boudica?"

Penny smiled. "How did you know?"

The receptionist glanced at the box Penny was holding before resuming scrolling down her phone display. "You want the Historical Antiquities Recovery Program."

"Where's that?" Dylan asked.

At the sound of Dylan's deep voice she looked up and straightened in her chair. "London Wall, between Barbican and St Paul's tube stations," she said, looping a piece of hair behind her ear. "They close at five." Dylan took the card she handed him. "Address and phone number is at the bottom. Any other phone numbers you need?"

Penny took the card from Dylan and tucked it in the pocket of her colorful jacket. "But Professor Jain works here. She'll want to see this herself," Penny explained before lowering her voice. "I really did find Boudica."

"That's what they all say." The woman snorted and turned her attention to a group of tourists behind them.

"Thank you." Penny unconsciously tightened her grip on the box that contained the precious shards of pottery and turned to Dylan. "Do you know how to get to where she's sending us?"

"Yeah, come on."

"Wait. Before we go there, I want to see the torcs."

Dylan looked bemused. "What's a torc?"

"It's an important necklace her tribe was famous for. They're on the second floor, I'll show you."

Dylan followed Penny across the massive enclosed courtyard of the museum. The crowds swirled around a center building that housed the museum gift shop on the bottom and a library on the floor above it.

"Who's that naked bloke on the horse?" Dylan asked as they passed a life-sized marble statue of a Roman mounted on a stallion.

"That's Caligula."

At a set of stairs Penny consulted a map and Dylan followed her up the wide steps to the second floor. They passed through crowded galleries until they came to a glowing display of golden helmets and shields.

Dylan stopped, his eyes wide.

"That's from Sutton Hoo. It's Anglo-Saxon, much later," Penny dismissed, not giving the stunning display a second glance.

"Wait... I know about that. They dug all that up. In some field in Norfolk."

"Yes, it was a ship burial mound, Anglo-Saxon, hundreds of years after Boudica. Totally different from what you've got."

"Bloody impressive nonetheless," Dylan chuffed.

They turned left and Penny headed directly to a large display case in the middle of the next room.

"This is the Snettisham Horde," Penny said, a faint smile tracing her lips.

Dylan looked at the display case filled with pieces of twisted wire and broken metal. "Looks like stuff from the scrap bin at the foundry."

"You're not the first person to think that. In 1947, a farmer in Norfolk was plowing a field and thought he had found an old metal bedstead. He threw it in the hedgerow."

"Don't blame him."

"It was only after his plow unearthed the torcs that he gave those a second look." They walked around the display until Penny stopped. "Those," she pointed to elaborate crescents of thick twisted wire, "are torcs."

"Those big metal bracelets?"

"They're worn around the neck. Like a necklace." The golden jewelry glowed softly in the subtle lighting. "The Iceni made these. At the time they were the most advanced metal workers in the known world. The Romans weren't even doing anything this good."

"But it's broken."

"Yes, most of the ones that are found are broken. Archaeologists have discovered they were deliberately broken before they were buried."

"How come?"

"No one knows."

They followed the line of tourists that moved slowly around the display case.

"That one, the big one on the box," Dylan pointed out. "That one's not broken."

"No. That's the Great Torc." It was larger than the rest, created from intricately twisted gold wires ending in large roundels. "It's the most beautiful one ever found."

"Was that hers? Boudica's?"

"No, she lived eighty years later. This was buried about 70 BC. They know that because a coin was buried with it. But it was probably part of the royal jewels of her tribe, the Iceni. After they found the Great Torc, they excavated the entire area and found a lot more torcs. Those over there, in silver, and in bronze as well. They seemed to have been buried in groups of three."

"How long did that all take?"

"I think they're still excavating."

Dylan muttered a curse under his breath. "Did they find chariots?"

The crowd shuffled around to another display case and Penny pointed to an impression of a wheel in dirt. "This is from a cart burial in Yorkshire. The wheels were made of wood that disintegrated, but they found the impression they left in the clay soil."

"Not very big," Dylan said, peering closely.

"The chariots weren't like you see in the movies, they were smaller and lighter and made of wicker. Much more maneuverable. The Iceni were experts at driving them—there was a driver and an archer and a very fast pony, and they would swoop in and let loose a volley of arrows at very close range and retreat. The Romans had never seen anything like it and were terrified."

"Did the wheels have those spikes on them, like the statue in front of Parliament?"

"Probably not. Prince Albert added those."

They continued winding their way through the rooms until Penny stopped by a bronze sculpture of a man's head. He had forward swept hair and big ears, and below his neck the metal was jagged and sharp.

"This was the Roman Emperor Claudius," Penny said. "It's the head of a statue that used to stand in Colchester. She had the head cut off when she burned the city, and probably took it with her."

"Were they mad at him?"

"Oh, yes. With good reason. Look, you can see where they hit it across the back of the head, and then sawed it off. They threw it in the Alde River, where it was found in 1907."

Penny stared into the empty eyes of the fallen emperor and felt a pleasant jolt of satisfaction.

Chapter Twelve

DYLAN'S KNOWLEDGE OF THE Underground was good, and they got to the HARP offices in London Wall in twenty-five minutes. The building was a nondescript urban edifice with an unwelcoming entrance. The security guard sent them to the second floor, which the British confusingly called the first floor. They wandered down a badly lit corridor filled with firmly closed doors until they found the one they were looking for.

Inside was a large waiting room filled with an assortment of people from all walks of life. Some wandered the room while others sat in chairs, and several were dressed in brightly colored robes.

A man wearing glasses was seated at a desk next to a frosted glass door, typing at his computer. He seemed to be in charge so Penny approached, Dylan close behind her.

"I'd like to see Professor Padma Jain, please."

The man sighed. "Is it too much to hope you have an appointment?"

Penny opened the box and carefully removed the pottery shard with the incised horse and set it on the desk. "I think she'd like to see this."

The man pushed his glasses up his nose and inspected the shard. "Fifth century AD Breton Samianware."

"No, there's no red glaze. First century AD Celtic. Iceni."

A woman with fluorescent pink hair wearing an emerald green cloak wafted between them. "Your jacket is very colorful," she told Penny. "I like it."

"Er, thank you. I like yours, too."

Penny took another piece of pottery from the box, eliciting a flicker of interest from the man at the desk. "Where did you find these?"

"On my property," Dylan said. "One of my buildings collapsed in the storm on Sunday night."

"What storm?"

People began to gather around the desk, craning their necks to see the pottery shards.

"Iron Age Britannic pottery is very rare," he sniffed. "It was only crudely decorated when decorated at all. At best these are late imports from Central Gaul."

"That's not true, Nigel, and you know it," a stout woman said. "There were at least five documented kilns operating in the Thetford area of East Anglia alone in 55 AD."

The man at the desk ignored her. "One has to deal with amateurs. The fact is, there is no reason to believe that what you've found is anything more than Victorian reproductions." He pushed his glasses back down his nose and resumed tapping on his keyboard.

Penny knew she had no choice but to tell the truth. "Look, I have every reason to believe I've found Boudica's tomb in Icelton."

"Oh, really?" he said, "Well you're in good company. Mrs Marshall here, has also found Boudica's tomb behind the Tesco in Clerkenwell. Mr Atwell has found her in his back garden in New Ash Green, and Mrs Bronstein is working on permission to excavate under Platform 10 at Kings Cross Station because she's buried under there."

"Platform 9!" the pink-haired woman corrected.

"But this really is Boudica's tomb!" Penny said in exasperation. "The last battle was in Edgware, where she was either killed or died soon afterwards. She was carried to Icelton and buried along with the rest of her people who were killed."

"You have no proof."

"The name? Hello? Icelton, Iceni, has no one ever made that connection?"

The man gave Penny a smug sneer. "My dear young lady, the village of Icelton derived its name from the Most Reverend I.C. Elton, Bishop of Willesden, who owned a large estate in the area."

Penny glanced at Dylan, who shrugged. "He's right."

"It's ridiculous to think that the last battle was in Edgware," a man next to Penny said. "Graham Webster, OBE, has proven convincingly that the location of the last battle, as described by Tacitus, was Mancetter, near Atherstone."

"He was wrong," Penny said.

The crowd began to mutter angrily.

Penny continued, raising her voice to be heard, "Webster based his hypothesis on the work of Oswald and Scott, as reported in the *Transactions of the Birmingham and Warwickshire Archeological Society* in 1964 and 1973. But they were wrong as well."

"All evidence points—" the man sputtered.

"They have no proof, it's all circumstantial. I know that's where Professor Jain is digging now and they have found exactly nothing. Everything in this box is more than they've found in five years. And," Penny said, warming to the subject, "there is no fresh water near Hartshill, the excavation site. The Anker River in Mancetter is five miles away. No self-respecting Roman commander would have ever chosen a battle site without fresh water very close to hand."

"But it's right next to Watling Street!" the pink-haired lady protested.

"Yes, and so is Edgware. The Romans chose the narrow gap in the hills between Highwood Hill and Barnet Gate, where the Moat Mount Open Space is now. Dollis Brook runs right behind it, and it opens onto the broad Edgware plain, a half a mile from Watling Street. It was a brilliant choice."

"But there's the Coventry Canal that goes right by Hartshill near Mancetter—"

"Which was built 1,708 years after the last battle," Penny corrected.

The stout woman next to her had listened closely to every word Penny said. "What university are you from?" she asked, not unkindly.

"I'm from a college in Indiana."

"What do you do there?"

Penny swallowed and stood straighter. "I'm on the custodial staff."

Any interest the man at the desk held disappeared at the news that Penny was a janitor. "Is there more of this? Have you found any gold? Coins? Jewelry?"

"Maybe," Dylan replied. "We dug this out and brought it here right away."

"I can show this to Professor Jain," the man said, reaching for the box.

Dylan's hand closed over the box before the man could take it. "You can come and see the rest for yourself."

"Look, Mr—"

"Rhea. Dylan Rhea."

A murmur rippled through the crowd.

"Mr Rhea. We are severely under-funded and can't be running out to investigate every bit of late Roman pottery people dig up in their gardens." The man handed Penny a three-page form. "You're welcome to fill this form out, and we might be able to have someone out to see it by…", he opened a log on his desk and began flipping through pages, "let's see… ah! Next March. How about Monday, March 16th at 9.00 a.m. Does that suit?"

"March!" Dylan exploded. "That's five bloody months!"

"Yes, as early as that. You're lucky because one of our field people lives in that area and will be able to squeeze you in. I've made a note, Boudica's tomb discovered at Mortager Park, Icelton, London NW9 7NE. I will pass this information along to Professor Jain. You have our thanks. Good day!"

Chapter Thirteen

BACK ON THE STREET Penny walked, head down, the box of pottery in her hands. Dylan walked beside her, covering the pavement at an impressive rate.

"Cup of tea," Dylan said, and ushered her into a café. He settled her in a bar seat at the window and returned momentarily with two mugs of tea and a large scone that he set in front of Penny.

"You didn't have any breakfast," was all he said by way of explanation.

The sweet biscuit was hot out of the oven and Penny realized she hadn't eaten anything in days. She slathered it with butter and dug in.

"Is this what you've had to deal with?" Dylan asked Penny as she devoured the scone.

"Yes," she said between mouthfuls.

"Right little wanker, wasn't he?"

Penny couldn't disagree with him.

"What was that bit about gold?"

Penny sipped the hot tea. "Unless there's gold, or a lot of coins and jewelry, they're not going to be interested."

"Would she have been buried with gold?"

"Probably."

"How much?"

Penny chewed for a moment, considering Dylan's question. "A lot."

"Jesus. What's up in Mancetter?"

"That's where everyone thinks the final battle took place, between Boudica and the Romans. Tacitus never says where it happened, just what the area looked like. Since Watling Street was the way groups of people moved around at that time it must have been near it. Tacitus says the Romans lined up in a defile, which is a gap in two hills, and Boudica's people were in a large plain. Unfortunately, there are a lot of places along Watling Street that fit that description."

"So what do we do now?"

"We?" Penny asked. "It's your property. I've done my part. I found her, now I'm going home."

"Don't you want to know if it's her?"

Penny shrugged. "I know it's her."

Dylan cursed and Penny sensed a fury begin to build in him. "So you lark in, find a ruddy King Tut's tomb under my foundry, and give me a pat on the back and tell me it's my kettle of fish to sort. What the hell am I supposed to do?"

"I don't know. Look, Dylan, a proper excavation takes a huge amount of effort. It's going to take months, maybe years to do it properly. And even then it's not like they're going to find a grave stone that says 'Here lies Boudica.'"

Penny opened the box and pondered the pieces of pottery, absently scratching the tattoo on her chest. "It has to be enough that I found her."

Dylan's foot began tapping a restless staccato. "When they found Richard III, up there in Leicester. How'd they know it was him?"

"Philippa Langley had funding, a large crew of excavators, and a major university behind her find, and even then it took them months to analyze his skeleton and do the DNA analysis."

"We don't have that."

"No."

"What do we have?"

"I have a return plane ticket back to America for tomorrow afternoon," Penny said. "Look, I'll help you cover it back up. No one knows about it, right? It should be secure until HARP shows up in March."

"I might not be there in March."

Somewhere nearby a church bell began to toll the hour.

"I'm sorry I can't help you," Penny apologized. "I don't have anywhere to stay, or any money. I've done my part. I've found her. Now I can go home and get on with my life."

"Well that's just lovely, isn't it?" Dylan finished his tea and crushed the paper cup in his fist. "If you'll excuse me, I need to brush my teeth."

Chapter Fourteen

IT WAS GETTING DARK by the time Penny and Dylan returned to Mortager Park. She followed him through the clubhouse to his cramped office, where he unlocked the bottom desk drawer and Penny placed the box with the pottery shards inside. Icelton had a league match that evening and players were beginning to arrive, making a loud clamor in the changing room next door.

"You're welcome to stay for the match," Dylan said, handing her a ticket. "I'll have one of the guys give you a lift back to Hendon afterwards."

Not having anything better to do, Penny took the ticket and thanked him. Dylan relocked the drawer and left without another word.

The foundry gates were still open, and Penny walked back to the tooling shop where the tattered outer door swung open easily. She stepped into the early evening shadows and tried to visualize the empty space filled with whirring machinery and busy workers, but her imagination failed. The place was nothing more than a hollow building, home to the birds that watched her from their roof truss nests overhead.

The backhoe had dug a shallow trench, no deeper than two feet deep and perhaps ten feet long. The surrounding dirt was unremarkable, just a few dark veins and bits of loose gravel. The support post they had been digging around, one of six that ran in a line down the middle, had only been sunk a few feet below the surface, with no reinforcing concrete footer whatsoever. It was remarkable the entire building hadn't collapsed years ago.

Penny stepped into the trench. She pressed her fingers into the dry soil, probing deeper around the area where they had found the pottery shards. Clumps of dirt fell back, revealing additional ceramic fragments no larger than her thumbnail. She left them in place.

There was no doubt that the right thing to do was to fill the trench back in and make the area safe, and trust that Dylan would keep it secure until the real archaeologists arrived in five months. They would recognize the site for what it was and things would be done properly. Her flight tomorrow was in the late afternoon—she'd get up early in the morning, come help Dylan shovel dirt back into the trench, and that would be that. It was a good plan, and now it was time to leave the tooling shop.

She sat in silence on the side of the trench until it was pitch black in the building, fighting an insistent urge to dislodge more dirt. When her watch said it was almost time for the game to start she returned to the stadium, where she found a seat in the ramshackle stands. Spectators arrived, taking seats around her as the teams began to warm-up on the pitch. Dylan stood on the sidelines with another man, probably an assistant manager, watching his players run drills. It got colder, and she blew on her hands to warm them.

The teams headed back to the changing rooms before filing out again to stand at midfield with the match officials.

The captains shook hands and the match started, the flood-lights illuminating the field.

Penny didn't know much about soccer, or football as they were calling it, but after twenty minutes it was obvious Icelton was struggling. There were a lot of missed passes and wild kicks, and on one occasion two teammates collided. Dylan stood, his expression grim, while the other coach yelled at the players, trying to whip up some enthusiasm.

Hoxton Borough was only marginally better and finally pushed the ball close to the Icelton goal. There was a flurry of short passes and the spectators in the stands craned their necks to see what was happening. It was only after the referee signaled a goal that the opposing team celebrated, followed by a smattering of applause from the stands.

"If they drop this one, where will we be in the tables?" A man in front of Penny asked his seat mate.

"Fifteenth, but close to the relegation zone."

"What's relegation?" Penny asked.

The man craned around to answer her question. "Relegation is where the three or four clubs at the bottom of the league table at the end of the season get dropped to the tier below. The league champions and playoff winners go up to the next tier. That's called promotion. Keeps the lads trying and the fans on their toes."

"You Americans could learn a thing or two about it with your professional football teams," his friend added.

Penny ignored that. "What league is this?"

"This is the Atlas League, Tier Seven. Founded in 1905, it's got twenty-two clubs around London and the southeast of England."

"How many tiers are there all together?"

"Eleven. Top tier is the Premier League, where all the big money is, then the Championship League, still lots of money, then League One and League Two. They're all professionals. Then comes the non-league tiers where the guys get paid a bit but work at other things. The bottom tier, eleven, is all the regional leagues. I think there's over a thousand clubs all together."

"And all the clubs in all the tiers can get promoted or relegated?" Penny asked, intrigued.

"Aye, they can. Perfect case being Kingsbury Town, right down the road, a Tier Seven club, just like Icelton, not fifteen years ago. Now they're in the middle of the Premier League table."

"They must be very talented."

"They've got Sir Frank Poleski's money behind them," his friend chimed in.

The teams lined up again and Icelton managed to make progress up-field for several minutes until the referee's whistle blew for halftime. Both teams trudged off the pitch into the restored player's tunnel, ignoring the taunts of the spectators who lined the rail.

Penny followed the crowd into the clubhouse. It was warm inside, and she found a seat at a table far away from a front counter loaded with fragrant meat pies for sale. They must be delicious, she thought, people were devouring them.

Taking her wallet out of her jacket pocket, she counted her money—there was a £10 note with a picture of Jane Austen, four pretty £5 notes, and some large and small coins. In total there was £39 and some change, which was about $50.

Her room was paid for until tomorrow, and she had an Underground ticket to get back to the airport. The flight to Chicago would take eight hours and the bus ride to Evansville another fifteen, and then a four hour wait for the connecting bus to Princeton. Her sister Angie was going to pick her up Friday morning after she got off night shift.

A dull ache started behind her eyes and Penny rubbed the bridge of her nose.

It had never occurred to her that she would find Boudica and that no one would believe her. The reality was stupefying. She had spent five years of her life solving one of the world's biggest mysteries and no one cared. Penny's fist curled and uncurled as the unreasonableness of the situation weighed on her.

The pounding in her head grew worse and Penny squeezed her eyes shut.

"Got a pound for the Snowball?" A chipper voice asked.

Penny opened her eyes and focused on the tall girl standing before her. She was wearing a green and grey tracksuit with *Crystal* embroidered on it and couldn't have been any older that sixteen. Her long hair was pulled back in a high ponytail and she was grinning from ear to ear.

"What's a snowball?" Penny asked.

"It's the club's lotto," the girl said, proffering a brightly painted bucket. "At every match you pay a pound and get a number, and if your number is called, you get a third of that day's pot. Then the club gets a third, and the Snowball gets a third. It started last November, so it's been growing bigger and bigger since then, like a snowball rolling down the hill. Get it?"

"How big is it now?"

"It's huge! Over £7,000, give or take a few hundred. The final drawing's tonight so everyone is tossing in wads of cash, and the winner gets half the pot. Whadda ya say?"

The girl's enthusiasm was infectious. "How much?"

"A quid."

Penny pulled coins from her pocket and held them out. "Which one is the quid?"

"That one. But for five quid you get six tickets."

"I'll take just the one, thanks."

"Right-o, here's your ticket. You print your name on it and drop it in the big glass bowl by the bar, or I can put it in for you."

Penny took the offered pen, printed her name on the ticket, and handed it back to the girl.

"The drawing will be in here after the match. Good luck!"

Chapter Fifteen

Back on the pitch, Icelton managed to even the score in the second half but Hoxton rallied and scored another goal, to win 2-1.

The mood afterwards in the clubhouse was sour as supporters sat at tables, grousing amongst themselves about the game while they waited for the Snowball draw. Dylan stood in a corner with the assistant coach, avoiding everyone.

Penny took the same seat at the back and was joined by an older man who sat down across from her and took a long draught of his beer.

"*It is quality rather than quantity that matters,*" he said, smacking his lips in appreciation, "and I must say the quality of this pint of bitter is exceptional."

"Seneca," Penny replied.

The man nodded approvingly and extended his hand. "The Stoic himself. I'm Len Case. And who might you be?"

Penny shook his offered hand, remembering him vaguely from Saturday night. His grip was cold, his gaze piercing. "I'm Penny."

"And to what does Icelton owe the honor of your visit?" Len asked, his smile keen. It didn't reach his eyes.

Penny shifted in her seat, feeling her stomach tighten with no explanation. "I'm a tourist. From America. I thought I'd stop in and see a real British football match."

"Well you came to the wrong place tonight, that's for sure," Len guffawed. "Although the lads do play better on occasion. You were at the game on Saturday as well."

Penny nodded. He was perceptive. "I go home tomorrow."

Len Case glanced at Dylan, standing in the corner. "Fancy him?"

Without waiting for a denial Len continued, "He's a washed up Premier League footballer. Quit last year, no one knows why. His girlfriend, a lovely girl, left him. Now he's here running his dear departed father's club into the ground." Len Case took another sip of his beer and shook his head and sneered, "He's got no idea what he's doing and he's going broke."

"*Wealth is the slave of the wise and the master of the fool.*" The Seneca quote spilled out of Penny's mouth without thought, her tone cold.

Len raised his eyebrows. "It is at that."

"Why did Dylan quit?"

"No one knows. He was with Kingsbury Town, they're the big Premier League club in these parts. Their stadium, Townsend Lane, is just down the road. Quite a local boy makes good story. Then his father died, and he came back here."

"When was this?"

"Last spring, didn't even see the season out with Kingsbury Town. Left them high and dry in their FA Cup run—they lost the semifinal to South Quay Road because they didn't have him. Pitiful. He had to shut the foundry down, but that was hardly his fault. His father had no head for business either."

"What did they make?"

Len shrugged and took a sip of his pint. "Specialty castings for airplanes."

"Aluminum alloys? A356? A357?" Penny noticed her question caused Len to flinch.

"You certainly know your aluminium castings. Unusual in a young woman." Len's eyebrows pulled together, and his icy gaze almost made her shiver.

"Not that unusual. There's a large automotive manufacturing plant in the town I'm from. My family works there."

Len's grip on his glass tightened. "I'm sure it's all automated. Charles refused to automate, had to do everything the old way. Not much call for that anymore, and what demand there is has gone to China. There's a man who wants to buy all of it and is willing to pay a very good sum. But our Dylan says no, he won't give it up."

Penny's mouth went dry. "What does this man want to do with the pitch? And the foundry?"

It might have been a trick of the light, but Penny saw Len hesitate a fraction of a second before laughing. "Ask anyone here!" he declared, sweeping his arm around the room in a grand gesture. "Build ten-story flats! An enormous mall! Or," he grinned, "how about run a new Underground line?

"But I tell you," Len leaned closer, and Penny realized she had never hated anyone so much in her life, "it's all rubbish. Reno, he's the investor, he's a smart man. He'll buy Icelton and invest money in it, bring in some quality players. He's done it with South Quay Road Potters, that's his Premier League club. Frank Poleski did it with Kingsbury

Town, and Reno can do it here as well. This area will benefit enormously. Dylan is just being stupid and selfish."

Penny didn't know how, but she was sure Len was lying. The foundry and stadium would be leveled and built up. The property was fifteen acres, and from what she'd already seen of London there was a lot they could cram on that much land. They would do it fast and with big equipment, and Boudica's resting place would be destroyed.

It all made sense now. Anger boiled through Penny's veins and it took everything she had to stay in her seat and control her breathing. Len continued his tirade against Dylan for several minutes, oblivious to her mounting rage.

At the front of the room a man clapped his hands. "Time for the Snowball drawing!"

The crowd grew quiet as the girl's team, dressed in identical green and grey tracksuits, marched in with a large fishbowl decorated with a festive snowman. Penny tried to figure out which girl had sold her the ticket, but it was almost impossible—although they were many shapes, sizes, and nationalities, they all had fresh scrubbed faces, their hair pulled back in ponytails, and huge smiles.

"Tonight's Snowball winner will be taking home half the pot, which is now £3,752. And to do the drawing, Icelton Football Club owner and manager, Dylan Rhea."

There was a smattering of weak applause as Dylan worked his way through the crowd to the front of the room.

Penny watched as Dylan, without further ado, plunged his hand into the bowl.

"No, Dylan, do it proper!" the girls admonished. "Like a snow globe!"

Dylan gave a half-hearted attempt at tossing hundreds of slips of paper around before withdrawing a single ticket from the bottom of the bowl. Everyone in the room sat at attention.

"And the winner is," he announced and then paused, looking at the ticket. The color drained from his face and his throat bobbled as he turned the ticket over, and then back, and then over again.

The crowd began to murmur as seconds ticked by and no announcement came. "Come on, Dylan, who won?" someone from the back shouted.

"The winner..." Dylan began again, before seeming unable to continue.

"Yeah, Dylan?" the girls encouraged. "Can't you read the name?"

They crowded around him but Dylan jerked the ticket away.

Penny rose to her feet, her chair clattering behind her, and walked through the crowd to the front of the room. She stopped before Dylan and handed him her ticket stub without looking at it.

"I won."

Chapter Sixteen

D YLAN STARED AT P ENNY like he'd never seen her before. She thrust the ticket stub toward him, her hand trembling with barely controlled anger.

He took the stub and compared it to the half he was holding, blinking several times before clearing his throat. "The winner is Penny."

"What?" A woman called from the back of the room. "Can't 'ear ya!"

"The winner," Dylan repeated, regaining his voice, "is Penny Adams."

There was a grudging round of applause and the girls gathered around Penny, patting her back and congratulating her. Her gaze never left Dylan's. The club secretary, who was introduced as Alan, brought out a sport bag of Penny's half of the winnings and the girls arranged everyone for pictures.

"Come on, Penny, you've won over three thousand quid! Let's have a smile!" One of the girls admonished. "And Dylan, give us a laugh at least."

Penny pulled her lips back from her teeth in what she hoped wasn't a snarl. Dylan appeared shell-shocked. When the girls were done with the photos, Penny turned to him. "I want to count it."

"What? Don't you trust us?"

"No."

"Okay, c'mon."

Penny grabbed the bag full of money and followed Dylan to his small office at the back of the clubhouse. He pointed at the cluttered desk and stood in the doorway as she upended the bag and began counting the bills, which had already been wrapped in tidy bands, along with a check for £2,000.

"All there?" Dylan asked when she finished.

She tucked a lock of unruly hair behind her ear. "Yes."

"How are you going to get it home? Checked baggage?"

"I'm not going home. I'm staying here."

It took Dylan a moment to process what she'd just said. "Excuse me?"

"I'm staying," she repeated. "Here."

"Whatever for?"

"Because she's here. This," Penny pointed to the bag, "is a sign that I'm supposed to stay and find her."

"I thought we agreed we're going to cover the area back up and wait for the inspector from HARP."

Penny shook her head. "No, it's not safe."

"Penny, it's been safe for two thousand years. Another five months isn't going to make any difference," Dylan reasoned.

"I don't mean it's not safe from burglars," Penny corrected him. "It's not safe from *you*."

Dylan blinked, appearing taken aback by the ferocity of Penny's statement. "Me? But it's my property."

"Exactly. And you're going to sell it to a developer who will come in here, tear all this down, and build high-rises."

Dylan frowned and shook his head. "I'm not."

"You are! It's why she called to me. It's why she wanted to be found," Penny drew a deep breath and continued. "To stop a new city being built on top of her. I'm not going to let that happen."

"Penny, I have no idea what you're talking about—" Dylan laid a consoling hand on her shoulder, which she immediately shook off.

"I have the money now. I can afford to stay. I'm going to do the excavation, find Boudica and her people, and then I'll call HARP and they'll come and see, and she'll be saved. From *you*," she added, poking his chest for good measure.

"Where did you get this bonkers idea from?" Dylan asked in genuine bewilderment.

"That bald man told me. The one who keeps quoting Seneca."

"Who?"

"Seneca. The first century AD Roman philosopher?"

"Yes, I know who bloody Seneca is," Dylan paced the cramped room, hands on his hips. "Oh, you were talking with Len Case. Look, I don't want to sell, but I might not have any choice. You have no idea how much it costs to keep all this running."

"I thought you were rich," Penny said. "You were a Premier League player. They all say you've got millions."

"I don't," Dylan said shortly. "Not even close."

"How long until you have to sell?"

Dylan exhaled. "End of the season. Probably April. Clubs at this tier are folding across the country, and the land is too valuable. You saw the way we played. No one will buy the club, and the foundry is shut down."

Penny nodded. "And the people from HARP will be here in March. So I've got five months to excavate that area, find what I'm supposed to find, and then everything will be great."

Dylan rolled his eyes. "You're delusional. How are you going to shift all that dirt yourself?"

"I'm going to rent the watchman's hut from you," Penny replied, as if it was the most reasonable thing in the world. "And stay there, and dig."

"The watchman's hut is just a shack. It hasn't been used in years."

"It has plumbing, and heat."

"Yes, but just that sink, and a nasty loo. And only a coal stove for heat."

"I can pay you a £100 a week," Penny reached in the bag and began pulling out notes. "HARP will be here in five months," she pointed to a calendar on the wall and counted. "That's twenty weeks at £100 a week. Here, take this check for £2,000."

"Don't be daft, girl. No one can live in that shack in the winter. Go buy a metal detector instead."

"This place has been a foundry for over a hundred years. There's aluminum and metal all over the place, there would never be a clear reading," Penny countered. "I'm moving in tomorrow."

Dylan ran his hands through his hair and blew out a deep breath. "There's no reasoning with you."

"No."

"You'll find out soon enough why it's called a hut," Dylan warned. "And moving all that dirt is the job for an army, not a slip of a girl who's had a bit of luck."

"I've already had all the luck I need. And I'm not afraid of work."

Dylan looked askance towards heaven. "Alright. This is already bizarre, but who am I to argue. What will we tell everyone?"

Penny considered this for a moment. "That I found some bits and am excavating them. Like more clay pots. But no treasure—maybe I'm digging around an old stone wall or hearth."

"You'll have to stay out of the way. I can't have people back there wandering around, wondering what you're doing."

"I will stay out of everyone's way, and I can rig up a security system. No one will notice I'm there."

Dylan stared at her, exhaustion lining his face. "You've got an answer for everything. I think I'm the one who's insane, but sure, why not?"

⋅◆⋅

Dylan insisted on driving Penny back to Hendon in the foundry van. He was right. It would have been dangerous to walk the mile, alone and in the dark, with so much cash. He carried it up the three flights of steps for her and waited while she unlocked her door and then made her relock it while he waited outside. Penny could hear him still muttering under his breath as he walked back down the stairs. She bit back a smile.

Penny sat on the bed, the bag of remaining money at her feet. The bottle of Leahzapine was on the night stand, and she unscrewed the lid and shook the contents into her hand. Five bright blue pills slid onto her palm, the same number she had left home with.

Penny closed her hand around them and gave in to the joy that welled up from within. She laughed out loud, and then buried her face in the bed pillow to muffle the sound, lest she disturb other people nearby. Emotions poured out of her and she let her convoluted emotions have free rein. Damn it, she deserved it.

She had no memory of taking the Leahzapine because she never did. She had collapsed on the bed and slept for an entire day and night from sheer exhaustion, not from a drug-induced blackout. The voice in her head had been real, the cup shard showed that. Winning the Snowball was just the icing on the cake.

Penny put the pills back in their bottle. She undressed and lay on the bed, pulling the blanket over herself and thinking with anticipation about the work ahead, her mind calm and the way forward clear.

She'd have no trouble staying out of Dylan's way; in fact, her preference was to avoid him. His mercurial mood swings were unnerving. There was no telling what he was on, but it was obviously something. He was, or at least had been, a very wealthy sports star and the tabloids said they did a lot of cocaine. New patients at Alms Park Psychiatric Hospital in Cincinnati, where she had been for a year, frequently came in addicted and he had the same symptoms—in the short time she had known him she'd seen him cycle between depression, paranoia, and bouts of energy, plus he was constantly grinding his teeth and didn't seem to realize it. He also said he was broke. Cocaine was an expensive habit.

Penny lay in the bed, considering what she needed to do next. First, she had to cancel her flight tomorrow, and then tell her parents she wasn't coming home as expected. That wouldn't be easy—it had taken Penny a long time to convince them her trip would be safe. Her sisters had wanted to come with her but couldn't get off work—the car plant was running three shifts a day and everyone needed the money.

Her illness had put them through so much and Penny hated the thought of causing them more worry. But the bag full of money under her bed and the pottery shards in the locked drawer in Dylan's office were proof she was right. The way things were going, Penny fully expected to do a bit more digging and uncover all the evidence she needed for HARP to pay attention. That should only take a week, or maybe two at the most.

She'd also have to let the college know she was staying here longer. She was letting people down and it bothered her, and she'd probably lose her custodian's job. But she was well now, and she'd enroll at Indiana University as soon as she got home. And then everything would be great.

Chapter Seventeen

PENNY SHOWED UP AT the foundry the next morning with her duffle bag and several shopping bags.

Dylan met her at the foundry gate, unshaven and looking like hell. "You're late."

"I had to cancel my flight and go shopping."

Across the foundry yard two workers were nailing plywood sheets to a frame around the portion of the tooling shop wall that had collapsed.

"It's not going to last forever," Dylan said, his breath forming cold puffs in the damp air, "but at least it will keep the wind out."

Dylan pushed open the rickety door to the tooling shop, the ancient hinges struggling to support the flimsy entrance. Inside the building Penny blanched when she saw a backhoe ripping up the last of the concrete floor and piling it outside through a double sliding door at the end.

"Relax," Dylan said, "the floor is only four inches thick and Alan is being careful. That pottery was buried eighteen inches deep, and we only found it because he was trying to pull out a post. You'd never be able to remove that concrete yourself."

Dylan was right, of course. But the dirt beneath looked just as hard.

Penny looked up in the dim light. "Those roof trusses are sagging."

"They're going to put up temporary support posts once the concrete floor is out." Dylan fished around in the pocket of his jeans and found a key. "This is the key to the watchman's hut outside door, and there's a sturdy barrel bolt on the inside of the door that leads to it. Alan will padlock the double doors at the end when he's done—we shouldn't need to use them at all."

Dylan turned to the door they had just come through. "Sorry, there's nothing I can do to secure this old thing."

"I've got that covered," Penny assured him, nodding to one of the shopping bags.

Dylan didn't look impressed. "You're going to need better digging tools than those toys you brought. There's stuff in the equipment room in the main foundry, help yourself."

"Thanks."

"People around here are nosy. We can say that you found some bits and are excavating them. It happens all the time around here. But they're going to want to see what you're doing."

"I thought of that. There's an odds-and-ends shop in Hendon and I bought a few pieces of old bric-à-brac." Penny pulled some items out of her duffle bag. "Here's an old tea cup, and some coins, and an ashtray. I'm going to break them up and put them in different spots in the dig."

Penny followed Dylan through the short hallway that connected the tooling shop to the watchman's hut. He jiggled a door handle in the passage way until it reluctantly gave way, revealing a utility closet and ancient commode. The white porcelain was stained and gaps in the floorboards showed the ground beneath.

"Does it work?" Penny asked.

"When it's not freezing."

He flicked a switch on a side wall in the watchman's hut and the uncovered bulb overhead glowed dim. "I'll get you a new bulb," he offered.

The room looked the same as it had on Sunday morning, which seemed like a million years ago. Penny dumped her bags on the floor and Dylan looked out of the grimy window, frowning.

"There's no mattress," Penny pointed out.

Dylan turned back to Penny. "What?"

"A mattress, for the cot," Penny pointed at the metal frame. "I'm renting this furnished. You're my landlord, you should provide one.

"Good point. Anything else you want?"

"Is there wood for the stove?"

"It's actually a coal stove. We're in a smoke-control area but the foundry still has an exemption. There's a pile of approved anthracite out back, help yourself."

Through the window Penny saw a white car pull into the foundry yard and stop. Dylan saw it as well.

"I have to go," he said, springing to life and tossing the key on the counter. "One more thing—there're showers in the clubhouse that you may use, but only when there's no one else around. Understood?"

Penny nodded. "You'll never see me."

Dylan grunted and left in a hurry. She saw him break into a run across the foundry yard to where the car waited. The driver passed him something and sped away. Dylan hurried into the clubhouse, the door slamming shut behind him.

⸺◦O◦⸺

While the backhoe continued to pull up the cement floor in the tooling shop, Penny rolled up her sleeves. There was a bucket and mop in the commode closet, and after several twists the sink faucets sputtered to life. Grey water swirled into the drain, which at least wasn't blocked.

A tattered portable radio sat on a shelf in the closet. She flicked it on and was pleasantly surprised when music began playing.

The coal stove looked in good shape. The wood Dylan had burned Sunday was fine ash and Penny remembered the metal chimney hadn't smoked. She found the coal pile outside and filled two buckets from the utility closet. It took several tries, but she managed to light a small pile and adjust the draft.

The little room was miserable and Penny had never much liked camping, but she consoled herself it was only going to be for a few days, until she found the gold or other precious objects. Taking a spray bottle and sponge from a shopping bag, she set to work cleaning the window and every surface in the room.

As she scrubbed, she decided that although she had paid Dylan for five months of rent she wouldn't ask him for it back when she left in a few days. And, as a reward for herself, she would buy a one-way plane ticket from Chicago back to Evansville, saving herself the fifteen-hour return bus trip. It was a luxury, but the idea cheered her up immensely.

By the time she finished cleaning the coals had begun to glow red and she could add more. The sound of the backhoe in the tooling shop had stopped, and she walked down the short corridor to peep through the connecting door. The long building was empty and silent.

The concrete floor had been stripped back to rubble, and the trench left undisturbed. Sturdy poles were jammed beneath the roof trusses, and a large blue tarp was secured over the missing part of the roof. Penny walked down to the wooden wall and saw it was anchored against the brick edge.

It was time to get to work. The question was, where to start?

Penny had seen pictures of excavations with real archaeologists and knew that they would run string in grid-lines to make quadrants, and that those would then be translated to a paper map. HARP needed to see this was a proper excavation, so that's what she would do.

The tooling shop was sixty feet wide by two hundred feet long. Penny took her hammer and the box of long nails and began pounding them in the floor-level wooden sill at even intervals until she had twenty-six gaps across both short sides. With a black magic marker she labeled them A to Z. She repeated this on the long sides, labeling each gap from one to eighty-seven.

Starting at one corner Penny tied off a spool of twine to a nail and began unwinding it across the width of the building to its opposite nail, then back across until she had even rows, tying a new spool to the end of the last one. The process of running the twine down the length of the building took longer as she had to carefully step between the rows already strung. It took hours, but when she was finished she smiled in satisfaction—the tooling shop was now divided into a grid of 2,262 squares, each about two feet square.

There was one last string to run. She attached one end of twine to a little spring and then tied that to a nail protruding from the bottom of the tooling shop door. Unspooling the twine she ran it ten feet to the watchman's hut door and threaded it under the door, tapping in some nails to keep it off the ground. Finally, she arrived at her cot and tied the end to another small spring and attached a little bell.

Back in the tooling shop she carefully opened and closed the exterior door, listening to hear the faint tinkle of the bell down the hall. The makeshift security system was crude, and Penny supposed any self-respecting burglar would laugh at it, but it would have to do.

Chapter Eighteen

The sun set at 4 p.m., effectively ending Penny's work day since there was no power for lights in the tooling shop. Across the foundry yard and through the fence she could see lights on in the clubhouse. She walked across, noting the car park was empty, and let herself in.

"Dylan?" she called.

"Back here."

She found him in his office, looking at piles of paperwork on his desk. "Sorry to bother you. I need to email my family and let them know I'll be staying. Is there a computer I can use?"

"Don't you have a mobile?" he snapped, not looking up.

"I left it at home. I didn't think I'd need it."

"Get one."

Dylan, Penny noted, was much more alert and energized than he had been that morning before the white car arrived. "It's expensive, and I don't need to talk with anyone. If I can send a few emails, and check them here, then I don't have to spend the money."

Dylan continued to read the paper he was holding.

"If it's a problem, I think there's a library in Hendon," Penny prompted. "They might have a computer I can use."

"You can use that," Dylan pointed to a laptop open on the desk. "Did the store drop off the mattress?"

"Yes, around three o'clock."

"Good to go?"

"It's great, thanks."

There was only a small stool tucked in a corner, so Penny sat on it, put the computer on her lap and logged into the email server. She composed an email to her parents, telling them that she had found some promising pottery and that she'd need a few more weeks to finish. "Then the historical people will come out and take over," she finished.

It would be better, she decided, to leave out the part about winning the lotto. "I have a safe place to stay and enough money for a couple of weeks. It's not fancy, but people here are nice and the food is okay. I will email every week. If you want to talk I can call, but it will be expensive. I haven't had to use the Leahzapine, but it's here if I need it."

The next email was to her boss at the college, explaining that she would need to be away a few weeks longer than she had planned. Her boss was a good person and Penny liked her, but Penny knew that she might have to fire her. The thought made her sad, but she didn't need access to the library anymore and she could get a job at Indiana University.

In the thirty minutes it took Penny to send the emails, Dylan had used the bathroom twice and chewed two sticks of gum. His foot tapped the floor in a constant staccato while he stared at the sheaf of papers in front of him.

Penny logged out and left the office. Dylan didn't notice her leaving.

Chapter Nineteen

It was Saturday afternoon and Penny had just sat down next to the coal stove in the watchman's hut for a tea break when the security bell by her bed jingled. Instantly alert, she shrugged back into her thrift shop sweater and gloves before creeping down the short hallway to the tooling shop. She pushed the door open and peaked around the corner.

A young boy wearing a winter coat and rubber boots stood in the middle of the empty building, surrounded by the string grid.

"Hello," Penny said.

The boy looked up from his perusal of a hole Penny had started excavating the day before.

"Who are you?" she asked.

The boy straightened and drew a deep breath. "My name is Arthur Gerald Pinkett-Harlow," he bellowed at the top of his lungs, "I live at 733 Sunnymead Road, London NW9 7NE." He added a long series of numbers Penny guessed was his phone number.

"Pleased to meet you. I'm Penny."

The boy nodded. "This is the third time Icelton have been in the FA Cup first round in ten years and twentieth time ever. Icelton have beaten Football League teams three times and reached the second round seven times."

"Really," Penny replied politely.

"In 2012, Alfie Curtis scored a hat-trick against Sunbury Town in the FA Cup," the boy added before returning his concentration to the hole.

"Arthur—" Penny began

"Everyone calls me Biscuits."

"Why?"

He pondered this question. "Cos I like biscuits."

"How old are you?"

"I was twelve at Michaelmas."

"Do you play soccer here?" Penny asked and then corrected herself. "I mean football."

Biscuits lost interest in the hole and began to step from one grid quadrant to the next. "My sister Kathleen plays for the Icelton girls' team."

"Which one is Kathleen?"

"She's tall and got long hair and a ponytail."

That narrowed it down.

Biscuits stopped in a quadrant and crouched down to examine a pebble. "What are you doing?"

"I'm looking for some things that might be buried here."

"Old things?"

"Yes."

Her explanation seemed to satisfy him. "Can I look too?"

Why not? Penny examined her expanding stock of tools stacked against the wall by the door to the watchman's hut and handed him a garden trowel. "You can start digging there," she pointed to a corner a few squares down. "Let me know if you find anything."

Biscuits stepped carefully through the string quadrants until he was in the square Penny had indicated. "Can we listen to Joe Lyons?" He pointed at the radio Penny had propped on a box in the middle of the building.

"Sure." Penny retrieved it and handed it to the boy, who tinkered with the dials until a man's well-modulated voice came through.

"... here today in Brighton at what I think is going to be the most interesting first round proper game of this season's FA Cup, where Tier Seven club Whitehawk are facing Tier Four Maidstone. Whitehawk, as we know, have been on fire since mid-September. Half of the eighty clubs in the first round will take home a very useful £20,000 and earn a trip to the second round next month.

"But first, to the other matches. In the Tier Seven, Icelton, mid-table in the Atlas League and on the back of two straight home defeats, are at home to the Pennine Premier League's leaders Dewsbury, who should have no trouble in putting their hosts away. That said, Icelton do have some talent in their two strikers Henry Collins and Tamba Taray, skipper and midfield dynamo Tommy Peele, winger Jeff O'Day, and goalkeeper Ned Winter.

"In other news, Rochester, top of the Championship and eyeing promotion to the Premier League, are seeing their financial problems persist despite reassurances to the contrary by their club chairman and owner. Players have complained of not being paid their wages, which the chairman is blaming on banking hiccups and the club's conversion to new administration software. Players are threatening to boycott their league match today if they were not paid."

A gradual commotion grew outside. Penny made her way to the door and saw a vast crowd waiting to enter Mortager Park. "There's a lot of people here today for the game. Is it something special?"

Biscuits nodded. "It's the first round proper of the FA Cup."

"What's that?"

"It's a football match. All the football clubs in the country can enter, or most of them."

"What do they win?"

Biscuits paused his digging and looked up at her. "The FA Cup."

"Anything else?"

Biscuits shrugged and continued digging. "Money."

"Does Icelton stand much chance?"

He shook his head. "No. They never get past the first round. They're playing Dewsbury today, who have Sam Robbins who's scored twelve goals this season and has five assists. But our Tom Peele, he's almost got as many, though not so many assists."

Biscuits continued to talk as he scraped, putting forth an amazing array of statistics.

A tingle began at Penny's hairline. "If Icelton wins the FA Cup, how much money would they win?"

"Lots." Biscuits examined a shard Penny had salted in the loose soil in case anyone had come snooping. "This looks like bits from my Grannie's tea cup."

"It is, but it's very old. How much is lots?"

"Millions of pounds, I 'spose. Kathleen says last year's winner got £3 million."

"How many rounds are there?"

Biscuits counted on his fingers. "Five, then the quarterfinals, semifinals, and the final."

"Biscuits!" A tall girl with a ponytail called from the doorway. "There you are! Dylan said it's not safe back here."

Up close Penny could see her green and grey tracksuit was embroidered *Kathleen.*

"I'm sorry if he's been a bother, miss," Kathleen apologized. "He wandered off. Biscuits, you're wanted in the press box, it's almost kick off."

Biscuits stood and brushed himself off.

"Are you going to the match, miss?" Kathleen asked.

It was three o'clock in the afternoon and the light was beginning to fade. *Why not*, Penny thought.

Chapter Twenty

PENNY FOLLOWED KATHLEEN AND Biscuits across the foundry yard to the back door of the clubhouse. People stood patiently in long lines at the ticket booths while more arrived on foot and by car. A gleaming bus custom painted in dazzling purple and yellow filled a good portion of the car park.

"That's Dewsbury's coach," Kathleen pointed, "they go all over in that. What us girls wouldn't give..."

Inside the clubhouse fans gathered at the long bar. Penny felt a stab of panic and glanced down the hallway to Dylan's office where the pottery shards were, and was relieved to see the door was closed. And, she hoped, locked.

"There's an extra seat in the press box, you can sit with Biscuits," Kathleen said and turned to her brother. "Look after Penny, do you understand? If you disappear again Mum will have your head."

Penny followed Biscuits through the crowd to the main stand where he took a seat in a small sectioned-off area with workbenches. A tattered sign on the metal rail in front read 'Press Box, No Admittance'. Penny took the seat behind him and watched people finish setting up broadcasting equipment and laptop computers.

On the pitch, Dewsbury ran synchronized warm-up patterns between orange cones. The visiting team's moves were sharp and precise, and the players exuded strength and vitality. Icelton was at the other end, running the same patterns, but looked disorganized and sluggish compared to their opponents.

"Biscuits, who's number seven, bloke with the mustache?" A distinguished man at the microphone asked, pointing to a Dewsbury player who was juggling a soccer ball from one foot to the other.

"Frankie Farley. Just signed with Dewsbury on Tuesday. Came from Edgwick where he played for two seasons and scored twice. His great-uncle played for Northern Ireland in 1964."

Penny stared at the boy in astonishment. He had recited the information off the top of his head, the way other people would give directions to the gas station.

The players tramped back to their changing rooms and re-emerged five minutes later with cute little kids decked out in Icelton colors.

"Welcome to Icelton Football Club," the announcer began, "and the first round proper of the Football Association's Cup. We also welcome the players, officials, and supporters from Dewsbury, who are having a great season in the Pennine Premier League."

"Biscuits, how many teams started the FA Cup?" Penny asked.

"748 in August."

"How many are playing today?"

"Eighty in this round between last night and Monday evening."

"What are Icelton's chances of winning today?"

Len Case plopped down in the seat next to Penny and said, "Zero!"

This got a big laugh from the people in the surrounding seats.

"You see," Len explained, "Dewsbury are top of their table up north. Those northern lads are fit and their manager is a cunning bloke who had five caps for England when he played for Sunderland. Icelton doesn't stand a chance."

The match started. Dewsbury, resplendent in purple and yellow stripes, seemed to easily dominate Icelton with long kicks and fancy dribbling skills. Within the first ten minutes Penny counted ten shots on the Icelton goal, with the last one going in.

The announcer leaned over to confer with Biscuits before announcing "Goal for Dewsbury scored by number ten, Chris Haines, his second this season and his eighth career."

Dylan paced the sideline, occasionally pointing to a player or consulting with his assistant whom everyone was calling Uncle Eddie. Both teams regrouped and this time Icelton managed to push the ball into Dewsbury territory.

The ball fell to Tommy Peele, who drove a shot towards the goal. The ball ricocheted off the post to hit the back of the head of the Dewsbury goalkeeper, who had been diving to make a save, and it rolled into the net.

"Goal for Icelton," the announcer said, and then added after a brief conference with Biscuits, "an own goal by Dewsbury keeper Rudolf Lutz. That makes the score Icelton 1, Dewsbury 1."

There was a huge cheer from the Icelton supporters and groans from the Dewsbury supporters.

"Got bloody lucky on that one," Len muttered.

At halftime the score was still 1-1 and fans shuffled into the clubhouse for a drink. As night fell, the temperature dropped and the teams returned to the pitch. The Dewsbury fans began singing a rather bawdy song that made Penny's cheeks turn red, and seemed to feel that victory was imminent as Dewsbury resumed its unrelenting pressure on the Icelton goal. The Icelton goalkeeper, Ned Winter, was outstanding and kept out shot after shot, only to see the ball flying back at him within a minute. Penny thought he must be exhausted.

The floodlights began to glow, changing the colors of the pitch, and the temperature continued to drop. Dylan made three substitutions in the last ten minutes of the match and Icelton became invigorated. An exhausted Ned Winter jogged off the pitch, replaced by a young man named Charlie Moore. Icelton's defense kept play at midfield but were unable to press further towards Dewsbury's goal.

"The referee has indicated there will be a minimum of three additional minutes," the announcer intoned.

"The referee is adding a few minutes to the clock for injury time," Len told Penny. "It's called added time, because there's no real break in the game. Now you'll see Dewsbury make their move."

Back on the pitch, Icelton managed to break through the Dewsbury defense. The ball rocketed between players while the Dewsbury goalkeeper tried to organize his defenders. The referee signaled a corner kick for Icelton and both teams spread out.

"Callum Williams will take this kick," Len told Penny in hushed tones. "He hasn't had a goal or an assist all season."

The player took the corner and curled the ball into the middle of the penalty area, where an Icelton player tried a shot. The ball ricocheted off three pairs of legs before again glancing off the head of Lutz, who hadn't seen the ball coming through the crowd of players in front of him. Lutz spun around in horror as the ball bounced into the net. The referee signaled the goal, then blew his whistle for the end of the game.

"A goal for Icelton, and another own goal by Rudolf Lutz. That makes the score Icelton 2, Dewsbury 1, and that is the final score!" The announced yelled at the top of his lungs.

The Dewsbury fans sat slack-jawed while the Icelton fans erupted with shouts of joy.

"Both of Icelton's goals were Dewsbury own goals!" the announcer blurted. After a quick consultation with Biscuits he added, "And we seem to have made history here today, as no club has ever won an FA Cup round with two own goals. That's a good £20,000 payday! Thank you for your attendance today and we wish you all a safe journey home!"

Len sat next to Penny in stunned silence. The Icelton players galloped to the center of the pitch, leaping into each other's arms in celebration while Dewsbury players silently watched, dazed.

◆

While the Icelton supporters flooded to the rail to cheer the team, Penny returned Biscuits to his sister and slipped out through the back door of the clubhouse.

Inside the watchman's hut she moved the cot aside and unscrewed the floorboard beneath, lifting out a new metal lockbox that fit between the floor joists. She dialed the combination and pushed back the lid, then took out £100 in banknotes. She closed the lid and locked it, replaced it in its hiding place, and screwed the floorboard back in place.

Celebrations were well underway in the clubhouse as Penny walked along the parking lot, where the morose Dewsbury players were getting into their beautiful bus. It passed her on the lane before turning right and speeding off into the night.

It took Penny twenty minutes to walk up to West Hendon Broadway to the betting parlor, Billy Dale.

"Evening, miss," the man behind the counter nodded as she stepped into the tiny shop.

"Can I place a bet on Icelton winning the FA Cup?"

"You can, miss."

"What are the odds?"

The man tapped a keyboard. "Fifty thousand to one."

"£100 on Icelton to win the FA Cup."

Chapter Twenty-One

PENNY SAT IN THE laundromat in Hendon, luxuriating in the warmth of the noisy space. Behind a dryer window her bright coat tumbled around in a pleasing blur of colors.

It was a Monday night, and Penny had held off doing wash as long as she could, but her clothing was filthy. It had been raining steadily, and the little sink in the watchman's hut could barely hold her hiking boots when she would try to rinse off the mud.

She had been digging for sixteen days now, believing every day would be the day she found the gold or other treasure that would bring HARP running. The days were excruciatingly monotonous—Penny would wake when the sun rose, have a breakfast of instant coffee and bread smeared with peanut butter, and then go to the tooling shop and begin digging.

She was working in concentric squares around the trench where the cup shards had been found. Three squares had yielded additional pieces, and she now had twelve shards in all. After that, nothing. She was able to dig two or three squares a day, and was trying to be methodical, but as each one came up empty her enthusiasm flagged. Swallowing the lump of disappointment lodged in her throat, she looked at the remaining 2,220 squares and her bones ached.

There was no electricity in the empty building—the dirty skylights in the roof provided the only light and the days were frequently overcast or raining. She would dig until she couldn't see anything in front of her, then retreat to the watchman's hut for a dinner of canned soup she heated on the coal stove. If no one was in the clubhouse she would run over to the showers, stand in the frigid water for as long as she could stand it, and then gallop back to the hut. She'd dry her hair in front of the coal fire, which once she got it going had pumped out a fair bit of heat.

⸺◆○◆⸺

The dryer beeped twice and the clothing inside settled into a heap. Penny stood, her sore muscles protesting, and began to fold her jeans, underwear, flannel shirt, and sweatshirt. Her wardrobe was expanding—she'd found a thrift shop and bought a sweater and another pair of jeans, and the lost and found at Icelton had yielded a scarf, t-shirt, and mittens.

A woman a few dryers down took a dress out of her dryer and shook it, the pretty fabric falling in soft folds. Penny sighed and wished she had done a better job scrubbing the dirt from under her fingernails.

Biscuits came by every morning on his way to school and worked the square she had given him with singular focus. They listened to Joe Lyons, the football prognosticator who had a radio show, and Penny began to learn just how football mad the British were.

Her parents had replied to her email and urged her to finish her work and hurry home. Her boss at the college had been sorry but Penny had been fired. Penny understood, and the knowledge that she'd be going back to Indiana University buoyed her.

She had £1,500 left, which she worked out was £75 a week if she had to stay the entire five months, which she would not. Things were expensive in London, and the risk of suddenly needing to spend a lot of that money made her queasy.

Penny finished folding her laundry and packed it in the duffle bag. She pulled the bright coat out of the dryer and put it on, relishing the enveloping warmth, and began the walk back to Icelton. As she passed the kebab shop a mouth-watering aroma wafted to the sidewalk and her stomach growled in reply. She diverted her attention from the partially steamed-up window and kept walking—there was a convenience store in the next block where she could get more bread and soup that would last her several days. She swung the duffle bag to her other shoulder and kept walking.

"Hey!" A voice called from behind her. "Hey, lass! You, in the coat!"

A beefy man chugged towards her on the sidewalk. As he got closer Penny recognized him as the counter man from the kebab shop. He was grinning from ear to ear.

"I say, you were in the shop two weeks ago when we had that foul up with the drinks, weren't you?"

Penny nodded.

"Excellent! We are sorry we hustled you out, and to show our contrition we would like to offer you dinner. On us."

Penny stood undecided as he reached out and shook her hand. "I'm Scott, by the way. My friend Jeff and I own the shop."

"I'm Penny. Penny Adams."

"Penny Adams," Jeff repeated. "You're an American?"

"Yes, Indiana."

"Pleased to meet you, Penny," Jeff said, and he really did seem pleased.

Jeff ushered her back down the sidewalk and into the shop, where the statue of Luciano Pavarotti held a sign announcing the day's special was something called lamb tikka and a soprano belted out an aria.

Scott came out from behind the counter and introduced himself, just as happy to see Penny as his partner. "You had the grilled chicken kebab and saffron rice last time, how about another plate of that?"

Penny wondered how he remembered her, but didn't argue. They piled a plate high and placed it before her with a soda and salad and she ate hungrily. It was delicious.

"Your coat, it's very colorful," Scott said, sitting down with her as she ate her dinner. "So what brings you to Icelton?"

"I, ummm," Penny wiped her mouth, "I'm doing a small geological dig over at the Icelton Foundry."

Scott and Jeff exchanged glances. "Oh yes? What are you looking for?"

"Variations in the stratification of a vein of Triassic sandstone with evidence of a fluvial deposition in the north London Bracklesham sub-group," Penny repeated from her memorized litany.

The men looked slightly crestfallen.

"So you like opera?" Penny nodded to the pictures on the walls of the two men with various opera singers.

"Oh, yes," Scott said. "We travel around the country visiting amateur opera productions. Last week it was Brighton, this weekend we're going to Salford."

"We're totally addicted," Jeff concurred. "This lass, singing the 'Tanto amore segreto' from *Turandot*, she's a lyric genius."

"The next Ana María Martínez," Scott agreed.

Penny knew almost nothing about opera but acknowledged the singer certainly seemed to be trying. "Thank you for dinner," Penny said, dabbing her lips. "It was very kind of you."

"You are welcome any time," Scott said. "Come back soon. We close at 9 p.m."

Penny glanced at her wristwatch. "Then thank you for staying open."

"How's that?"

Penny nodded to the clock on the wall by the counter. "It's nine thirty. I think your clock has stopped."

Chapter Twenty-Two

"We have Icelton manager Dylan Rhea on the phone now," the radio host announced, "to chat with us about his Atlas League club getting past Dewsbury in the FA Cup first round. Icelton is now onto the second round, ten days from now. Dylan, how are you doing?"

"Fine, Eric, and yourself?" Dylan lied as he huddled in Dad's office chair, keeping an eye out of the window to the car park.

"Just great, Dylan, thanks. You've drawn Mudford Town for your second round opponent. They've just been promoted to the Football League. How do you feel about going up against a side three tiers above you?"

Dylan had seen this question coming. "Just glad we're playing in their new stadium, Eric, and not in The Bog."

That got the intended chuckle. "You know The Bog all too well," Eric agreed, "and Mudford Town supporters are just as happy to see the last of their seventy-eight-year-old stadium as well. This will be the first match in their new stadium, which the builders have guaranteed will never flood."

"Might have to find another name for the club," Dylan quipped, trying for some levity.

"Ha ha, yes indeed. Now Dylan, we know you're used to playing in front of huge crowds, but are your lads looking forward to playing in a stadium with 10,000 spectators?"

Not really, truth be told they're scared shitless. "Yes, indeed. It's an electric feeling that can really energize a team." He cracked his knuckles and tried to still his bouncing leg.

"To remind our listeners, Icelton defeated a dominant Dewsbury side in the first round when Dewsbury scored two own goals, one in the last minute of added time. Their manager has said they are feeling pretty stupid, especially judging by Icelton's level of play. Thoughts, Dylan?"

Zlatan Ahmic could go fuck himself. "Well, Eric, I think you'd agree we were very strong and played well. Dewsbury didn't take their chances, and we played as a team. Tamba Taray had a marvelous low shot that only narrowly went wide, and our defense held up."

"You have to admit though, Dylan, that your goalkeeper Ned Winter was the hero of the game. The stats say that he made more than a dozen saves."

"Absolutely," Dylan agreed. "He was player of the match." *Although it should have been Rudolf Lutz,* Dylan smirked to himself.

"How are you gearing up for Mudford, then? They've got a tricky front four."

Alan came to the door and stood listening. "Eddie and I are watching tapes of Mudford and we'll be ready for them next Saturday," Dylan said.

"The best of luck to you and Icelton!" the announcer said and rang off. Dylan slapped his mobile on the desk and looked out the window again. There was no sign of the white delivery car with his refill of energy drink powder, and he had been out for almost a day.

Alan raised his eyebrows. "You and Eddie are watching tapes of Mudford?"

"Yeah, I've got their last three matches up on YouTube," Dylan nodded to the open laptop on his desk. "I've got the players' wages here, if that's what you've come for."

"With the bonuses for the first round win?" Alan asked.

"Yes, as stipulated in their signing agreements. I wish it could be more. But I was able to give Len a check as well."

"By rights we should be sending it to the Dewsbury lads," Alan grinned. "Eddie said to ask if there's any money left over to pick up an extra player?"

"A bit, who's he thinking of?"

"Barney Bannon is sitting on the bench at Hastings. We might be able to get him on loan."

Dylan put his fingers to his lips and blew a sharp whistle. "Oi! Biscuits!"

The glum lad appeared in the doorway.

"Barney Bannon at Hastings United."

Biscuits stared into space for a moment and shook his head. "Cup-tied."

"When?"

"Second September against Evesham."

"Alright, thanks."

"Kid's like a computer," Alan said after Biscuits left. "It's spooky sometimes. But he saves the club a boatload of admin work trying to figure out who is eligible to play for us."

From over Alan's shoulder, Dylan saw Penny scoot down the hallway to the changing room.

"Alan, did we get an estimate for the boiler repair?"

"Yeah, let's see..." Alan paged up his mobile phone, "three hundred quid."

"Let's get that going."

"You're sure?"

"Might as well."

Alan left and Dylan nipped into the bathroom to brush his teeth. The interview had gone well. He was sure he'd sounded relaxed and confident, which was the exact opposite of the way he was feeling.

It was five o'clock and still no delivery. He started pacing.

The water heater clanged to life as Penny ran the shower, and he was pretty sure she'd gotten about a full minute of lukewarm water. She didn't complain, though, and he had to admire her grit and determination. Biscuits seemed to have glommed onto her, and the girls liked her as well. Sue never had time for them.

A few minutes later Penny was at the door to his office asking to use his laptop. Her hair was tied up in a towel and she was bundled in a huge sweater and the jacket he had given her.

"Things going okay over in the tooling shop?" he asked.

She nodded and pulled a small package wrapped in toilet paper from her jacket pocket. "I've got a metal bit that looks old, can we put it with the rest?"

"Sure," Dylan unlocked the desk drawer and held out the box. She carefully checked that everything was in there, added the new piece, and watched as he relocked the drawer. "That's it? Find anything more?"

"Unfortunately no. I've got the area around the trench pretty much dug out and there's nothing else there."

Her eyes, Dylan noticed, kept darting away and returning to the area under his nose. "What are you looking at?"

"Nothing."

"No, you keep looking at my nose."

Penny shrugged. "You've got some coke on your upper lip."

"Excuse me?" Dylan's eyes widened.

"The white powder, there, on your upper lip." She pointed to an area directly below his nostril.

Dylan stepped into the tiny loo and inspected his reflection in the mirror. He laughed. "That's my tooth powder."

"Oh."

He wiped it off with a swipe of his hand. "It's not cocaine. I don't do drugs."

Penny shrugged and looked away. "Of course not."

"You say that like you don't believe me," he accused.

"It's none of my business."

"It's not anybody's business!" Dylan heard himself raise his voice and tried to tamp it down. "I mean, of course there have been rumors. But there are always rumors. It's quite unfair." There was something about the way Penny raised her eyebrows that incensed him. "If I was found to be on drugs, I would lose the club."

"Really."

"Yes, really. The FA doesn't mess around. And I'll be going back to playing soon," he said, his voice quavering, "very soon actually. As soon as I get Icelton sorted. I'd be mad to jeopardize that."

"Sounds like a plan, Dylan. Good night."

As Penny turned to leave he saw the white car zooming down the lane. He followed her into the hallway and caught her hand. "Penny, I need you to believe me."

"Okay. If you need me to believe you, I will."

As he raced to the car park, it occurred to Dylan her statement wasn't the actual vote of confidence it sounded like. What kind of fool did she think he was? As if he'd risk his livelihood and reputation.

Chapter Twenty-Three

PENNY BIT INTO THE succulent chicken kebab, ignoring the warbling tenor working his way through a complicated piece of Italian opera. It was Monday night, laundry night, and her clean clothing was folded in the duffle bag next to her.

"This one singing, he's a school teacher from Liverpool," Scott said, piling a second helping of chicken kebabs on her plate.

"We heard him two weeks ago at the amateur festival in Cardiff," Jeff said, humming along to the singer's lament that had a curious nasal quality to it. "Knocked his riff from Verdi's *Otello* out of the park. He's an up and comer, that one."

Penny gave what she hoped was an appreciative smile and continued eating. The Monday night dinners at Ye Olde Kebab Shoppe had become her biggest meal of the week.

"Excavations going well over at the foundry?" Scott asked.

Penny concentrated on the plate in front of her. "Yes, great."

Which was a lie. She had now excavated forty-two squares which had yielded nothing. She'd even broken down and started in a new area closer to the outside door, but they had turned up empty as well. It was taking everything she had to keep her hopes up. It was November 29th, and the deadline to register for the spring semester at Indiana University was December 15th. There wasn't much time left.

The muted television on the wall had been playing the news, but now showed a serious-looking woman standing in a field, speaking into a microphone. *Fraud War* was written in an aggressive army-type stencil over her head.

"There's a piece of work," Scott said, nodding towards the screen. "She and Dylan were an item last year."

Penny stopped eating and paid more attention to the television. The camera zoomed in and Penny could see her better. Her blue eyes were piercing, and her shiny blonde hair was cut like a bowl around her head with long bangs in the front, like a helmet. The tailored military-style jacket she wore heightened the effect.

Scott clicked the remote and she began to talk. "Welcome to *Fraud War*, where we battle fraudsters. I'm Sue Paulin, your host."

"We all went to Charles Rhea's funeral, but she wasn't there," Jeff said as the show's theme music played.

"Tonight on *Fraud War*," Sue continued, "we expose a vile ring of thieves who are scamming pensioners out of millions of pounds. All in the name of charity."

The show cut to a television control room with Sue standing in the middle of multiple camera screens, playing the director. The premise seemed to be that Sue directed strategy, ordering staff to do interviews with people and visits to the places where the fraud happened. The drama was heightened by pulsing music and dark lighting. At the end, they found the bad guys and handed them over to the police.

"Is this a popular show?" Penny asked, finishing her dinner.

"Oh yes, it's one of the most popular in Britain," Scott said. "Millions watch every Monday night. Say, I need to run some takeout deliveries, would you like a lift?"

Penny gratefully accepted the ride, and Jeff drove her back to Mortager Park in the kebab shop's little car.

"Good night, Jeff, thank you," Penny said as she pulled her duffle bag out of the back seat.

"Right-o, good night," Jeff said, and drove away.

The parking lot had a half a dozen cars in it and the lights were still on in the clubhouse. A few people loitered by the clubhouse entrance and nodded to her as she walked by.

The gate to the foundry was open, which wasn't that unusual. Dylan seemed to forget to lock it quite a bit, but Penny always checked before going to bed. She fished the small flashlight out of her jacket pocket and walked to the watchman's hut, unlocked the door, and turned on the naked overhead bulb. The room was warm, and she was adding another scoop of coal to the stove when the little alarm bell by her bed gave a sharp ting.

It was past nine o'clock, too late for it to be Biscuits. Penny looked out of the watchman's hut window to the outside door of the tooling shop—it looked firmly closed. She took the heavy flashlight from it's place next to her bed and moved down the short hallway, taking care to prevent the floorboards from squeaking. She pushed the door open slowly.

The full moon lit the empty building through the roof windows, and she could see the silhouette of a person at the far end, bending over an excavated square. She brought the flashlight to her shoulder and snapped it on.

The strong beam of light illuminated Len Case's startled face. "What do you want?" Penny asked.

Len straightened and blocked the light beam with his arm. "What you got going on here then? And get that light out of my face."

Penny kept the light beam trained on his eyes despite his discomfort. "I'm excavating."

"Do you have permission to do all this?"

"Ask Dylan."

"You expect to move all this yourself?"

"*Difficulties strengthen the mind, as labor does the body.*" Penny quoted Seneca and saw him flinch.

"It will take you forever."

"*Time discovers truth,*" Penny replied.

Len glowered and stepped into the next square. "You're not a real geologist, you know."

"I'm not?"

"No, you're one of them looking for buried Roman gold or coins. You're an *amateur,*" he spat the word out, "and a bad one at that. There's been rumors about buried treasure in these parts for years but it's naught but twaddle. You can't move a stone in this country without finding some leftover from another century. You're wasting your time."

"It's mine to waste."

"Oh, ho ho, I see what's really going on," Len leered, "you're after Dylan. Well, he'll soon be finished."

"You can leave now."

"I'm leaving, I'm leaving," Len muttered, stepping on the low mesh of string. He let himself out through the dilapidated door, slamming it behind him, and Penny heard the bell tinkle back in the watchman's hut.

A bad feeling settled around her. She went back inside the watchman's hut and slid the barrel bolt into place.

Chapter Twenty-Four

Penny's little radio was perched on a crate in the middle of the tooling shop, tuned to Joe Lyons's show.

"It's a cloudy December 6th across most of England today, as we welcome you to the second round proper of the FA Cup," Joe Lyons began. "Four weeks ago, round one left us with forty clubs moving forward, ranging in rank from lowly Ealing in Tier Eight to fifteen Tier Three clubs. Let's talk about the twenty matches to be played over this weekend and early next week. We'll start off with a Yorkshire derby..."

Penny scraped through a layer of hard-packed dirt as Joe Lyons continued his prognostications, her fingers already stiff from the cold. Everyone had left for the match, groaning that the trip would take an hour each way. The girls had stopped by to offer Penny a ride, insisting she come along, but she had declined. Today was going to be the day she discovered the gold, or whatever else she was supposed to find, that would bring HARP running.

"... and it's back to The Bog for Atlas League Icelton, who are visiting League Two Mudford Town. Despite Mudford's best efforts to have their gorgeous new stadium ready for today, we received word a few hours ago that it had failed its final inspection when a serious sanitation issue was discovered. Mudford and Icelton have agreed to move today's game match back to their old stadium Boggy Marsh Lane, unaffectionately known as The Bog."

Penny paused to blow warm air on her stiff fingers.

"While Icelton shouldn't cause Mudford too many problems, this development does level the playing field, or should I say playing bog, for the underdog club. The weather report is predicting rain for later today and we'll see if it holds off.

"In other news, Championship Rochester's troubles continue. Players have reported that they received a payment on Wednesday, but none of their arrears, while the groundstaff and some administrative staff report their paychecks have not been cleared by their banks. The club owners claim there was a snafu at the bank, which has refused to comment, and it is rumored that the police have launched an investigation. Just to remind you, if salaries remain unpaid the players can become free agents and Rochester might be left without a squad."

The sound on the radio began to wobble and Penny went back to the watchman's hut for some new batteries, but the package was empty. She turned it off and worked in silence.

⸺⬥⸺

At some point in the afternoon, rain began to patter against the roof. The soil in this area was particularly hard, and she'd only gotten two squares dug in the last three days. The vast expanse of untouched string grid surrounded her like a jail cell.

Penny rocked back on her heels and peeled off her gloves. Her fingers were chapped and cracked, her nails worn down to the nubs. Her nose was running in a continuous stream in the damp cold. Discouraged, bone tired and freezing, it was hard to imagine being any more miserable than she was right at that moment.

"Look," she said out loud, her breath making white puffs, "I know I'm supposed to be here. You've made that clear."

Her voice echoed around the empty building, interrupting the chirping of a family of sparrows that had built a nest in the rafters.

"Discovering the pieces of the cup was great. And it has the same design that you told me to get tattooed—that was a nice touch. But no one believes that I found you." Penny wiped the sleeve of her sweater across her eyes to catch the tears that were spilling down her cheeks, and drew a deep breath.

"I'm only one person, and this area is immense. Dylan doesn't want to sell the property, but he doesn't seem to have much choice. I have to get back to register for my college classes. This can't be my life. I have to go home, and go to college, and help my family."

The birds were silent now, giving Penny their full attention.

She raised her voice, her tone firm. "I have five cans of soup, a half a loaf of bread, and four apples left. That will last me until Tuesday. If I don't find anything HARP thinks is important by then, I'm leaving. You can't ask me to do any more."

She paused. The sound of the rain beating on the metal roof grew louder as the storm drew nearer.

"I know it's crazy that I'm asking someone who has been dead for two thousand years to pull their weight, but there you have it."

⚬

By four o'clock it was too dark to work. Penny grabbed her towel and ran through the rain to the deserted clubhouse.

She had perfected the routine of showering in the changing room—strip, run in the shower and turn the hot water on full blast, wash her hair and body, and rinse in the cooling water. It took her under three minutes, but today the lukewarm water lasted an extra minute, she guessed because there had been no one in the clubhouse all day.

She toweled off and put on a pair of thick sweatpants and a sweatshirt from the thrift shop. They engulfed her but were warm. Wrapping the towel around her head she headed back to the watchman's hut, holding her jacket over her head as an umbrella. She ate her soup for dinner next to the coal stove, listening to the rain become a downpour, while the heat dried her hair.

At seven p.m. there was a loud knocking on her door. "Penny! It's us!"

Penny opened the door and Chloe, Kathleen, and Charvi piled into her room, dripping wet. "You'll never guess!" Kathleen announced.

"No, you'll never!" Chloe agreed, hugging Penny.

Charvi clapped. "It was incredible!"

"Girls, what happened?" Penny said.

"Icelton beat Mudford Town!"

Penny sat down hard on the cot. "No way."

"Way!" the girls trilled in unison.

"Tell me what happened."

"Well," Kathleen began, "you know we was supposed to be playing in Mudford's big, beautiful new stadium?"

Penny nodded.

"It seems the local inspectors found a patch of damp, smelly ground between the main entrance and the toilet block and didn't think it was safe."

"The old pitch," Charvi picked up the story, "Boggy Marsh Lane, was dry as toast so they did a pitch inspection there and it passed. But it floods easy, which is why they call it The Bog."

Chloe continued, "So the mums drive us to The Bog, and it's nasty as all get out—"

"I swear I saw a rat—" Kathleen confided.

"Kathleen, we told you it was a Chihuahua," Chloe rolled her eyes. "Anyhow, because they didn't think they'd be using it, it wasn't clean or anything. And then there weren't enough seats for those that bought tickets for the new stadium. It was a mess."

"So the match starts," Charvi picked up the story, "and Mudford gets a corner and the ball goes in over Ned's head. Then Icelton starts waking up, and it's pretty good football for the first half but nobody scores again."

"At halftime the mums are trying to get tea and it starts raining. The guys go back on the pitch and it keeps raining, this time buckets. The pitch turns into a bog."

"Because the drainage is so bad?" Penny asked breathlessly.

"Yes. We thought Henry Collins had scored, but it was disallowed for offside," Kathleen said. "Then Tommy made a great pass to Tamba, and he scored."

"So we're still drawing," Chloe grinned, "the ref says only one minute of added time, I think because everyone wants to get off that pitch, and the score is 1-1. Everyone is covered in mud and it's still pouring with rain."

"Mudford has a corner that Ned catches," Kathleen continued, "Then the referee puts his whistle to his lips but doesn't blow. Ned takes the ball and, with wind blowing a gale behind him, boots it the entire length of the pitch..."

"... Their keeper had come up for the corner—he must have forgotten Henry's goal had been disallowed—and was racing back towards his goal..." Chloe drew the story out, smiling broadly.

Penny held her breath. "What happened then?"

"It went in!" the girls crowed in unison.

"The ball flew high over his head and bounced into the net." Chloe laughed. "And everyone started cheering. It was incredible!"

Chapter Twenty-Five

Later that night, Dylan flicked on the lights in Dad's office at the clubhouse. There was, he knew, a bottle of Scotch locked in the bottom drawer, next to the box with Penny's bits and bobs. He hated the taste of the stuff but it was time for a toast.

He found a paper cup, poured in a small draught, and raised it in silent salute. Icelton was in the third round of the FA Cup for the first time ever. He wished Dad was here to see it, he would have loved it.

Dylan held his breath and swallowed the dark liquid in one gulp, coughing as it burned its way to his stomach. Which was empty, but he didn't care. Because winning felt good. Not just good, it felt fucking great.

He'd won a lot as a player and there was no denying the euphoria. But it was different as a manager, he realized. He owned this win—they were his lads, his club, his training. The prize money and TV money might not save the club, but it would certainly keep things going for more than a year. He was doing something right. *Finally.*

Yes, Icelton had gotten some lucky breaks in the match. Going into the last ten minutes the rainwater had been up to the players' boots, and they looked like they were closer to swimming than playing football. But Icelton had adjusted better and showed fantastic team spirit. They were the same conditions for Mudford, but they'd buckled under the weight of expectation. Icelton hadn't given in.

"In the last minute, I saw that their keeper had come up for the corner," Ned had said on the coach ride home, still in shock. "There was no one within ten yards of their goal so I took a chance, and just kicked it. Like me and Alan used to do when we were little, to see who could boot it the furthest."

Dylan smiled, remembering the almost surreal moment. The Mudford players were in the penalty area and no one tried to stop Ned taking the quick downfield clearance. He had watched from the sideline as they sprinted after the ball as it bounced along, splashing in the sodden pitch. Then it just rolled in the goal.

Remarkable. Almost unbelievable.

A few supporters had followed the coach back to Mortager Park and cheered them off, but everyone quickly dispersed in the filthy weather. Harry Goodnaught was the only one bitching as he was responsible for washing the team kit, and Dylan conceded he was going to have his hands full. The guys had gone out to celebrate and wanted him to come along but he'd declined. Now he wished he hadn't. He knew he wouldn't be able to sleep.

Dylan crushed the cup in his hand and threw it in the trash, then locked the bottle back in the drawer and brushed his teeth. The tooth powder had a bitter edge, but the peppermint flavor evened that out. It was refreshing, and he even rubbed a bit on his gums.

He stood on the front porch of the clubhouse. The rain had stopped but the clouds enveloped the moon. The light was off in the watchman's hut, and as he watched a faint plume of smoke wend up from the chimney, it occurred to Dylan that Penny might not know they'd won. It was one o'clock in the morning, but he wanted to tell her about it.

Leave the poor girl alone, Dylan, he chastised himself. She was probably exhausted, and he could tell her in the morning. He should go home and get some sleep himself because tomorrow was going to be a busy day. Yes, that was the best plan... until he heard a scream.

Chapter Twenty-Six

ONE MINUTE PENNY WAS asleep, and the next she was awake.

She opened her eyes and blinked, fully alert. Her glowing watch face said it was one a.m. The cramped room was pitch black, the single outdoor security light was a hundred yards away and pointed in the opposite direction.

The little bell by her cot jingled again.

Kathleen and the girls had left hours ago, and Biscuits knew he wasn't allowed in the tooling shop without Penny. She had locked the foundry gate herself after the girls had left.

Easing herself up to keep the creaking cot springs as quiet as possible, Penny pushed the blanket back and slid her feet to the floor. Without making a sound she pulled on her jeans and sweater and slipped into her boots.

The watchman's hut had two doors, one to the foundry yard and the other to the hallway that led to the tooling shop. Both were locked, and if she stayed where she was she was relatively safe.

Relatively.

The only window in the hut looked out on the foundry yard and the exterior door to the tooling shop. Peering out, Penny saw something propping that door open. It was small and block-like, and after a moment she realized it was a plastic container, like the kind her father used to store gasoline for the lawnmower at home.

Someone was trying to burn down the tooling shop. Her tooling shop.

Oh, hell no.

Grabbing the heavy metal flashlight, Penny unlocked the door to the hallway and edged down until she reached the tooling shop door. She paused and waited. The little bell jangled again—the exterior door had been closed.

She had no plan, other than to scare the arsonist away. Whoever was breaking in wouldn't like being discovered, she reasoned, and didn't seem to know she was staying in the watchman's hut. Or maybe didn't care. Surprise and light were the only two weapons she had.

Taking a deep breath, she swung the door open and raised the flashlight to her shoulder, directing the beam into the dark building.

A large figure ten feet away was caught in the strong light. It seemed to be a man, dressed in black, with a knitted mask pulled over his face. He was holding the gas can, trying to unscrew the cap, but dropped it to shield his eyes from the bright light.

"Get out of here!" Penny yelled, lowering her voice to make it sound gruff and masculine, while keeping the fierce light trained on his eyes.

Just run away, Penny prayed, *just run away*. Instead the man charged at her.

In three steps his feet got tangled in the string grid and he lurched sideways, giving Penny a moment to reach behind her to the wall where she stored her digging equipment. She kept the flashlight trained on him while the other hand frantically groped for the handle of the pick-axe. She found it and closed her fingers around it.

Penny didn't feel brave, but she also didn't feel scared. Anger pulsed through her—she was *not* going to sort through the smoldering remnants of a destroyed building, she was going to keep digging and find what she was supposed to find and go home. This thug had no right to burn down her work.

Freeing himself from the string grid, the man lunged at Penny. She brought the heavy flashlight crashing down on his head and he yelled out in pain, but his hair under the mask absorbed some of the concussion from the blow. In retaliation he brought his arm down on hers with a vicious chop. The flashlight clattered to the dirt floor and rolled away.

Penny screamed in pain. She had never fought anyone in her life, but memories from a high school self-defense class came roaring back. The flashlight beam at her feet now pointed across the long building, so with the cloak of darkness she jumped to the left and kicked the man hard on the shin.

He cursed and hopped on one foot. There wasn't much hope there would be anyone around to help, but the instructor had said to make as much noise as possible so she screamed, and kept screaming. Aiming a kick higher up, she was rewarded with her assailant bending over with an audible "ooof".

If she could drive the pick-axe into his thigh that should stop him, she reasoned, and with two hands on the handle she pulled it back to strike.

"You fucking bitch!" he shouted before dropping his shoulder and barreling into her, driving her back against the brick wall and knocking the breath from her. He ripped the pick-axe from her hand and swung it over his shoulder where it flew in an arc, landing somewhere at the back of the building.

With a savage motion, his hands went straight for her throat, jacking her up against the wall so high her toes struggled to make contact with the ground. There was no air, and in terror Penny scratched wildly at his face and kicked her legs. The man was strong and easily avoided her feet, twisting his head to elude her hands.

His grip tightened on her throat and Penny felt her body weakening. She clung to consciousness, refusing to give in to despair, and felt a flicker of satisfaction when she managed to scratch at his eyes.

I'm going down fighting, she thought. *That should count for something.*

With an abrupt jerk, the attacker was pulled off her. Penny dropped to her knees, gasping lungfuls of air, while her attacker fought someone else. Close by, Penny could see two large shapes struggling in the darkness. There was the sound of meaty punches being thrown and deep-throated groans before one fled through the door, followed by the other.

Penny knelt in a heap on the dirt floor, gagging. Strong arms wrapped around her and she flinched, ready to fight again.

"Penny!" Dylan was at her side, crouching next to her. "Dear God, talk to me girl!"

"I'm okay—" she managed to get out, desperately trying to draw deep breaths.

Dylan grabbed the flashlight and helped Penny to sit up, his arm wrapped behind her, and began checking her over.

"Are you bleeding, where are you hurt—"

She couldn't reply but clung to him, her courage deserting her now that he was there. The enormity of what happened crashed around her and she gave in to the terror engulfing her. She began to shake uncontrollably. *Oh my God, I almost got myself killed.*

"There was a man, he was breaking in," she stuttered, trying to piece together what happened, "He had a gas can. Dylan, he was trying to burn the tooling shop down—"

"It's okay now, he's gone, you're safe," His arm tightened around her as he turned the flashlight in the direction Penny was pointing and saw where the gas can had been dropped. "I heard you scream and came running. The lock on the gate had been broken."

After a few moments her heartbeat began to steady. "There were two men. One stopped the other from attacking me and they began fighting each other. Was that you?"

"No. When I got here, there was only you in here."

"Did you see anyone run out?"

"No, no one. Good thing you kept screaming. We need the police, and an ambulance—"

"Not an ambulance," Penny countered. "I'm not hurt. And we can't call the police."

"Why not? An arsonist broke into the foundry."

"I have my money hidden in the watchman's hut. And they might take the pieces of the cup we found." Penny's panic began to grow again. "And I can't give any description of the guy who attacked me, or the person who pulled him off me."

"Maybe they can get some fingerprints?" Dylan suggested.

"He was wearing gloves. There aren't any security cameras either. The police will crawl all over my excavation, see I'm living here, and maybe make me leave. Word will get out and people will think I'm finding valuable things and there will be more break-ins."

Dylan didn't seem convinced but there wasn't much choice. "Look, I can lay on a bit of security. Not a lot, but we won a bundle today."

"The girls came by and told me, congratulations," Penny paused. "Do you think it had something to do with that?"

"You mean like a disgruntled Mudford Town supporter? I should hope not..." Dylan thought for a moment. "Whatever is going on, it's not safe for you to stay here, even with security. I was insane for letting you talk me into it in the first place. You need to move in with me."

Penny shook her head. "I can't leave. They'll come back. I have to protect this."

"But there's nothing here. You said you haven't found anything."

"They weren't trying to steal anything. They wanted to burn the tooling shop to the ground. And maybe the other buildings as well. I'm going to keep going. I'm not going to stop until I find what I'm supposed to find."

Dylan sighed and helped her to her feet. "Well then, I can't get the security arranged until tomorrow, so you're coming home with me."

Chapter Twenty-Seven

Sunday morning Penny stood in the open doorway of the tooling shop biting her trembling lip. The old door, which had been ripped off its hinges sometime last night, was on the ground before her. Her carefully laid out string grid was now hopelessly tangled, ripped from the nails and was bunched in tangled heaps around the building. It was going to take ages to put it back to rights.

The sparrows overhead chirruped shrilly, breaking the morning stillness. Penny sat down on the crate in the middle of the building and felt hot tears build up. What was she supposed to do? This dig was a sitting duck for thieves and it was impossible to secure. Her arm ached from where the intruder had hit it, and the mirror in the bathroom at Dylan's house had shown black and blue marks starting on her throat.

After several minutes the swallows settled and the tears passed, and her breathing returned to normal. She looked up to see Biscuits standing in the doorway, surveying the mess.

"Freddy Young left Hampstead Football Club for Hendon Football Club after ten years in 1931," he said, Penny supposed by way of condolence. He shuffled around for a few moments, then stooped and picked up an end of string and began to wind it.

Penny watched his slow, patient motions and realized there wasn't any alternative but to do the same. She found another end and began winding as well. The process of untangling the mess was tedious but Biscuits didn't seem to mind. Penny put the new batteries Dylan had given her in the portable radio, and together they listened to Joe Lyons's match report from yesterday and the analysis of the Sunday games that would soon be played.

Biscuits wound patiently for three hours before Kathleen came to fetch him. "Oh, miss! Your nice string grid, what happened?"

"I think an animal got in here last night and got tangled up," Penny said, not all together untruthfully. "Biscuits has been a big help setting it straight."

"As long as he's not being a pest. Mum says to come along, Biscuits, we're out to Grannie's for lunch."

The boy trotted after his sister, leaving Penny alone. Dylan came an hour later with two men in technician uniforms.

"Penny, these guys are here from the private security firm I've just hired. They'll be installing security cameras that they'll monitor remotely, add some more lights, and put a better lock on the gate. I'll make sure you get a key. And I guess we'll be getting a new door here."

Penny nodded.

"Sure you don't want to spend the night again at my place until they get the security sorted?" Dylan asked.

"Thanks, but it's best I stay here."

"Do you need anything else?"

"I wish I had my dad's 20-gauge Winchester loaded with rock salt," Penny grumbled.

Dylan blanched. "Guns are illegal here."

Penny rolled her eyes. "I'm joking..."

——◄O►——

Penny finished rolling the ball of string she was working on and lined it up next to the others; by her estimate she was halfway through the arduous process. She started winding the next row of twine and followed it to the far end of the shop, an area Penny had so far ignored. Her stomach rumbled again.

The pick-axe had landed here, point down, thrown by her assailant the previous night. It had been thrown with force and the sharp tip was embedded in several inches of soil. Using two hands, she pulled. It released easily, and Penny could see the soil here was softer and darker. She cleared a few inches with her foot, and then retrieved an old screwdriver and began to probe the area. The dirt gave way easily and Penny went back to her tools and grabbed a trowel, whisk brush, and soft-haired brush.

Within ten minutes the hole was eight inches deep and again as wide, with no sign of any rocks or clay. She probed again with the screwdriver, and on the third push it hit something with gentle impact.

Her hunger forgotten, Penny cleared a broader area and revealed the rim of a wide clay pot. It was the same color as the horse pot, and intact. Using the whisk brush she cleared away an inch around a thick rim. The dirt inside the pot was soft, and she pushed her fingers in and felt cold metal. Brushing further, Penny saw two strands of heavy wire, a dull brass color, formed into a semi-circle with tightly curled ends.

Hands trembling, she ran her fingers around the edges and tugged. It freed easily and emerged from the dirt in one piece. It was a torc.

A glorious smile broke out on Penny's face. "Thank you," she breathed.

Her focus intent, Penny set the torc to her side and probed deeper in the pot. She knew she should be documenting everything—the depth of the soil, the orientation of the torc, but she didn't care. She was too excited.

She did, however, have the presence of mind to run and grab some newspaper she'd been keeping and placed the soil she removed on it. Who knew, there might be clues in there as well. Using her fingers she probed deeper until she felt another metal ring. This one was larger and thicker than the first, but the metal was blackened and Penny didn't dare scratch it to see if it was silver. It, too was a torc, and also unbroken.

A stillness settled around her efforts, and even the sparrows were quiet. The only sound was her own deep, steady breathing. The pot walls were holding firm, and she didn't dare remove any of the supporting soil around it. Penny continued digging, knowing full well what lay at the bottom.

Two inches further down she felt another metal coil. Curling her fingers around it she lifted it easily, and even with the dirt that clung to it Penny could see it was a golden torc. Gold never tarnished and never faded, and the elaborate piece glinted a bit in the thin light. It was sturdy and much heavier than the first two, and just as magnificent as the day someone had buried it.

Penny sat back on her heels, elation spreading through her body like a drug. They were torcs. They were all intact. She looked around the tooling shop, feeling a sense of belonging. She loved this place more than anywhere else on earth.

Taking off her sweatshirt, Penny folded it around each torc, taking care that they did not touch. She put a layer of newspaper in the hole the torcs had come from and filled it with soil from the other end of the building—it would help the pot stay stable yet not be mixed with the dirt she had removed. That should please the real archeologists.

She carried the torcs to the watchman's hut, spreading more newspaper on her cot and laying the torcs on it. Pulling up a crate to sit on, she began the painstaking process of brushing away the detritus that had settled into the crevices, taking care to save it on the newspaper spread beneath.

The bronze torc, she saw, was the lightest and smallest, a collar of simple double-twisted thick metal wire that ended in tightly coiled spirals.

The blackened torc, she noted, was covered in a fine grey ash. If this find was in keeping with Iceni practices, it was silver. It was made of finer strands that were tightly woven into a thick wire cord, with round knobs at the ends. They seemed more elaborate but their detail was hidden by the encrusted soot. Penny noted this torc was slightly misshapen and looked like it had been worn—flat here, and out of curve there.

Penny set the two torcs aside and put the gold torc front and center. The soft brush dislodged flecks of dirt and she saw it, too, was made of hundreds of strands of metal wire floss woven smoothly into an inch thick coil. It was like the Snettisham Great Torc, but bigger and with more complex detail. The diameter was slightly larger than the other two torcs and it was easily three times the weight, almost two pounds by Penny's estimate. The terminals on the ends were elaborate, and even crusted with dirt she could tell they were magnificent horse heads. They faced each other, each with a ring in its mouth, possibly for a chain to go through. Penny had never seen anything like it in her research. It was going to give scholars heartburn for years.

"I've given up five years of my life to find this," Penny whispered reverently, slipping the torc around her neck.

The torc fit snugly but was not uncomfortable, and the gold warmed quickly against her skin. Penny inhaled, feeling a pleasant wave of relief wash over her. She stood up taller and caught her reflection in the window glass.

Not a bad look.

It was very important that she call HARP right now. This was treasure, important treasure—gold, and probably silver and bronze. She should borrow Dylan's phone and take a picture and send it to them, and they would see for themselves. The torcs were obviously early Britannic, almost certainly Iceni, and had been buried for a very long time. Within hours her tooling shop would be crawling with professionals who would know what to do. Maybe even Professor Jain herself would arrive and take over, and tell Penny she'd done a great job.

And then Penny would be free to go home.

It was funny, Penny thought, how the torc rested more on her shoulders than her neck. You'd think a heavy necklace would be uncomfortable, but it was actually very pleasant. Keeping one eye on her reflection in the window glass Penny turned her head left and right, then unbraided her hair and let it fall around her in a curly auburn mass.

It was entirely possible, Penny considered, that the fruitless excavations in Mancetter might be taking up all of HARP's resources. If she sent them the pictures, there was every chance they'd keep ignoring her. Today was December 5th, and HARP said they would be here on March 21st. That was only 106 days, which was practically next week. It wouldn't hurt anything if she kept digging a bit more, and it might even help HARP when they finally arrived.

The Penny that stared back at herself in her reflection knew that calling HARP was not only the honorable thing to do, it was the right thing to do.

Just not yet.

Penny gently removed the gold torc and wrapped it in her sweatshirt with the other two, debating where they would be safest. After some thought she emptied her duffle bag and placed them carefully inside, and added her money from the lockbox, toothbrush, toothpaste, towel, and a change of clothing.

She walked the three blocks to Dylan's house, taking pains to appear unconcerned, stopping leisurely at the intersections while casting furtive glances at passers-by. When she reached his street, she gave in and ran the last hundred yards, arriving breathless on his door stoop and leaned on the doorbell. From behind the door she heard the scraping and clanking of locks until finally the door opened.

Dylan looked surprised to see her. "Penny, are you alright?"

"Yes. I'm going to take you up on your offer."

"Offer…"

"You're right, it's safer here. I've paid you rent for the watchman's hut but I can afford a bit more for the room I stayed in last night—"

"No, no," Dylan shook his head, "not a problem." He dragged a hand through his hair. "I'm sorry, but what are you doing?"

She barged through the door. "I'm moving in."

Chapter Twenty-Eight

WATER GUSHED OUT OF the showerhead in the bathroom Penny was using at Dylan's house, plentiful and steaming hot. Penny rotated slowly, letting it hit every part of her body and reveling in the abundance. She had been living at Dylan's for four days now and this shower had become the highlight of her day.

The shower stall was tiny but she didn't care. The bathroom was clean and warm, and attached to the small bedroom Dylan had let her use. Compared to the cot in the watchman's hut, the single comfy bed and nightstand were luxurious.

The torcs were hidden in a box she had secreted at the back of the closet under a stack of empty suitcases. She would have preferred hiding them under the floorboards, but the room was carpeted, so that was out of the question. And judging by the wide array of locks on the doors and Dylan's security system, they were safe enough.

In fact, the state-of-the-art security system was so complicated Penny had to consult the directions she'd written for arming and disarming it every time she came or went. This was a curiosity in itself—at home in Indiana they had never locked the doors.

She dressed and went around the corner to the kitchen and poured herself a cup of coffee from the coffeemaker Dylan never used. In the four days she'd been living there she'd learned a lot about him, although she rarely saw him. He suffered from insomnia—she could hear him watching television in the wee hours of the morning. He kept almost no food in the house, seeming to subsist solely on the jar of energy drink powder on the counter. His mother was living in Spain and called to check on him regularly. He seemed to enjoy talking with her and would assure her everything was fine.

Penny made herself toast for breakfast and was just finishing it when the doorbell chonged. She navigated the series of locks. "Good morning, Biscuits."

"Rod Baider scored the first goal in the 1979 Middlesex Charity Cup Final on a cross from Greg Sewell," Biscuits replied by way of a greeting.

Penny got her coat and together they walked to the foundry, Biscuits chattering about obscure Icelton statistics for the five-minute walk. It was mid-December now, and the air was brisk.

At the dig Penny opened the watchman's hut with the key and they meandered through the hallway to the tooling shop. She checked the makeshift security system she had set up—a piece of tape over the new outside door—all remained untouched. The grid had been restrung, and Biscuits went to his square and began scraping.

After Biscuits left for school, she switched to working the squares next to where she had found the torcs. They hadn't yielded anything yet, but the clues were there.

Later that afternoon Penny stopped work early and carefully refilled the holes. She walked to Hendon, stopping first to say hello to Scott and Jeff at Ye Olde Kebab Shoppe. Jeff waved from behind the counter.

"What happened to your arm?" Penny asked.

"Slipped and fell on the way home the other night," Jeff rolled his eyes as he negotiated the cash register with one hand.

"Must have been some fall," Penny observed, noting the black and blue smudges on his face.

"I made a shambles of it," Jeff agreed. "How are you?"

"Doing well, thanks."

"Can we drop off some take out at the foundry?"

"I'm, ummm, staying at Dylan's. It's safer," Penny smiled and Jeff gave her a thumbs up.

She walked on to the Hendon Post Office, stopping first to buy a Christmas card for her family. In the Post Office she opened the card and wrote "I'm including your Christmas present. Make sure you put this in a very safe place. Missing you all, love Penny".

She placed the betting slip from Billy Dale inside the card and sealed it. At the counter she bought an overseas stamp and carefully affixed it and handed it to the person at the counter.

"Will it arrive by Christmas?" she asked.

"Shouldn't see why not."

Penny walked back to Dylan's house, sad she would be missing the holidays with her parents. As she turned down Elthorne Road, a white car passed her and pulled into the driveway in front of the house. It was the same white car she'd seen multiple times at the Icelton grounds. Penny picked up her step.

The driver was looking at her mobile phone and didn't see Penny approach. The car was still running, and Penny opened the passenger side door. "Do you have something for Dylan?"

The woman behind the steering wheel jumped. "Who are you?"

"I'm staying here," Penny replied and snatched the bag on the car seat. "This is for him, right?"

"Yes, but—" the woman's eyes widened, and she lunged for the bag, but Penny had already slammed the car door shut.

"Not a problem, I'll take it in. See ya!" Penny bolted to the door and began pressing buttons on the keypad to unlock it.

The woman rolled down the window. "Hey! Bring that back!"

Penny forced herself to focus on entering the sequence codes Dylan had given her and in seconds the door beeped and the locks released. She burst through and slammed it shut behind her, terrified the driver was hot on her heels.

Penny waited twenty seconds and then peeped out the side window. The car was still there, and the woman was tapping madly on her mobile, then slammed the car into reverse and sped backwards into the road, ignoring an approaching car that honked in disapproval. She shifted forward and sped away.

In the kitchen Penny opened the bag and took out a small bottle. Without hesitation she unscrewed the top and sniffed, detecting peppermint. She wet her finger and dipped it in the white powder, leaving a tiny bit on the tip. She dabbed it on her tongue and immediately tasted a bitter and metallic taste. Penny rubbed a tiny bit on her gums and the sensation was instantaneous. She went to the sink, rinsed her mouth and spat it out.

Chapter Twenty-Nine

Dylan came home twenty minutes later. "I forgot my mobile, had to come back for it. Did the chemist deliver here?" he asked the moment he came in the door.

"Yes," Penny nodded to the bag on the kitchen table and he reached eagerly for it. "Dylan, this isn't any of my business, but I think this is mostly cocaine."

He paused. "What?"

"The stuff in the bottle. It's mostly cocaine."

"That's ridiculous. It's tooth powder, for brushing your teeth."

"I'm not judging you. But you said you didn't do drugs."

"I don't. Never have." His eyes narrowed. "How would you know its cocaine?"

"I don't know. I've never done cocaine, either. But my roommate at the hospital where I was treated had a serious cocaine addiction problem. She told me it tasted like metal and was bitter. Her boyfriend was also a drug dealer. She saw a lot of it."

Dylan stared at the bottle like he had never seen it before.

Penny looked at the large plastic jar labeled Energy Drink on the kitchen counter. "They deliver that as well?"

Dylan nodded slowly. Penny unscrewed the lid and dipped a finger in. The powder tasted disgusting, and she made a face.

"Acquired taste," Dylan tried to joke as a torrent of emotions contorted his face. "So you're saying there could be drugs in here?"

"Yes."

"Why would they have cocaine in the tooth powder?" Dylan asked.

"I don't know. Maybe we should go ask them."

—◦—

"Malnutria Chemists? Never heard of 'em," the London cab driver said.

"They're in Chelsea," Dylan said.

"I know, I'm reading the label. 729 Danvers Street, Chelsea," The cab driver repeated, looking at the address on the bottle label. "Doesn't exist, mate."

"What do you mean?" Penny asked.

"I mean, there's a Danvers Street in Chelsea alright, but it's short and doesn't go as high as 729. It starts at the Thames Embankment, near Albert Bridge, and goes two blocks up to Paulston Square. It's all houses."

"Can you take us? Maybe it's on King's Road," Dylan said.

"I know Chelsea like the back of my hand. And I've never seen nor heard of any Malnutria Chemists, certainly not around Paulston Square," the cabbie reiterated.

"Let's go there."

The driver shrugged. "You're the boss."

———◆◇◆———

It was as the cab driver said. Danvers Street was a leafy London side street with rows of houses and people walking their dogs around a green square. There was no pharmacy in view.

"Take us to a real chemist, please," Penny asked the driver.

Dylan stayed in the cab while Penny went inside and bought the most expensive over-the-counter drug test they had. Once back in the house she handed the bag to Dylan. "You need to take this drug test."

He looked at the box for a long time. "I've taken it before."

"Then you need to take it again."

Dylan disappeared upstairs and returned to the kitchen a few moments later with the test kit. Five minutes later Penny read from the results panel.

"You're positive for cocaine, amphetamines, benzodiazepines, and barbiturates. I guess the good news is that the marijuana and methadone is negative."

"Jesus..." Dylan muttered, rubbing his temples.

"Dylan, if you're telling the truth, then someone is drugging you."

"Why do you think I'm not telling the truth?"

Penny shrugged. "Druggies lie."

"I'm *not* a druggie. You have to believe me."

"I do believe you. But who is sending you this stuff? Where does it come from?"

Dylan sat on a kitchen chair. "Sue got it."

Penny snorted. "Your girlfriend. The one on television."

"Yes."

"So she takes it as well?"

"She did. But Sue doesn't do drugs. She's a vegan, for God's sake. Made me eat all that nasty stuff."

"Okay, where did she get it?"

"I don't know. It just showed up at the flat in Chelsea. I wouldn't touch it until Duncan, our team physio, gave it the green light. He said it was just an expensive jar of plop, full of herbs and needless dross. It didn't do much in the beginning. But pretty soon I couldn't stop taking it."

"Are you still paying for it?"

"Every month on my credit card, hundreds of pounds." Dylan rummaged in a drawer and pulled out a paper statement. "There."

Penny read the statement, it did indeed say Malnutria Chemist. She used Dylan's mobile phone and called the number. "It says it's been disconnected." She chose her next words carefully. "You said you'd taken this drug test before."

Dylan nodded, staring at the floor. "Right after Dad's funeral."

"And?"

He drew a tormented breath. "Penny, no one can know about this."

"I won't tell anyone."

"Dad hadn't been feeling well for a bit," Dylan began. "Mum was worried. I was playing close to here, over at Townsend Lane Stadium, and I'd get over to see him most nights. I loved it cos we'd talk about Icelton. The club meant everything to him. I was playing like crap and I knew it, and it was a relief he didn't want to talk about that—which made him just about the only person around who wasn't on my case. Then one day he didn't wake up.

"I was right gutted. I only remember bits of the funeral. Afterwards Gwen, she's my godmother, and she's also a doctor, came round. Gave me a hiding for the ages, told me I looked like shit and she wanted me in her office Monday morning."

"Did you go?"

"Course not. I refused, point-blank. She said she figured I wouldn't go and tossed a bag in my lap. She told me it was an at-home drug test and to take it. Said I'd be shocked at the results."

"Did you take it?"

"No. I left it here. I was back and forth between Sue and my flat in Chelsea helping Mum close this house up—she was going to their place on the Costa del Sol to rest, and I was helping her get Dad's affairs in order. I was actually feeling a lot better. Then right before a Liverpool match I started getting the shakes. Giles yanked me at halftime and I sat on the bench for the rest of the game. It was a disgrace. That night I came here and took the test."

"And?" Penny asked.

"Lit up like a bloody Christmas tree," Dylan snorted. "Of course it was defective, right? So I went to the chemists and bought another one. Same thing. I went back out and bought three more, each one from a different shop, each one a different kind. Drank gallons of water the night before, then the next day took all the tests, an hour apart. Nailed every single fucking one."

"I thought athletes got random drug tested all the time," Penny said.

"They do, both the FA and Kingsbury Town. Players get called in at random everyone once in a while but I hadn't. I'd only been with the club for a little less than a year at that point."

"What happens if someone tests positive?"

"For the rank and file like me, you're done. You're fired and your career is as good as over."

Penny's eyes widened. "Everyone?"

Dylan nodded. "Sir Frank has a zero-tolerance policy. He's a good man, but he has no time for drugs. Then the FA, they can ban you forever. You can't be a manager, you can't own a club, you can't be a referee. You are out on the street."

Penny considered this for a moment. "What did your girlfriend say?"

"Sue wasn't around, she was in Dublin working on a story." Dylan drew a deep breath and released it slowly. "I knew I was sick, but my brain was in a fog and it felt like mush. Still, I knew I had to get ahead of it. The next morning I went in to see Sir Frank and I told him I was retiring, effective immediately."

Dylan stopped, unable to go any further. Penny took his trembling hand in hers.

"He was shocked," Dylan continued, his voice choking up. "He's a good man, he really cared. I was crying like a babe but couldn't say anything. Sir Frank said 'Look, you don't have to tell me anything, but we can get you help.' I refused."

Tears were running down his cheek. "I had no idea how the drugs were getting into my system. I couldn't tell anyone."

Penny handed him a tissue and waited while the storm passed. "What did your girlfriend say?"

Dylan gave a sharp laugh. "She got home the next day. I sat her down and told her, and she went berserk."

"You told her about the drugs?"

"No, I couldn't. I couldn't tell anyone. You don't understand, once word got out I'd be finished. My plan was to figure out how the stuff was getting in my system and get rid of it, and then go back to being a professional player. Come out of retirement, get fit, get a spot at a good club. Maybe not Premier League level but at least Championship.

"When I wouldn't tell her why I retired, Sue flipped out. Started crying and yelling, not making any sense. When she finally calmed down, she said she needed time to think. Told me to leave. I came here."

"And you never once suspected that someone was giving you doctored stuff?"

Dylan shook his head. "No one's ever accused me of being smart. But I had Duncan check them and he sent them out and it was all okay. Useless in his opinion, fancy dross, said it was my money to waste."

"So someone started fiddling with the ingredients later." Penny looked at the bottle of tooth powder on the table. "Did Sue take this?"

"Yes, but she had her own concoction. Said she didn't fancy peppermint."

Penny turned everything Dylan had said over in her mind. "Something isn't adding up. If someone wanted you to test positive, so you'd get fired and kicked out of football, they would have stopped after you retired. And if they wanted to kill you they'd have done it by now."

Dylan swallowed. "I guess."

"What do you want to do now?"

"I want to get clean."

"Okay. Let's get you clean."

Chapter Thirty

Dylan sat with Penny in Gwen's examining room the next morning, haggard after another sleepless night. He was so dehydrated it took the nurse forever to find a vein from which to draw blood, and the girl who took his blood pressure blanched. He had puked twice, and it had taken him forever to give even a few drops of piss.

Gwen sat on a stool across from them, tapping on her laptop computer. "I'll have your blood and urine results by this afternoon, and I'm ordering a full panel that we should have back in three days. You've got samples of the stuff?"

Penny handed her a bag with the jars of tooth powder and energy drink.

"I've got a good lab that can find out what's in here but it's going to take longer, at least two weeks. But in the meantime we'll assume it's the works. Now, symptoms. Insomnia?"

Dylan nodded.

"Headache?"

Dylan nodded again, the pounding in his head increasing as if on cue.

"Vomiting? Diarrhea? Anxiety?"

"Yes, yes, and yes."

"Erectile dysfunction?"

Dylan flushed, totally humiliated. Penny turned to politely stare out the window.

"Come on, lad," Gwen snapped, "I've known you since you were in diapers."

"Uh, maybe," he muttered. Never had he felt so damned embarrassed.

She pointed to the bag. "Dylan, where did this stuff come from?"

Dylan tried to focus but his brain felt like it was in a fog bank. "It was after I started with Kingsbury Town. We had it at the flat in Chelsea," he said, his tongue thick.

"Did that girlfriend of yours give it to you?" Gwen asked.

"She drank it as well," Dylan protested.

"Was she sick? Headaches? Vomiting?"

"No." Sue had never been sick a day in her life.

Gwen reached for a clipboard and began writing things on it. "You're lucky to be alive, Dylan. You're very sick. I'm sending you to hospital. Eddie can manage the team while you're gone."

"No. No, I can't do that," Dylan panicked. "We've got the next FA Cup round coming up. They can't find out about the drugs, Gwen. You know they'll drum me out."

"Detox is serious business and can be life-threatening. You need to be monitored." At his continued refusal Gwen sighed and folded her arms. "Have you gone to the police?"

Dylan shook his head. "No! Whoever is giving me this stuff is doing it for a reason. They need to think I'm still on it."

"How long will the detox last?" Penny asked.

"It depends what's in there. If it is mostly cocaine, a few days. I'm guessing there're some amphetamines as well, and that's longer, about a week. You should be over the physical effects in about seven days. I can prescribe something that will help with the withdrawal symptoms—"

Dylan gritted his teeth to silence the chattering. "No," he finally got out. "Nothing. No more drugs. I'm doing this cold turkey, at home."

⚫

Dylan hadn't left his house in five days. At least Penny said it was five days. For all he knew it could have been five months or five years.

They'd let everyone know he had a terrible bout of the flu and Gwen backed them up. Uncle Eddie had taken over the squad, no questions asked. Penny made him soup that he left untouched and kept careful watch over him. Gwen had been round to see him, taken his blood pressure and listened to his heart, and said that he was doing okay but he had to keep up his liquids so he didn't become dehydrated. That was easier said than done, because he was puking up everything in his system. The drugs weren't leaving without a fight, but he'd be damned if he'd let them win.

Biscuits would come to the door every morning to get Penny. He'd ring the doorbell, the sonorous CHONG splitting Dylan's brain. The lad seemed to delight in it—if the door wasn't opened fast enough he'd ring CHONG-CHONG and then CHONG-CHONG-CHONG. Dylan felt like his head was going to crack open.

On her second visit Gwen brought his preliminary test results with her, confirming the cocaine and amphetamines. "There's also Valium, progesterone, estrogen," Gwen ticked off, "digitalis, and amitriptyline. It's like they cleared the shelves for you."

Dylan grunted, feeling another bout of nausea approach. "What about that chemist in Chelsea?"

"No record of it anywhere in London nor the UK, I had it checked."

"How's the team?"

"Eddie says to tell you they're doing great, they won at Ickenham Town and will probably beat Highgate at their place in the next game."

Dylan nodded and bolted for the loo.

⋯⋯◄○►⋯⋯

The insomnia, blessedly, began to disappear and he welcomed the bliss of unconsciousness. When he woke, the sheets were soaked with sweat and he could smell himself. It was dark outside, his only indication of the time. He had no clue what the date was. Gingerly he sat on the side of the bed, and then staggered to the shower where he stood under the water for a long time, rubbing a bar of soap listlessly over his body.

When he emerged his bed linen had been changed and a glass of cold water was on the nightstand. He dragged on a pair of sweatpants and t-shirt that hung limp on his body, and slowly made his way downstairs.

Penny was in the kitchen, unpacking her duffle bag. A grid map of the tooling shop was unrolled on the table.

"What did you find today?" Dylan asked, his voice rough.

He could tell it was something very exciting by the way her eyes danced, but she quickly shook her head. "Oh, just a shard from a pot, it might be something but probably nothing."

Dylan held the back of the chair to steady himself. "Do you need the key to the drawer in the office?"

"No. Here, sit down," Penny guided him, and poured a glass of water. His legs gave out from under him and he plopped into the chair.

Dylan pushed the glass away but Penny pushed it right back. "Gwen says—"

Reluctantly he took a sip, then forced himself to take another.

"I've made chicken soup," Penny added and ladled a small bowl. Dylan focused on bringing the spoon to his lips without spilling but didn't have much success.

Penny dabbed his mouth with a tea towel. "I found Ritz crackers at the market. This is what my mom gives us when we're sick. I can even toast them and put butter on top."

A wave of nausea pushed up his throat. "Maybe later. Thank you for changing the sheets."

"Not a problem, happy to do it. Did you get much sleep this afternoon?"

"Some." Dylan pushed the soup bowl away and looked at the grid map where Penny was recording her finds. "That's where you found the new shard?"

"Yes, but I think I'm on to something else that's really stupendous. Remember at the British Museum the impressions of chariot wheels they found in the clay? The wood had rotted away but the impressions were still in the dirt?"

Dylan nodded, his recollection clouded at best.

"Biscuits found an area where the dirt was markedly different colors. I went over and saw a curve, and what looked like spokes."

"Good for Bis—" Dylan got out before staggering to the hall toilet, just in time. When he was finished retching his guts out, he splashed water on his face and rinsed his mouth.

Penny was outside the door and put a gentle hand on his arm. "Come on, let's get you back to bed."

"No," he grasped her hand, his eyes squeezed shut. "Keep talking. What do you miss most from America?"

"Kentucky Fried Chicken," Penny said, leading him back to the kitchen where he collapsed in a chair.

The thought of it turned his stomach and he was afraid he was going to retch again. He drew several deep breaths. "We've got that. There's one on Camden High Street."

"That's not around here."

"Why do you like it so much?" he asked, clenching his jaw to keep his teeth from chattering.

"My older sisters, when they were in high school, worked there. They'd come home at midnight and their clothing would smell of fried chicken, and I'd be asleep in our room and start dreaming about it. They'd have to take showers to get the smell out of their hair."

"What are your sisters' names?"

"Ruth and Angie."

"Tell me about them."

"Only if you let me help you up to bed."

A string of angry curses flew out of Dylan's mouth and he immediately felt remorse. "I'm sorry. You don't deserve any of this. Thank you for being here, for helping me."

"Of course."

He struggled to his feet and allowed Penny to help him up the stairs to his bedroom. He hated being so fucking useless. "T-tell me about Ruth," he said, relieved to be back in bed.

"Ruth was third runner-up in the Miss Indiana pageant when she was nineteen," Penny said, pulling the blankets up over him. "She got to wear beautiful gowns, and get her hair done. I used to paint her nails for her. I wore one of her gowns for my prom."

Dylan lay back against the pillows. "Do you have a boyfriend?"

"I did."

"What happened?"

"He didn't want a girlfriend in an institution."

Penny handed him the glass of water and he took a sip. "What do your parents do?"

"Everyone does shift work at the automotive plant in town. My Dad was a test driver, he's a maintenance engineer now. My mom and Ruth work on the assembly line, and Angie works in the quality control department."

"Sounds like they're all hard workers."

"Shift work pays the best. We're still paying off the year I was at Ash Park Hospital. It was really expensive."

He must have dozed off because she was still sitting next to him when he woke. "Thirsty," he got out.

She handed him the water. This time she had added ice and a straw. He pulled on it gratefully. "You're really good at taking care of people going through detox."

"I saw a lot of people go through it at the hospital in Cincinnati."

"How long were you there?

"A year."

"Why were you there? Because of the voice you were hearing?"

"Kind of. The rest of the patients, they definitely hear voices. With me it's more of a feeling that someone has their hand on my back and is pushing. Pushing very hard."

"But it was right," Dylan countered. "You're here. You found the pot shard with the horse on it. You're finding more stuff."

Penny shook her head. "She's still not satisfied."

A thought occurred to Dylan. "You're not happy about having been right."

"I am, I guess," Penny gave a half-smile. "But it's kind of like getting to the top of a huge mountain you never had any intention of climbing in the first place."

Dylan was struck by her fortitude. "What are you going to do when you get home?"

"Get my life back."

"What—" A bout of shivering interrupted him, "—what does that entail?"

"Go to college. Make new friends," Penny said, tucking the blankets closer around him. "The worst part about getting sick was losing friends. People don't want to hang out with you. And then when I was at the facility, people forgot about me."

Dylan reached out to clasp her hand. "Penny. That first night, when I met you. I'm sorry."

"Sorry?"

"For kissing you."

"It's okay. You were on drugs."

"No, it was out of line," Dylan continued, feeling a desperate need to apologize for his atrocious behavior. "And I knew it was out of line and I did it anyway. But the thing is, when I met you, I suddenly felt good. I hadn't felt good in a long time."

Penny looked confused, as well she should. "I'm glad."

"No, you don't understand..." Dylan needed to explain more, to tell her how much her coming into his life meant to him, but all the energy drained from his body and he surrendered to the tidal wave of sleep that rolled over him.

Chapter Thirty-One

THE BEACH BAR IN Marbella, on the Costa del Sol in the south of Spain, was starting to fill up. Dylan sat on the patio, enjoying the evening breeze off the Mediterranean that lifted the heat left over from the day. On the television behind the bar, Kingsbury Town was giving South Quay Road a lashing for the ages, which cheered him up immensely. South Quay Road had beaten Kingsbury Town in the semifinal of the FA Cup last year, right after he had retired, and he knew his sudden departure had been a major contribution to the loss.

Dylan took out his new mobile and tapped a few keys to get updates on the other matches that were being played that day. He'd accidentally dropped his old one in the pool when he'd fallen asleep on the inflatable lounger the day before, and gotten an earful from Mum about it. But there hadn't been an issue—he'd gone out that morning and gotten a new one without much fuss. At this time of year there seemed to be more Brits on the Costa del Sol than Spaniards.

A group of Scottish girls waved to him from another table, giggling as they held large glasses of tropical cocktails. They were wearing Santa hats and dressed for a night out, and obviously up for a good time. Dylan ignored them and took his glass of lemonade to a quiet table in the back.

He caught his reflection in a mirror across the room. He'd gotten some sun that day, a decided improvement over his previous pallor. But the bright holiday shirt Mum had given him hung on his frame, and even from a distance he could see dark circles remained under his eyes.

Penny said the trembling would stop and it had, and the fog was finally lifting from his brain. He still didn't have much energy, and he could tell his mother was worried. The spicy Spanish food turned his stomach but the fresh fruit tasted good. The chicken soup Penny had spooned into him for ten days straight was the only other thing that had stayed down.

Penny. Remarkable girl.

She'd insisted he get on the plane, to be with his family for Christmas. He sort of wished she was here now, but good Lord the girl needed a rest after nursing him night and day. Last year Sue had insisted they go to St Barths in the Caribbean instead of joining Mum and Dad here, calling the Costa del Sol tacky. Tacky it might be, but at least you didn't need a second mortgage to pay a restaurant tab.

His cousin Andrew walked in and Dylan waved him over.

"Order me a beer, there's a good chap," Andrew said, collapsing his large form in a chair and wiping his brow. "Your mum, bless her, is putting the kids to bed. My poor wife is knackered, too much sun."

A television nearby flashed the news that the owner of Rochester Football Club had just been arrested, and showed video footage of him being led from an opulent house to a waiting police car.

"Isn't that who you drew in the third round?" Andrew asked.

Dylan nodded, following the story with interest. "Yeah, they've got eight days to clean up their finances and pay their players or they're threatening to all become free agents."

"I don't blame them," Andrew grunted. "What happens if they can sort themselves out?"

"They'll beat us like a drum."

"You've had a good run of it, though," Andrew accepted a glass of beer from the server and toasted Dylan. "Heard you got some pretty young American digging back in the foundry. What's she found?"

Dylan shifted uneasily. "A few bits and bobs." Remembering Andrew was a history teacher, he added, "She's looking for Roman stuff."

"Oh yes?" Andrew said with obvious interest. "That area you're in along Watling Street, there was plenty of Roman activity, according to Tacitus."

"Tacitus," Dylan repeated. "She keeps going on about him. Who is he?"

"Who was he," Andrew corrected. "He was a Roman. He wrote a series of books, *Works of Tacitus*. His father-in-law was Roman military staff in Britain in the first century AD, and later he was governor of Britain. He would have given Tacitus a first-hand account of the rebellion."

"Do you mean Boudica's rebellion?"

"Yes, Queen Boudica," Andrew said. "Now there was a woman. Tacitus hated her guts."

"Why?"

"Romans hated a woman in power—they just couldn't conceive of queens. Cleopatra, Zenobia, Boudica—any woman in charge of anything made their heads explode. They liked their girls pretty and at home, keeping their tongues in their mouths."

"But Boudica beat the Romans."

"Almost, but not quite."

Dylan sat back in his chair, ready for a good story. "What happened?"

"You mean with the Romans and Boudica? It's a grand tale," Andrew smiled. "Around 'bout two thousand years ago, Britain was a whole bunch of small tribes, each with a king or queen. They squabbled amongst each other and got up to mischief, but for the most part they raised sheep and worshipped their gods, led by the Druids, who were the priest class.

"The Druids were educated—they could read and write, and they studied the stars which helped them make some accurate predictions. But most of all, they were respected and could move between the tribes, which meant they could organize.

"So Julius Caesar showed up in 55 BC thinking Britain had huge amounts of gold and silver. It was a disaster—the Romans had no idea about the tides being so big and his fleet got wrecked. He stayed in the south, met with a few tribes that said they'd be friendly, and went back to Rome considering Britain done and dusted.

"Nothing much happened for a hundred years, then in 43AD the Romans came back to get serious about con-quering. Emperor Claudius showed up and cut deals with the tribes in the south and east. He said 'You lot become clients, pay us taxes, show us where the gold and silver is, and we'll protect you and trade with you. You get all the lovely things from Rome like wine and olive oil and culture, and the missus gets pretty jewelry and nice fabric.'

"Those tribes took one look at the Roman legions Claudius had brought with him and decided that was a good deal. Claudius and his generals congratulated themselves on a job well done and went back to Rome, leaving a governor and several legions to make sure everything ran smoothly."

"What about the tribes in the north?" Dylan asked.

"They were a lot cooler to the Romans, as were the Druids. As the Romans pushed further north and west, the Druids started stirring up resistance. The Britons would attack them in forests and marshes, guerilla-style, and then melt away. The Roman legions fought like machines and were very good at hand-to-hand combat, but they needed space to maneuver as a group. Also, the Britons had chariots, which the Romans didn't use. The Romans were terrified.

"By 54 AD the Romans were getting knackered. The resistance was taking up a lot of resources and the gold and silver Julius Caesar had raved about turned out to be muck. It was rumored that Emperor Nero had had enough and was ready to chuck the whole lot.

"Now this didn't go down well with the rich back in Rome, who had invested a lot of money in Britain thinking they were going to get even richer. Toffs like Seneca—the same guy that Len keeps quoting—were in it up to their ears. They weren't going to walk away from it.

"They convinced Nero to keep at it and get serious about bringing the Britons to heel. He sent Suetonius Paulinus, who was an excellent general and had lots of experience putting things right. Paulinus arrived in 58 AD and immediately set about eliminating the Druids."

Dylan signaled the server for another beer for Andrew, anxious to keep him talking.

"In the meantime, the Romans built Colchester, which they called Camulodunum, as their capital and started settling retired soldiers there—you know, you do your twenty years in the army and Rome sets you up in a nice garden flat. Since it was full of retired soldiers, the Romans didn't even build a wall around the city. Didn't see the point.

"The land they built it on was controlled by the local Iceni tribe, ruled by a guy named King Prasutagus. He had a wife, Queen Boudica, and at least two daughters, and they lived around Thetford, ninety miles to the north of London. The king was cooperating with the Romans and they gave him a lot of independence, but he had his hands full with these pensioners who were arrogant, rowdy arses.

"The Romans decided that what Colchester needed was a big temple dedicated to Claudius. Not only did they force the Iceni to build it, they also forced them to *pay* for it. King Prasutagus said 'See here, we don't got that kind of money,' and the Romans said, 'not a problem, we'll loan you the money.'

"The temple got built very fast. It was huge and had proper columns like a Roman temple and a bronze statue of Emperor Claudius out front. At the same time, Suetonius Paulinus had his legions up north and was pushing the Druids further and further north and west.

"Now King Prasutagus died around 60 AD, and left a will saying his daughters and Nero would inherit his kingdom, which was pretty much par for the course at this time."

"Why not his wife, Queen Boudica?" Dylan asked.

Andrew laughed and sipped his fresh beer. "No one knows. But I think it was because Prasutagus knew she was a hot-head who hated the Romans and he wanted peace. He probably figured one of the daughters would marry well and become queen, and that Nero would be the overseer. Sort of like it was when he was king.

"But what he didn't plan on, see, was that after he died, the Romans would ignore his will and go in and confiscate everything. They said, 'Not so fast, your king died and the kingdom is now imperial property', and sent in the retired veterans from Colchester to do an inventory. Boudica must have put up a resistance because they flogged her—and this is the really tragic part—they raped the two daughters. Miserable bunch of brutes."

"Tacitus said that?"

Andrew nodded. "Who's the barbarians, I ask you? Now the Iceni are basically slaves on their own land and they were not happy. Things start going wrong in Colchester. The citizens, who were Roman citizens, which was a very big deal, saw bad omens—the big statue of Victory in the main square fell down, it rained blood, and sundials cracked. Some of the people left, but most stayed.

"The good news for the Romans was that the Druids were cornered in Anglesey, three hundred miles away and at least five days away on foot. Paulinus needed to march west to finish them off, but he couldn't trust the Iceni, could he? So he made them hand in all of their weapons. When they didn't do it voluntarily, the Romans sent in the retired soldiers again. It seems that was the last straw.

"Paulinus is no sooner marching west, when the Iceni revolt. Tacitus, he says Boudica was their leader, and she took them straight to Colchester. Remember, even though it was the capital of Roman Britain it was undefended—no wall, and only two hundred retirees to defend the city.

"The Iceni attacked the town and strolled right in. The citizens managed to send a messenger on horseback north to the 9th Legion, over a hundred miles up the road in Lincoln, telling them to come rescue them. They were the closest and the only legion available, since the rest were with Paulinus in Anglesey. Then everyone ran to the new temple and barricaded themselves inside.

"For three days the Iceni burned the town, and then they burned the temple with everyone inside. You can still dig down six, seven feet in Colchester and see a big black streak. No one survived."

"But where was the 9th Legion?" Dylan asked, completely absorbed by the story.

Andrew's lips pressed into a sly smile. "They never made it to Colchester. Boudica and her people were waiting for them. They ambushed the soldiers and cut them to pieces. Only the general and a few cavalry survived—it was a complete rout and the first time an entire Roman legion had been wiped out. That was 2,500 soldiers massacred. *And by a woman.*

"On their way out of Colchester, the Iceni cut off the head of the statue of Claudius for good measure."

Dylan remembered that from the British Museum. "What happened next?"

Chapter Thirty-Two

"NOW PAULINUS," ANDREW CONTINUED, "he's just fought a big battle in Anglesey and defeated the Druids. Huge victory, but then he gets word that Boudica has burned Colchester to the ground, wiped out an entire legion, and was marching sixty miles down the A12 to London."

"There was no A12 back then," Dylan pointed out.

Andrew rolled his eyes and laughed. "No, it was just a glorified marching path the Romans built to get them around the country. There's a problem—Paulinus is three hundred miles away from London. And even though at that point London was just a settlement on the Thames, it handled a lot of trade. It wasn't nearly as important as St Albans and Colchester, but it was full of merchants who were Roman citizens. It was an important port.

"Paulinus tells his army to start marching east, and that he'll meet up with them at Lichfield. He took a few hundred men and somehow, nobody really knows how, got to London fast. As soon as he arrived, he took one look around and saw it was hopeless. London's a sprawling shanty town with no walls and he can't defend it.

"He said, 'Sorry mates, I only brought a few guys with me, you're on your own'. The citizens were like 'Not bloody likely! We're Roman citizens, you have to stay here and defend us!' and Paulinus said, 'Look, she's going to torch this place to the ground and nobody can stop her. Best get out while the going is good.' Then he marched out of London like the hounds of hell were on his heels and left Boudica to it."

Dylan leaned forward, his elbows on the table, anxious to catch every word. "What did she do when she got to London?"

"Ten times worse than what she did in Colchester, if you believe Cassius Dio who wrote about it a hundred years later. He said, 'All those left behind were butchered and London was burned to the ground.' Then Dio gets very, very detailed about all the atrocities Boudica and her army did, and it was nasty.

"After the Britons were done destroying London," Andrew continued, "they looted their way back up Watling Street towards St Albans, which was the second largest city in Britain, with lots of good things to steal. But here's the thing—St Albans wasn't full of Romans, it was full of Britons. They were locals who had cooperated with the Romans, and who were living in really nice Roman-type houses and dressing up like Romans and acting all Roman-like, lording it over the Iceni.

"Boudica's army looted the city and burned it to the ground. But nobody's found any bodies, like what they found in Colchester and London, so historians think the citizens saw her coming and high-tailed it out of town."

Dylan was beginning to really like Boudica. "So what did the Romans do? A woman was kicking their ass."

"Exactly!" Andrew laughed. "She'd wiped out three Roman cities and massacred an entire Legion. They were furious. Getting repeatedly trounced by a woman was the biggest insult they could imagine. The Roman citizens were furious and Paulinus knew Nero would want him dead if he didn't defeat this woman. He had to fight her, and win.

"He had three legions left in Britain—the 2nd, 14th, and 20th—and he knew Boudica knew this too. He had to meet up with them before she found them—or before she found him. He must have been terrified.

"Paulinus rendezvoused with the legions he'd told to meet him near Lichfield. He only had 10,000 men because the 2nd never showed up, and he thought Boudica had over 100,000 people because other tribes might have been joining her. He knew she was going to attack him but he didn't know where. So he had to attack her first.

"He also had to pick the battle ground, not her. Romans liked to fight their enemies in tight quarters, so he looked around and found a good site. Tacitus is very clear—Paulinus wanted a place with woods to his back and a narrow opening in front of him, like between two hills, and a plain in front so the Britons would have to funnel in to him with no cover. We also know Roman commanders picked battle spots near fresh water and grass for the horses.

"Tacitus says Boudica showed up and the Romans let her get very close. Her people, which included the old and the young, had all their stuff in wagons, which she formed in a semi-circle behind her before she and her people at-tacked. The Romans unleashed the javelins, then went in with their short swords. The Britons retreated, but their wagons blocked them and they were crushed between the wagons and the Romans. It took all day, but the Romans won. They massacred everyone."

Andrew sat back in his chair and took a long sip of beer while Dylan sat on the edge of his seat. "What happened next? What happened to Boudica?"

"No one knows for sure. Tacitus says she poisoned herself, but he would say that. Cassius Dio says she took sick and died and was given a magnificent funeral."

"So where did the battle take place?"

"Ah, that's the question. We know both Boudica and Paulinus were sticking to the A5, so it was somewhere along there, anywhere between Marble Arch in London to Wroxeter, up near Shrewsbury. They've been looking for years. They've been able to rule out the flat bits."

"But that's over one hundred and fifty miles!"

"There are four areas that match Tacitus's description, but each has something wrong with it. And no one has ever found the huge amount of bones that must have been left behind."

"Some people think she's buried in London," Dylan said.

"Aye, back in the Victorian time they were building the Underground and unearthing all manner of old Roman stuff, especially around Kings Cross Station. There's even Battle Bridge, which no one remembers how it got its name, but it doesn't fit the description Tacitus gives of the battle location, although it's very close to Watling Street."

Dylan sat and thought for several moments. "What about Icelton?"

"Eh?"

"She might be buried in Icelton, and the battle took place nearby. The A5 runs right through Hendon," Dylan pointed out, "and the narrow valley could be a bit to the north near Barnet Gate, with the Edgware plain in front, and water from Dollis Brook."

"Where've you come up with all that?"

Dylan realized he might be giving up more information than he intended. "Just, you know, some people talk."

Andrew broke into a wide grin. "If you've got Boudica buried in your backyard, my good man, you're going down in history."

Chapter Thirty-Three

PENNY SLEPT LATE, A luxury. It was Christmas Day after all.

It was still early in Indiana, but she had planned on emailing her family Christmas wishes around six p.m. Dylan's laptop was here and he'd given her the passwords before he'd left to visit his mother in Spain.

Penny hoped Dylan was getting some sun and rest. He'd been stable for three days before he left but was still weak and underweight. Gwen had not been thrilled about the trip but in the end agreed. "His mum will pile food into him until he can't walk," she'd confided. "And he needs a change of scenery."

Penny made herself scrambled eggs and bacon for breakfast and then decided to binge-watch British television. She was on her third movie when the doorbell chonged.

She set her plate on the coffee table and went to answer the door. "Biscuits, it's Christmas Day, I don't think—"

Dylan stood on the door stoop, bundled up and holding a bucket of Kentucky Fried Chicken in each hand. "Happy Christmas!"

"Dylan! I thought you were staying in Spain until New Year?" Penny said, a flush of happiness spreading through her.

"It was really crowded, I came home early," Dylan said as she helped him in the door. He looked tanned and disheveled, but cheerful. "I slept in the airport in Madrid last night to get on the first flight back to London this morning."

"What's all this food?"

"Christmas dinner, of course!" he laughed. "Are you hungry?"

"For the Colonel? Always."

Penny set plates and utensils on the kitchen table and opened the two buckets of fragrant fried chicken. "You got the mashed potatoes and gravy as well!" she inhaled with delight.

They sat down and dug in. "My word, I haven't had this in ages," Dylan said, devouring a fried chicken breast. "It's delicious."

Penny gnawed on a drumstick. "I'll never take it for granted again. How was your vacation?"

"Lovely seeing Mum," he said between bites, "and the rest of the family. My cousin Andrew was there with his family—he teaches history. We had a long talk about Boudica. He told me the whole story, what Tacitus wrote, and the other guy, about who she was and what she did. You and she are a lot alike."

Penny helped herself to another serving of mashed potatoes and gravy. "How so?"

"You're tall and she was tall," when Penny nodded he continued, "you have long tawny hair and she had long tawny hair. And you're a fighter, like she was."

"To a point," Penny added. "I guess he didn't tell you what she did in London?"

"Not really. That bad?"

"Really bad. But I'm pretty sure she knew that being subtle wasn't going to convince the Romans she meant business."

After they had finished their meal and cleaned up, Dylan went to his bag and took out a festively wrapped gift and gave it to Penny. "I saw this in Marbella, and thought of you."

Penny unwrapped the box and removed something wrapped in delicate tissue paper. Inside was an elaborately carved tortoise shell hair comb.

"They call it a mantilla comb, and it's not real tortoise shell," Dylan cautioned. "Those are outlawed."

Penny turned the beautiful comb back and forth, admiring it with delight. It had a wide wedge shape, with carved flowers at the top and long teeth.

"The Spanish women wear them. You've got a lot of hair and I thought you might like it. For dress up."

Penny piled her hair on top of her head and slid the comb down to secure it. The prongs held her hair easily, and she ran to the hall mirror to see her reflection. Penny loved the way the decorative top fanned above her head like a crown. "It's beautiful!"

"You like it?"

"I love it, thank you," she said, and impulsively kissed his cheek.

Dylan caught her hands in his. "Penny, I can't thank you enough for what you've done for me. I'm feeling a lot better. I mean it—I think you saved my life. For the first time, it seems like in forever, I can think clearly. My strength is still coming back, but that's happening."

"That's wonderful."

"We're going to lose to Rochester next week in the FA Cup, but even still, with the loser's share I think I'll be a lot closer to paying back Len. And now that I'm getting healthy, I'll be able to play again and earn a living."

Penny smiled. "That makes this a really great Christmas, then."

Dylan took out his mobile phone and handed it to her. "Why don't you call your parents and wish them a happy Christmas?"

Chapter Thirty-Four

Two weeks later Dylan stood on the scale in Gwen's office, stripped down to his briefs and socks. "Christ, Gwen, ever think of getting some heat in here?"

She ignored him. "You're up a full stone," she said with satisfaction. "Any nausea?"

Dylan laughed. He had been eating everything in sight. "None."

"Insomnia?"

"Sleeping like a log."

"Deep breath—" Gwen said, holding a stethoscope to his chest. "Fourth round draw tomorrow?"

"Yeah."

"Rochester having to forfeit the third round was quite a gift."

"They had no choice," Dylan grinned, "the chairman was under arrest, all the board members either quit or were arrested, and the players hadn't been paid and are now free agents. With all the debts and no board, the club had no choice but to go into receivership. And without enough players to raise a team, they had to forfeit the game."

"Same prize money regardless, though?"

"It cleared the bank last week," Dylan said with satisfaction.

Gwen dropped her voice. "Any more deliveries from this rogue chemist?"

"Not since I got back from Mum's. No sign of them."

"Interesting. Get dressed and meet me in my office."

Dylan pulled his jeans back on and buttoned his shirt. He'd gotten a haircut before he left Marbella and still had a bit of tan left. Penny had noticed, and that made him happy. He passed a pretty nurse in the hallway who winked at him. Managing a club in the FA Cup fourth round will make a guy pretty popular, he guessed.

He took a seat in Gwen's office and she turned her computer screen towards him. "These are your lab results from last week. White blood cell count excellent, liver function tests going back to normal, and your albumin is excellent which shows your body is getting the nutrition it needs. How's the erectile dysfunction?"

"For fuck's sake, Gwen..." Dylan glanced out the window, feeling his face turning red. Gwen was only his godmother, but still. She was looking at him with her eyebrows raised and he knew he was not getting off the hook. "Well, since you ask, lately there's been some improvement."

She nodded. "Glad to hear it. Erectile dysfunction in a man your age can indicate serious damage. I was worried. Were you able to sustain it?"

The memory of Penny bending over to take a casserole out of the oven Sunday night flashed through his mind. "Er, yes."

"Has it happened more than once?"

Dylan shifted in his seat, remembering her sitting on a chair in the living room last night, brushing her hair while they watched a show on the TV. "Yes."

"Good." She clicked to the next screen. "Your urine has cleaned up remarkably. Look, here, you don't flag for anything in this test. And this panel here—this is showing the basic toxicology panel—all negative and normal."

"The cocaine?"

"Gone."

"And the Vyvanse?"

"Not a spec. All the amphetamines are back to negative."

Dylan exhaled deeply. "Thank God. I can go back to Kingsbury Town."

"Not so fast." Gwen clicked through several screens and pulled up more charts. "You tested positive for diazepam, which is a benzodiazepine. It's still showing up here, in the N-desmethyldiazepam levels because it's a metabolite, in significant quantities."

"Which one is the diazepam again?"

"The Valium."

"Bloody hell. So another week?"

"No, longer than that. They found a substance similar to meldonium in your system, and that can remain in your system for months. I've done some research—the newest versions the testing labs are detecting can take up to a year. We don't know what you got so we don't know how long it will stay."

"How can you not know?" Dylan asked with annoyance.

Gwen rolled her eyes. "Sorry, Dylan—the rogue lab that created it for the cheating athletes hasn't submitted it to the UK Medicines and Healthcare Products Regulator Agency yet, so I don't have the full information on it."

Dylan ran his hands across his scalp and blew out his cheeks. "Sorry."

"All I can tell you is that if your blood were tested again today, they'd easily detect at least three things. But the very good news is that your heart and liver don't seem to be showing any long-term damage. You must be feeling better."

"I can go twenty minutes without taking a piss, if that's what you're asking."

"That was the birth control. Your estrogen and progesterone levels are in range." She tapped a few more keys. "Your blood pressure is remarkably good for a man who's taking a team into the fourth round of the FA Cup."

Dylan shrugged. "The guys look good, and if I'm relaxed, they're relaxed. There's no way we're going to get past Plymouth United so we've all decided to take the beating like men, collect the loser's check, and then go for a jolly booze-up."

Gwen laughed. "I've got seats on the halfway line and £20 on Icelton to win."

Dylan folded his arms over his chest. "Test me again next week."

"No, Dylan."

"Yes."

"Dylan, you were drugged, almost poisoned, and who knows for how long? It's going to take your body a while to recover, and you still don't look well, especially for an athlete. I need you to relax and focus on something else." Gwen paused. "How's Penny?"

"She's well."

"Smart girl. I was impressed."

"She's a decent sort," Dylan said, trying to remain non-committal.

"You need to keep a watch," Gwen warned. "Whatever she's poking around at in the old tooling shop, she's raising some interest. I know, I know," Gwen continued, "she is being as invisible as a ghost. But I tell you, Len is grumbling. I don't like it. There's something up."

"Win or lose, I'll be able to pay him off after Saturday."

"Yes," Gwen agreed, "and for some reason that seems to be the last thing he wants."

Chapter Thirty-Five

Saturday morning Penny was finishing her coffee when the doorbell chonged. She grabbed her jacket and hurried to open it before Biscuits could press the doorbell button again, or again-and-again, or again-and-again-and-again. He seemed to delight in the sonorous sound of the bell which could be heard from outside.

They began their walk to the foundry, Biscuits chattering about a football match that had been played fifty years ago in Cornwall. At the main road Penny saw the street was gridlocked with cars, vans, and buses.

"Biscuits, is everyone trying to get to Icelton for the FA Cup fourth round game today?" When he nodded, she blanched. "Mortager Park will never be able to hold this crowd."

"Wealdstone beat Golders Green four to one in the 1940 Middlesex Red Cross Cup final," Biscuits replied. "Attendance was 3,000."

At Mortager Park, two enormous luxury buses painted in the Plymouth United colors were trying to turn around in the narrow confines of the car park. People were yelling and tempers were high.

"Is that the visiting players' bus?" Penny asked Cassie, who was helping at the gate.

"No, that's Plymouth United's supporters and club officials. The players's coach is stuck up on the high street. There's too much traffic and the lanes are too narrow, and their fancy coaches can't get here," Cassie laughed. "It's a zoo!"

Kathleen rushed over. "Biscuits, you're wanted in the clubhouse. Joe Lyons wants to meet you."

For the first time since she had known him Biscuits smiled. He followed his sister into the throng and Penny walked back to the foundry gate. The security guard opened it for her and said good morning.

Inside the tooling shop Penny turned on the radio and began work on the wagon wheel impressions Biscuits had discovered. There were now four of them spread across eighteen grid squares. Penny worked these areas whenever there were people around, like today. When things were quiet and she knew she wouldn't be disturbed she went to the back of the shop and continued digging in the area she'd found the torcs.

"Today is January 24th, and it's the FA Cup fourth round," Joe Lyons's cultured voice filled the empty building. "Thirty-two clubs will be playing sixteen matches over the weekend, and the winners will take home £180,000. The losers will still get a £90,000 pay day, but no one wants to be the loser today. We are at Mortager Park, home of Tier Seven club Icelton who are hosting perennial Championship League power Plymouth United. Icelton, who have won only one of their last three Atlas League matches, are the David in this fight against a tough Goliath.

"I'm here in Icelton's away dressing room and it's a far departure from the luxury of Plymouth United's home stadium. And I must say, it goes to show the FA's commitment to the FA Cup that they rejected Plymouth's demand for a neutral venue and instead said 'Suck it up, you're playing grass roots football today, boys.'"

Penny laughed, thinking of the huge buses in the car park.

"Fans here at Mortager Park might be disappointed to not see Plymouth United's first team today. In an interesting turn of events, legendary manager Nicholas Reef announced yesterday that he was sending his club's Under-17s side, citing first team 'other commitments'. The Under-17s side is, of course, comprised of brilliant young players and their manager is with them."

This news made Penny pause. *The other team had sent a bunch of kids?*

"I have to give Icelton Manager Dylan Rhea kudos here," Joe Lyons continued. "He has several diamonds in the rough in his lineup including captain Tommy Peele, who works by day as a butcher, striker Tamba Taray, who drives a delivery van for a bakery, and a beast of a keeper in Ned Winter. Ned, of course, is the brother of Alan Winter who made several appearances with Reading in goal several years ago, and who is now club secretary. Ned and Alan have a small business machining custom aluminum canisters for engines."

"Social media has labeled the trio 'The Butcher, The Baker, and the Canister Maker'!" Joe Lyons laughed at the joke. "It's going to be quite a match."

—◦—

Four hours later, Dylan cupped his hands over his ears, trying to hear Joe Lyons's question over the pandemonium around him. Joe handed him a set of earphones which helped and the cameraman pointed his lens in their faces.

"Plymouth United left their first side at home and Icelton has just given their replacements a nightmare ninety minutes of outstanding play," Joe Lyons yelled to be heard. "I have the winning manager, Dylan Rhea, here with me—Dylan, can you explain your strategy?"

Well, I bloody well didn't plan on Nicholas Reef sending a bunch of teenagers today, Dylan thought to himself. "We trained well this week and even brought the boys in for an extra session," Dylan lied. "And once we knew the draw, we studied Plymouth closely and knew we wanted an attacking formation. It worked out very well for us."

"Do you think Nicholas Reef is rethinking his decision to leave the first team at home?"

Dylan knew he was grinning like an idiot but didn't care. "His kids did a great job. Even though they had to run a mile from the high street to get to the ground, they still they put up a fight, didn't they, Joe?"

Actually, Dylan knew, even though some of those kids were barely shaving, they were cold-blooded assassins who were Premier League caliber. But today, experience beat youth. He'd seen quickly that the kids were only thinking one or two moves ahead, and while their precision and fitness were lethal, it was possible to fake them out. They had three goals disallowed for offside. He'd quickly determined it wasn't possible to exhaust them but they could out think them. Something clicked in his head, and Dylan knew they could beat these kids.

"Last week you lost an Atlas League match to a team of mainly retired schoolteachers," Joe Lyons was pointing out.

"To be fair, Joe, we had Tamba Taray out with a knock on his ankle and Zaki Dunbar was unable to get off work. But today more than made up for it—we were in excellent form and everyone played to their peak."

"They did indeed! And we will see you on Monday for the fifth round draw!"

Dylan met up with the team back in the changing room, wedging himself in around the camera crews and fans.

Harry Goodnaught came to the door, wheeling two cases of champagne bottles. "Plymouth sent these over before they got on the buses," Harry told Dylan, "It ain't the real thing cos them kiddies aren't old enough to drink, but a nice gesture none the less."

Dylan grabbed a bottle, shook it, and then popped the plastic cork to shower his team. "We did it!"

The players gave a roaring cheer and did the same. Someone cranked up a speaker and loud music began to blast, and soon news reports around the world were showing video of the little football club from north London singing and dancing joyously under a rainstorm of sweet fizz.

Chapter Thirty-Six

UNABLE TO CONCENTRATE ON the dig with the huge commotion of the FA Cup match going on, Penny had given up and walked back to Dylan's house. She'd made herself a cup of tea and spent the afternoon working at the kitchen table, updating the grid map with her finds.

It was close to 8 p.m. when Penny heard the front door open. Dylan appeared in the kitchen doorway dripping wet and disheveled, his cheeks sporting at least three different shades of lipstick.

"I demand to know," Dylan began, "what the hell is going on?"

Penny sat back in her chair and mentally sized up the situation.

"We win by own goals," Dylan continued. "Then Neddie boots one in. Rochester goes bankrupt. And today Nicholas-Bloody-Reef decides to send a bunch of youngsters who aren't old enough to drive."

"You won," Penny surmised.

Dylan swallowed tightly. "Yes. Yes, we bloody well did win, against every odds-maker in Great Britain, and every sane person on this planet. There's something more going on. Something you're not telling me."

"Follow me. I'll show you."

Penny went to the closet in her bedroom and pulled out the empty suitcases, behind which was hidden the lockbox she had brought home from the watchman's hut. She laid it on the bed and opened it, and gently unwrapped the three torcs and placed them on the bed.

Dylan came closer to see what she'd laid out. The gold torc glowed warmly in the overhead light.

"These are necklaces," Dylan finally said, "like the ones at the British Museum."

Penny nodded. "Torcs."

Dylan whistled through his teeth. "They're a lot nicer than what the museums got."

"Yes," Penny agreed.

He reached out to pick up the bronze torc but hesitated.

"Go ahead," Penny said. "They're yours, anyway."

"It's like someone made them yesterday." Dylan cradled it in his large hands. "You found these in the tooling shop?"

Penny nodded. "The day after the arsonist tried to burn it down. I went back in to untangle the guide lines and I found the hole where the torcs were buried an hour later."

"The day after you were attacked? That's when you came here and said you wanted to move in."

Penny nodded. "I had these in my bag. They're safe here, at least safer than the foundry."

Dylan put the bronze torc down and lifted the golden one. "Is it solid gold?"

"It's probably an alloy of gold and silver. Professor Jain says the Iceni goldsmiths hammered several kinds of metal sheets into the gold, to give it flexibility. It's how they were able to make such delicate coils."

He turned the golden torc over carefully, then back. "It's not broken. You said most of them they find are broken."

"That's right. These are intact."

"How long do you think this stuff's been buried out there?"

"A very long time."

"Are they hers?"

"Nothing says 'Boudica' on it, but it all fits. If nothing else, they belonged to someone very, very important."

Dylan blew out his cheeks. "Is there more?"

Penny unwrapped more items from the lockbox. "I've found four gold coins, and this ring, and I think this bit of wire is part of a bracelet."

"Oh, hell. This is a bit more than some pottery shards." Dylan put the gold torc back on the bed and rubbed his hand over his chin. "That git at HARP said to call them if you found gold."

Penny met his eyes. "Yes."

"What would happen if you called them?"

"And they sent someone out? They'd take one look at these and take over the entire dig in a heartbeat. Probably the entire site."

Dylan paled. "Including the football ground?"

Penny nodded. "I'm pretty sure this is a very big deal."

Dylan began to pace the hallway from her bedroom to the front door and back again. Penny could hear him talking to himself.

"Look," he said, coming to a halt before her, "I have no idea what's going on here. But for some reason things are going very, very well."

"They are," Penny agreed.

"I don't want that to stop. We have no business being in the FA Cup fifth round, none at all. We've had an extraordinary run of luck, but we've been playing really well, too."

Dylan paced another lap, his muttering growing louder.

"Maybe I'm being greedy but fuck it, I'm not in the habit of looking a gift horse in the mouth. The fifth round is in three weeks and we will absolutely get our arses kicked because no top tier club is going to make the mistake Nicholas Reef made today. But until then we need our playing ground."

"What do you want to do?" Penny asked.

Dylan stared down at her, his gaze dancing with mischief. "I want to keep playing. What do you want to do?"

Penny picked up the golden torc, stretching the ancient necklace between her fingers. "I want to keep digging."

"Alright then," Dylan breathed. "After the win today I can keep on the security, and maybe even beef it up. But we can't leave the stuff here, in the closet."

"Where can we put it?"

"There's a safe upstairs in my bedroom, a small one, for Mum's jewelry. It's old but it's sturdy."

"You'd have to give me the combination."

"I will. I'll let you change the combination to whatever you want. You don't have to tell me."

"Can we use your phone to take pictures of everything?"

"Of course."

Penny grinned. "It's a deal."

Chapter Thirty-Seven

THE EARLY FEBRUARY WEATHER had turned foul. A security guard slid open the tooling shop outside door, letting in a blast of cold wind. "Miss, can the girls come in?"

Penny looked up, brushing a stray lock of hair from the braid that hung down her back. "Yes, of course."

The girl's team filed in and lined up behind their captain.

"Penny," Chloe announced, "we'd like a word."

She sounded serious, so Penny stood, her joints stiff, and wiped her filthy hands on her equally filthy flannel shirt. "What's up?"

"The Supporters Association is planning a Valentine's party for tomorrow night. It was Dylan's idea and the mums are organizing it," Kenna said. "It's going to be fancy."

"Fancy schmancy," Carlie added.

"Totally posh," Cassie concurred.

Penny blew her nose in her handkerchief. "Sounds like fun. Where?"

"Here at the clubhouse," Kathleen said. "We think you should go."

"I'd like to, thank you for inviting me."

Kiva frowned. "You need to get cleaned up."

"Of course, I think I've got a clean pair of jeans. If not I can do a wash tonight."

Eleven heads shook in simultaneous disagreement.

"No," Kristie said. "We mean really cleaned up. Like spiffy."

"Dead classy," Crystal added.

"Dime piece," Lindsey winked.

Penny looked at her grubby hands, which were cut and had soil embedded under the nails. "Girls, this is about as good as it gets right now."

"Not a problem," Chloe said. "My dad says we're to bring you to his shop at half six tonight. He'll do your hair."

Kathleen turned to Chloe. "Thought your dad was a solicitor?"

"That's my other dad," Chloe said.

Karis unzipped a long garment bag. "And my mum is giving you this dress."

An approving murmur arose as she pulled out a red sequined dress. The dress bodice sparkled in the weak February daylight, while the chiffon skirt billowed gently above the dirt floor.

The breath caught in Penny's chest. The dress was exquisite but obviously costly. "I can't accept that."

"She wants you to have it. She said after the last baby she's never squeezing into it again, and that you look to be the same size she used to be."

"And my mum sent shoes," Charvi pulled out a pair from her bag, "she's pretty sure you're the same size."

The strappy red high heels were a perfect match for the dress. "Why can't I just wear a clean top and pants?" Penny protested.

"Because, silly, it's fancy! Icelton has never made the fifth round of the FA Cup before and likely never will again. It's a celebration, so you need to look good," Cassie said.

"Really good," Kenna agreed.

"Hot as a potato," Carlie added.

That evening, Penny sat under a drying hood in Chloe's father's salon in Hendon, her freshly washed and trimmed hair pinned up in rollers.

"Dad likes to do things old-school here," Chloe laughed, pointing at the rollers.

Chloe and Kanti pulled up manicurist tables and insisted on painting her nails. Penny picked out a soft pink polish and Kanti soaked her hands while Chloe filed, both girls keeping up an amusing chatter.

"I used to do this for my older sister Ruth," Penny said. "She was in scholarship pageants."

"Like Miss America?" Chloe asked.

"State pageants, Miss Indiana. She was third runner-up five years ago."

"Did you do them as well?"

"No."

Kanti began buffing the tops of her nails. "How come?"

"I got sick."

"What kind of sick?"

"First very sick with influenza, and then mentally sick," Penny said.

Chloe carefully brushed on the polish. "You seem okay now."

"I had very good doctors," Penny said. "But I had to go away, to a hospital four hours from my home."

"How long were you there?" Kanti asked.

"A year."

"What was wrong with you?"

"A bad flu was going around and I caught it. My fever got very high before I started to recover. After that I started hearing a voice in my head."

Chloe nodded. "My cousin's like that. They give him meds. Do you take meds?"

"No, I tried them and they didn't work, even some of the stronger experimental ones. But they did work for a lot of the patients at the hospital."

"Whose voice was it?"

"A woman."

"What was she telling you?"

"To come here."

"Really?" Chloe chuckled. "Fancy that. 'Go see beautiful Icelton, Penny.'"

"Chloe, you shouldn't laugh. It's not polite," Kanti chided her.

"I'm sorry, Penny."

"No, it's okay. I know it's a weird story, especially compared to the other patients. Their voices were telling them to harm themselves. Some people were really sick and had a lot of problems going on at once. But for most people it's just a matter of learning how to cope. I was a pretty easy case."

Chloe began a second coat of polish. "Did they cure you?"

"I kind of cured myself."

"How?"

"Well," Penny began, "I cut a deal with the voice. I was out in the garden—the hospital has a beautiful garden—and started talking back to her. I told her that if she would leave me alone, I would get a job and make the money to come here."

"Did it work?"

"Sort of. I guess we reached a compromise. Her voice became quieter, and I was able to leave the hospital. I got a job at the local college as a custodian at night for four years. I made enough money and here I am."

"And she wanted you to dig up the old tooling shop?"

Penny nodded. "Evidently."

The girls accepted this without comment. "You're not going back to America, are you?"

"I'll have to. I can't stay here."

"But you won the Snowball!" Chloe protested. "You've got boatloads of cash, so you can stay here a long time. We don't think Dylan minds you staying with him. He's so much better since you moved in with him. He's nice now, and fun."

"And doesn't look like a scarecrow," Kanti added, blowing on Penny's nails to dry them.

"And doesn't yell at everyone," Chloe agreed.

"We don't want you to go back," Kanti said. "Call your parents and tell them you're staying here. They can come visit if they want."

⸻ ◆ ⸻

Before leaving the shop that evening, the girls made Penny promise not to go to the dig the next day.

"We're leaving from Mortager Park car park at nine a.m. sharpish, and you're to go with us. Dylan got us all tickets," Kanti instructed and Penny agreed.

Back in her bedroom at Dylan's house, Penny stared at her reflection in the mirror on the wall. Chloe's dad was a magician—her hair hung in loose, shiny ringlets around her face and down her back, moving easily when she shook her head. She fingered a soft tendril and smiled.

The beautiful red dress hung on the door, and she gave in to temptation and tried it on. The fit was perfect. The high heels slid on her feet like gloves, and she tottered around the tiled hallway, loving the way the chiffon swished between her legs. A test pirouette almost landed her on the floor, and she whooped with laugher as she caught herself on the stair railing. Five minutes later she was striding around the house with confidence, twirling like a ballerina. If there was music at the party and Dylan asked her to dance, she'd be ready. The thought filled her with joy.

Somehow she had begun to feel at home.

Chapter Thirty-Eight

"You're coming today, right?" Dylan asked Penny the next morning, wolfing down a third bowl of cereal at the kitchen sink. "I got tickets for everyone and I think the mums are driving the girls out."

"Yes, they offered me a ride," Penny said. "How far away is Newbury Town?"

"About sixty miles to Berkshire, a two-hour trip."

"What's going to happen today?"

"Newbury are going to clean our clocks," Dylan said with certainty. "Their manager, Tom Wharton, is a miserable first-rate bastard who enjoys humiliating the opposing team. His players hate him, the FA hate him, his own brother, who owns the club, hates him. Which is saying something because he's an even bigger bastard than Tom is."

Penny took another box of cereal from the cabinet and handed it to Dylan.

"But the punters at home watching telly *love* him," Dylan continued, "he's a one-man theatrical performance. Newbury's matches always make *Match of the Day* because of it. At least this game is being shown live so we'll pick up £150,000 whatever happens."

"Did you ever play against Newbury?"

"Not since the Whartons bought it and Tom became manager. He humiliated Swindon Town last year—they'd already won the game, but they scored three more goals in added time."

Penny frowned. "That's not very nice."

"Nice has nothing to do with it. I am fully expecting him to let us think we have a chance and then in the last five minutes make it rain footballs on poor Ned Winter's head."

"Why would he do that?"

"For the drama, keep the punters glued to their TVs." Dylan made a mocking expression "'Ooohh, look Penny, Icelton has a chance! No, here's Newbury waking up and showing exactly what they are capable of.'"

"What can you do about it?"

"Absolutely nothing. Get poor Neddie an umbrella. Pick up our consolation check and go to the party tonight." He glanced at her. "You are going, right?"

"Yes. The girls say it's dress up."

Dylan nodded. "It will be a right blow out, everyone deserves it. Did you do something different to your hair?"

Penny reached up and self-consciously touched a smooth lock. "I washed it."

"Looks good," Dylan said, checking the now empty cereal boxes. His mobile beeped, and he checked his message. "Right, I'm off. See you there." He leaned in and kissed her cheek. "For good luck," he winked and was off.

⚬

At noon a platoon of SUV's, driven by the mothers of the girls' team, waited in traffic outside Newbury's stadium. Biscuits had been afforded the honor of riding in the team bus, and Penny sat in a backseat, admiring the leafy suburban neighborhood of well-kept houses that backed on to the stadium. The brick houses were covered in ivy and shaded by lovely trees and looked like something out of a movie.

The car radio was tuned to Joe Lyons, and Penny noted a distinct upbeat change in his tone.

"Today is the fifth round of the FA Cup—sixteen teams, eight matches, winners take home £360,000 and the losers half that. We are at Lister Lane in scenic Newbury, Berkshire, where Newbury Town will face the last non-league club in the FA Cup, Icelton.

"It's a sellout crowd with all 19,459 tickets sold, and an absolutely perfect day for some football. And since it's Newbury, we're guaranteed some entertainment. Manager Tom Wharton and his twin brother, club owner Tim Wharton, are known for their showman tactics. They beat Tier Four Shrewsbury in the fourth round with a manufactured cliffhanger ending and earned a frown from the FA. Will they try it again? Manager Tom Wharton keeps his boys very organized and, some would say, very arrogant."

Penny listened closely as Joe Lyons played a clip from an earlier interview with the Newbury manager. "Icelton is a fine club, Joe, you've said so yourself," Tom Wharton said sadly. "I don't know what we're going to do. We're racked with injuries."

"This is a club that likes to wait out their opponents," Joe Lyons continued. "They are famous, or may I say infamous, for letting a team enjoy lots of pressure and possibly even score just to see how they tick. And then wham, in the final minutes, they take complete control and dominate. Especially on their home pitch. Merciless.

"Icelton has had a good run of luck so far but I dare say Newbury Manager Tom Wharton is not going to make the same mistake Nicholas Reef did in the fourth round and send a youth team. Icelton are clearly playing above their level but are putting in solid performances. Midfielder Tommy Peele and striker Tamba Taray are shining beacons, and keeper Ned Winter has played brilliantly. But I fully expect Newbury to make short work of them."

⸺◆⸺

The girls poured out of the cars and headed towards the narrow gates where they presented their tickets and were directed to Icelton's section of the stadium. They found their seats, and Penny was pleased to see a respectable showing of fans dressed in Icelton's green and grey amongst the sea of Newbury black and white. She herself wore a green and grey striped scarf she had gotten from the lost and found bin at Mortager Park.

Both clubs were on the pitch doing their warm-ups. Dylan stood on the sideline, his expression intent, calling out a few remarks, while Uncle Eddie stood behind the goal coaching the keepers.

The teams ran back to their changing rooms, and soon walked onto the pitch, each holding the hand of a young child, a mascot for the day. The sun came out and the breeze settled into pleasant puffs.

"That's Tom Wharton over there on the sidelines. He's the Newbury manager," Crystal pointed to a ruddy faced man who seemed to be glaring at his own players. "Proper bugger he is. Won't let their Girls Under-18s team train on this lovely pitch."

"Only one worse is his brother, the owner. That bloke standing behind the goal, in the black and white get-up," Chloe pointed.

Penny squinted. "They look like twins."

"They are. Tom and Tim, the 'Terrible Twins'. Tempers like volcanoes when they don't get their way. Creeps."

"Jerks," Cassie agreed.

"Successful jerks," Kristie corrected, and they all nodded.

Tempers flared ten minutes into the game when a Newbury player was shown a yellow card. Tom Wharton leapt to his feet and began hurling abuse at anyone who would listen. The referee pointedly ignored him.

The first half passed quickly, with Icelton getting possession of the ball frequently, but Newbury easily broke up plays. Dylan stood with Uncle Eddie on the sideline, arms folded, while the Newbury manager stalked the technical area yelling loudly, only pacified when Newbury scored. Behind the goal, his twin nodded in satisfaction and celebrated.

⸻◦○◦⸻

"Newbury doesn't seem to be trying very hard," Penny said, watching Dylan follow the team into the tunnel at halftime. The score stood at 1-0 and Icelton looked exhausted.

"It's what they do," Kenna said. "They toy with the other team, feeling 'em out. The last ten minutes are going to be a bloodbath." The other girls nodded sadly in agreement.

The second half started fast and the ball was rarely out of Icelton's half. Ned saved shots from all angles and they became even more frequent as Newbury increased their pressure.

Suddenly, Icelton moved downfield and Henry Collins passed to Tamba Taray, who managed to deceive the Newbury goalkeeper and scored, tying the game at 1-1.

"It's going to get ugly now," Carlie predicted.

The home fans were enjoying themselves, Penny noted. Some had taken their jackets off in the afternoon warmth and were sunning themselves in the stands. From her seat high in the stand, Penny saw red lights flashing in the neighborhood behind the south end of the stadium.

Dylan made his last two substitutions, and the crowd clapped politely for the Icelton players being replaced. Play resumed and the Icelton players gave it their last effort. The Newbury supporters struck up a loud song which almost drowned out the sound of sirens approaching from a distance. Almost, but not quite.

Flashing red and blue lights could now be seen several blocks behind the stadium. Tamba Taray broke down the wing and began dodging Newbury players and was almost on the edge of the penalty area when the referee, his hand to his earpiece, blew the whistle and halted play. He jogged off the pitch to meet with stadium officials, who then motioned for the managers to join them.

The crowd went quiet and the sunbathers in the stands stood and looked towards the emergency to the south, the sirens seeming to compete with each other in an elevating blare. The referee sprinted back to midfield and blew his whistle, making a sweeping motion with his arm.

"Ladies and gentlemen, this match has been abandoned." The stadium announcer, whose voice had been jovial a moment before, intoned. "You are asked to form an orderly queue and exit at the north end of the stadium with all haste."

Initially no one in the stands moved, surprised and confused by the order.

A woman in the next section stood and yelled at the top of her voice, "I've just heard from my sister who lives over there. We have to evacuate, there's a bomb!"

Penny looked back to the pitch. Dylan was running, gesturing to Icelton players to get off the pitch, while Tom Wharton was screaming at the referee and gesturing wildly. Penny couldn't hear his words over the pandemonium but his face was red.

The stadium announcer continued his instructions for fans to leave, and Penny and the girls followed the crowd down the steps and through the short tunnel which immediately backed up. Ahead Penny could see the other twin, Tim Wharton, locking the north gate while two security guards stood next to him, mystified.

"Go back to your seats!" Tim Wharton yelled. "We are finishing this game!"

"He's not letting us out!" A woman began to scream. "We're trapped in here with a bomb!"

Chapter Thirty-Nine

THE NEWBURY MATCH, DYLAN recollected later, had begun on a civil note. He was being interviewed in the media room before the game when Tom Wharton strolled by, the encounter seeming to be by coincidence, but Dylan knew better.

"Dylan," Tom had extended his hand and turned so the cameras could catch his good side, "Welcome back to Lister Lane. Good to see you at this level again."

"Good to be back," Dylan shook the man's hand, "Congratulations on your promotion last year."

Tom shook his head, to all appearances a worried manager. "Aye, we're zooming up the charts. But go easy on us today, lad, half my team is laid up with injuries."

Injuries my arse, Dylan thought. "I'm sure you'll give us a show today, regardless."

Tom Wharton didn't bother to conceal the glint in his eye. "Let's give the punters an exciting match, then."

———◆———

In the 85th minute Dylan stood with Uncle Eddie on the sideline, mildly surprised at how well things were going. True to his word, Tom Wharton had every player with an injury on the pitch, leaving his stars as substitutes for the beat down that would begin any minute.

But for all Newbury's hobbling around, Icelton was holding its own. Tamba was on fire, and Callum and Jack in defense were breaking up plays like clockwork. The score was 1-1 Icelton and he could not fault anything.

"I wonder what's up over there," Uncle Eddie pointed to the south end of the stadium, where the neighborhood beyond seemed engulfed in blue and red flashing lights.

"Somebody's cat is up a tree," Dylan laughed. "Or somebody's Range Rover got jacked."

Play continued as the sirens got closer and louder. The referee listened to his earpiece, then blew two short toots on his whistle and signaled a stop of play.

The players rested where they were stopped, and after a moment the referee waved for the managers to join him. Tom Wharton jogged over, puffing hard.

"Bosses, we have been instructed to evacuate the stadium due to a bomb found nearby. This match will be abandoned."

"Like bloody hell it is!" Tom Wharton erupted.

The referee ignored him and ran back to the center circle, blowing a long whistle signaling the end of the game. The players began to wander off the pitch in confusion while the stadium announcer told spectators that the stadium had to be evacuated.

Undeterred, Tom Wharton followed the referee back to midfield, yelling at both teams, "You ruddy bastards stay right where you are! We're finishing this game!"

Dylan followed Tom, motioning to his team to get to the sidelines.

"We are not bloody well leaving this pitch!" Tom bellowed at the top of his lungs, pointing at his bewildered team. "Get back out there!"

A policeman of considerable size ran towards them but Tom was undeterred. "And you!" he pointed a pudgy finger at Dylan, "this is all your doing! If you think you're going to steal another win in the FA Cup over me, you've got another thing coming!"

"Sir, I must insist—" the policeman loomed over Tom, trying to usher him off the pitch.

"Get your hands off me!" Tom pulled back to punch Dylan, but Dylan ducked, and the sharp blow connected with the policeman's face, knocking him to the ground.

Incensed, Tom Wharton swung at the referee but Dylan tackled him to the grass. Tom flailed while Dylan made short work of subduing him. More police arrived and Tom was hauled to his feet, handcuffed, and led off the pitch.

The referee gave Dylan a hand up and pointed to the gates at the north end of the ground where the police had Tim Wharton in handcuffs as well. "C'mon, let's get everyone out of here."

⬥◉⬥

Dylan followed his players towards the gate, keeping to the side of the rush of spectators exiting. Ahead of them, Harry Goodnaught was tossing the team kit bags from the changing room and the players grabbed them before leaving the stadium. Everyone scrambled on the coach and the driver began easing into the departing traffic, directed by the emergency services around the maze of local roads. Soon they were on the motorway, speeding back to Icelton.

"Holy hell," Jeff O'Day, the left winger, exhaled.

"Did all of our supporters get out?" Dylan asked. "Where's Penny?"

"I just got a text from Claire," Tommy Peele called out, "they're all out and back in the cars but stuck in traffic. They're safe, and Penny is with them."

Dylan relaxed back in his seat. "Good Lord, I have never seen anything like that. Where's this bomb then?"

"Neighborhood at the south end," Alan read from his mobile phone, "an unexploded bomb. Seems some chap was planting a tree in his garden this afternoon and found it. They're evacuating the entire area."

"Why would anyone plant a bomb in someone's backyard?" Henry Collins asked.

"It's from World War II. It happens now and then. They landed, never went off, and then got built over," Alan explained.

"What we gonna do now? Do we replay the match?" Zaki Dunbar asked.

"Yeah," Callum Williams, a midfielder said, "and this time Newbury won't be dogging it till the last minute. Right, Dylan?"

Dylan sat in his usual seat at the midpoint of the coach and considered this question.

"Right, Dylan?" Callum repeated.

"I don't know about that," Dylan said as thoughts raced through his head.

Charlie Moore, the reserve goalkeeper, turned around in his seat. "What don't you know?"

"I don't know," Dylan said in measured tones, a grin on his face, "how the policeman that Tom Wharton punched feels about it."

The entire coach sat in stunned silence.

"Tom Wharton slugged a copper?" Callum asked.

Dylan nodded. "And I heard one of the emergency police say that Tim Wharton had wrapped a chain around the north gate to lock everyone in."

"That's insane," Alan said.

Dylan nodded. "They were counting on the added time to do their usual blitz. It backfired."

The team digested this news for a moment.

"We was tied," Tamba Taray remarked.

Dylan's mobile beeped. A text message from FA OFFICE read:

`Pls confirm you and team all present and accounted for`

Dylan texted back an affirmative and then added: `Situation with finishing match?`

The cursor on the message flashed for several minutes.

`Under review you will be apprised at the earliest`

"That was the FA," he told the players. "They don't know what's going to happen."

⸻ ◆ ⸻

The rest of the trip back to Icelton was silent as the players scoured the internet for the latest news. Pictures were spreading like wildfire of Tom Wharton punching the policeman, of Dylan wrestling him to the ground, and of both brothers being led away in handcuffs.

By the time they arrived back at Mortager Park a large crowd had gathered in the car park, and Dylan could see news cameras and reporters.

Dylan stood at the front of the bus and addressed the team. "Right then, no comments to the press. We all evacuated in an orderly fashion, and our concern is for the supporters and people whose houses are around the bomb. Got it?"

The players nodded nervously.

"But Dylan, what if—" Frankie Rhys-Davies began but Dylan cut him off.

"No what if's," Dylan said, "keep your mouths shut. Get in there, get changed into your party togs and be ready for the soiree the ladies have laid on. Or they will have our arses."

"Yes, boss."

————◆————

The clubhouse was packed and the mood raucous. Glittering red hearts celebrating Valentine's Day hung from the ceiling and red and white streamers crisscrossed the room. Table after table was laden with savories and confections of every kind which the players were helping themselves to liberally.

"Glad to see you eating again, Dylan," one of the mums said as Dylan reached over Biscuits' head for another sandwich from the huge stack, the sixth by his count. He was famished and knew he'd been eating like a horse, but the weight was coming back on, and the associated energy along with it. His custom tuxedo was still a bit loose on his frame but the suspenders helped.

"They're delicious," he said, woofing it down with a large swallow of lemonade and looking around for Penny. "Where're the girls?"

"They want to make an entrance," the mum said with a laugh.

Dylan checked his phone again. No messages.

Catching sight of two old friends he grabbed their hands in a firm shake. "Jeff! Scott! Good to see you, lads! Glad you could make it tonight. Who's watching the kebab shop?"

"We closed up early just to be here," Jeff roared, "wouldn't miss it for the world!"

"Okay, it's time!" A mum grabbed Dylan and directed him to the kitchen where the players had been corralled. He went through the door and halted, blindsided by the group of gorgeous girls in front of him. They were no longer eleven girls in identical tracksuits, instead standing before him were elegant young women dressed in glittering evening gowns, ready to be escorted into the party by a player. The transformation was astounding.

He searched the group until he found Penny, a vision in a red sequined dress. He knew she was a beautiful girl but tonight she was dazzling. She'd even piled her hair up and secured it with the mantilla comb he'd given her for Christmas, which made it look like she was wearing a crown.

Dylan swallowed, unable to take his eyes off her. "Penny, you're beautiful. May I escort you?"

"Thank you, so are you. Last time we saw you, you were rolling around in the grass at Lister Lane with the other manager." Penny laughed as each couple was being announced to loud applause.

Dylan grunted. "Did you get out of the stadium okay? What happened at the north end zone?"

"It was scary," Penny said. "The one twin locked the gates and wouldn't let anyone out, but the police arrived right away and cut the lock and we all left."

"Jesus."

"What are they going to do with the bomb?"

"They'll take it in a field somewhere and blow it up," Dylan replied, and then dropped his lips to her ear. "Was this *her* doing?"

He inhaled the fresh scent of her hair and saw an attractive flush spread across her smooth skin. "I don't know."

They were the last to be introduced. Dylan stood straight, adjusted his bowtie, and offered Penny his arm. "Let's go have some fun."

Together Dylan and Penny walked into the room to deafening cheers. He waved happily and noticed Penny's eyes sparkling as she enjoyed the well-wishes. Someone had set up a makeshift podium, and he drew her along with him and kept her by his side as he began a speech.

"First off, I'd like to thank everyone for their support. We've been very fortunate this year, and..." he paused, "Dad would be proud."

There was a rousing chorus of 'Hear! Hear!' and he paused to brush away a tear that had sprung up in his eyes, noticing many in the room did the same. He continued to talk about the team and the club before wrapping up with what he knew would be the crowning moment.

"And last but not least..." Dylan pulled an envelope from his tuxedo coat pocket and went to stand by Len Case, "a check for the full amount owed to our generous benefactor, Len Case. With interest. Icelton is now debt free!"

A loud cheer went up and Len stood to shake Dylan's hand, looking less than thrilled. He stood unsmiling for pictures.

Dylan's mobile rang and he raised his hand. The room fell silent as the party-goers watched him withdraw it from his jacket pocket and answer it.

"Yes, sir," he nodded and listened. "Of course, sir. There's nothing to be done for it, I agree. Yes, I'll inform the club. Thank you, sir."

Dylan hung up the call and faced the room, his expression sober. "That was the Lord Lambton, the president of the FA."

The crowd digested this information in silence and waited.

"What does he want, Dylan?" a voice finally called out.

Dylan blew out his cheeks and broke into a wide grin. "He has invited me to attend the FA Cup quarterfinal draw on Monday evening."

Chapter Forty

Penny had heard loud sounds in her life but the roar from the Icelton party-goers topped it all. "We're in the FA Cup quarterfinals!"

Someone turned on the large-screen TV at the end of the clubhouse. "Newbury Town manager Tom Wharton is under arrest tonight for punching a Newbury police officer," the news anchor intoned, "his attack was stopped only when Icelton manager Dylan Rhea intervened."

Video of Dylan tackling Tom Wharton was repeated several times, twice in slow motion, and Penny watched Dylan smother a grin.

"This behavior is completely unacceptable," a stone-faced Football Association official frowned. "We will view the television footage carefully and receive reports from officials at the match before we take further action. However, we can announce that Newbury Town Football Club have declared that they will withdraw from this season's Football Association Challenge Cup competition and, as a result, Icelton Football Club will advance to the quarterfinal stage and will receive the prize money awarded to the club winning in the fifth round proper."

The screen returned to the news anchor. "And we have a statement, just released, from Newbury Town FC, that reads in part: 'Our club wishes to apologize to the Newbury constabulary, The Football Association, Icelton Football Club, and all spectators attending today's match. We concede the match to Icelton and wish them the best of luck in the FA Cup quarterfinal."

"Newbury have also announced that their share of gate receipts will be forfeited to the Newbury Police Benevolent Fund," the announcer added.

Dylan let out a whoop of joy and grabbed Penny and swung her around, clasping her so tightly her dress left red sequins on his tuxedo jacket.

The party was still going full steam two hours later when Dylan took Penny's arm and whispered in her ear, "Icelton is the toast of London tonight. I'm taking the guys into town to have some dinner. C'mon, I'm treating."

A long line of taxis were lined up outside and the players and their wives and girlfriends piled in. Space was short and Dylan pulled Penny onto his lap. "Comfortable?" he asked, his lips close to her ear and his hands around her waist.

Penny settled into his arms. "This is a lot of people. Can we really get into a restaurant without reservations?"

"I called an hour ago and they said no problems," Dylan grinned. "Being in the FA Cup quarterfinals opens a lot of doors."

The chic restaurant in central London had indeed prepared large tables, to which the players were escorted with hearty applause from the other patrons. The team waved with unreserved delight and bottles of champagne were delivered and popped with great fanfare.

Penny, seated next to Dylan, was handed a glass and tried her first taste.

"Bubbles tickle your nose?" Dylan laughed after she had a tentative sip.

They were indeed the toast of London that night. A continuous stream of well-wishers stopped by their tables, many of whom Dylan knew. Penny was introduced to everyone in a blur of names and faces.

As they were finishing their dinner an athletic young man stopped by and was introduced as Yaba Owusu, a handsome Ghanaian who was playing for South Quay Road.

"Hey Dylan," Yaba said, "Reno is having his birthday party tonight down the road at the Colosseum. He wants you all to come."

Tom Peele and his wife Claire begged off, "Thanks, Yaba, but we've only got the sitter till midnight."

"Me and Nick here are going to hit Jesters first," Tamba said, "We'll catch up to you later."

Other players and their partners peeled off, leaving Dylan and Penny to walk the block to the imposing hotel. Dylan wrapped Penny in his overcoat and offered her his arm.

The Colosseum was indeed a grand hotel. The three-story marbled entrance was easily the most impressive thing Penny had ever seen. Inside, security guards dressed as Roman soldiers stood before a firmly shut double-door off the foyer, equipped with shields and lances.

"This is a birthday party, Dylan," Penny said. "We didn't bring a present."

Dylan pressed his hand to the small of Penny's back and kept walking. "Reno doesn't need presents. He already owns everything."

The guards pulled back their lances and the doors swung opened. As they passed, Penny noticed the lances were real in every detail. Inside a ballroom was filled with hundreds of people. The Roman theme continued with a huge fountain in the middle of the room, around which scantily clad women lounged like nymphs. Penny's eyes grew wide.

A bare-chested man appeared before them with a tray of champagne. "Just an orange juice for me," Penny said faintly.

"Same," Dylan said before being surrounded by well-wishers.

"Dylan!" A man draped in a toga bellowed from across the room. "*Mio amico*!"

The crowd parted to let him through, and Penny saw the toga was edged in purple and he wore a laurel leaf crown on his head of thick black hair. He was smiling widely.

Dylan shook his hand but the man brushed it aside and wrapped Dylan in a huge embrace. "The man of the hour! Today we both have wins to celebrate!"

"Congratulations, Reno, you made short work of Chelsea."

"Bah, my manager," the man sputtered, "he's a fool. We could have scored more goals if he had picked a more attacking formation. But it's 4–4–2 all day long, blah, blah, blah. Maybe I need to become manager, eh? And who is your friend?"

"This is Penny Adams, from the United States," Dylan kept his hand on Penny's back as he made the introductions. "Penny, this is Renato Tedesco, who owns the South Quay Road Potters."

"It is my pleasure, *signorina*." Reno bowed deeply and took Penny's hand, placing a warm kiss on it.

A cold shiver raced down her spine as Reno continued to clasp her hand. "Happy birthday," was all Penny could think to say.

Dylan's hand moved to her waist and pulled her gently against him.

"What luck you always have, Dylan," Reno commented, noticing the movement. "Today a bomb and an unhinged manager. Tonight a ticket to the FA Cup quarterfinal and a beautiful woman."

"I am a lucky man," Dylan smiled at Penny, and then at Reno. "Maybe soon the FA Cup as well?"

Reno laughed, but Penny noted the joviality didn't reach his eyes. He clapped his hands loudly and turned to the gathered people. "Tonight I share my celebration with Dylan! *Salut*!"

Chapter Forty-One

AT DAWN A TAXI delivered Penny and Dylan back to the house on Elthorne Road. Dew clung to the grass edging the pavement so Dylan swept Penny up in his arms and carried her effortlessly to the front door. Setting her back on her feet, he negotiated the security system, and they stumbled inside.

"I'm starving. How about you?" Dylan asked, heading for the kitchen.

"But they served that breakfast at five am," Penny said. "You ate an entire plate of eggs and bacon."

"I know, but that was two hours ago," Dylan grinned and helped himself to a slice of cake Penny had made the day before. "Did you have a good time?" he asked between forkfuls.

Penny smiled. "I did. I don't think I'll ever have another night like that again in my life."

"You mean they don't have women gladiator battles at birthday parties in Indiana?" Dylan expressed with mock surprise.

"Weren't they incredible? Those swords looked very real."

"I think they were. And the arrows the guy dressed up in the Cupid outfit had were sharp as well. Reno does like to walk the edge." Dylan finished the cake and put the plate in the dishwasher. "Do you want to go out again?"

"Where?"

"I don't know. Anywhere... a walk around the block, the bus stop, the market... I'm not tired and I don't want the night to end. Are you tired?"

"I've never felt more awake," Penny smiled and made a decision. "But my scalp is getting sore from having my hair up for so long. Would you help me take it down?"

She moved close to Dylan, so close that she could catch the scent of him—warm, slightly spicy, and very male. He reached out to clasp the mantilla comb and pulled up slowly until it was free. She shook her head, releasing the cascade of tawny hair around her. She heard his breath catch in his throat.

"Penny, I'm trying to be a gentleman," he said, his voice sounding strained.

"You are," she assured him as she turned around to face him.

"And that time I kissed you, the night we first met—"

"—I'd like you to kiss me again," Penny interrupted, her eyes sparkling. She wrapped her arms around him and drew him against her. He leaned into her and dropped his lips to hers, tasting her, taking his time. The feel of his lips on hers was electric, and she felt his desire as the kiss deepened. She ran her hands across the muscles in his back and heard him moan softly.

The doorbell chonged, breaking the spell.

"Bloody Biscuits," Dylan whispered against her lips and Penny laughed. He moved to feast hungrily on the smooth skin of her neck, his lips scorching her skin.

The doorbell chonged again, followed immediately by another chong.

Dylan sighed and nibbled the fine skin of her bare shoulder. A triple chong insisted someone open the door.

"Damn it, Biscuits, it's ruddy seven o'clock in the morning, can't you give it a rest—" Dylan yelled over his shoulder.

"I'll take care of it." Penny reluctantly disengaged herself from Dylan's arms and walked to the foyer. She tapped the security control buttons, slid back the deadbolts, and then opened the door. "Biscuits, it's too early to go to the—"

"How do you do, you must be Penny!" A blonde woman stood on the door stoop, her face a wreath of smiles. "I'm Sue."

Chapter Forty-Two

PENNY RECOGNIZED THE WOMAN immediately from her television show. She was dressed in a tailored navy blue coat, her blonde hair short and glossy. A leather messenger bag was slung over her shoulder, and behind her a red Porsche convertible was parked at the curb.

A burst of cold wind hit Penny, blowing her long hair in her face and making the folds of her gown rustle. She shivered involuntarily, trying to frame a suitable greeting.

Behind her, Dylan was sauntering down the hall towards them. "Biscuits, it's too early to go to the dig, and we've been up all night—" He froze in his tracks when he saw who was standing at the door.

Sue's focus switched from Penny to narrow on Dylan. "Hello, Dylan."

"S-Sue..." Dylan stuttered, his mouth agape in astonishment.

Seconds ticked by as Penny glanced between the former lovers.

"Aren't you going to introduce me?" Sue prompted.

"This is my, ah..." Dylan fumbled, "my friend, Penny. Penny, this is..."

The woman didn't wait for Dylan to finish his thought. "I'm Dylan's friend as well. I'm Sue Paulin. It's a pleasure to meet you."

Penny choked off a reply as Sue clamped her fingers in a vice-like handshake. The woman only came to Penny's shoulder, but her erect carriage and air of command made her seem much taller. Up close Penny could see her teeth were dazzlingly white.

"Don't you two look sharp!" Sue said, taking stock of Dylan's suit and Penny's gown. "Reno said you'd dropped by his birthday party. The 'Football Manager of the Hour' out living it up in London, good for you!"

Dylan ran his hand through his hair, and Penny saw a red flush at his neckline. "What are you doing here?"

"I was in the neighborhood and wanted to stop by and congratulate you," Sue replied.

Dylan stared at her, his expression blank. "On what?"

"On your win yesterday!" Sue laughed, and with a grand gesture swept by them. She made a bee-line back to the kitchen where she began to make tea.

"I just came back this morning from Anglesey. Reno—" she said, directing Penny to take a seat in a chair at the table, "that's my boss, Reno Tedesco, he owns the network that produces *Fraud War*—he got a tip the captain of the ferry that ran aground last week had faked his mariner's license and was seen smoking marijuana with the crew shortly be-fore the accident."

Dylan stood in the kitchen doorway, his arms crossed and his expression thunderous.

Sue maneuvered around the kitchen without hesitation, taking mugs out of the second cabinet on the left and spoons from the top drawer next to the sink. "We found a neighbor who agreed to go on camera and say that he thought the guy had anger issues, and an ex-girlfriend who knows the guy who sold him the weed."

"Is it true?" Penny asked.

Sue paused dropping tea bags into the mugs and shrugged. "Who cares? It's explosive, and that's all that matters. But it took a lot longer than I expected. Bloody Welsh, it takes them ages to get to the point."

She poured the boiling water from the electric kettle into three mugs. "Anyway, I got the exclusive and came back to London as quickly as I could. This is where the action is. And you, my good friend," Sue grinned, poking Dylan sharply in the chest, "are the biggest action there is!"

Dylan rubbed his hand over the faint stubble on his jaw. "How's that?"

"You're in the quarterfinals of the FA Cup! You're the hottest news on the planet! And Reno wants an exclusive interview." Without waiting for agreement she whipped out her mobile phone and began scrolling. "Jade Haskins is available, she's always fancied you—no? Monica Birley-Hatton? Too posh? You're right, of course, let's see..." she snapped her fingers. "Jo-Beth Wharton. Why didn't I think of her in the first place?" Sue's manicured finger began tapping the screen. "She can be over here in a jiffy—"

Dylan's hand shot out and closed over Sue's. "No. No interviews."

Penny saw the woman's eyes narrow before she recovered herself. "Of course not right now, not when you have a friend over. Penny is welcome to join us, of course."

Penny shrank back. "I don't want to be in any interviews."

"Suit yourself, love, but you may not have a choice," Sue advised. "Our Dylan here is the biggest story in England right now, and I can make sure you're treated right. Other producers might not be so friendly."

Friendly was the last word Penny would use to describe Sue Paulin.

Sue tapped a few times on her phone before presenting the screen to Penny. "See, you're already all over the news."

A headline scrolled before her, *Icelton Out on the Town!* Penny continued scrolling, feeling a surge of pleasure as she looked at the pictures of her with Dylan dancing last night, his arm wrapped around her as she leaned back, her dress a blur of red sequins. They were both laughing and looking in each other's eyes, a beautiful, happy couple.

"What newspaper is this?" Penny asked.

"The *Sunday Mirror*. It's already gotten over a million hits." Sue handed her a mug of tea and put one on the table for Dylan. "That's an interesting tattoo you've got there, Penny."

Penny looked at her chest, where the gown's neckline revealed a part of the horse. "Thanks."

Dylan ignored the tea and took the phone from Penny. He scrolled through the pictures with a cursory movement before putting it back on the table. "Penny's not involved in any of this."

"Don't be ridiculous. She already is."

There was a loud trill from Sue's mobile and Penny saw BBC SPORTS flash across the caller ID with a phone number. Sue answered and said she'd call back in five minutes.

"Penny, would you give us a moment?" Sue asked, somehow making it sound like an order instead of a request. "Dylan and I need to talk."

"No," Dylan said when Penny began to stand. Instead he laid a hand on her bare shoulder and gently pressed her back in the seat. "Penny stays."

"Alright." Sue put her hands on her hips and took a deep breath. "I know I've been horrid, and I'm sorry."

Dylan nodded, and it occurred to Penny that the sharp tone of Sue's apology sounded like something a bank robber would say when they got caught red-handed.

"But I'm here to help," she added.

"I seem to have done very well without your help," Dylan countered.

"Yes, and you bloody well know it's been a fluke."

"We don't need—"

"Don't be stupid, Dylan," Sue cut him off. "I meant what I said—you and Icelton are the biggest news out there. There are only seven other clubs left in the Cup and they are all Premier League powerhouses who will not make the mistakes Plymouth and Newbury did. You need to lock down sponsorships and deals as fast as you can and you need to start now.

"I'm not here to interrupt what you have going on," Sue continued, jerking her head in Penny's direction, "and we can talk about us after you get your ass kicked in the quarterfinal. In the meantime, let's make this work."

Sue drank the last of her tea in one swallow and checked her watch. "You've got the draw tomorrow morning and the BBC Sports department wants you on *Sportsline* at 9 a.m. Shave, put on a fresh shirt, and meet me at your clubhouse in thirty minutes."

Sue swung her expensive leather messenger bag over her shoulder and glanced at Penny as if she had forgotten she was there. "You're welcome to come along as well."

Dylan followed her to the front door and closed it behind her, and from the kitchen Penny could hear the loud roar of the Porsche's turbo engine rev and drive off.

Penny fought a sudden urge to go upstairs to Dylan's room to check the torcs, even though she knew they were safe. Instead she found Dylan in the living room, sunk into a deeply upholstered chair.

"I'm sorry," he said when he saw Penny. "She comes in and takes over, and orders people around. She's like that."

"She's right, you know. About you needing help."

"She's always right. About everything." Dylan shook his head as if trying to clear it. "I never expected her to show up, here, today. I haven't seen her in almost a year."

"What are you going to do?" Penny couldn't stop herself from asking.

"I don't know." Dylan said, his confusion evident.

What about us? Penny wanted to ask, but bit the question off because she was too much of a coward to hear the answer. "I think you need to do as she says."

Penny excused herself and went to her bedroom. She slipped out of the gown and wrapped it in its cover, and placed the shoes back in their box. In the bathroom she scrubbed off her makeup before pulling on a pair of jeans and flannel shirt, socks, and boots. Finally she brushed out the beautiful curls Chloe's father had so carefully set and twisted them into a tight braid down her back, securing it with a rubber band.

Penny returned to the living room where Dylan hadn't moved. "I need to get back to the dig."

"Penny, wait. I'm sorry."

She saw her confusion mirrored in his face. "It's not a problem. I had a really great time last night, thank you."

"Stay for breakfast at least," Dylan said, struggling to free himself from the depths of the cushions.

As if on cue, Dylan's mobile began to chirp and he cursed under his breath. Penny placed her duffle bag over her shoulder, slipped out the door, and headed to her dig.

Chapter Forty-Three

When Penny got to Mortager Park, she saw the red Porsche was parked in the handicapped spot closest to the clubhouse. The guard let her in through the foundry gates and they chatted for a few minutes about the surprising change in Icelton's fortunes.

Although tired from having had no sleep the night before, Penny worked all day, steadfastly ignoring the bustle outside the foundry gates. The red Porsche was still there when she began her walk home that evening, and she had dinner and tried to go to bed early. Sleep was elusive until she heard Dylan come in after midnight, and she strained listening for the sound of a second pair of feet. She fell asleep somewhat happier that there was just his.

Biscuits came to the door Monday morning in a cheerful mood. "In 1873, Wanderers were exempt until the FA Cup final and Queens Park from Scotland had byes until the semifinal and then they withdrew." He kept up the running commentary as they passed the clubhouse, oblivious to Penny's glum mood.

Monday evening Penny was making dinner when Dylan came through the door, looking exhausted. He greeted her and helped himself to a huge plate of spaghetti with ground turkey Bolognese sauce and plopped down at the kitchen table.

Penny looked up from her own plate. "Was the quarterfinal drawing today?"

Dylan nodded, eating hungrily. "We drew Layer United."

"Where are they from?"

"Colchester. It's about seventy miles northeast of here."

Penny nodded. "I know where Colchester is."

"That's the city Boudica burned to the ground, right?"

"The first one, yes. It was called Camulodunum back then. Are they a strong team?"

Dylan went back to the stove for a second helping. "They got promoted to the Premier League two seasons ago and have been doing well. They have a new manager, some very experienced players, and although their administration has been a bit disorganized, they're figuring things out. But they are still a top-flight club."

Penny looked at the logo'd shirt Dylan was wearing. "New sponsor?"

"Yes, it's great," he enthused. "The largest luxury car dealership in the UK. They've sent over a Porsche Cayenne SUV for me to drive, even had it painted green. Beats the hell out of taking a cab or using the foundry van."

"Sue fix that up?" Penny couldn't stop herself from asking.

"Yes." Dylan shoveled a few more forkfuls of spaghetti in his mouth and chewed, eyeing Penny speculatively. "Do you not like Sue? She is a little brash, but she says she wants to be friends with you."

"She seems nice." It was the only polite thing Penny could think to say.

Dylan looked hopeful. "You think so?"

Penny pushed her plate back, unable to lie. "Actually, no."

His shoulders slumped. "A lot of people say that."

"I don't want her near my dig."

"No, of course not."

"And don't tell her what I'm doing here."

"I haven't. I've told her I've laid on extra security because of Alan and Ned's equipment. She doesn't seem interested."

I'll bet, Penny thought to herself. "You two were living together?"

"Yes, for a year."

"So it was serious."

Dylan put his fork down and considered her question. "I guess, yes. Look, Penny, I don't want to put you off."

"We don't need to talk about anything."

"I need you here."

"Because you want the good luck to continue?" The second the words were out of her mouth Penny wanted to take them back.

"No. Believe me, our luck will end on March 15th at 3 o'clock in the afternoon. Sue is right about that."

"She's also right that in the meantime you need to make hay while the sun shines. It's an old farming metaphor," Penny explained, seeing Dylan's quizzical expression. "It means you need to put all your efforts into getting as much set up now as you can. We can talk about us when things are over."

Dylan reached across the table and took Penny's hand in his. "You're sure?"

His fingers closed around hers, strong and warm, and Penny nodded, doing her best to keep eye contact and not look away. "I'm sure you don't need any more complications in your life right now."

He shook his head, his lips curving in a smile. "I appreciate it, but you're not a complication. You're the best thing that's ever happened to me. My mind feels like it's going in a million directions, but I want to make sure you and I are okay. If that's what you want, that's what we'll do."

"We're fine. But there is one other thing I want. The safe in your room, where the torcs are. Can we move it down to my room?"

"Yes, I suppose. It's not bolted to anything. When?"

"Right now."

Dylan didn't ask why, and Penny wasn't sure she could give him an answer if he did. She just knew she needed to keep her treasure close.

Chapter Forty-Four

"HERE YOU ARE, YOUR favorite," Scott said, setting a heaping plate of chicken kebab and rice in front of Penny. It smelled like heaven and she dug in.

Fraud War played silently on the television on the wall. Sue Paulin was standing on a ferry dock in Wales, the wind whipping her short blonde hair, her microphone thrust towards a woman in a shapeless rain slicker.

Penny ignored the television and went back to eating. Three amateur tenors belted out a lusty rendition of Verdi's *Libiamo nélieti calici* from *La Traviata* over the restaurant sound system, and the statue of Luciano Pavarotti on the counter advertised the daily special of Mixed Kebab Roll with a drink for £6.

Scott slid into the empty booth seat across from her.

"Icelton have drawn Layer United in the quarterfinals," he said, and Penny nodded. "At Townsend Lane Stadium as a neutral venue. I guess the FA learned their lesson having Premier League clubs try and navigate the streets around Icelton's ground."

"It was funny," Penny agreed, and scratched her tattoo.

"What's Dylan think?"

"I don't know. I haven't seen him in almost a week."

"I guess he's been inundated. It must be a zoo over there."

Penny nodded, not mentioning that she was going out of her way to avoid him. That wasn't difficult; he was putting in eighteen-hour days running between team training, interviews, and appearances. The story of Icelton being in the FA Cup quarterfinals had sparked international interest, and Sue was keeping him on a grueling schedule that included 2 a.m. broadcast interviews in Asian countries, followed by British morning shows at 6 a.m. and American ones at noon. For the last two weeks the red Porsche had been parked in the handicapped spot closest to the Icelton clubhouse, and seemed to be keeping the same hours Dylan was.

The club itself was also transformed. Once waspish Icelton supporters were now smiling and ebullient as they were interviewed by news crews for local interest stories. Icelton's Tuesday night and Saturday afternoon league matches were now nearly sold out, even though Dylan was using a lot of his non-regular squad members. The girls had reported their games were also attracting much bigger crowds, and they were thrilled.

Penny breezed past it all, grateful that no one was paying any attention to her or the security guard behind the foundry fence. Dylan had made sure that the doors to the watchman's hut and tooling shop had been updated with high-tech digital combination locks that Penny changed every two days. The security company had even brought in a small trailer for the guard to take breaks in.

A mother came into the restaurant with several children in tow and Scott went back behind the counter. Penny ate her meal, chewing slowly and trying to avoid looking at the television. Behind her there was a thud, followed by a loud crash and the children screamed. Penny jumped to her feet and spun around, seeing the statue of Luciano Pavarotti lying shattered on the floor.

"Everyone alright?" Jeff ran in from the back room.

"Yes!" the mother said, checking the children.

"Mummy the statue fell over on its own!" The children wailed. "We wasn't near it!"

"No, of course not," Scott said. "I was running her card and didn't see what happened."

"But the statue was in the middle of the counter," Penny began, looking at the shattered remains strewn across the floor, "nowhere near the edge..."

"You alright, then?" Jeff asked the kids as Scott hurried to get a broom and dustpan. "How about a nice soda with them kebabs?" At a warning look from the mother he added "—on second thought, have some crisps."

Penny slid back into her seat, feeling unsettled. Behind her the restaurant door opened and a cold wind blew in, making the back of her neck tingle. A woman tossed an expensive leather messenger bag into the seat across from Penny and slid into the booth, uninvited.

Penny looked up and patted her lips with the napkin. "Hello, Sue."

"Hello, Penny!" Sue said brightly. "Fancy running into you. Come here often?"

"Every Monday evening. Like clockwork."

"I admit I did know that," Sue grinned. "What's good?"

Penny forced herself to relax her grip on the plastic knife in her hand. "Everything."

"I'll just have a Diet Coke, then," Sue called to Scott.

"You order at the counter," Penny said.

Sue rummaged in her messenger bag for her wallet and found a few coins, and got up to toss them on the counter as

Scott handed her the can. She waived her manicured fingers in helpless supplication so he pulled back the tab for her, releasing a furious hiss of carbonated gas. It took several seconds for the pressure to relieve.

"Thanks," Sue said and rejoined Penny at her table. Penny fought to keep her expression neutral.

Sue looked at the television where she was on the ferry crossing the water, spray breaking over the bow. "There, that's the episode with the Anglesey ferry. God, it was cold."

"So the captain was at fault?"

Sue shifted in her seat and shrugged. "Don't know. He went missing a week ago when he found out we were up there filming. The national papers have picked up the story."

The television switched to an advertisement and Sue lost interest. "So! You're from Ohio, I understand."

Penny got the feeling Sue already knew the correct answer. "Indiana."

"That's quite a long way from here."

"Is it? Gosh, I hadn't noticed."

Sue ignored her sarcasm. "How is it? I mean, being here in London, a Midwestern American girl alone in a huge international city?"

Penny shrugged. "Everyone is nice."

"You've been here a while. Since November?"

"Is this an interview, Sue?"

Sue laughed, as if the question was uproariously funny. "Sorry, no. It's my day job, it just spills over. Sometimes I find myself interrogating the bin lady!"

Penny's appetite had disappeared, but she forced herself to eat a forkful of rice. Sue's lacquered fingernails tapped an impatient staccato on the rim of her soda can in time to the opera. "Dylan says you're doing some digging back in the foundry. When can I come have a look?"

Penny raised her eyebrows with pretend surprise. "You're interested in Quaternary alluvium subcrop distributions over Palaeogene bedrock strata?"

"Ha, no, not really," Sue admitted, and pushed forward when it was obvious Penny wasn't going to volunteer anything else. "I did an interview over at Middlesex University a while ago. They've dug up quite a few artifacts in that area, including some gold. In Roman times it was used as a burial ground. 'Beyond the pale' they called it."

With measured movements Penny finished her soda and checked her watch. "Oh yes? I'll be on the lookout for any of that stuff."

"Penny, wait. Don't leave yet. I wanted to talk to you about Dylan," Sue said. "Me, showing up now, it must seem very odd."

Penny looked at her stonily. "It's none of my business."

"I want to be clear, I'm not here to cause any trouble," Sue continued, her expression contrite. "Dylan's very fond of you. He talks about you a lot. And you...?"

Penny remained silent, refusing to be drawn in.

"We are," Sue continued, "I mean we were... involved. I thought we were in love, but then he changed. Isn't that strange?"

Penny shrugged. "Whatever he was going through before, he seems healthy now."

Sue sighed and nodded.

"Very healthy," Penny added. "And very successful."

"Yes, now. Do you know what changed?" Sue asked, unable to keep a sharp edge off the question.

"I have no idea," Penny lied, and didn't care if Sue knew she was lying.

"People were talking," Sue continued, the fingernails resuming their tapping, "and said it must be drugs. I told everyone that was silly, Dylan would never do drugs. The possibility of being tested was too high and he would never risk it. But his behavior was so strange, and then he quit Kingsbury Town."

"Retired," Penny corrected.

"It's the same thing," Sue snapped before resuming her lament. "I didn't know why. He wouldn't tell me. I begged, but he wouldn't say a word. Why wouldn't he tell me?"

Because he didn't trust you, Penny thought to herself. Instead, she answered, "I don't know."

Sue's shoulders slumped. "I felt terrible and wanted to help him, but he wouldn't let me. And then his dad died, and I was so confused. I needed time to think."

"And now you've had that time?"

Sue dropped her lashes. "We're not sure what we're feeling. I just worry about him—this wild FA Cup run and all the media attention. I think he needs me around. I just want to help."

"Well, good luck with that," Penny said and stood to leave.

"See you around?" Sue called after her.

Once outside on the sidewalk, Penny drew in lungfuls of the cold night air and began the walk back to Icelton. At the end of the block she passed the red Porsche, which was parked directly behind a white car.

Chapter Forty-Five

M ORTAGER PARK WAS A ghost town the Sunday morning of Icelton's quarterfinal match against Layer United, a welcome change from the beehive of activity it had been the last four weeks.

Sue had been a constant presence and had even brought in her assistant, who had set up a temporary office in a corner of the clubhouse. Biscuits had chattered Layer United statistics and historical facts all day yesterday, and the girls had stopped by to model their new club tracksuits, ordered specially for the occasion.

That morning Penny had found a ticket for the day's match on the kitchen table, with a scribbled note from Dylan saying the mums had a seat for her in one of the SUV's but she might just be better off walking the mile to Townsend Lane Stadium because the traffic would be horrible. She considered going, but the thought of seeing Sue and Dylan happily together outweighed all other considerations. Besides, she had work to do.

Penny walked along the foundry fence and the guard let her in the gate with a friendly hello, followed by a yawn. In the tooling shop she pulled back the tarp that covered the cart wheel indentations she was working on, seeing better in the morning light the clues she had detected yesterday of a thin cart yoke between the wheels. The wood had disintegrated centuries ago but the indentations in the clay soil remained remarkably clear.

This was the third cart she had uncovered, running in a diagonal line from the first one Biscuits had found. She was methodically identifying each one, drawing it on her map, refilling the area with loose soil, and covering it with a tarp before moving on to the next. Professor Jain would have a field day with them.

At noon Penny turned on the radio to listen to Joe Lyons's show, followed by the match commentary.

"Today Colchester's Premier League power, Layer United, faces amazing Tier Seven Icelton, the club that just will not lose," Joe Lyons intoned.

"Icelton has now made FA Cup history by progressing further than any non-league club at their level, though, of course, Tottenham Hotspur won the FA Cup in 1901 as a non-league club. And regardless of the twists of fate that have brought them to this point, I must say Icelton just keeps getting better and better. Standouts include Tamba Taray, captain Tommy Peele, and of course keeper Ned Winter."

Joe Lyons continued his glowing report of Icelton before switching to Layer United. "Layer has fielded their full line-up, including brilliant Bulgarian stars Bontcho Borisov and Lubomir Dmitrov. New this season is left winger Dermot O'Sullivan, and the squad is strengthened by the two young-sters who have shone since coming back from half-sea-son loans to Ipswich, Robbie Portman, and Geoff Carrow. Also added is young backup goalkeeper Rae McGrath, who signed from Crystal Palace a few weeks ago."

The match began, and it was obvious from the start that Icelton was in for a thrashing. The score was 4-0 at the half, and 6-0 midway through the second half.

Joe Lyons was prosaic. "Icelton could never have expected to have come this far, and they have their place in the history books by becoming the first Tier Seven club to get to the quarterfinals of the FA Cup. They've had a great run, some extraordinary luck, and they've played jolly good football to boot. But Layer has been very professional and Icelton can go home knowing they tried their best. Along with a very nice check in their pocket."

As the match wore down to the final minutes, Penny packed up and secured the site, anxious to avoid the team bus when it arrived back at Mortager Park. Even though they lost, there was a clubhouse party planned to celebrate Icelton's historic run. Sue would be there with Dylan, and Penny couldn't stomach the thought of seeing them together.

"Icelton has an Atlas League match on Tuesday, away at Fairlop, to go home and prepare for," Joe Lyons was saying. "They'll leave here today with their memories and should be proud of how far they've come. Because for many, Icelton represents the true meaning of football in England..."

Penny turned off the radio, locked the tooling shop door behind her, and waved to a few supporters who were setting up a huge banner on the fence where the team would see it when they arrived back at Mortager Park. A single television news truck pulled in and parked next to a low podium that had been erected in the carpark.

Back at Dylan's house, Penny was making herself dinner when the doorbell began to CHONG CHONG CHONG repeatedly. When she opened the door she found Biscuits standing on the stoop, breathing hard, his face red from exertion and his eyes wild.

Alarmed, Penny crouched down next to the boy. "Biscuits, what is it? Are you alright?"

Unintelligible words flooded out of the boy's mouth as he tried to catch his breath.

"Take your time. Whatever it is, we'll figure it out," Penny assured him but it only seemed to make him more frantic. "Biscuits, did you run here all the way from Townsend Lane Stadium?"

He nodded, gripping her arms. Good Lord, that was over a mile away.

"P-P-Penny," the boy stuttered, "Mmmm-McGrath, mmmm-McGrath..."

Penny nodded. "Yes, Biscuits, tell me about McGrath. Was he a player?"

"Is a p-player! Now! R-r-right now! For Layer! McGrath is c-cup-tied!"

So far this made as much sense as anything he usually said. "And?"

Biscuits paused and took three deep breaths before blurting out, "August 14th Sherborne Town leading Deptford United 4-nil at 91 minutes and McGrath comes on for Deptford. So McGrath is cup-tied, Penny. McGrath is cup-tied—"

The boy stopped to draw another breath, his agitation growing as Penny did nothing. "PENNY McGrath is cup-tied. McGrath is—" he continued, his voice steadily rising to a scream, "CUP-TIED, PENNY! McGRATH IS—"

"Yes, it's okay. I heard you," Penny assured him. "McGrath is cup-tied."

Satisfied that Penny understood, Biscuits grabbed her hand and started pulling her towards the road.

"Wait, Biscuits, I need my jacket and I have to lock the house—"

"NO! NO, PENNY! McGRATH IS–" the little lad bellowed at the top of his lungs.

"Just give me two seconds and I will be right back out," Penny promised. "Stay here."

Penny grabbed her jacket and locked the door behind her, and then ran to keep up as Biscuits dragged her to Mortager Park like the hounds of hell were on their heels.

Chapter Forty-Six

THE ICELTON TEAM COACH rolled into Mortager Park after nightfall. The trip was only a mile from Townsend Lane Stadium but the route had been lined with well-wishers and taken almost an hour. There was no feeling of sadness in the coach, in fact the sense of relief was palpable. The future was looking bright.

Dylan sat back in his seat, relaxed and happy. It had been good to be back in Townsend Lane Stadium. His old team-mates Hugo Auchincloss and Mick Carr had stopped in to visit, and Sir Frank had thoughtfully had the Icelton players' names mounted above the lockers. His team had wandered around the cavernous locker rooms in awe, taking pictures.

"Blimey this is luxury," Tamba had remarked, marveling at the state-of-the-art physio room. "What's that?" he asked pointing at a large tub.

"That's the ice bath," Dylan had said. "Fifteen minutes in there after each match. Torture, but effective."

The game against Layer had been a whipping, but still his team had played well. Vahid Sistani, Layer's manager, played his strongest team, but Icelton hadn't let them have an easy time of it—Layer had been forced to work for it. At halftime Layer led 4–0, and when Callum Williams had knocked one in for Icelton at the 85th minute the crowd had given him a rousing cheer. The final score was a well-deserved 7–1. There were no hard feelings.

The FA would be sending a check over in a few days for the consolation prize money and the cut of the gate receipts, and television fees would be banked in a month. Icelton Football Club was solvent for many years to come. There were ten games left in the rest of the Atlas League season and it would appear they would be finishing in the middle of the table. Yet here they were, playing in front of 32,000 spectators today, and not making a disgrace of themselves. Remarkable.

Being back at Townsend Lane Stadium had brought back a flood of memories. That was the thing—even though Dylan knew he had every intention of going back as a player, today that idea had been distinctly less appealing.

He was starting to enjoy being the manager. It was like something in his head had clicked. The game unfolded before him and he just knew which way things were going to go. He sensed the opposing teams' weaknesses and saw the holes in their defenses. He knew where his team needed heat and where they needed to press.

Dylan smiled and thought about Penny. He wished she'd been there today, and he'd been tempted to wake her up at dawn to give her the ticket in person. But he wasn't surprised when he'd looked up into the seats and saw her seat empty—she was doing a very good job of avoiding him.

Not that he could blame her. Sue had been a constant presence and Dylan had to admit she was making herself very useful. The media attention had been explosive and with his attention focused on coaching the team, he would have had no way of dealing with it. Sue organized the sports writers, the cameras, his wardrobe, everything. He had for-gotten how good she was at ordering people around.

It had been easy getting back into a routine with her. They had shared a few late night takeout dinners, but he had to be honest with himself—he had no desire for Sue. Maybe it had been the drugs, but he had no idea what he ever saw in her. Around Penny his arousal felt inflamed—it wasn't just sexual, he wanted to make her laugh. He wanted to tease her. He wanted to know what she wanted so he could get it for her.

For the past four weeks Dylan had caught glimpses of Penny. Her dig was now behind eight foot tall fencing with a chained and locked gate so it was impossible to just stroll over and visit with her. But he knew she was near, sensed her, and was comforted.

Feeling bone weary, he decided he needed a real vacation. God knew they'd all been working like dogs and deserved it. He had money in his pocket now, and Penny could use a vacation as well. Maybe she'd go somewhere with him.

From his seat at the front of the bus, Dylan could see the crowd that had gathered to welcome them back to Mortager Park. The coach slowed to a crawl as it passed through the well-wishers before coming to a halt in the spot Sue had set up. Portable spotlights had been erected to highlight the players as they emerged from the coach, and a news crew was there to film the event. Supporters were cordoned on either side, waving flags, and cheering.

The players descended one at a time and stood on the steps of the coach, enjoying their last minutes of notoriety. Someone had even brought a trumpet to herald them. Alan and Uncle Eddie got off and waved, and then it was Dylan's turn.

He stood on the bottom coach step, tears welling in his eyes as he accepted the thunderous accolades. Someone struck up a rousing cheer of 'for he's a jolly good fellow', and he saw a banner draped over the clubhouse that read ICEL-TON WILL ALWAYS BE CHAMPIONS IN OUR HEARTS. A lump formed in his throat.

Sue slipped next to him and put a hand on his. "It was to be expected," she consoled.

Dylan shrugged, looking out over the crowd for Penny.

"You did an amazing job." Sue's eyes were tentative, searching, her hand ice cold.

"Day's work," he replied.

Sue motioned to her assistant to let a group of supporters through the cordon rope. "I need a thirty-second speech. BBC is camera two on the left, then look at the NBC camera one on the right."

Dylan watched his team with pride as they hugged the supporters and posed for pictures. Cameras flashed, illuminating the night, and the girls' team waved green and gray flags. Len was nowhere to be seen.

"I wish your dad had been here for this," Gwen said, hugging him. "I know he's so proud of you."

Sue pinched his arm, the cue for him to give a short speech. He stepped up to the podium and took the microphone her assistant passed over. As the cameras followed him, he saw a movement at the back of the crowd, and squinted to make out what it was. Bloody hell, it looked like

Biscuits bobbing and wading through the throng, dragging Penny behind him.

"Start talking—" Sue hissed.

Dylan watched in surprise as Biscuits made it to the rope cordon, ducked under it with Penny still in tow, and past where the girls' team was assembled.

"Biscuits, where have you been?" Kathleen scolded. "We've been going mad looking for you! Mum's frantic!"

Her brother ignored her and didn't stop until he and Penny were before Dylan. Up close he could see the little lad was frantic. Sue's grip on his arm tightened.

"What is it?" Dylan asked. "What's the matter?"

Penny, disheveled and out of breath, looked to Dylan, and then to Sue, and then back to Dylan. "What does cup-tied mean?"

Chapter Forty-Seven

Sue's hand dropped from Dylan's arm like she had been scalded.

"What?" Dylan yelled over the chattering of the crowd.

"Cup-tied!" Penny yelled back, and people around them began to fall silent. "What does it mean?"

"Who's cup-tied?" Dylan asked. He turned to Biscuits, who was pale as a ghost. The boy's mouth worked soundlessly, and no words came out.

Dylan's heart began to race. *Jesus Christ.* "Bloody hell, Biscuits, who is cup-tied?"

"A player named McGrath," Penny said when Biscuits was unable to speak.

Dylan's pulse leapt. "When?"

Biscuits whispered and Penny bent to listen. "August 14th, I think he was playing for Deptford."

Mobile phones were whipped out and time seemed to stand still as the crowd feverishly searched.

"Bloody hell," Alan muttered in disbelief.

"Sub keeper—" Gwen shouted, reading from her mobile phone, "—came on in the 91st minute when Ribeiro, their starting keeper, was taken off, injured."

The crowd began to chatter with excitement that built into a rumble. Penny looked around in confusion.

"No, no—" Sue began, "Wait just a goddamn minute. All the players are vetted. This can't happen."

"It happens all the time!" came a sharp retort.

"No! All the players are vetted," she insisted, spinning around to confront Penny. "Listen to me, you idiot, you can't come in here with some wild story—"

"I don't understand," Penny said, genuinely mystified. "What's cup-tied?"

"FA rules say clearly that once a player appears for team in a cup competition, he can't play for another club in that season's competition," Gwen replied, glaring at Sue. "McGrath was on a half-season loan from Crystal Palace with Deptford United from August 1st to December 31st. He returned to Palace on January 1st, and was transferred to Layer at the end of the January transfer window."

"Layer substituted him in at the 83rd minute today," Alan said, and then swallowed hard. "Layer played an ineligible player."

"Why would they do that?" Penny asked.

"Players forget, clubs forget." Alan replied.

"What does this mean?"

"It means," Dylan said, swallowing hard, "Icelton is almost certainly in the FA Cup semifinals."

Chapter Forty-Eight

IT SEEMED TO PENNY that no one in north London slept that night. The news that Layer United might have played an ineligible player spread like wildfire, and the news crews at Mortager Park snagged the sports story of the year.

More media descended on Icelton. Vans full of equipment jammed the narrow drive while reporters set up lights outside the clubhouse and reported live. Sue gave interviews, one after another, downplaying the probability of a cup-tied player and emphasizing Layer's dominant win over Icelton.

Penny listened and wondered whose side she was on. But she heard the rising panic in Sue's voice loud and clear.

Kathleen and her parents stood with Biscuits while reporters tried to interview him, but once everyone understood the enormity of his discovery, he'd reverted to his normal stoic demeanor and offered only random statistics from Icelton matches played thirty years ago. They eventually gave up.

Inside the clubhouse, Dylan had spoken to the FA and was in conversation with Alan Winter, discussing the necessity of filing a formal protest and getting the proper documentation. But the answer seemed to be a foregone conclusion; Layer would be thrown out of the competition.

The night guard arrived and after seeing the crowds, ended up calling in two more guards. Penny stayed at the clubhouse, keeping an eye on the foundry gate, which was firmly closed.

At 1:30 a.m. Sue found Penny drinking coffee and munching on a sandwich from a party tray. "Penny, we need your security guards to help with the crowds out front. Problem?"

Penny's gut reaction was to deny her request but she couldn't think of any reasonable way to do it. "No, not at all," Penny said, trying to sound helpful.

Sue paused, apparently listening to a person speaking in her earpiece. "Okay," she replied, "I'll tell the guards to open the foundry gates and the TV camera trucks can park back in there."

Penny glared at her. "If that's okay with you, Penny?" Sue added.

Penny fought back the wave of panic that threatened to engulf her. She told herself the tooling shop was adequately defended—it was over a hundred feet from the foundry yard, had good locks on the doors, and was completely inconspicuous. The foundry was Dylan's property, after all, and he needed the space.

"Let me go do it for you," she said, and began to walk towards the door.

"Thanks, you're a dear. And Penny?" Sue called after her, "What's the passcode for Dylan's house? He wants me to stay tonight."

Penny swallowed hard and scribbled it on a piece of paper before fleeing the building. She pushed the gate open wide and waited while television trucks and vans filed through. They came equipped with their own mobile lighting and generators that were soon bathing the foundry yard in harsh light.

She walked back to the tooling shop and dou-bled-checked the locks, noting that her primitive alarm string still ran from the exterior door back to the watchman's hut. It might be redundant with all the security Dylan had laid on, but it had proven effective and Penny didn't see any reason to detach it. She followed the string through the short hallway back to her former room and flopped on the cot.

At least here she was happy. The dig had proven that she was right. She was making new finds every day, some of them quite important. Professor Jain's hypothesis that there were first century AD cart burials outside of Yorkshire was correct, and she had found the most beautiful torcs ever discovered. The fact that Dylan and his maybe-ex-girlfriend were back together, and at the center of the biggest sports story in the world was something she was just going to have to deal with.

Penny laid down, pulled the comforter up, and felt very, very sorry for herself.

<hr>

The hum of portable generators in the foundry yard woke Penny the next morning. The sun poured through the small window in the watchman's hut promising a pleasant day, but her back hurt from the stiff cot and she had a headache. Through the window she saw more trucks had arrived while she slept, and there were now eight television vans parked in the foundry yard. The gate was still open and news crews were walking back and forth.

Hoping there would be fresh coffee in the clubhouse, Penny pulled on her boots and jacket and walked over. There was no sign of Sue or Dylan, and the handicapped spot where the red Porsche was usually parked was empty.

Inside the clubhouse an Asian film crew tried to convince Penny to give an interview and followed her around as she poured coffee despite her polite decline. More reporters arrived and she fled to Dylan's office, pulling the door closed behind her. She sat in his chair for half an hour drinking her coffee, trying to wake up. The desk was covered in stacks of paperwork, and she smiled when she saw her letter from Princeton College among the papers. It seemed like a million years ago she had left it there.

There was a knock on the door. "Someone to see you, miss."

Penny opened the door, not recognizing the security guard who stood there. "I'm not expecting anyone."

The guard shrugged. "You're Penny Adams, right? They said you was back here. Guy asked for you by name, said you were expecting him today, Monday morning at 9 a.m. Said he was supposed to see the tooling shop, so I let him in."

Penny's pulse jumped, and she bolted out of the clubhouse and across the foundry yard. The door to the tooling shop stood wide open, and inside a man, dressed in work khakis and a windbreaker, knelt in the middle of the string grid looking at the pottery bowls Penny had uncovered.

Penny froze. "Who are you?"

At the sound of her voice the man stood up. "My name is Thomas Mitchell," he said, looking around in disbelief. "I'm from HARP."

Chapter Forty-Nine

IF MORTAGER PARK HAD been a zoo before HARP showed up, by Monday at noon it was a certifiable asylum.

Thomas Mitchell had wasted little time summoning his field team and supervisors, who in turn alerted what seemed to Penny like every archaeologist in Great Britain. It didn't take long before a crowd of distinguished academics descended on the Icelton foundry.

The news people, sensing a new vein of energy, mobbed the door of the tooling shop demanding entry. The security guards had their hands full shepherding them back to the other side of the foundry gate and, at Thomas Mitchell's command, moving the news vans out. The foundry gates slammed shut, leaving the television presenters to shout their questions through the chain-link fence.

Thomas Mitchell surveyed the fence around the foundry buildings. "This is all good," he said, "but the security is abysmal. We'll be bringing in our own."

Penny followed him doggedly around the site but was consulted on nothing and introduced to no one. A woman wearing a HARP jacket caught up to them, out of breath. "Someone has been staying in the room over there with the coal stove," she reported, pointing to the watchman's hut. "There's a cot with a mattress."

"Yes, I am," Penny said.

Thomas Mitchell shook his head. "No, can't have it. This site has to be secured."

"But I want to stay here. You can't kick me out."

"The only person that can make that determination is the property owner. Where is he?"

"I'm not sure where he is," Penny said. "He's Dylan Rhea." At Thomas Mitchell's blank stare Penny elaborated, "This is Icelton Football Club, and he's the owner. They just found out they're in the semifinals of the FA Cup."

"I follow cricket," Thomas Mitchell shrugged, indifferent. "We need to speak with Mr Rhea."

Penny went back to the clubhouse where Sue's assistant was frantically typing on a laptop, a collection of mobile phones scattered on the table before him.

"Yes, love?" the harried man didn't bother looking up at Penny.

"Where's Dylan?"

"He and Sue went back to his place to get some sleep—" he paused to listen to his earphones. "Yes! Yes! Dylan is meeting with the FA at 3 p.m. today, he'll have a statement directly afterwards—"

"When will they be back?" Penny interrupted.

"No clue. Look, make yourself useful and give an interview to that lot. They're desperate for footage." He pointed across the room at a television presenter and her crew who looked up hopefully.

Penny instead went back to the tooling shop, where another HARP member politely asked her to wait in the watchman's hut while the supervisors looked over her site. She slumped on the cot while the little bell next to the bed tinkled repeatedly for two hours as people came and went through the tooling shop door. Finally she was summoned into the dig where cursory introductions were made. Penny lost track of the dozen directors, assistant directors, field coordinators, and advisors assembled before her.

"Is Professor Jain coming?" Penny asked after everyone had been introduced.

A woman, whose titles included 'Lead Specialist', 'Assistant Acting Director', and 'Methodology', ignored her question and cut to the chase. "Where's the treasure?"

Penny was taken aback by the directness of the question. "How do you know I've found treasure?"

"Because we're professionals. We know what we're looking at. There are empty clay vessels dating from at least the first century BC and they would have been buried with material wealth."

"The stupid girl has removed them from the site," an important-acting person told another important-acting person when Penny hesitated. "Who knows what we'll be able to reconstruct."

"I marked everything. I was careful," Penny protested. "I have a grid map."

"This is exactly why amateurs should not be involved," the woman scolded. "I'm sure you meant well, but you know you were instructed to call us the moment you found gold, coins, or jewelry."

"All that's water under the bridge now," another said. "Where are your findings?"

This wasn't going the way Penny had always imagined it would, and she felt the need to stall. "Findings?"

"The gold. You've found gold, haven't you?"

Penny heard the certainty in their voices. Afraid of getting in deeper trouble than she already seemed to be, she reluctantly replied, "Yes."

"Where is it?"

"Somewhere safe."

A dozen pair of eyes bore down on her. "We need to see it. Now."

"I have to go get it."

"We'll come with you."

"No! Stay here. I'll be back in an hour."

⸺◦⸺

The archaeologists had argued but in the end had let Penny leave. She walked back to Dylan's house with trepidation. It was now 2 p.m. and the red Porsche was still parked outside. Her heart sank. She wanted to turn around and go back to Mortager Park, or be anywhere else, but the archeologists were demanding to see what she had found and she had to return to the foundry with something. She punched the keypad buttons and let herself in the front door.

Sue was in the kitchen talking to someone on her headset, her voice low and urgent. She jumped when she saw Penny. "Hello!"

Penny nodded. "Is Dylan up yet?"

"No, he's still asleep. What do you want?"

"I'm just going to get some stuff from my room."

"Don't make too much noise. He's exhausted."

Penny opened the door to her room and saw Dylan laying full length on her bed, fast asleep. He was wearing only gym shorts, his chest rising and falling, his breathing deep and even. A rush of relief flooded Penny's heart. The bed was narrow and Dylan took up all of it. His bed upstairs was at least three times as wide, and she knew instinctively that Sue would have commandeered it.

Penny exhaled and began to move quietly around the room, taking down the large grid map of her site, rolling it, and securing it with a hair elastic. Kneeling in the closet, she opened the safe and placed the collection of little boxes in her duffle bag.

Dylan muttered something in his sleep and rolled over.

The boxes with the torcs were at the bottom of the safe. Penny hesitated before leaving them where they were, closing the safe door, and spinning the combination dial. She took one last look at Dylan and tucked her duffle bag under her arm, shutting the bedroom door soundlessly behind her.

"Things hectic over at Mortager Park?" Sue asked, not bothering to look up from her mobile.

"You wouldn't believe," Penny said, and hurriedly left the house.

※

Back at the dig, the archaeologists gathered around a portable table they had set up in the watchman's hut. Penny unrolled her excavation map, noticing that her cot had been removed. They used push pins to mount it on the wall and then Penny opened boxes, one by one. A notable frisson ran through group as the contents of each was revealed.

"Bloody hell, that's an Irstead Quarter Stater," someone said as she lay a small gold coin on the table.

"And six Bury Face Horse Half Units!" a woman yelped when Penny opened the next box and removed several larger coins.

"Dear God, dear God, please let there be a Bury C Diadem..." a man said under his breath, and then let out a squawk when Penny laid ten of the little disks on the table.

The crowd surveyed her findings. "All late denominational, minted right before the rebellion. And all three Iceni mints."

"I've never seen so much late denominational gold," another whispered.

"Where are the denarii?" a woman demanded, frantic. "There must be denarii."

"Are these denarii?" Penny opened a box and laid out twenty-two silver disks.

"Holy shit, they're all Claudian. There's no Nervan. No Hadrian." Penny listened as they named the Roman dynasties that came after Boudica.

Penny laid out the final bits of jewelry and the pottery shards. By the time she finished the room was silent.

"That's it?" the lead specialist asked.

"Except for the impressions of cart wheels and traces, like in Yorkshire. I reburied them. They're under the blue tarps in the tooling shop."

One of the men's eyes rolled back in his head and his knees crumbled.

"Catch him!" someone yelled.

It took several moments to revive him, and his co-workers took him outside for some fresh air, a beatific smile on his face.

When things had settled down the lead specialist faced Penny. "We want the torcs."

"What are they" Penny asked, feigning ignorance.

"Twisted wire necklaces. About yeah-big," she made a circle with her hands. "In gold, silver, and bronze."

"Professor Jain says that not all Iceni burials —"

"Yes, we are bloody well aware of Padma Jain's view of Iceni funeral practices," she snapped. "Where are the torcs?"

Penny could not outright lie, but she was also not handing them over. "If I find any, I'll let you know."

The lead specialist stared at her and then seemed to come to a decision. "Well, congratulations Miss Adams, you have done a very nice job here," she said, placing a firm hand on Penny's back and guiding her to the door. "We will be taking over now."

"But this is my dig!" Penny protested.

"Yes, of course, thank you, after we talk with the land owner we will be in touch."

Without further ado, Penny was hustled out of the watch-man's hut and the door shut firmly in her face.

Chapter Fifty

Having nowhere else to go, Penny returned to the clubhouse. There were now guards at the doorway but they recognized her and allowed her into the packed room.

Dylan, freshly showered and shaved, stood at a makeshift podium surrounded by camera crews, photographers, and reporters. Sue stood by his side.

"Dylan, have you heard from the FA?" a reporter called out.

"Yes, we just spoke. Layer United admitted they'd played an ineligible player, but said they didn't know he'd appeared in an extra preliminary round tie on loan with a Tier Nine club. They accept they will be expelled from the competition and aren't going to appeal the decision."

"So your draw is going to be either South Quay Road, Leicester City, or Kingsbury Town. Who'd ya fancy?" This question drew a laugh from the crowd.

"I want to see my old mates!" Dylan replied, grinning.

Sue stepped in front of Dylan and spoke into the microphone. "Okay, lads, that's a wrap for right now. We'll have more news when we hear it. In the meantime, Icelton has an Atlas League match to prepare for tomorrow. See you then!"

Sue shepherded Dylan back to his office and stood guard in the corridor while chatting with a group of reporters. When Penny tried to step past her, Sue blocked her way.

"Sorry, love, Dylan's up to his eyeballs."

"I need to see him," Penny said.

Sue made a production of checking her mobile phone. "Of course, not a problem. Let's see... tomorrow morning at half past ten?"

Penny swallowed the curse on her tongue. "Now."

"No, darling. But I'll let him know you stopped by."

A hot burst of hatred flashed through Penny and she squared her shoulders and stood erect, glaring down at Sue. From her fight with the intruder, Penny knew that her height was an asset. Surprise was as well.

Dylan emerged from his office as Penny was sizing Sue up. "I just got a call from Lord Lambton, he's offering us—oh, Penny! Good to see you. What's the matter?"

"I need to see you." Penny spoke over Sue's head, her eyes narrowed. "Now."

"Dylan," Sue interrupted, her jaw set, "Sky Sports News needs you in ten minutes—"

Dylan glanced between the two women. "Yes, not a problem, be just a jiffy." He pulled Penny in to the little office and shut the door.

Penny continued through the office to the boiler room, silently indicating Dylan should follow her, and pulled the door shut behind them.

"Penny, what's the matter?" Dylan asked, pressing against her in the cramped confines.

"They're here," she whispered.

"Who's here? And why are we whispering?"

"HARP. HARP is here."

Comprehension slowly dawned on Dylan. "Bloody hell. When?"

"This morning."

"Great timing."

"Actually, it is almost exactly when they said they would show up, back when we went to see them in November. It's Monday, March 16th."

Dylan exhaled. "I guess it is. What have you shown them?"

"The coins. And the jewelry, and the pottery."

"But not the torcs?"

"No."

"What did they say?"

"Their eyes jumped out of their heads." Tears began to roll down Penny's face and she couldn't stop them. "And then they kicked me out."

Dylan pulled her into his arms. "They're not taking over," he whispered in her hair. "But the timing is horrendous."

"You're in the semifinals," she smiled.

"Yeah, thanks to you and Biscuits."

They heard an insistent knocking on the office door. "Dylan, I need you out here now," Sue commanded.

Dylan wiped Penny's tears away with his shirt sleeve. "This is something I can make better right away. Come on."

Dylan led Penny by the hand into the hallway, heading toward the tooling shop. "I have to go talk to some people," he told Sue. "Tell Sky Sports News I'll be back in an hour."

She began to protest but Dylan added, "That's an order, Sue."

Forty minutes later Dylan emerged from the tooling shop. Penny jumped up from the crate she'd been sitting on outside the door, and he motioned for her to follow him around the corner of the watchman's hut.

"You're right, they know you've found something major," he told her once they had some privacy.

"What did they say?"

"Not much, but we cut a deal. In exchange for access to this property and control of security, you will be given a role in the excavation work."

Penny's spirits lifted.

"You're to be my representative here. What you say, goes. You won't be able to stay here, though," Dylan cautioned, "That's my rule. They agreed it's for the best."

Penny frowned. "It's going to be a little crowded at your house."

"No, it's not. I'm taking the team out to Goffs Oak Country Club until the semifinal. They've got lodging and a decent pitch, and it's private. Lord Lambton over at the FA set it up. You'll have my house to yourself."

"Is Sue going with you?" Penny couldn't stop herself asking.

"No, of course not," Dylan smiled, and pulled her close. "Would you go with me? I'd rather you did."

Penny smiled as Dylan kissed her, his lips warm against hers, his strong arms holding her tightly. The play of his mouth across hers was thrilling, and she heard herself sigh. There was a loud sound from inside the tooling shop as the HARP people attempted to open the sliding doors at the far end, making the heavy portals squeak in deafening protest.

Dylan buried his face in her curls. "Come with me," he breathed against her ear.

Penny opened her eyes and saw Sue at the clubhouse back door, staring at them through the fence. She felt a prick of intuition. "I'm sorry. I think I need to keep an eye on things here."

Chapter Fifty-One

PENNY DUMPED THE WHEELBARROW full of clay dirt into the large sifting box, her nineteenth of the day by her count, and wiped her brow. April 5th was a hot, stifling day in northwest London and she had peeled down to a t-shirt. This seemed crazy, because yesterday she'd been freezing in her sweatshirt.

The industrial-sized generators HARP had rented chugged next to her, powering the banks of computers, lighting, field laboratory, and the portable digital photography studio they had erected in a sturdy tent nearby. From the few glimpses into the tooling shop she'd been allowed, Penny saw that her excavation site had been transformed. Scaffolds held industrial lighting that made the building glow at night. She took it as a compliment that the professionals had kept the grid system she had established, and were even using the same string layout. Dozens of colored and numbered flags now dotted the squares and yellow tape cordoned off the areas where she had discovered the cart pieces.

"Is it Boudica?" Penny continued to ask, but they refused to answer.

Biscuits sat next to her, poking at the dirt in the sifting box. His chatter lately had pertained to devastating losses suffered by British football teams in the last century, and Penny could tell he was brooding. There had been a run in with Thomas Mitchell on the second day of HARP's presence at Mortager Park, when Biscuits had wandered into the dig as he normally did. He had been quickly ejected.

"Miss Adams, we cannot have children crawling all over this site," Thomas Mitchell had informed her.

"He's the one that found the cart wheels," Penny had countered.

"I will make sure his contribution gets proper acknowledgment. But he may not cross that threshold."

Biscuits had looked at the pullover Thomas Mitchell was wearing, which bore the emblem of Lord's Cricket Ground. "England lost to Bangladesh by fifteen runs in the 2015 Cricket World Cup at Adelaide."

Thomas Mitchell's eyes had narrowed. "Jos Buttler kept us in it."

"And the coach, Peter Moores, took you out."

Penny had no idea what the exchange entailed, but the man had stalked off and Biscuits had looked, if possible, smug.

⬥

Kathleen swung by after the girls' team practice to collect Biscuits and chat. With the men's team now training at Goffs Oak Country Club, the media circus had quickly left Mortager Park and the girls delighted in having it to themselves.

"Did we tell you, Miss, that Sue is arranging for us to be interviewed on the pitch at the semifinal at Wembley on Saturday?" Kathleen asked.

"That's wonderful."

"Yeah, me and all the girls are chuffed. You'll be there, right? We're all going to be in a skybox. Dylan's set it up."

"Yes, I'm looking forward to it."

After Kathleen and Biscuits left, Penny leaned back against the fence, closed her eyes and let the sunlight warm her face. She hadn't seen Dylan since the day HARP had shown up, almost three weeks before. Sue had disappeared along with him, and regardless of the fact that Dylan had kissed her before he left, Penny still felt distinct unease.

A car honked nearby. When she didn't move it honked again, this time with more insistence. She opened her eyes to see Reno Tedesco sitting behind the wheel of a purple Corvette convertible, waving to her.

"Hello, Penny!"

Penny sat up and waved back. "Hello, Reno. How are you?"

"I am well!" He hopped out of the car and approached the gate. "May I come in?"

What was one more person? Penny held the gate for Reno, who caught her in a bear hug and kissed both of her cheeks with lusty smacks. He wore a starched white linen shirt, pressed jeans, and gorgeous leather loafers.

"*Ciao, bella*! Let's go see what you have going on here."

Without waiting for her, Reno strode to the door of the tooling shop where he was unceremoniously halted by one of the HARP workers. "Not so fast."

"No? But I am a friend of Dylan's!" Reno smiled. "I have just come for a look. No? A tiny peek?"

Penny watched his cajoling with amusement. When nothing worked, Reno drew himself up to his full height, which was still shorter than Penny. "It is just as well," he said, his tone imperious, "I have seen excavation sites much grander in Rome and I'm sure this would bore me."

He turned to Penny. "But this visit is not a failure. I am going to have dinner with a very beautiful woman," he confided.

"Oh? Who?"

"You!"

Penny laughed at his joke, but seconds later her eyes widened as she found herself escorted to his sports car. "I am starving. I haven't eaten in two, perhaps three hours! Look at me," he patted his flat stomach with the hand that wasn't holding Penny's arm, "I am fading away to nothing. Penny *amore mio*, you must have pity on me."

"I'm not dressed," Penny protested, pointing to her dusty jeans and t-shirt.

"You look like a supermodel. Besides, we are going to a family restaurant. Working people's food. You will like it, you will see."

Reno helped Penny into her seat in the Corvette. Penny knew it was brand new, a Z51 3LT 6.2 liter V-8 that he must have imported directly from the assembly plant in Bowling Green, Kentucky. She rubbed her hand over the stitched leather dashboard with approval.

Reno slipped into the driver's seat and the engine roared to life.

"You got the eight-speed dual-clutch automatic?"

"*Si,*" Reno nodded with mock sadness, "the manual was not available."

With a spray of gravel he whipped the sleek automobile around the car park, hitting forty miles an hour down the long, rutted Mortager Park driveway. The car was a miracle of suspension and the bumps were barely noticeable. In the winding streets of Icelton, the car's maneuvering was tight.

"Reno, there's no rear-view mirror," Penny observed, loving the feel of the wind in her hair.

"No," Reno shook his head and confided, "The first rule of Italian race car driving: What is behind me, does not matter."

There was a slight lurch as the car downshifted at the traffic light onto the main motor way.

"It's the torque converter," Penny pointed out. "It's clashing with the active fuel management system. You can order an AFM disable device. The bump will still be there but you won't feel it as much."

Reno looked at her with undisguised adoration. "You like fast cars, Penny?"

"I love fast cars."

"Then we go fast!"

Chapter Fifty-Two

OTHER CARS ON THE M1 wisely vacated the passing lane, leaving Reno and his purple Corvette an open road. A Paganini violin concerto blasted at top volume on the stereo as Reno drove with one hand while conducting with the other.

"Paganini is the king, yes? The greatest violinist who ever lived. Yes, he was from Parma, but I know in my heart he was a Roman," Reno thumped his chest for emphasis. "And you know what they say? His expertise with the violin was only surpassed by his expertise with women."

Reno wagged his thick eyebrows but Penny ignored his innuendo and enjoyed the drive. "Where are we going?"

"St Albans, it is just up the road here. That is where my football club is, the South Quay Road Potters."

Twenty minutes later they arrived in St Albans—much faster, Penny suspected, than most drivers headed in the same direction. They drove through a suburban area and Reno turned left onto South Quay Road.

Penny looked around, seeing nothing but a pond and pokey stream. "Where is the quay? Isn't that a dock or something?"

"They tell me a long time ago there was one, along the river Ver. There was an old inn here called The Potter, I had it knocked down to build my masterpiece."

Reno drove down a broad road and motioned towards a hulking stadium surrounded by acres of parking lots. Although clearly modern, Penny realized the clumsy elliptical design was meant to evoke the Colosseum in Rome, complete with three levels of arched colonnades. As they drove closer Penny could see a huge marble statue looming in front of the entrance.

"Who is the statue of?" Penny asked, craning her neck to see from the car.

"Me!" Reno said with pride. "I sculpt it myself."

The base was over ten feet tall, and was topped by a statue that rose another twenty feet. Penny saw it was indeed Reno, bare to the waist, wrapped in a Roman toga with a laurel wreath crown on his head. His extended arm held a soccer ball.

"It's, it's..." Penny groped for words. "It's enormous."

Reno sighed with satisfaction. "*Si*. I would have made it bigger but they couldn't find enough marble."

"You chiseled that yourself?"

"Yes and no, I draw out what I want and hire the sculptor. We work together. Then he gets mad and walks off job and I finish. It is perfection, no?"

"It's something else." Penny looked around the rest of the stadium. "Have you sculpted any more statues?"

"No, there was a tragedy." Reno held up his right hand, showing her where the middle and ring fingers were noticeably crooked. "I had trouble with my first Corvette, I run off the road. In the wreck I break all these fingers. The doctors, they tell me I will never sculpt again. What an artist the world has lost!"

Closer to the town, Reno pulled into an empty space in front of a modern restaurant called L'Imperatore and hopped out.

He pointed at the sign and grinned. "L'Imperatore means The Emperor. That's me!"

He opened Penny's door and helped her out, tossing the keys to a young man who was sprinting towards them. They exchanged greetings in Italian before Reno swept Penny into the restaurant.

Staff and diners hailed him as they sallied through the main dining room and Reno laughed, waving back, while maneuvering Penny up the open stairs to an intimate second floor balcony table. Two servers welcomed them, and Reno settled Penny into a velvet banquette and himself across from her in a massive wooden armchair, replete with purple tassels.

A bottle of red wine appeared, followed by fresh bread and a bowl of olive oil. Reno poured them each a generous glass, ignoring Penny's protests that she didn't like wine. "You will love this," he assured her. "From my vineyard in Tuscany. It is the best Tignanello ever bottled. I drink it ten years ago and fall in love and try to buy the vineyard, but the owner wouldn't sell."

Penny took a sip and liked it. "What did you do?"

A sly looked passed over Reno's features. "He suddenly has a bad tax situation with the Italian government. Then he is happy to sell." Reno raised his glass to Penny. "I propose a toast—to a remarkable woman who seems to bring luck to all around her."

A server appeared with more appetizers, including something called Pizza e Mortazza and Crostini alla Romana, which had anchovies on it. At Reno's urging, Penny tried a bite and found it tasted delicious.

Reno tore into the pizza and rolled his eyes back as he chewed. "Heaven."

"This is an amazing dinner," Penny agreed.

"Is not dinner!" Reno corrected her, horrified. "We are just getting started. And no menus, we eat what the chef, Gino, sends out. This is my restaurant. You trust me? Yes? Good, you won't be disappointed. But here's the thing—I make them bring all the dishes at once. In Rome, at Mama's house, it takes hours to eat. I love it, but here I want it all at once."

"Sounds good to me," Penny laughed.

"But—" Reno raised a warning finger, "No antipasti. I hate antipasti. Is for lunchtime."

Reno kept up an amusing dialog as plate after plate arrived, each with an Italian name.

"I sculpt. I make statues," Reno told Penny as a bowl of truffle pasta, called Tagliolini al Tartufo con Taleggio, was placed next to her. "But no, Papa says 'Reno, you must go into the family business'. So I take over Papa's newspaper, and I buy another newspaper. And a television station. And then more. Until I wake up one morning and have an empire. That makes me the emperor."

Penny nodded and helped herself to a serving of rare beef carpaccio with mustard and lemon dressing that Reno called Carpaccio de Manzo.

"But my life is art. Italians love to make art. I paint these—" Reno waived his fork around the restaurant, gesturing to the enormous scenic paintings on the walls. They reminded Penny of the artwork on the carnival canvas at the Indiana State Fair.

"Am I a brilliant businessman?" Reno asked, and Penny paused in her appreciation of roast lamb with new potatoes before realizing the question was rhetorical. "Yes. But here," Penny blanched as he unbuttoned his shirt and displayed a large tattoo of the Mona Lisa over his heart, thumping it for emphasis, "—here is the heart of a true artist."

Dinner continued until finally the plates were whisked away and a tower of tiramisu was placed before her. "Reno, I can't, I'm stuffed."

"We wrap up and you take home. For a midnight snack," he waggled his eyebrows. "Café!" he commanded.

"I buy South Quay Road five years ago," Reno continued. "I need a challenge. I need to do something hard. I want the FA Cup."

"Didn't you almost win it last year?"

"*Sì*. We lose to Leicester City, again, and I know it is too soon. I don't have the right players. I look at Dylan but I pass on him. Sir Frank take him though, and I think he's *pazzo*—" Reno made a comical twirl with his finger against his temple, rolling his eyes wildly. "Crazy."

Penny flinched.

"But it turns out Sir Frank is good *pazzo*! Crazy like a fox." Reno tapped his finger to his forehead to emphasize his point. "Crazy smart. Sir Frank sees what we all miss. He take Dylan and give him a chance."

Tiny cups of espresso arrived and Reno became contrite. "But now I am boring you, all this talk about me. So, Penny. What are you doing here?"

It took Penny a moment to realize this was the first direct question Reno had asked her in two hours.

"I know you find something at the Rhea family's *fabbrica* because HARP people are there. They have taken over the entire Icelton foundry, where you were digging. What have you found, Penny Adams?"

His eyes locked with hers, suddenly losing all their warmth.

"Gold," Penny replied bluntly. Why not, she figured, it would be common knowledge soon enough.

Reno digested this piece of information. "You pick a poor place to find it."

"I didn't bury it in the first place," she pointed out.

"No. But you knew right where to look." Reno leaned back in his chair, taking his measure of her. "Perhaps I hire you, bring you here to St Albans to dig. And you make me lucky, like you make Dylan lucky."

Penny took her time sipping the strong coffee, and Reno's fingers began to drum the white tablecloth.

"I hire you right now," he said abruptly. "This minute. I pay you a million pounds a year."

Penny did the calculations in her head. He was offering her over a million and a half dollars.

Reno misinterpreted her silence. "It is too little? Okay, two million pounds."

"But I'm not a British citizen. I can't work here."

Her concern make Reno laugh. "I can hire who I want. When we build the new stadium, we uncover lots of stuff. But I need to get it built fast, so we kind of ignore it. Now we can spend the time. Lots of time."

"How much time?"

"Years."

"I appreciate the job offer and all, but I'm going back to Indiana."

"Oh yes? When?"

Good question, Penny thought. "I can't give you an answer right now. I'm not sure."

A group of important looking people approached the table to say hello to Reno, and the discussion was over. After a few moments he made his farewells and drove Penny back to Icelton.

<hr>

Dylan was waiting for them when they arrived at Mortager Park. Reno drove into the car park with none of the flourish he had earlier in the afternoon, parked, and helped Penny out of the car.

"Dylan! Good to see you. I come by earlier to say hello but you are at your new training camp. I see Penny, she looked so hungry, I take her for a little snack. Why you no feed this young lady? You need to take care of her."

Penny's eyes widened at the taunting, which Dylan ignored.

"Reno," Dylan nodded, and shook his hand.

"I wish you luck this weekend against Kingsbury Town," Reno said.

"Good luck to you against Leicester City."

"Toussaint Badeaux is ready for them," Reno said dismissively and kissed Penny's hand. "*Ciao, bella.*"

"Thank you for dinner," she said.

"I am looking forward to the next time," Reno winked before getting in his car and driving away.

"He's nice," Penny smiled, watching the Corvette go down the long lane.

Dylan turned to her, his irritation clear. "I was worried about you. You disappeared."

"No, I didn't. I went for dinner."

"Without telling anyone?"

"Who was around to tell?"

Dylan didn't have a suitable reply to that. "What did he want? Reno always wants something."

"He offered me a job."

"Doing what?"

"Excavating near his stadium in St Albans. He offered to pay me two million pounds a year."

"He was joking," Dylan said dismissively.

In the distance Penny could see the Corvette had reached the end of the long driveway and turned right without stopping, making an oncoming car slam on its breaks to avert a disaster. "I don't think so."

Chapter Fifty-Three

THE SKYBOX AT WEMBLEY Stadium had two large-screen televisions, both broadcasting Joe Lyons.

"Today we are broadcasting the FA Cup semifinal live from Wembley Stadium," Joe Lyons said, a broad smile on his face, "featuring perennial bridesmaids Kingsbury Town and the upstarts, Tier Seven Icelton. A fascinating note—both clubs are based within two miles of this stadium. It's almost a northwest London derby!

"This is, of course, the second match of the weekend. Reno Tedesco's South Quay Road Potters yesterday evening defeated Leicester City 2-1, with the Haitian international Toussaint Badeaux scoring twice, both with assists from Yaba Owusu, the rising star from Ghana. Will they be meeting Kingsbury Town in the final, or will Icelton's amazing run continue?"

The camera panned back to show Biscuits sitting next to Joe Lyons, a lopsided grin on his face.

"I am joined by my friend and amazing statistician, Arthur Pinkett-Harlow, who has just informed me that whilst Kingsbury Town is a frequent visitor to Wembley, this is Icelton's first visit in more than fifty years. Icelton were runners-up in the now defunct FA Amateur Cup played at the old Wembley Stadium in 1956 and again in 1968, the closest they have ever come to winning a national cup competition.

"And while you might think this match is a David versus Goliath, in reality it is a lot more of a level playing field than you would suppose. Icelton boss Dylan Rhea was a Kingsbury Town player for almost two seasons until almost exactly a year ago and knows their system well. Kingsbury Town boss Giles Roberts always has a bizarre trick or two up his sleeve, but Rhea knows his quirks. Icelton standouts include skipper Tommy Peele in central midfield, striker Tamba Taray and their hero in the early rounds, goalkeeper Ned Winter.

"I admit that I have given in to my obsession with Icelton. Whatever the reason, they have made it further than any non-league team in the history of the FA Cup since the Football League expanded to four divisions one hundred years ago. Some say it might be due to luck, some say it might be due to mistakes on their opponents' parts, but right now I am seeing dogged determination and a sense of destiny. And all of this from a club that can't move out of mid-table in their own league. Astounding."

Joe Lyons chuckled, a beatific smile on his face. "I must say, this is the most fun I've had in ages."

⸺◆⸺

"They're going to be ground meat today," Len predicted, taking the seat next to Penny in the Wembley sky box. "Kingsbury Town is a proper club and this is a proper stadium."

"How are you, Len?" Penny asked with real concern. She hadn't seen the man in weeks. His skin was pale and his forehead had an unnatural sheen.

Len squinted at the pitch below. "Never better, my dear, never better. Although I wouldn't mind a pint, if you'd be so kind?"

Penny nodded and made her way through the crowd to the bar at the back of the room, where one of the enormous television screens was broadcasting a live interview.

"I'm joined by Sir Frank Poleski, owner of Kingsbury Town. Tell us, Sir Frank, have you fully vetted your squad for any cup-tied players?" A stylish reporter asked.

The distinguished man chuckled. "Yes, Jade, I've had the staff go back through the records and everyone is legal today. The weather is beautiful, and as far as we know there are no unexploded bombs within a mile of the stadium."

While the bartender poured the beer, the girls came bouncing in to the room. They were dressed in their green and grey Icelton tracksuits with matching ribbons in their pony tails, making them look even more identical, if that was possible.

"Penny!" Carlie called over to her. "We were just featured on the pre-game show! Sue set it up."

"Alex Scott interviewed us. She played for England and has 140 international caps," Lindsey said.

"Me grandma just texted," Kenna added. "They all watched it on the BBC. Can you imagine? It was spectacular!"

"Totally spectacular," Carlie agreed.

"A dream come true," Lindsey added.

Penny congratulated them and returned to her seat. She handed Len his beer and he mopped the sweat from his face and took the glass, draining it in one go.

"Can I get you a glass of water?" she asked.

Len brushed her off. "No. I'm fine. Just thirsty. Hot as blazes in here."

Penny frowned, noting the doors were open, and it was actually rather chilly.

The match began and Penny watched Dylan on the sideline, where he stood with the new assistant coaches and support staff. He was wearing, she noted, the same grey tailored suit and white shirt, open at the throat, he'd been wearing to all the FA Cup matches and she smiled to herself. Obviously he wasn't as inured to superstition as he let on. His expression was implacable while the coaches traded comments.

After two minutes, Fernando Garcia-Lopez of Kingsbury Town made a dangerous tackle just outside the Icelton penalty area. The referee had no hesitation in showing him a red card. Garcia-Lopez looked horrified and after a brief complaint, head bowed in shame, walked slowly off the pitch while his manager Giles Roberts and teammates stared furiously at him.

"That's a lucky break," Gwen said, sitting next to her husband Eddie, who was clearly happy to be in the skybox and not on the field and under pressure.

The match continued with both sides showing good speed and fast moves. Eddie kept up an amusing commentary on the action. Penny began to have hope that Icelton really did have a chance.

At halftime Penny stood and went to the bar to get a soda. Chloe motioned to her, "Penny, can we have a word?"

Penny walked with Chloe, Kanti, and Kathleen to the back of the room. They gestured into the hallway but Penny shook her head. "They said the doors locks automatically, and we won't be able to get back in. What's up?"

The girls glanced at each other. "We got interviewed down on the pitch before the match," Chloe began.

"Yes, I know. Kenna said it went well," Penny said.

"It did," Chloe nodded, staring at the floor. "Very well."

"Excellent," Kanti frowned.

"Best ever," Kathleen echoed without conviction. "Only, it felt funny."

Penny looked at the girls in confusion. None of them would meet her eyes.

"We was waiting to go on the pitch—" Chloe began.

"—were waiting," Kanti corrected.

"We were waiting to go on the pitch with Alex Scott," Chloe began again, "and Sue was with us. She started talking about the foundry and what you were doing there."

Penny's breath caught in her chest.

"She said how it was funny how you showed up," Kanti continued, "Out of the blue, not knowing anyone."

"And began digging up Dylan's old foundry," Kathleen added. "She said people were saying you were crazy. And that people back where you come from in America said you'd been locked away in an insane asylum for years."

"I got really angry," Kanti continued. "We all did."

"We told her it wasn't an insane asylum, it was a hospital to help people. Like you told us," Chloe added. "And you weren't there for years, but just a year. 'Til you got better."

"She said people like you, that hear voices in their head, get violent and hurt others," Kathleen continued. "She asked if you had done that. We said no, of course not. And that people at your hospital were there to get better, and you did. That you learned to manage the voice in your head."

Penny blinked several times, hoping the girls were almost finished.

"Then the producer woman called us on the field and we ran out. We didn't think any more about it until afterwards, that it didn't feel right," Kanti looked at Penny with shame. "We went to find Sue but we couldn't."

"We're sorry we talked to her. We don't want her to cause trouble for you. You're our friend." Chloe said.

"It's okay," Penny said, fighting down nausea at the girls' words.

"Why is she talking to people back in America about you?" Kanti asked.

"I guess because Dylan is a big story. And the dig might be a big story," Penny said.

"I don't trust her," Chloe said.

"Neither do I," Kenna agreed.

Kathleen nodded. "She's a snake."

Penny didn't disagree.

Chapter Fifty-Four

At halftime the mood in the Icelton changing room was tense. Kingsbury Town was up 1–0, although Icelton was having flashes of brilliance. Dylan's blood coursed through him like ice. The clarity—he knew how to win. It was crystal clear to him.

"They are down a man and we are holding our own," he began, pacing the spacious changing room like a caged tiger.

Tommy Peele lay on the trainer's table getting his hamstrings massaged. "They're toying with us, Dylan."

"No, they're not. That's not Giles' style. Alright, what do we think?"

"We need more speed on the left wing," Nick Cooper volunteered. "Auchincloss is faster than lightning."

"No, he's not," Dylan countered. "He's an old man with three kids who's just smarter than you. Drive him out to the corners, make him use his left foot. He's got an old injury that's crippling him."

"I was talking with him," Zaki said. "He told me I need to get into a more attacking position. And he said it in French."

"He's doing that to mess with your head."

"Really?" Zaki frowned. "His French is excellent. He's really a very nice man, I don't know why people say such mean things about him."

Dylan rolled his eyes upwards, as if looking for divine assistance. "Henry! You were late releasing the ball twice. What the hell were you thinking?"

"I'm trying to get through Mick Carr and Darius Rutledge but I can't. They're like brick walls."

"Yes, you can. And we're letting Will Currie run roughshod over us."

"It's like the kid has eyes in the back of his head," Nick complained, "he sent a pass to Jason Edu and never even looked."

"I know that because we used to practice it," Dylan snapped. "Now listen to me. Cantamessa is the key. I've been watching him. His old groin injury is flaring up."

"He's been trying to outflank me all half," Tommy said.

"Right, keep the pressure on. Giles doesn't have a good sub for him; Cresbow got a concussion on Tuesday and hasn't been cleared. Cantamessa is the key.

"Remember what we said before the game, keep possession, play simple passes. And don't try to match them for physicality. Rutledge and Carr have done this for years, but they don't have your pace, Tamba, and they don't want to be dragged too far forward to stop you, Henry.

"Trust the process. You are as good as they are—better, in fact. You've all been in the pro system at some point. You take care of yourselves. You're in better shape than they are because you only play half the games they do, and you're younger.

"They are going to try and win this in ninety minutes, but remember, they are a man short and have made one substitution, taking off a forward to fill the gap left by Garcia-Lopez. They still have three players nursing injuries and they can't all be replaced, so by ninety minutes they might be down to nine and a half men. They are tired old men. All we need is one goal to tie this up. We just need to outlast them."

Tamba raised his head. "You really think we can beat Kingsbury Town?"

"I *know* we can," Dylan said, and for the first time, he believed it. "Get it tied up, and then I'll tell you how we're going win."

The second half was very cagey. Icelton, playing the game of their lives, took the game to Kingsbury. Carr and Rutledge were fully stretched to keep out Tamba and Henry.

Then, with just under ten minutes remaining, Icelton broke up a Kingsbury Town attack and Callum Williams broke downfield. Marco Cantamessa pulled up and fell to the ground, his groin muscle failing him completely. The Kingsbury Town players looked to the referee to stop play for the injured player, but he let the game continue as it was not a head injury.

This momentary loss of concentration was disastrous for them, because Callum Williams sent a beautiful pass to the feet of Henry Collins. Darius Rutledge came to him, but Henry Collins took the ball around him. Mick Carr suddenly had Henry Collins in front of him to his right, and Tamba a few yards off his left shoulder. The pass to Tamba was on Mick Carr's wrong side and Tamba sprinted past him, dummied a shot to make Brian Bathurst dive early, and then lifted the ball into the open net.

The score was now tied and Kingsbury Town made their second substitution. Marco Cantamessa was replaced, and soon a third as Hugo Auchincloss's left foot injury returned. The final whistle came and Kingsbury Town's worst fear—extra time—was realized.

Fifty minutes later, the referee raised his whistle to his lips and blew a long trill, indicating the end of extra time. Lacking forward players, Kingsbury Town were forced to be more defensive, and this suited Icelton perfectly. There had been no more goals so a penalty shoot-out would decide the second FA Cup finalists.

The Wembley skybox was completely silent and no one moved.

"They're still tied. What happens now?" Penny asked.

"Penalty shoot-out," Gwen whispered.

Penny glanced at Len. His face was pale and beads of sweat dotted his forehead.

"Can I get you something, Len? Some water perhaps?" Penny asked.

Len's eyes remained fixed on the pitch below where both teams were gathered around their coaches. "Shut up you stupid girl."

Penny flinched when she heard the searing anger in Len's voice, and she stood to move a few seats away from him.

The goalkeeping coach stood with Ned Winter and Charlie Moore, the backup goalkeeper, discussing strategy. After a quick meeting they slapped hands and Ned took his place in goal.

"Shooting first for Kingsbury Town will be Samuel Nkomo," the television commentator announced to the watching world. The Kingsbury Town player ran to the ball and swung his leg sharply left. Ned dove at full stretch, but the ball missed his fingertips by inches and went into the net, just inside the post. The crowd roared. 1–0 to Kingsbury.

Mark Chiedoze lined up to face Kingsbury Town goal-keeper Brian Bathurst. He took his time positioning the ball on the spot and then jogged up slowly to the ball, lifting his shot high to his right but without much power. Brian Bathurst leapt to block it. Still 1–0 to Kingsbury.

Mick Carr powered a shot into the Icelton net, but Callum Williams hit a goalpost and the rebound came back towards him. The score was now 2–0 to Kingsbury Town.

Ned kept cool and collected as Pozny Gorlinski attempted to fake a shot to the left that instead went right and low. He caught it and held it, and the crowd cheered. 2–0 to Kingsbury, but Icelton still had a chance.

Henry Collins scored with his attempt for Icelton and Jason Edu missed, lifting the ball over the crossbar. Tommy Peele powered a shot past Brian Bathurst just inside the post. Now it was 2–2, both teams having failed twice. This was the last kick for each team before sudden death. Ned blocked a powerful shot by Darius Rutledge. Finally Tamba Taray took a very slow walk to the penalty area, knowing that if he scored, Icelton would be in the FA Cup final.

Penny held her breath and watched Dylan on the side-line. To her surprise, he was smiling. Tamba also looked supremely unconcerned and took his time placing the ball on the spot before walking slowly to the edge of the penalty area. Behind him, on the halfway line, both teams were in huddles, their arms linked together. Some players from both teams turned their heads, unable to watch the drama unfold forty yards downfield.

The referee raised his arm and blew his whistle. Tamba bolted towards the ball, grinning, and slammed it to the right.

Brian Bathurst got his hands on it but the power was too much and the ball punched the back net.

"Icelton has won! 3–2 on penalties! They will play in the FA Cup final. I don't believe what I just saw," Joe Lyons bellowed.

Tamba's teammates engulfed him and Dylan looked up at the sky box, a huge grin on his face. The stadium rocked with pandemonium and Penny cheered wildly along with everyone else, amazed at the team's accomplishment. Gwen hugged Penny, tears streaming down her face, and the girls hugged everyone.

Behind Gwen, Penny saw Len lurch out of his seat and grope his way up the aisle, sweat streaming down his face and his breathing labored. He pushed through the door to the corridor and stumbled outside.

Penny worked her way through the cheering fans and followed him out the door. She found Len in the hallway, leaning against the wall for support.

"Len, let me help you," Penny said, rushing towards him.

"Get away from me," Len gasped. "This is all your fault."

Penny ignored him. "You need help—"

"It's all your fault," he repeated, his voice a ragged whisper. "You should have never shown up."

Len lurched towards Penny, his eyes wild. He was taller than she was and outweighed her by at least a hundred pounds, but was unsteady on his feet and toppled against her. Penny braced her outstretched arms to steady him but didn't have the strength to stop their fall. The best she could manage was to twist them both so Len hit the wall and they both crumpled to the floor, Penny controlling the slide as best she could.

She freed herself from Len, who was unconscious, and rolled him on his back when she saw he wasn't breathing. With frantic movements she tried to find a pulse in his neck but there was none.

"Len! Len!" Penny yelled, loosening the buttons at his collar.

Penny jumped to her feet and ran to the skybox door but it had locked behind them. The hallway was empty, and she pounded on the door but the cheers of tens of thousands of spectators drowned her out.

Rushing back to Len, she opened his shirt the rest of the way and knelt beside him. His skin was cold and damp as she placed her hands together over his sternum and began CPR, counting to twenty, praying someone would come to help. It had been ages since she'd taken first aid at summer camp, but she remembered the basics and pushed her palms down repeatedly with all her strength. Seconds ticked by and Len remained motionless while Penny prayed someone would hear her calls for help over the thunderous rapture of the crowd.

At last the skybox door opened and she heard someone gasp, "Oh my God, Penny, what's happened—"

"Get help! Get Gwen, Len's had a heart attack."

"Yes, yes—" Within seconds the hallway was filled with people and there was a man at her shoulder.

"Here, I'm a nurse," he said, "let me take over."

Penny fell to the side, exhausted. Gwen knelt next to Len and a medical team appeared moments later. The medics surrounded him, directed by Gwen, while the nurse continued CPR. A portable defibrillator was rolled out and pads slapped on Len's chest, one above his collarbone and the other on his chest.

"Clear!" they yelled and everyone moved back. Len's body leapt as the current surged through.

"He has a pulse and breath sounds!" Gwen called, monitoring the machine. "Let's get him to hospital."

"Is he going to be okay?" Penny asked as Len was lifted onto a gurney, an oxygen mask strapped to his face.

"We got a heartbeat," Gwen said. "There's a pretty good first aid station in the stadium but the ambulance is already here and can take him to Northwick Park Hospital. They've got an excellent cardiology department."

"He looked terrible. He was stumbling outside, so I followed him to make sure he was alright. He collapsed."

"Good thing you were there," Gwen said, patting her back.

"Gwen, Len was saying some very strange things before he collapsed."

"He wasn't in his right mind, Penny," Gwen consoled her. "He's not going to remember any of it. But Penny, you probably saved his life."

Chapter Fifty-Five

DYLAN PUSHED THROUGH THE doors of the hospital, the reporters hot on his heels.

"He's family," Gwen waived him through while security blocked the trailing press and photographers.

In the waiting room, Dylan rushed to Penny and wrapped her in his arms. She looked exhausted and had been crying.

"Congratulations," she whispered, holding him tightly.

"Thanks, but more importantly are you okay?" His eyes searched her tear-stained face. He hadn't realized what a toll the last few weeks had taken on her. She was thinner, pale and appeared more than exhausted—almost fragile, which was crazy since she was the strongest woman he'd ever known.

"Yes, I'm okay."

"What happened?" Dylan asked the assembled group, keeping a firm arm around Penny.

"Len was looking bad all day," Gwen said. "He's been hypertensive for years, since his wife died, yet has refused all treatment. He's also gained at least a stone since the autumn. I think your win sent him over the edge,"

Dylan nodded. "How long until we know anything?"

"He's in bypass surgery right now. It will be several hours," Gwen said.

"Does he have any family?" Penny asked.

"No, his wife passed away five years ago, no children."

With no additional news, they settled down to wait. Dylan took the seat next to Penny and held her hand.

Penny smiled. "Tell me about the match."

"The lads were brilliant, weren't they?"

"I've never been so nervous as during the shoot-out."

"I wasn't," Dylan grinned. "Kingsbury Town has an awful record in shootouts. Brian Bathurst has lightning reflexes and works best in a crowded penalty area. In one-on-one situations, like a penalty shoot-out, he makes mistakes, so I told the lads to take their time, stroll up, let Brian stew. It worked a treat."

"And you're in the FA Cup final."

"We are. And Penny," Dylan dropped his voice, "we did this without her. I knew how to win, it came to me clear as a bell. There was nothing weird about this. This was all us."

"That's wonderful."

Dylan was ravenous, so they found the hospital cafeteria and had a leisurely dinner of soup and sodas. When they returned to the waiting room, Dylan was surprised to see Tommy Peele waiting for them.

"Dylan, can I have a word?" Tommy asked.

Dylan squeezed Penny's hand, and led Tommy into the hall. "Sure, mate. Why aren't you and Claire out on the town? Where's the rest of the squad?"

"Oh, they're all at Jesters," Tommy said, looking out the window to some point in the distance.

"What's up?"

It took Tommy several moments to answer. "After the match I got a call."

Dylan didn't like the sound of this at all. Tommy continued to not make eye contact. "Oh, aye? Who from?"

"Reno Tedesco."

Dylan crossed his arms and waited for Tommy to finish.

"He's offering me a contract with South Quay Road."

"It's after March 31st. You can't play."

"I know. It's for next year, but I have to sign now."

"How much?"

Tommy blew out his cheeks, and it was a moment before he could speak. "Eight million pounds. Three years."

The words hit Dylan like a sledgehammer. "Jesus."

Tommy faced Dylan, his expression a combination of amazement and shock. "It's more money than me and Claire have ever seen. Or are likely to see in our lives."

"Tommy, you're good but you're not that good. He's just throwing money at you to get you off the Icelton squad. So you can't play in the FA Cup final."

Tommy nodded. "I know."

"You'll ride the bench for three years. You'll never see a minute playing time. Is that what you want?"

Tommy ran his hands through his short-cropped hair. "Dylan, I have to. For Claire and the girls. We can buy a house."

"You're all getting a share of the winnings. It won't be as much as what Reno's offering, but it will be a huge check. With the television rights it will be close to three-quarters of a million pounds each for all of you. And when we win the FA Cup, it will be even more. Think about the endorsements this will garner."

"Dylan, we will finish the Atlas League in mid-table," Tommy reasoned. "We're not close to the title or even the playoffs. You've got Sergey—he's solid, he'll get the job done. He was better than me at Newbury."

"Sergey is a good lad, but he's not you," Dylan retorted. "He's not had the experience with Nick and Jeff."

"I'll work with him."

"No," Dylan paused, and shook his head and sighed, resigned. He couldn't do this to Tommy, he couldn't be selfish. "You need to do this. Call them back, say yes. Get a lawyer and get that contract reviewed. Sign it tomorrow."

"Really?"

"Yes, really. Get it locked down. Reno will be good for it, regardless of what happens."

Tommy stood taller, as if a huge weight had been taken off his shoulders. "Thanks, Dylan."

He shook Tommy's hand. "Best of luck, mate."

—◆◇◆—

Dylan took a long walk around the ground floor before returning to the waiting room where Penny sat alone.

"Len's out of surgery, Gwen's back talking with the doctors," she said. "What's the matter? You don't look so good yourself."

Dylan collapsed in the chair next to her. "Tommy's out. He's signing with South Quay Road tomorrow. Reno offered him a huge contract, and he has no choice but to take it."

"Is Reno allowed to do that?"

"Yes, but Tommy can't play for him until next season. But he can't play for Icelton anymore, either."

Penny rubbed his shoulders while he ruminated over the situation. "Is he going to hire anyone else away?"

Good question, Dylan thought. "Reno is ruthless. I have no idea what else he's going to do."

Chapter Fifty-Six

Sunday evening Dylan let himself into the small apartment he was using at the country club, bleary-eyed after spending hours watching tapes of Kingsbury Town with the coaching staff. The lights were on in the room and he heard noises coming from the kitchenette around the corner. His heart jumped—maybe Penny had gotten a ride with one of the wives or girlfriends and come out to visit him.

He rounded the corner with eager anticipation but stopped short, disappointed. "Sue. Didn't see the Porsche outside."

She spun around at the sound of his voice, holding a casserole and looking charmingly domestic in a neat apron over her usual uniform of crisp blouse and pressed trousers.

"It's in the shop, time for the 50,000-mile maintenance. We finished filming early today, so I decided to come over and bring you dinner." She dipped the spoon in the dish and held it out, batting her eyelashes. "Care for a taste?"

It was cassoulet, a favorite of his. "No, thanks. I ate with the guys in the cafeteria."

"But I made it for you myself," she pouted prettily. "I knew you wouldn't be eating well. Here, try a bowl."

He took the offered spoon and sat down at the little table that had been set for one. At her urging he brought the spoon to his lips and tasted a bite.

"Well?"

"Good."

She slid into the chair next to him. "I've missed this. The two of us, eating dinner, sharing the day."

Dylan could count on one hand the number of times Sue had cooked for him when they lived together; both their lives were so hectic it had been easier to eat out.

"How's training going without Tommy Peele?" she asked.

"We're going to get thrashed. Your boss has seen to that."

"He is ruthless," Sue concurred, helping herself to a roll. "Sergey isn't bad. He's a good playmaker."

She was right, of course. Dylan looked at the food. "You're not eating?"

"I ate earlier. And I've gained two pounds!" she laughed, and pushed the plate a little closer to him. "You go ahead."

Sue watched him, the overhead lighting reflected off her makeup. Penny's skin glowed with good health, while Sue's looked like it was clad in cheap paint. Dylan took one more bite and set the spoon down. "What are you doing here, Sue?"

"We need to talk."

"What about?"

"I'm not sure about Penny," she said, her tone serious.

"Penny is none of your business," he replied tersely.

"She's dangerous, Dylan. She's been institutionalized."

"How did you find that out?"

"It's my job, remember? She hears voices in her head."

"A voice. One voice, that happened to be right," Dylan corrected, but then immediately regretted saying anything. It felt like a betrayal of Penny.

"Don't you see? That's just crazy. She's crazy, and she has convinced HARP there's some amazing discovery buried under that dilapidated old building of yours. It's a scam."

"Oh, yes? How did she do that?"

"She's been in there by herself for months, creating things for the archaeologists to find. It's fraud. I know she faked a letter from Princeton University to get you to let her in. She pretended to be a geology student."

Anger surged through Dylan. "You stole that from my desk."

Sue ignored that. "And she also attacked Len."

"Don't be ridiculous, he was having a heart attack! She saved his life."

Sue shook her head. "He's saying she attacked him first. Broke two of his ribs. I got the surveillance video from Wembley and it's damning."

It took Dylan a moment to realize what Sue was driving at. "What are you going to do with all this evidence, Sue?"

"We've filmed an episode of *Fraud War* about her. It's going to air tomorrow night."

Dylan's eyes narrowed, and he knew he had never hated anyone so much in his life. "It's all lies."

Sue shrugged. "It's going to show everyone how crazy she is. But you can stop it."

"How?"

"Forfeit the FA Cup."

Dylan rocked back in his chair as everything fell into place. "So that's Reno's price."

"He'll pay you the loser's portion, there's no need to get greedy. He just wants the Cup."

"Then he's bloody well going to have to earn it."

"You're willing to sacrifice Penny for your ambition? You played well against Kingsbury Town and really did beat them. But you knew how. You have no chance against SQR," Sue pressed on. "Right now, Penny is some nameless redhead you were dancing with at a party. After my show airs, millions of people will know the truth about her."

"You're very sure of yourself," Dylan said. "No chance this could backfire on you?"

Sue ignored the taunt and pulled on her jacket. "Talk with Penny. She's been exposed, and my guess is she'll be on the next flight out of Heathrow and back to oblivion. Call me before noon tomorrow and I'll make sure the show never sees the light of day."

She shouldered her messenger bag and left.

Dylan went to the toilet and forced himself to throw up.

Chapter Fifty-Seven

THE TOOLING SHOP WAS buzzing with activity Monday morning as HARP staff bustled about. Penny sat outside at the long table that had been set up for her, shaking loose dirt through the mesh sieve. She looked up to see Dylan walking through the foundry gate and smiled.

He dropped a kiss on her forehead and pulled up a camping chair next to her. "How's it going in there?"

Penny shrugged. "If it was important Professor Jain would be here by now."

"Are they being nice to you?"

"They are, as long as I don't get in the way."

Dylan looked at the second field tent that had been added next to the first and the large trailer for the security. "It's like they brought an army in."

"I know. What brings you by?"

Dylan stood and offered her his hand. "Come on, let's go someplace quiet."

Penny brushed herself off and walked with Dylan to the clubhouse. The girls' league matches were done for the season so the building was empty. Dylan unlocked the door and followed her in, held a chair for her at one of the long tables, and took the one next to it.

Penny sat down and watched Dylan carefully. His shoulders slumped and he looked exhausted. "What's the matter?" she asked softly.

"I've something to tell you. And I want you to hear it from me first."

A cold band tightened around Penny's heart. "It's about Sue," she said, wanting to get it over with as soon as possible.

Dylan blew out his cheeks. "Yes."

"It's okay, I understand."

"You do?"

"Of course. You two were together for a long time. It makes sense that you've gotten back together."

Dylan shook his head and reached for her hand. "That's not what I'm trying to tell you."

"There's something else?"

"No. I mean yes. I mean, there's only one thing. I'm forfeiting the FA Cup."

"Excuse me?" It was the last thing she expected Dylan to say, and it caught Penny by complete surprise.

"The FA Cup final, in four weeks. I've decided Icelton is going to forfeit to South Quay Road."

Dylan's words weren't making sense. Penny shook her head. "Are things not going well at the place you're training? You think the team can't do it?"

"No, that's not it. I think there's a chance. Not a great chance, but a chance."

"Then why?"

Dylan drew a deep breath. "Sue told me that you're the target of tonight's *Fraud War*."

Penny laughed, the sense of relief palpable. "Me?"

"Penny, this is serious. Sue found out about you being hospitalized. She stole the letter you gave me that first night, that you forged. I guess they've been dredging up stuff about you for the last few weeks."

"I'm not surprised. The girls told me she had been asking them questions about me. I didn't expect this, though."

"She told me that if I forfeit, they won't run the show."

Penny's mouth dropped open. "That's blackmail."

"Yes. Reno has promised to pay me the runner-up fee, along with whatever television rights and our portion of the gate receipts would be. That's almost £5 million right there."

"But, but—" Penny sputtered, "It's letting him win. You can't do that."

"It's not about me, it's about you. I can't let her go on *Fraud War* and smear you like that."

"What's the worst she can say?"

Dylan looked at her in askance. "You've seen her shows. They will stop at nothing to reveal the most incriminating things about you, and she doesn't care if they're true or not."

"There's nothing to dig up. I am the most boring, uninteresting person in Indiana. And that's really saying something," Penny added.

"You're not," Dylan countered. "You're a wonderful, beautiful person and I care about you a lot. I'm not going to let her drag you through the mud."

Penny drew herself up. "Dylan, you cannot give up now. I am not giving up. We have to see this to the end."

"Penny, you have no idea what you're saying."

She sat up straight and lifted her chin. "We are not going down without a fight. I want to watch this show."

Chapter Fifty-Eight

Ye Olde Kebab Shoppe closed early that night, the door locked and the security curtains pulled down outside. Inside, Dylan sat with Penny at a booth while Jeff and Scott stood at the counter, arms crossed, frowning as they all watched the large television on the wall.

"Tonight, a very special edition of *Fraud War*," Sue intoned from the middle of a wheat field she was standing in. "I'm here in Patoka, Indiana, the heartland of the United States. A place of wide open spaces, vast horizons, and unfortunately, a fraud."

The camera panned around the flat farmland vista before switching to footage of pickup trucks driving by and a woman setting pies on her window sill. A group of children running a lemonade stand waved at the camera.

Penny's high school picture flashed on the screen. "Victoria Adams is from this small town. There's a grocery store, a furniture store, and a little church. Life here seems idyllic. But the question is, what happened to Victoria?"

A mailman smiled and nodded. "Penny Adams? Nice girl. Sad what happened. Haven't seen much of her lately."

A woman in a flannel shirt said, "She just cracked up. One day she was totally sane, the next she was hearing voices."

"That's my cousin Janice," Penny said sharply. "I haven't seen her since I was ten."

"Penny Adams?" An older woman said, "I was her Sunday School teacher. I heard she had a nervous breakdown. Her poor family. We prayed for her."

"She's always been interested in English history," a woman identified as her eighth grade English teacher said. "She took out every book on the subject and had me get in books from around the state."

"In fact," Sue added ominously, "that interest is more of an *obsession*. But what is Victoria Adams doing in London?"

"She thinks she's found Boudica!" a woman Penny vaguely remembered from the HARP office cackled.

"That's right," Sue continued, "the first century heroine of the Britons, the mighty Boadicea. Her name, in fact, was Boudica, and she did a good job of almost chasing the Romans out of England. But she was killed in the final battle and her grave has never been found."

After a long segment on the history of the Romans in Britain the show returned to Sue standing outside the gates of the foundry. "This is the home of Icelton Football Club, currently the luckiest football team in Great Britain. A Tier Seven club that can't seem to win more league matches than it loses, but yet finds itself in the final of the FA Cup."

"Bitch," Dylan muttered under his breath.

"Behind me is the building where Penny has been digging since she arrived in November. She thinks she has found the grave of Boudica. With me is Councillor Benjamin Indra, who represents the local ward on the borough council. Councillor, what do you think of this idea?"

"Icelton Foundry is nothing but a blighted urban eyesore," Councillor Indra said with distaste. "The land needs to be developed to bring jobs to the area. The idea that a custodian from a small college in Indiana could come to our country, dig for ten minutes and find Boadicea is utterly ridiculous."

"Ridiculous, indeed," Sue agreed. "And, perhaps, one of the most massive frauds ever perpetrated. We've asked Mr E.G. Finch-Prendergast, a pre-eminent amateur archaeologist who is actively involved in the search for one of Britain's greatest queens, why there is no chance she's found Boadicea."

A nervous-looking man wearing thick-rimmed spectacles appeared on the screen. "If Penny Adams thinks some old bits of glass and pottery means it's the grave of Boudica, she is indeed crazy," Mr Finch-Prendergast declared. "Tacitus has clearly said the location of the battle was near a large hill. There is no large hill in Icelton."

"No, the battle didn't take place in Icelton, you idiot—" Penny spat.

"We don't know definitively, but the recent findings at Mancetter are very promising," he continued. "I've been volunteering with the Historical Antiquities Recovery Program for the last five years and we have found many clues."

"Oh?" Sue said. "Gold? Pottery?"

"Not as such," the amateur archaeologist cautioned, "but enough to make it the premier Boudica excavation in the United Kingdom. Things are going slowly, though, and it takes so much time and money."

Sue's eyes widened with shock. "So Penny is actually stealing the resources of HARP to continue this fraud?"

"Oh yes, undoubtedly. They could begin by *paying me*, for a start."

The camera returned to Sue. "What would make a woman travel more than 4,000 miles to perpetrate a huge hoax? We traveled to Cincinnati, Ohio to find out."

Video footage of a hospital campus with lovely grounds was shown and Penny stiffened. Dylan pulled her back against him and wrapped his arm around her.

"At the age of eighteen, Penny was diagnosed schizophrenic," Sue said, standing by the entrance. "She was held here for a year, at the Alms Park Psychiatric Hospital in Cincinnati. It's a four hour drive from Patoka."

"I wasn't held, I was a patient," Penny protested.

"You sodding whore," Jeff muttered.

"We don't discuss our patients," a woman captioned as a hospital spokeswoman said, "but Alms Park is the foremost in-patient mental health care facility in the Midwest, and one of the best in the nation."

"We weren't allowed to film on the grounds," Sue continued, "but locals assure us that this hospital treats the most violent and delusional patients."

"That's a lie," Penny said.

Scott patted her shoulder. "We know it is, love."

"By the time she was admitted to this hospital, Penny's obsession with Boadicea had been going on for years. After she was deemed safe enough to discharge, Penny obtained a job as a custodian at Princeton Community College. This is not the famous Princeton University that we all know, but a small school in the middle of nowhere. Penny targeted this school so she could steal a piece of letterhead to create her own credentials. She used the letterhead to fool Icelton team owner Dylan Rhea into letting her dig." A photograph of Penny's letter flashed on the screen and Penny cringed.

"But there is a problem," Sue intoned. *"She is still very dangerous."*

Len's face appeared on the television, a breathing tube attached to his nose. "I don't remember much. Just that Penny attacked me." He paused, and the camera pulled back to show him lying in a hospital bed. "She sat next to me at Wembley for the entire match, as sweet as pie. Then as I was leaving, she followed me out. And she just went berserk."

"You miserable old bastard," Dylan swore.

Len lifted his hospital gown to show the bypass scar on his chest. "She broke two of my ribs."

"I didn't," Penny felt tears begin to spill down her cheeks. "I was trying to help him. Gwen said I saved his life."

"I'm better now," Len continued, "no thanks to her. She has to be stopped."

"That lying piece of shit," Dylan spat. "That was a heart attack. You did save his life, Penny."

"Why would he lie?" Jeff asked.

After a commercial Sue reappeared, this time sitting in a studio where she introduced a panel of experts. "Dr Martin Frankel, you're a dermatologist from Surrey. In your opinion, is this a serious situation?"

The doctor smiled cheerfully. "Absolutely. Miss Adams needs serious help. In my opinion, she needs to be sent back to the hospital that was treating her."

Dylan lunged for the remote to turn the television off but Penny stayed his arm. "No. We have to keep watching."

"Some people are wondering if Penny has duped everyone into believing there's another dead king in the car park," Sue smirked. "Doctor, is this possible?"

The doctor nodded heartily. "Mass hysteria is very common. Icelton had some lucky breaks that were not that unusual. Penny used her psychosis to feed these, let's just say, flukes. She's wasting valuable HARP resources that are already stretched thin. It's positively criminal. All for digging up a few pieces of Victorian glassware and some wartime dross."

"Let's also remember that Icelton is not just any other Tier Seven football club," a sports journalist on the panel added. "They have a former Premier League footballer as owner and manager, and several very talented squad members."

"Who can't fucking get out of mid-table!" Dylan roared at the television.

"It's a regrettable hoax," Sue announced sadly. "But one that seems to have come to an end. Join us next week, when we—"

Scott snapped off the television with distaste. "That was all utter horseshit. Why is she doing this?"

"She works for Reno. They're going to do anything to stop us," Dylan spat out, his face thunderous.

"Reno wants that land, I bet. He needs to make it seem worthless," Jeff said.

Penny turned to Dylan. "You said there's a press conference tomorrow, with you and Reno, for the FA Cup final."

"Yes, at 10 a.m. at Wembley Stadium. Why?"

"I want to talk."

"No, Penny—" Jeff began.

"I have to set the story straight. I cannot let them smear mental health patients like that."

"You're not unstable. It's all bullshit."

Penny's jaw was set. "I want to talk. I have to talk."

Chapter Fifty-Nine

THE NEXT MORNING, FIVE tabloids were stacked on Dylan's front door stoop. HOAX! screamed the *Mirror* in huge letters. The *Observer* headlined SHE'S A NUTTER!, accompanied by unflattering pictures of Penny from her high school yearbook.

"Don't look at them," Dylan ordered as he scooped them up and dumped them in the trash.

Dylan drove them to Wembley in the loaned Porsche Cayenne SUV. Penny sat in the passenger seat next to him, her face pale. Paparazzi were waiting for them at the stadium's main entrance, cameras snapping.

"Penny. You don't have to do this," Dylan tried to convince her one last time. "I still don't think it's a good idea. Please, we can turn around and go home."

"I need to set the story straight."

Inside the building, staff ushered them into a large auditorium that was already full of people. On the stage a podium was set up facing the audience, and a long table with chairs was arranged next to it. Dylan introduced Penny to a distinguished older man, Lord Lambton, the head of the FA.

"Please, call me Richard," Lord Lambton said. "I've been following your story with a great deal of interest."

"Oh, really?" Penny winced.

"Yes, my great-grandfather's sister-in-law was Lord Carnarvon's niece. She was with him in Egypt when they discovered King Tutankhamen's tomb. I saw a little statue she pilfered from the excavation. I've always loved archaeology," Lord Lambton enthused.

Penny wasn't quite sure how to react to this but smiled weakly. Dylan gave her a last hug before taking his seat at the table, next to Reno. The two men shook hands while the cameras clicked. Sue stood against the wall halfway across the room, wearing a crisp suit and looking smug.

Lord Lambton took the microphone first. "Before we begin, Miss Victoria Adams has asked to make a statement."

As Penny approached the podium cameras began to click rapidly, the flashes temporarily blinding her. In her hand she held the index cards she had written the night before.

Penny cleared her throat and took a sip of water, and glanced down at the first card. "My name is Victoria Adams. People call me Penny."

The reporters immediately started calling questions. "Are you crazy, Penny?"

Penny turned to the second card. "There was a show on the television last night about me. Yes, I have been diagnosed with schizophrenia."

"So you are a nutter?" another reporter called, but shut up when Lord Lambton raised his arms to restore quiet.

Penny looked up and saw Sue smirk. She turned the third card. "Maybe I am crazy. You can say whatever you want, I don't care. But I do care very much what you are saying about people suffering with mental illness."

Penny waited for another interruption, but when none came she continued. "A lot of people have health issues. Diabetes. High blood pressure. They learn to deal with it because they have to. They learn how to take care of them-selves, and see the warning signs. They learn how to get help, and how to help themselves."

By the time she turned the fifth card the room was com-pletely silent. "Mental health is no different. Some days are good. Some are not great. At the Alms Park Hospital in Cincinnati, I learned how to deal with the voice in my head. The voice that told me to come here and dig up Dylan's parking lot."

That got a laugh. Penny waited for more screamed ques-tions but the crowd waited patiently for her to say more. She turned the next card.

"Most people with mental health challenges are not vi-olent. With the right treatments we learn to live happy, productive lives. And it's not always medications. We learn breathing techniques and other ways to cope.

"I was lucky enough to be at one of the best hospitals in America. The doctors and staff there never made me feel bad about myself. They are supportive. It cost my family a lot of money, money they didn't have. But it made all the difference. And I'm truly grateful to both my family and the staff."

It was getting hot under the beating spotlights and Penny brushed back a lock of hair that had fallen in her face. "The worst part of having a mental health issue, though, is the stigma. You lose friends. Your family suffers. Little things stop happening, like just hanging out, or going to get a pizza with friends. The loneliness is far worse than the actual problem you have."

She looked up at the people before her who two minutes ago had been behaving like savage beasts and saw one wipe a finger under his eye. Sue and Reno stared at her, their faces stamped with fury, while Dylan beamed with pride.

"I told the voice in my head that I would go to Icelton and dig for one day, just to prove it wrong. And then I would go home and try to get my life back. But instead, I've found friends, a home, and love. People here accept me for who I am."

Penny turned the final card and looked directly at Sue. "The show last night said I came 4,000 miles on a wild goose chase because a voice in my head told me to. That part is true. But I am not violent. I saw Len Case having a heart attack after Icelton won the FA Cup semifinal and I tried to help him. I gave him CPR. The doctor said I saved his life, and I—"

The stillness of the auditorium was broken by a loud commotion in the corridor. The double doors at the back of the room swung open and a group of well-dressed people swept up the aisle. The reporters whipped around and began talking.

A tall, dark-haired woman wearing a beautiful suit swept onto the stage and took the microphone from Penny. She arranged a sheaf of papers on the podium, put on a pair of reading glasses, and looked critically at the crowd before her. Penny glanced at Lord Lambton and was surprised to see a broad smile on his face. He winked at her.

"Good afternoon," The woman spoke into the microphone with authority. "My name is Professor Padma Jain, and I am the director of the Historical Antiquities Recovery Program, part of the British Museum's research into ancient Britain."

Penny's jaw dropped. Professor Jain's voice rang loud and clear and the rabble stilled as she took complete control of the room.

"I am here today to discuss the preliminary findings of the investigation into the antiquities discovered in the area of northwest London, at the Icelton Foundry. Lights, please?"

The auditorium was plunged into darkness and then lit by a projector directed above Reno and Dylan's heads. The stark light showed Reno's shocked expression and Dylan's amused one.

Professor Jain clicked a remote and a recent aerial photograph of the foundry displayed on the screen. "The fieldwork presently being conducted at and around the Icelton Foundry grounds in north London, a heavily urbanized area, has revealed evidence of a large-scale high-status Iron Age interment area adjacent to Mortager Park Stadium."

She clicked again and a picture of the interior of the tooling shop appeared. "Test excavations initiated by Miss Adams have revealed the presence of an indigenous tribal Romanic-Britannic burial, consistent with the paleoclimatic and paleoenvironmental features of the time."

Several more slides followed in rapid order. "Due to the size and lack of disturbance of the site, we have been able to perform an initial analysis of the artifacts recovered and note they indicate that a narrow timeframe can be determined, most definitely to the early post-Roman occupation."

Penny stood enraptured next to Professor Jain, happiness spreading through her like a bubbling wave. Slide after slide clicked by as Professor Jain continued a methodical review of what they had uncovered in the tooling shop, including the now clear cart indentations and even more pots. Finally, beyond all hope, a portion of a skeleton had been unearthed close to where Penny had found the torcs.

Penny wiped hot tears away from her eyes and glanced at the reporters, and she almost laughed out loud when she realized they had no clue what Professor Jain was saying. They seemed to be struggling to decipher the meaning of her presentation, and in particular what in the world she was doing delivering it at the FA Cup press conference.

Finally a reporter raised a meek hand.

"Lights, please," Professor Jain snapped. "Questions?"

"Professor—sorry to interrupt, but we're on a deadline," a journalist from the *Sun* stood up looking nonplussed, "so I gotta ask—can you give us working stiffs a break and tell us in regular talk what you're trying to say?"

The elegant woman gazed down from her podium at the motley group before her, appearing to size up their intelligence. Seeming to come to a decision, she leaned into the microphone and spoke a short and succinct sentence.

"Penny Adams has found Boudica."

Chapter Sixty

After Professor Jain's announcement there was a pause as everyone in the room tried to wrap their heads around what she had just said. People stared, jaws hung open, and Penny saw Professor Jain struggle not to smile. A surge of thrill coursed through her, something beyond relief and joy. She rolled her eyes heavens-ward and exhaled.

Across the room Sue Paulin stood ramrod straight, her brows gathered in an ugly scowl while her mouth formed silent curse words. An enterprising photographer got a shot of her at that exact moment, which went viral an hour later on social media. The *Mirror* carried it in their featured story on Penny the next day under the heading: NOT SO MENTAL AFTER ALL!

Journalists and broadcasters jumped to their feet and began yelling questions, while the photographers and TV cameramen in the front surged towards them, targeting their lenses on Penny and Professor Jain. Penny took an involuntary step backwards, shocked by the intensity of their advance. Dylan jumped to his feet and rushed across the stage to her side while Lord Lambton raised his hands to quell the mob but was ignored.

"Come on, you two follow me," Dylan yelled over the mayhem, taking Professor Jain and Penny by the arms and ushering them off the stage. A security guard opened a back door and they fled down an empty hallway.

Dylan opened doors until he found an empty lounge. "Let's duck in here."

Inside the room Dylan swept Penny into his arms, and Penny clung to him, not knowing if she was laughing or crying.

"Dear Lord," he panted, his face buried in her hair, "was that real?"

"I'm not sure," Penny said.

Professor Jain swept her dark hair back from her face, her eyes dancing. "That was fun," she laughed and held out her hand. "We haven't been introduced. I'm Padma Jain."

Keeping a firm arm around Penny, Dylan shook her hand. Penny shook the offered hand as well and forced herself not to drop into a curtsey.

"Quite some timing you have there, professor," Dylan said.

"I called Richard Lambton as soon as I saw that terrible television show last night," the professor snorted contemptuously. "He's on our board of directors, and I've been keeping him apprised of our progress. He suggested this would be the perfect place to announce our findings. A bit dramatic, but I think it went well, don't you?"

Penny listened to Professor Jain, speechless. "I can't believe you're here," she finally blurted out.

There was a sharp knock on the door and an FA staffer stuck her head around. "Dylan, Lord Lambton would like to try to finish the press conference with you and Mr Tedesco. Can you come back?"

"Are you okay?" Dylan asked Penny. "It won't take long. Wait here and I'll come and get you afterwards."

Penny nodded and Dylan kissed her cheek and left. "Professor Jain, did I really find her?"

"Call me Padma," the woman grinned, "and you most certainly did. May I be the first to congratulate you?"

A broad smile spread over Penny's face, and the feeling of relief was palpable. Her knees felt weak and she sat down on a sofa, not sure her legs would support her.

The elegant woman flopped in a club chair across from her. "And do you know what the real kicker is? I grew up not two kilometers from where you found her. My family are members of the Shree Swaminarayan Mandir up on the hill, overlooking Mortager Park. I never had a clue."

"The white castle?"

"The very same," Professor Jain said. "What's up with that television presenter?"

"She's Dylan's ex-girlfriend."

The professor rolled her eyes. "Quite a piece of work, that one. It's nice to have a hand in making something that terrible backfire so spectacularly. Although her timing was right. We've only just gotten confirmation on the skeletal remains."

"That's the body you found?" Penny asked.

"Yes. We discovered her three days after we arrived. I'm sorry they kept you blocked out, but until we got the forensics back, the tooling shop was technically a crime scene," Professor Jain explained. "She's in great condition, though, for a two-thousand-year-old body."

"Are you sure it's Boudica?"

"As sure as we'll ever be. It's a woman, between 35 and 50 years of age, about six feet tall. Wounds consistent with battle. If nothing else, judging by the arrangement of funeral artifacts, this was a very high-ranking person. The coinage you uncovered narrows the dates significantly."

Penny nodded. "You said that you thought the Iceni didn't always cremate, and you were right."

"That is a definite win," the professor grinned. "A lot of my colleagues will be eating crow on that one. But I have to ask, how did you know exactly where to dig?"

"The show was right about one thing," Penny said, "I did hear a voice. I was very sick with the flu, and Boudica came to me in a dream, when I had a high fever. She said she needed to be found, and that she was buried by a stream called the Silk, and that they had built a white castle above her."

Professor Jain accepted that without comment. "How did you know it was Icelton?"

"I didn't. I had to research everything and it took years. She also insisted that I get this tattooed on me somewhere so I didn't forget." Penny pulled the fabric of her neckline down to show Professor Jain the horse tattoo on her chest.

Professor Jain's eyes widened. "That's the Iceni horse from the AV stater, minted between 20 BC and 10 AD."

"It's also on the cup fragment Dylan found, the morning after the big storm. But I guess I should start from the beginning."

Professor Jain listened intently as Penny told her the entire story. "That's quite an astonishing feat of scholarship, and from four thousand miles away," she said when Penny finished. "You've suffered quite a bit for this."

"My family as well."

Professor Jain nodded. "So I have to ask you, where was the last battle?"

"I think Moat Mount Open Space."

Professor Jain blurted out a curse before catching herself and smiling sheepishly. "Sorry, but I've driven past there a thousand times, back and forth up the M1 to Mancetter." She shook her head in disbelief for several moments. "But it makes sense. Yes, right off Watling Street."

"Barnet Gate and Highwood Hill are two of the highest points in London. The Edgware plain lies to the west in front of it. There's still an open space between the hills where the battle took place. That's the narrow defile Tacitus mentions."

"That's not much of a defile," Professor Jain grunted. "But then again the Latin translations are a mess. What about the water supply? Was it enough for a force the size of Suetonius's army?"

"His army was rather small, so Deans Brook and Dollis Brook were adequate. Moat Mount Open Space was all they needed—it was less than two miles from Watling Street, it was easily defendable, and it was hidden until you were almost on top of it. And they knew Boudica would be bringing her people back that way."

The professor shook her head. "I was so sure it was Mancetter."

"She wouldn't have gone north to Mancetter. The 14th Legion was based there. She wasn't going to march up there."

"Then Cuttle Mill in Northamptonshire, surely? Or Silchester?"

"No. They never got that far."

"Why did she turn around? Everyone thought she kept going north and west."

"There was no reason for them to go west—those tribes were friendly to the Romans. And in the north there were still remnants of the 9th Legion she had wiped out. They also weren't going back to their homeland in Norfolk because she knew that after the havoc she'd wreaked in Colchester, they'd never have any peace there. Remember Tacitus said the Iceni didn't plant any crops that year? It was because she knew she was going to move them, and scorch the earth behind her. She had planned it all."

"But why Icelton?"

"I think she was a Catuvellauni, from the north London area. Tacitus said she was of noble birth but he also didn't say she was a local. The Catuvellauni tribe was friendly with the Iceni, and relatively close by. I think she knew the area, had connections, and was moving them there. She burned London and St Albans to clear out the Romans who were causing trouble for the Catuvellauni."

"No one has ever given much thought to what tribe Boudica was originally from," Professor Jain nodded. "This hypothesis might hold water. So that's why they had the wagons with them at the final battle?"

Penny nodded. "And the women, children, and elderly. I think she had ordered them down from Norfolk, and she was taking them back to Icelton. They met up in St Albans."

"Which she sacked as well."

"I think that was more her people wanting a last bit of revenge on the Britons, who were acting like Romans."

Professor Jain's brows knitted together. "She must have known Paulinus was coming for her."

"Maybe. But things were happening quickly all over the country, and the Druid communication network had been knocked out by their defeat at Anglesey. I wonder if Paulinus didn't spread the word that he had been killed in Anglesey, fighting the Druids," Penny said.

"Bloody hell," Professor Jain exhaled. "Did she poison herself, like Tacitus says?"

Penny shrugged. "I don't know. But she died soon after. Maybe you'll find out."

"The remains show mortal wounds, like Cassius Dio said. And the burial is as he said as well. His stock will certainly go up," Professor Jain smiled, and then considered Penny carefully. "Have you found the torcs?"

Penny clamped her lips together but couldn't stop them from curling into a smile. "Yes," she finally admitted.

"How many?"

"Three."

Professor Jain seemed to be holding her breath. "Intact?"

Penny nodded. "Yes."

"When can I see them?"

The quiet of the lounge was broken by the sound of a large crowd coming out of the auditorium, their voices loud and rushed.

"Soon."

Chapter Sixty-One

BACK IN THE AUDITORIUM Lord Lambton was trying his best to settle the frantic members of the media. On the stage dais, Dylan sat next to Reno, who was keeping a somber game face. Under the table Reno's foot tapped impatiently.

"Any idea where Sue disappeared to?" Dylan asked Reno, his expression equally nonchalant.

Reno ignored him.

"She certainly left in quite a hurry. Seems like your attempt to get me to quit the FA Cup backfired," Dylan taunted, his tone pleasant.

Reno checked his wristwatch and crossed his arms over his chest.

"I mean," Dylan continued, "nice try and all that. I guess you didn't expect Penny to have been right after all."

Reno said something under his breath in Italian. Dylan doubted it was complimentary.

After another two minutes Lord Lambton gave up trying to restore order. "Right, chaps, we're going to have to try this another day," he told the two club owners over the din. "Reno, we'll have you exit through that door behind you, and Dylan, why don't you go out that way."

They both stood, but before Reno could move, Dylan made a show of wrapping his arm around Reno's shoulders and forcing the shorter man to face the photographers and reporters.

"C'mon, Reno, let's give these hard-working folks a smile!" Dylan grinned and grabbed Reno's hand in a crushing shake.

Reno stood stiffly while the cameras clicked a thousand times, and Dylan muttered into his ear "Come after my girl again, Reno, and you'll need a bigger pair of those designer sunglasses to cover your black eye."

—◆—

Dylan followed Lord Lambton back to the lounge where they found Penny and Professor Jain in deep conversation. Dylan sat next to Penny on the sofa and took her hand.

"Well done, ladies," Lord Lambton said, mopping his brow. "I have no doubt that this will go down in FA history as one of our more interesting press conferences. Padma, I think your staff is anxious to get back to the relative safety of the British Museum."

Professor Jain jumped to her feet. "Good heavens, I forgot all about them."

"What's going to happen now? With the dig, I mean." Penny asked.

"The Crown will buy the land, all of it," Professor Jain said.

Dylan frowned. "Mortager Park as well?"

"They didn't find anything under the pitch when it was replaced three years ago—" Penny added.

"—and it was bombed in the Blitz and they found nothing." Dylan added.

"We're going to need it all, the foundry, and Mortager Park," Professor Jain apologized. "They're out there now setting up a new security perimeter."

"Will Dylan be treated well?" Penny asked.

"Oh yes, they'll deal fairly. And it will be preserved as a conservation site. We'll be digging for years. Decades. Who knows how long?" Professor Jain shrugged. "Dylan, we've begun the process of drawing up an agreement with you, but it's going to be a few days before we can start negotiations."

Dylan grunted. "I can't do anything until after the FA Cup."

"Absolutely. This is quite a coincidence, your discovery of Boudica and Icelton's dramatic wins. Almost another Richard III and Leicester City situation! I don't think there's a car park in Britain that's going to be safe going forward," Professor Jain laughed. "Penny, I'd like you to work with us at the dig. It will have to be in an unofficial capacity at the moment, until we get the site property certified, but I'm guessing you're going to be around for the next few weeks? Yes? Right, then. See you tomorrow at the site."

Penny nodded, and Lord Lambton escorted Professor Jain out.

"Did the press conference end?" Penny asked Dylan after they had left.

"It was a circus. Lord Lambton said we're going to try to do it again next week."

"What did Reno say?"

"Nothing, but he didn't look happy."

Penny gave a snort of disdain. "Good. Sue disappeared."

"I don't think we'll be hearing from her for a while," Dylan said. "Let's get out of here and go celebrate you making the biggest archeological find in Britain in a hundred years. You haven't even seen London yet, have you?"

The idea of taking a day off with Dylan sounded like a very good idea to Penny. "No, I haven't."

"Alright, then. Fancy being a tourist?"

Chapter Sixty-Two

PENNY HAD GOTTEN USED to the attention Dylan attracted whenever people saw him. But that afternoon it was a jolt to have passers-by on the streets of London recognize her with excitement as well.

"Those teenagers over there are pointing at me," she whispered to Dylan as they walked around Trafalgar Square.

"Social media works at lightning speed, but it's just the young kids who pay attention. It's going to take a while for everyone to know who you are," Dylan assured her.

They quickly realized just how wrong he was. A crowd of all ages began to follow them as they walked along The Mall towards Buckingham Palace, filming with their mobile phones and calling out congratulations. Penny stood for pictures with people at the memorial to Queen Victoria in front of the Palace, but by the time they had walked to the Admiralty Arch she'd had enough.

"Maybe we should go back to Icelton," Penny said, massaging her jaw. "I'm tired of smiling."

Dylan called Alan and put him on speaker. "Do not come back here!" Alan advised, "The lanes to Mortager Park are jammed with sightseers and the police were called in to direct traffic."

"Can you still work?" Dylan asked.

"We have two deliveries to make today and I'll try to get them out. But I think you're going to have to find me a new shop."

"Sorted, mate."

"Heat and a working loo would be nice," Alan added.

Dylan checked his watch. "It's morning in Indiana. Let's go find someplace quiet so you can call your parents."

Penny brightened up. "Oh yes, Mom and Dad should be getting off back shift and will be home soon."

Finding some place quiet was more difficult than they had anticipated, but eventually they found an out-of-the-way park near Waterloo Bridge that was deserted. Penny spent an hour on the phone, first with her parents and then her sisters, trying to explain what was happening with the discovery of Boudica and the FA Cup.

"What did your family say?" Dylan asked after Penny hung up.

"They're in shock," Penny smiled, handing him his phone back. "They don't really understand what's going on. And when I tried to explain, it started sounding bizarre, even to me."

"Their daughter is famous."

"Yes, they found that out when they got off shift and news crews were in the parking lot. A network called and wants to fly them over here."

"That would be wonderful. I'd like to meet them," Dylan said.

Penny shook her head sadly. "They can't. They have to work. The plant is running three shifts a day. But they were very happy that I'm well, and that I was right."

"There's a load of messages on my mobile requesting interviews," Dylan frowned, scrolling down the screen. "Do you want to do any?"

"I'd rather eat. I'm hungry."

"Too right there. Let's get some dinner."

"Where should we go? Everywhere is going to be mobbed."

Dylan took out his mobile phone and began tapping a message. "I'm not sure, but I know someone who might help."

Two minutes later Hugo Auchincloss messaged Dylan back:

`Table for two at Whitehall 1212, it's off Whitehall CT by Scotland Yard. Matthew is the manager he's waiting for you`

Dylan navigated them through a lovely park and along a majestic road until they found the address. A large man greeted them at the door, his face a wreath of smiles.

"Mr Rhea and Miss Adams! A pleasure to see you. Right this way, please."

The restaurant was the most beautiful Penny had ever seen. Mirrors reflected subtle lighting and the chairs were deep and plush. Matthew escorted them to a table with a view of the River Thames.

Dylan held Penny's seat for her and Matthew began to recite their daily specials, but Dylan waved him off. "You choose, we're starved. Bring it on."

"Yes, sir!"

The food was amazing and Matthew waited on them personally. There were shrimp, which Matthew called prawns, followed by the best steak Penny had ever eaten. They put butter on it, an unheard-of luxury, and the mashed potatoes were even better than her mother's. Finally Matthew wheeled out a dessert cart with a jaw-dropping assortment of cakes and confections. Penny pointed to a glistening chocolate globe balanced on a pedestal, its surface like a dark mirror.

"What's in there?" she asked, entranced.

Matthew made an elaborate production of solemnly placing the globe before her and handing her a small golden hammer. Penny gently tapped the side of the globe, which broke open to reveal a mound of chocolate mousse topped with fresh strawberries in a puddle of chocolate sauce.

"It's like a piñata!" she clapped with delight.

Dylan chose the cheesecake and held a forkful for Penny to try. She nibbled the piece and savored the richness. They declined the cheese tray and instead ordered coffee, lingering while the sun began to set over the Thames.

"That was one of the best meals I've ever had," Penny said. "Can we go for a walk? I feel like I've eaten Thanksgiving dinner."

"Of course. Where to?"

"If that's Big Ben, then we're close to the statue of Boudica, aren't we?"

"Yes, that's Westminster Bridge over there."

"Then let's go see her."

The setting sun glinted off the front of the Parliament buildings as they walked down the Embankment to the corner of the bridge, where Boudica stood in the chariot with her two daughters, proud and defiant.

"It's funny they put up a statue of her, after she burned London to the ground," Dylan observed, holding Penny's hand in his. "You're sure there weren't any spikes on her cart wheels?"

"Pretty sure. I didn't see any indentations in the dirt, at least. And the cart would have been made of wicker. It was Prince Albert's idea to have this statue made, and put it here," Penny said. "He wanted people to equate her with Queen Victoria. Boudica is Celtic for Victory."

"And your name is Victoria," Dylan remarked. "I have to stop thinking that things are a coincidence."

"I was named after my Aunt Vicky," Penny apologized. "She lived close by, so everyone called me Penny because my hair is copper red."

"Go stand in front of the statue," Dylan said, "I want to take your picture."

Penny raised her arms in victory, a huge smile on her face, and Dylan snapped the picture. A tourist nearby offered to take their picture, and Dylan scooted next to Penny, grinning.

"Go ahead and give her a kiss!" the tourist called.

So Dylan scooped Penny into his arms and kissed her lustily, taking her breath away.

"Let's walk across the bridge," Dylan suggested, leading her by the hand. They stopped in the middle and looked over the Thames. Big Ben chimed eight o'clock and the lights began to illuminate the Parliament buildings, reflected in the river's water.

"I need to ask you something," Dylan said, turning to Penny.

"Yes?"

"Did you mean what you said at the conference? That you've found a home here, a family, and love?"

Penny nodded. "I have."

Dylan moved closer to her, the nearness of his body intoxicating. "You said you'd had a boyfriend."

Penny flinched. "He dumped me."

"I'll sort him out later. How serious did it get?"

A faint blush tinged Penny's cheeks. "Not very."

Dylan leaned in to brush his lips against her ear. "The next eighteen days, until the FA Cup, are going to be mad. I want you to stay out at Goffs Oak with me."

His arms wrapped around Penny and she leaned against him, stroking the muscles of his chest. "I don't trust Reno," Dylan continued, "I need to protect you. But I don't want you to feel pressured. I don't want to take things fast. I want to do things the right way."

"Do I have a say in this?" Penny murmured. "I have some questions as well."

"Alright, I guess that's fair."

"Has there ever been anyone else? I mean, besides Sue."

The question seemed to amuse Dylan. "Do you mean, was I like Mick Carr, before he got married? Not likely. I was quite boring, to tell you the truth. Football was my life. I'd go on a few dates but none of the girls liked it when I'd drop them back at home at nine p.m. and be in bed by ten myself."

"Were you in love with Sue?"

Dylan stared into Penny's eyes, brushing his knuckles gently along her jawline. "I thought I was, but now I see it was all rubbish. Because now I know what love really feels like."

Penny's pulse took a delightful leap. "How does it feel?"

"It feels like peace," Dylan kissed her lips tenderly. "It feels like hope. It feels like happiness."

Penny gave herself up to Dylan's passionate kiss. "I can't get enough of you," he murmured hoarsely against her ear. "Come back to Goffs Oak with me."

Penny paled. "We can't leave the torcs at your house. Can I bring them with us?"

"Aren't you going to give them to Professor Jain now?"

"No, I was going to wait until after the FA Cup."

"You don't think we can win it on our own?" Dylan asked, amused.

"I don't know. I don't want to take the risk," Penny confessed. "What do you think?"

Dylan thought about it a moment. "The stakes are a lot higher now. I guess I don't want to risk it either. So yes, let's go back to my house and get your stuff, and take them with us. If that's what you want."

Penny pulled his lips down to hers. "You're what I want."

◄O►

Dylan drove them back to Icelton and parked in front of his house.

"Why are all the lights on?" Penny asked, immediately alert.

"The lights always come on at night, remember? They're on a timer."

"I know, but there're more lights than that on."

Dylan peered closely. "You're right. What the hell?"

As they ran up a path, a tanned woman threw the front door open. "Darling!"

Dylan skidded to a halt. "Mum?"

Chapter Sixty-Three

After embracing Dylan, the woman turned to Penny. "You must be Penny! Gwen's told me all about you. I'm Janice Rhea, Dylan's mum."

Janice smothered Penny in a warm embrace while Dylan looked on in astonishment.

"What are you doing back here?" he asked.

"We called her!" Gwen announced from the living room where she was sitting with Eddie. "Right after your press conference this morning. Quite the to-do. I figured you needed some help."

Dylan's mother nodded. "What a remarkable coincidence! Boudica buried at Mortager Park, fancy that. I dropped everything and got on the first plane back."

Penny and Dylan followed his mother to the living room. "That old girlfriend of yours is a nasty piece of work, Dylan," Gwen said darkly. "I think she was behind you being poisoned."

"But she was taking the stuff as well," Dylan reasoned.

"Two different batches, I'd wager," Gwen said. "Look, you've seen what she's capable of. And Len had a hand in this somewhere, I'm sure of it. He lied through his teeth last night on that television show."

"Where is he?" Janice asked. "I have a few choice things I'd like to say to him myself."

"I don't know," Gwen said. "I went 'round his house this morning, no answer. Neighbor said they haven't seen him in over a week."

"Where are you staying, mum?" Dylan interrupted.

"Here, of course," Janice answered brightly. "With Penny. You said on the phone last week you're out at the training camp, with the team. She needs someone here with her."

Dylan's face dropped. "Of course."

Janice squeezed Penny's hand. "We'll have a wonderful time, won't we, Penny?"

Penny looked at Dylan with regret. "I can't wait."

⬤

Penny met Professor Jain at the dig the next morning, and together they walked through the tooling shop, where a small army of workers were carefully constructing scaffolding over the dirt floor. A colorful blanket, in a rough plaid design, was neatly spread over the ground close to where Penny had found the torcs.

"It's a traditional wool Celtic blanket, obviously handwoven. We found it this morning when we arrived," Professor Jain said.

"You didn't put it there?" Penny asked.

"No. The guards didn't see anyone enter or leave the building, and the security cameras showed nothing," Professor Jain frowned. "It's like there're ghosts around here."

Outside the tooling shop, Penny was surprised to see Biscuits sitting at the sorting table, deep in conversation with Thomas Mitchell.

"Belinda Clark was the first person to score a double hundred. She scored a 229 against Denmark in Mumbai in 1997 in the Women's Cricket World Cup," Biscuits was insisting.

"Biscuits, I'm telling you, it was Sachin Tendulkar against South Africa!" Thomas Mitchell laughed.

"But you didn't say 'just in men's cricket'!" Biscuits retorted, and Penny was shocked to see him smile.

"Hello, Biscuits," Penny ventured.

"Hello, Penny," he replied, and then returned to his animated discussion with Thomas Mitchell.

Penny paused a moment to appreciate Biscuits' newfound friendship before turning to Professor Jain. "Can we go in the watchman's hut?"

Inside the little room Penny put her duffle bag on the table and motioned for Professor Jain to stand next to her as she pulled out two carefully wrapped packages. "Go ahead, open them."

Professor Jain took a pair of cotton gloves from her pocket and carefully unwrapped the first package, which contained the bronze torc. "Oh, my goodness—" was all she could say when she could finally form words.

She swiftly unwrapped the second package, which held the silver torc, turning it over multiple times to examine every facet of it. Penny watched with delight as she kept an excited running monologue with herself, noting every detail of both torcs. Finally Professor Jain put them down and turned to Penny. "They're exquisite. And the gold one?"

"After the FA Cup," Penny said apologetically.

Professor Jain swallowed gamely and nodded her head. "Alright. Let's get these down to the British Museum."

Chapter Sixty-Four

A WEEK LATER DYLAN stood watching the team begin the training session at Goffs Oak, enjoying the lovely May afternoon. The squad was on the pitch stretching out in the warm sunshine, and he knew they felt cheerful as well. Training had been going well, the bonus checks from the semifinal win over Kingsbury Town had hit everyone's bank accounts, and the wives and girlfriends were being feted around London like royalty. Down the hill from the pitch, the country club car park was full of shiny new cars.

Dylan blew the whistle, and the assistants lined the team up for drills. He'd told them he wanted a light workout, nothing challenging. The FA Cup final was in ten days, and this was more to keep everyone limber and their minds on business.

His phone chirped and he glanced down at it, noting it was from Tamba.

`I'm going to be a little late`

`Traffic?` Dylan tapped out with his finger and waited for a reply. None came.

He ignored the pang of anxiety that brushed his spine like the flick of a panther's tail. Even though many of the guys had been granted generous leaves of absence from their day jobs, Tamba insisted on doing deliveries for the bakery when they couldn't find other drivers.

The players moved through the routines with ultimate smoothness, their eyes alert and their bodies relaxed. Dylan followed Tommy Peele's replacement, Sergey, a student from Uzbekistan whose English was limited, but who had a great talent delivering long and short passes. Still, he missed Tommy and knew the rest of the club did as well, especially Tamba.

Where the hell was Tamba?

The passing drills began, and Dylan paid special attention. He and the assistants had been watching hours of South Quay Road film, looking for patterns and weaknesses. There was no doubting that Reno had brought SQR far in the last five years, and Dylan knew from playing them himself that they were tough and disciplined.

But unlike Kingsbury Town, they were a team of individual talents, none of whom seemed particularly disposed to pass the ball. Their set plays were solid, but once play opened up into having to think on your feet, they didn't rely on their teammates. Toussaint Badeaux was a brilliant midfielder and Yaba Owusu a striker who dominated by sheer size and strength. The official club statistics said he was six feet one inch tall, but Dylan knew he had at least three inches on that. He was literally a locomotive.

In a phone interview this morning, a sports reporter had asked, for what seemed the millionth time, if Dylan really thought Icelton had a chance against South Quay Road. It had been the same question he'd been getting all through the run up to the final, and he didn't have to lie anymore. The answer was yes—barely, but yes. It wasn't obvious, but

South Quay Road's defense was weak at several points. If they could distract enough players, they could find a hole.

The assistants signaled for a break and Dylan checked his messages again. Nothing from Tamba, but his mother had sent a picture from that morning, when she had taken Penny to visit Andrew's family. Penny was smiling broadly, holding the newest baby. Dylan had to hand it to his mother—subtlety had never been her strong point. He was missing Penny badly, but he was glad she approved.

After the break the squad picked up sleeveless tops for five on five practice. Ned stood in one goal while his backup, eighteen-year-old Charlie Moore, was in the other. Dylan couldn't help but smile. Charlie had a wingspan like an albatross and seemed to love nothing more than diving into the grass.

The lads took the ball and began dribbling downfield. Jeff O'Day passed to Henry Collins, and Henry took a neat shot on goal. Charlie was a second too late, and it flew in. Dylan checked his mobile again from any messages from Tamba.

`You're bloody well playing in the FA Cup in 10 days when can you fit in training??` He messaged.

Again, there was no reply.

The assistants called out a set-piece and the squad lined up again and began play. Frankie Rhys-Davies was handling the right-back position well. Dylan nodded to himself—Frankie was much more comfortable as a central defender, but moving him to this position was making him think a bit.

There was a flurry of deft passing and a slick pass to Nick Cooper gave him a chance to shoot, but Ned quickly anticipated it. He was already in position and leapt to catch the ball as it reached his outstretched hands, but landed awkwardly on the grass and collapsed in a heap.

And then he began to scream.

Dylan froze, unsure of what he had just seen. It was impossible—seconds before Ned had been flying above the ground, a huge grin on his face. This couldn't be happening.

He sprinted across the pitch to where Ned lay on his side, his face contorted in paroxysms of pain. "Ned! Bloody hell, what happened?"

Nick Cooper knelt next to Ned. "He got the ball and then came down on his left foot, just like he always does, but it just crumpled. I heard a snap. I think it's broken."

"Jesus, Dylan," Ned bit out through clenched teeth, "it hurts—"

"We've got this, Ned," Dylan assured him as they were surrounded by the physio and assistants.

Within seconds, the physio was calling for a stretcher. "Not good, Dylan," she called over her shoulder as she worked to immobilize Ned's leg. "Not good at all. We've got to get him to hospital."

Dylan dragged his hand across his scalp, still not believing his eyes. "Is he going to be okay?"

"We'll do our best, Dylan, but I'm sure this is going to be surgery."

Chapter Sixty-Five

Dylan called Gwen, who directed him to a hospital five miles up the road. It was decided that it would be fastest if Dylan drove him there in his SUV. His teammates carried Ned to Dylan's car and carefully loaded him in the back.

"You're a brick, Ned," Dylan said, starting down the long drive.

Ned gave a wan smile. "Watch the bumps, Dylan."

Even though he drove as carefully as he could, Ned's gasps of pain were audible from the backseat. What should have been a short trip took almost thirty minutes. Dylan was afraid Ned had passed out for part of it.

Hospital staff met them at the door with a wheelchair and whisked Ned through the double doors for x-rays. Dylan called Alan and then paced the waiting room impatiently while he waited for news.

Alan arrived shortly thereafter. "Brought along a treat for you," he winked before heading back to see his brother.

Penny followed Alan through the door and ran to Dylan. Dylan engulfed her in his arms.

"I was at Mortager Park when you called Alan," Penny said. "I thought you might need some company."

"I've never been so happy to see anyone," Dylan said. "What happened?"

Dylan shook his head. "Freak accident. We were having a small-sided training game, not pushing it, just a light session, and Neddie jumped for the ball. He came down wrong and snapped his ankle."

"Had he been injured?"

"No, not at all, that's the thing."

They sat to wait, and ten minutes later Alan reappeared. "It's bad, Dylan. Poor Neddie, the doctors are saying it's one of the worst breaks you can have, a bimalleolar ankle fracture, which means he broke it two different places."

"He just landed on it wrong. How could that happen?"

"The doctor is saying there might be some underlying issues, like bone density or stress fractures. We won't know that for a few days. They're taking him to surgery now. It's going to be plates and screws."

"How's he feeling?"

Alan grinned. "They gave him some good pain meds and there's a pretty nurse back there, so for the time being he's okay. I'm going to call Mum and Dad and get them out here. And you're going to need another keeper."

As shocking as it seemed, Dylan had completely forgotten about the FA Cup. "We've still got Charlie..."

"Charlie Moore is only eighteen years old," Penny said. "How can he play in the FA Cup final?"

"I'll get on the blower and see who I can dredge up while Ned's in surgery," Alan said. "We might be able to get an emergency signing, but at this point everyone is going to be cup-tied. I'll call you when we know something."

After Alan had disappeared into the back Dylan turned to Penny. "I want to talk with Mr and Mrs Winter. Let's wait for them to get here."

"Dylan," Tamba looked around the corner to the waiting room where Dylan and Penny stood. "They said you'd come here. How's Ned?"

Dylan shook his head. "Not good. The first x-rays show two breaks in his left ankle."

"How'd it happen?"

"He landed funny. He just crumpled."

"Jesus," Tamba winced. "That's awful. But Charlie, he's been doing well."

"Very well," Dylan agreed, beginning to get his head around the setback. "He got quite a bit of playing time while I rested Ned for a few league matches. Tomorrow at training, I want you and Connor to do lots of shooting drills with him, give him everything you've got."

Tamba glanced at the floor. "Dylan, I need to talk with you about that."

"The drills?"

"No. Training tomorrow. And the final."

There was something in Tamba's tone, usually so friendly and upbeat, that made Dylan's heart sink. He felt Penny's hand slip around his. "What's up?"

"Do you remember that movie I read for back in November? The new James Bond film?"

"Yes? You got a part?"

Tamba nodded.

Dylan exhaled, relieved. "Not a problem. You're filming what, two or three days, like before? We can work around that."

"No, Dylan," Tamba gave a half-smile, like he was in a daze. "I got a big part. They're casting me as one of the villains."

"The villain of what?"

"The story. Of the movie, the entire thing." A grin broke out on Tamba's face. "I'm going to be a movie star."

"When does production start?" Penny asked when Dylan remained speechless.

"This Friday."

"Okay... okay..." Dylan sputtered as his brain tried to grapple with the enormity of what he was hearing. "That's in two days. So, fittings, rehearsals, a few hours a day? You'll have to get off for the FA Cup. But we'll make this work, Tamba."

"No, Dylan, they're not filming here in London."

Dylan didn't want to ask the next question. "Where are they filming?"

"Some place called Patagonia," Tamba said. "Ain't that where that Paddington Bear came from?"

Penny's eyes grew wide. "That's Peru."

Anger swept through Dylan. Violent, pointless anger. "Who in the hell ever heard of a five foot six inch, ten stone Bond villain?" he roared, jumping to his feet and stalking the small waiting room.

Tamba looked crestfallen and Dylan immediately felt terrible. He paused his rant and took several deep, savage breaths. "How much are you making?"

"Almost a million pounds. Plus residuals. My agent—it's so much, he can't figure it out."

Dylan took Tamba by the shoulders and stood him up. "Look, mate, take it. Get a lawyer, and another agent, and lock this deal up. Call Tom Belleville-Howe, he'll know what to do."

"He will?"

"If he can sort out Mick Carr, he can sort out anyone. But tell him to get it locked up fast. Like by tomorrow."

Tamba nodded, listening to every word Dylan said. "Everything is happening so fast, Dylan. I don't want to mess it up."

"You have to get that contract signed before word gets out about Ned. And then get on that plane to Patagonia."

Tamba shook his head in confusion. "Where's Patagonia?"

"I don't know, but it sounds cold."

⁂

After Tamba left Dylan collapsed in the chair next to Penny and buried his face in his hands. "Is this her doing?"

"Who?"

"Boudica," Dylan muttered.

Penny patted his back consolingly. "Of course not."

"I lost two of my best players today."

"Ned was an accident," she reasoned.

"I'm stretched so thin. We're going to humiliate ourselves."

"You can't let this get to you." Her fingers began to massage the stiff muscles in his neck, and he closed his eyes and felt the stress begin to drain away.

"Can you stay? Can I take you for dinner?" Dylan asked after a few minutes.

"Your mom is having Gwen and the neighbor ladies over to play Contract Whist tonight, and wants me to play," Penny apologized. "I said okay."

Dylan's shoulders slumped further. "I am truly cursed."

Chapter Sixty-Six

Two days before the FA Cup, Dylan sat on the stage in the press room at Wembley Stadium between Charlie Moore, Ned's replacement, and Connor Shaw, a Scottish striker who was Tamba's replacement. Reno sat further down the table, flanked by his prized players Yaba Owusu and Toussaint Badeaux, while the South Quay Road manager sat on the end, almost an afterthought. Before them was a packed auditorium of media and reporters from around the world.

Blazing lights beat down on the dais. Dylan took another swig of bottled water and checked his watch impatiently. He had an appointment in Mayfair he needed to keep and this circus was supposed to have started forty minutes ago.

Lord Lambton, who looked like he had aged ten years since the last press conference, signaled the questions could begin.

"Dylan! If it wasn't for the discovery of Boudica at Mortager Park, would you be here today, playing for the FA Cup?"

Dylan leaned into the microphone, ready for the question. "Yes, we would. I knew our players had it in them from the beginning."

The next question came through a translator. "No," Dylan replied tersely, "we have not built an altar or made sacrifices to any gods to ensure our victory. Next question."

"Dylan, you lost Ned Winter last week to a broken ankle at training. Did Boudica have anything to do with that?"

Dylan exhaled slowly—it was going to be a long day. "No. Ned's injury revealed he has early onset osteoporosis, but is recovering well, thanks for asking. Next question."

"Dylan! You finished the Atlas League in mid-table, yet you're playing in the FA Cup final. Do you think Boudica doesn't like Non-League football?"

Lord Lambton had advised him to stay calm but Jesus, this was getting ridiculous. "I have no idea what she does and does not like, because she's been dead for almost two thousand years. The lads have been playing very well, and—"

"Ye might give a bit o' credit to the gaffer!" Connor Shaw interrupted in an almost unintelligible northern Scottish accent. "All this blether o'er some deid wummon, can we no tak a pint an agree it's a load a shite?"

The crowd laughed uproariously and Dylan saw Lord Lambton wince.

"Dylan has been instrumental in our success," young Charlie Moore added, sounding like a college professor lecturing a classroom of introduction-level students. "And until last week we had a full squad. Our defense has been solid and strong, and we haven't lost anyone in that position. We've great counter-attacking skills but, most of all, we're flexible in our formations and quickly adapt to different situations if necessary."

Dylan smothered a grin as the reporters, many of whom he had never seen before and guessed had never been to a professional football match in their lives, attempted to decipher Charlie's excellent analysis. They failed and turned to Reno.

"Reno, there's been a huge blowback from the mental health community over the show you own, *Fraud War*, and the depiction of people suffering from mental health issues. Care to comment?"

Reno leaned into the microphone. "I am here to talk football today."

Another reporter jumped to her feet. "Alright then, do you think Icelton got here by skill, luck, or the hand of Boudica?"

Reno winked conspiratorially. "I must be careful how I answer this, or I could get hexed by every witch in Great Britain!" When the crowd had finished laughing, he added "Look, we must give Dylan credit. He has been very clever, and very cunning. A worthy opponent. But I think he will recognize he is over-matched and do the smart thing." Reno sat back and glanced slyly at Dylan.

"Reno, South Quay Road supporters are complaining about a lack of tickets for the final. The ticketing agency has said it has software issues and is struggling to solve them. The match is only two days away, yet many SQR fans say they haven't been able to get tickets. Care to comment?"

An ugly rash sprouted around the collar of Reno's tailor-made white linen shirt. "Yes, this I have heard. We are working with the FA on it. I have been assured the situation will be corrected."

—◆○◆—

The traffic from Wembley to Mayfair was jammed as usual, and the ten-mile drive took Dylan more than an hour. He took the scenic way knowing the other routes wouldn't be any faster, past Hyde Park, left onto Piccadilly, and left again onto Albemarle Street.

This was an area of London he wasn't familiar with, and he checked the written directions Hugo Auchincloss had given him. Finding a parking spot was no mean feat, but he got lucky with a spot close to Malbrey Jewellers and walked to the main door. The doorman nodded and opened the portal with a subtle flourish, welcoming Dylan into the deeply carpeted store. Towering glass display cabinets showed off a spectacular collection of watches, clocks, and even handbags.

A gentleman met him in the foyer.

"How do you do, Mr Rhea," the man bowed. "I'm Robert Paulson and it will be my pleasure to serve you. Come right this way."

Chapter Sixty-Seven

Dylan woke on the morning of the FA Cup final in his own bed, feeling rested and refreshed. He'd wanted to sleep at home, close to Penny—or at least as close as his mother would allow. It had become obvious she had decided to appoint herself Penny's unofficial chaperone, and while he knew she meant well, and that it was only until the final, he still chafed at the enforced chastity. Penny for her part seemed to be enjoying his mother's company and the whirlwind of social activities she had organized.

He heard noises in the kitchen below and quickly showered, shaved, and dressed in the same suit he'd worn to go to every FA Cup match since November. He knew Penny would understand the superstition, and at this point if it wasn't broke he wasn't going to fix it.

Amazing aromas from below met him on the stairs. In the kitchen Penny was removing a large tray from the oven, and he slid up behind her silently and kissed her neck. She jumped in surprise.

"Dylan! Don't sneak up on me, you almost made me drop breakfast."

"Sorry," he apologized. "Just trying to get a minute alone with my best girl. Mum and Gwen out for their walk?"

"Yes," Penny said, "have a seat. Let's send you off to make history on a full stomach."

Penny set the golden casserole on the table and Dylan eagerly dug in. "My word, this is amazing."

"It's called a strata. It's sausage, and eggs, and bread, and cheese—"

Dylan leaned over and kissed her. "You had me at sausage."

"Could you turn off your mobile while we're eating?" Penny asked, helping herself to a plate. "It's blipping every five seconds."

Dylan rolled his eyes. "Of course. I get immune after a while."

He was finishing his third plate when his mother and Gwen came in.

"I've had the strangest text message from Len," Gwen said. "He wants to come over and talk with us."

Dylan snorted. "I've got nothing to say to him. He can salve his conscious some other place."

Janice nodded. "I agree."

"I messaged back and told him we need to be getting to Wembley, but he's insisting. Says he'll be here in ten minutes."

Penny stood up and took the dishes to the sink. "I don't want to see him. He lied on television and said I attacked him."

"He might want to apologize for that," Janice said.

"He can apologize to all of you. I'm supposed to be meeting the girls at Mortager Park to walk over to Wembley, and can't be late."

Dylan walked her to the door and handed her the duffle bag. "See you soon."

"Good luck," Penny said, and pulled his head down and kissed him soundly.

"With a kiss like that I could win the World Cup," Dylan grinned.

* * *

Although Len had said he would arrive in ten minutes, it was almost forty minutes after Penny left that he finally knocked at the door. Dylan barely recognized him—Len had lost a lot of weight and looked a shadow of his former self. He walked with a discernible limp as he followed Dylan into the kitchen where his mother and Gwen were waiting.

"I wanted to apologize to you all," Len said, sitting down heavily in a kitchen chair. "Especially you, Janice."

"For what, Len? For lying about Penny attacking you?" Gwen asked, her tone scathing.

Len took out a handkerchief and blew his nose loudly. "No. I need to come clean about this. I loaned Charles a quarter of a million quid for improving Mortager Park because I knew he wouldn't be able to repay it."

Anger pulsed through Dylan and his fists doubled up.

His mother reached over and put a hand over his, stilling his rage. "Why, Len?"

"I thought it was for the best. The foundry was close to bankruptcy, Charles wasn't listening to reason, and you were all going broke."

"We were not going broke," his mother objected. "We had all the money we needed. It wasn't much, but we were fine."

"And I was helping him pay you back," Dylan added heatedly, "while I was at Kingsbury Town."

Len shook his head. "You don't understand, you could have had more. Much more. We all could have been millionaires."

"So you tried to force Charles into bankruptcy, just to get him to sell? That's awful," Gwen said.

"It would have worked out," Len assured her. "Reno would have paid top dollar for the land, and the club."

"And what would he have done with the place?" Gwen prodded. "Be honest, for once."

"There has been some talk, some top-secret talk, of London Underground building a spur of the Jubilee Line into Icelton. Land prices will soar. Reno wanted to snap up the foundry grounds and Mortager Park before anyone else did. He approached me and offered a stake if I could help make it happen."

"You greedy bastard. Charles was your best friend," Janice bit out.

"It wasn't going to work, though, if Dylan kept playing for Kingsbury Town, was it?" Gwen asked, looking pointedly at Dylan. "He was due to sign a new contract with them, and get a huge pay rise."

Len's eyes shifted away. "I don't know anything about that. I was just supposed to get you to the bargaining table."

"How far were you and Reno willing to go to make this happen, Len?" Gwen demanded. "Who else was involved with this?"

"I don't know. You have to believe me, I thought I was doing the right thing," Len beseeched. "For everyone."

"Luckily, thanks to Penny, that didn't work out," Janice said.

Len's shoulder's sagged. "Please tell Penny I'm sorry. Please accept the apology of an old, sick man."

Penny walked down Elthorne Road towards Mortager Park, so deep in her own thoughts that she didn't see the van that had pulled into a driveway in front of her until she was almost upon it. It was white and detailed with yellow lines and black and white squares, and the windows were darkened. Immigration Enforcement was written along the side facing her.

Two men dressed in official uniforms got out of the van and approached her. "Miss Adams?"

Penny halted. "Yes?"

They reached in their jackets and flashed badges. "Her Majesty's Immigration Service. May we see your passport?"

Penny rummaged in her duffle bag and pulled it out. "What do you want?"

"You entered the country on October 31st and today is May 16th," one officer said, flipping through the pages of the passport. "You've overstayed your six months visitor visa by fifteen days. Please come with us."

Penny shifted uneasily. "But... does it have to be today?"

"Yes, miss." They opened the door to the van and pointed in the backseat. "Please get in, Miss."

Penny looked frantically up and down Elthorne Road but the sidewalks were deserted. "Where are we going?"

"We're taking you to the Immigration office at Heathrow to get an extension of your visa."

She paled. "Can I go tomorrow? Or Monday?"

"No, Miss. You need to come with us now."

"What happens if they won't give me an extension?"

The officer shrugged. "Then they put you on a plane back to where you came from."

Penny held out her hand. "Give me my passport back," she demanded with as much force as she could muster.

"At Heathrow, miss. Now please, get in the van."

Penny knew she had no choice but to do as she was told. "May I borrow your cellphone? I need to call my, my boyfriend."

"Yes, Miss. At Heathrow," they said, and took her by the arm to guide her into a seat in the back, sliding the door closed behind her. The two officers got in the front seats, which was separated from her by thick plexiglas.

The driver sped through Icelton and got on the A5 motorway, heading south. "Wait, Heathrow is north of here. We're going south," Penny said loudly, to be heard through the partition. There was no acknowledgment the men heard her.

Penny's heart began to pump with terror as the miles flew by. There were, she saw, no handles on the inside of the van doors, and the windows were sealed shut. "Are you guys really from Immigration?" she yelled, to no avail.

The van left the motorway and began a circuitous route around large towns. According to Penny's watch they had been on the road for almost an hour. She was supposed to meet the girls at Mortager Park—would they have been able to get hold of Dylan to let him know she was missing?

The blood continued to pound in her ears. She considered beating her fists on the windows to try to attract attention but remembered they were tinted. Through the plexiglas she could see the driver and the other man talking with each other and consulting the GPS map.

The van continued deeper into the countryside, where the road turned into twisting lanes. Eventually it turned down a narrow stone drive surrounded by overgrown hedges, with deep potholes that tossed Penny around the bench seat. At the end of the lane was an abandoned farmhouse.

The van stopped and Penny unsnapped her seatbelt. "Where are we?" she demanded, pounding on the plexiglas divider.

The driver got out of the van, followed by the other man. They stood to the side, ignoring her, while one checked his watch and the other lit a cigarette. Looking from window to window in the back, Penny could see the place was deserted. If she screamed, there would be no one to hear her.

Penny fought back the tears that threatened to choke her. She knew she had to stay focused, that she could not let the terror distract her. There must be something she could use to defend herself and break free. They had put her duffle bag in the front seat with them, and she wasn't wearing any jewelry, just her wristwatch. But her boots had laces, maybe she could do something with them.

The men continued to smoke their cigarettes, their backs to the van. Penny slipped out of her boots and sat back on the seat, quickly unlacing them with deft movements. When she was finished, she slipped her boots back on and stuffed one lace in her jacket pocket. The other she wrapped around each palm, leaving a foot of cord between them, and had no idea what she was going to do with it.

They had been in the clearing for almost twenty minutes when a car appeared, speeding down the lane towards them. As it pulled up next to the van, the van driver came around and slid the door by Penny open.

Penny considered making a dash for it but froze when the newly arrived car doors swung open.

Jeff and Scott got out and walked over to the van. "Nice work, lads. We'll take her from here."

Chapter Sixty-Eight

THE MEN FROM IMMIGRATION tossed their cigarettes and ground them out with their shoes. "Right, Jeff. Cheers, Scott."

Jeff and Scott popped their heads into the van where Penny continued to sit, her mouth gaping open. "Hallo, Penny!"

Penny knew her mouth was moving, but it was a moment before she could form words. "What are you two doing here?"

"Saving you from Sue!" Scott said.

Jeff nodded, and then seemed to notice Penny's look of abject terror. "What, didn't the guys tell you?"

The Immigration men looked at each other. "We had to make it look convincing. She came along without a fuss."

"Sorry, Penny," Scott apologized. "We had to get you out of harm's way for an hour."

"You're not kidnapping me?"

"Good heavens, no, just the opposite, actually. Sue was going to try to kidnap you but we saved her the trouble. It's time to take you back."

Penny's hands relaxed around the boot lace she had been holding taunt. "Is Dylan safe?"

"He's fine. He's at Mortager Park."

"I should call him. He'll be worried."

"Good idea, but would you mind texting?" Scott asked. "He's tied up at the moment."

At Penny's look of concern Jeff added, "He meant that metaphorically! He and Sue are having a chat."

Penny unwound the boot lace from her hand and took the phone Jeff offered. `It's Penny. I am OK, I think. Jeff and Scott say they are taking me back to Mortager Park.`

A message appeared twenty seconds later. `Good. You're safe with them. See you soon. I love you.`

Penny exhaled and handed the phone back to Jeff. "Okay. What's going on?"

"Let's get on the road and we'll explain."

Penny tripped getting out of the van and almost crashed to the ground.

"Good Lord, girl, what happened to your boots?" The men laughed, helping her to her feet. When she showed them the shoelaces in her pocket, they patted her on the back. "Sue would have never stood a chance."

Penny folded her long legs into the back seat of the little car while Jeff got in the passenger seat and Scott wedged himself behind the steering wheel and began driving back towards the road. "Tell me what's going on."

"Sue seems to have tried a last-ditch attempt to get Dylan to forfeit the FA Cup by kidnapping you," Jeff explained. "She was waiting for you at the end of Elthorne Road. We had to break that up so we sent Gerald and Ken. Now Sue is trying to kidnap Dylan, but he doesn't seem to be having any of it. It's her final chance to show Reno she can get the job done."

Penny stared at the men, puzzled. "How do you know Reno? How do you know any of this?"

Scott glanced at Jeff. "You'd best explain."

Jeff turned around in his seat as best he could and faced Penny. "We're Druids."

This was so absurd Penny laughed out loud. "There's no such thing as Druids. Not anymore."

Jeff smiled. "Still, here we are."

Penny struggled to comprehend what they were saying. "But... Druids have long hair. And beards. And wear... I don't know... cloaks and tall, pointed hats."

"Some do," Jeff said.

Scott wrinkled his nose. "Posers."

"Can you do magic?" Penny whispered.

"Magic?" Jeff laughed. "We can barely work the bloody grill at the shop without setting the place on fire."

Her eyes widened. "Human sacrifices?"

"That was all vastly overblown. Although in Sue Paulin's case I'd be willing to make an exception," Jeff added darkly.

"It's a bit more subtle than that," Scott explained as he drove. "Let's just say we pay attention. The secret of the Druids, if you can call it that, is we know what we're looking for and we keep an eye out. We also have an extensive network and pass information along. Coordinate, if you will."

"Guys, you run a kebab shop for heaven's sake," Penny said.

Jeff nodded. "It's a very important job. We had to work our way up to it."

Maybe it was an aftereffect of the stress she'd been under, but Penny burst out laughing again. Scott waited until she finished. "Yes, we get it, not very glamorous. But Icelton is one of the top posts. It's been on our radar, so to speak, for a long time. Druids have always had a presence in the area."

"What's a long time?"

"Going on two thousand years now."

"So Ye Old Kebab Shoppe is really old?"

"There's been a shop there in one form or another since the Romans left, run by Druids or people friendly to us. The area has always been... energized."

"Yes," Scott agreed. "That's a good way to describe it."

"The amateur opera is the excuse for us traveling all around Great Britain," Jeff continued. "We visit forest groves and have meetings. Worship, if you like. Druids are the original networkers. Back then, in Roman times, the Druids were the ones who could move around between warring tribes and were always welcomed. We coordinated things, which is why the Romans needed to get rid of us."

"And they almost did, when Suetonius wiped them out at the battle of Anglesey. But they pulled together and within two hundred years were back in business," Scott said. "We knew the day you showed up that things were starting to happen. Big things. The biggest yet."

"Do you remember the first time you walked into the kebab shop? The sodas turning red?" Jeff asked.

Penny nodded. "You kicked everyone out."

"Yes, didn't need that getting all over social media. But after you left, we opened every can and they were fine. Lemon soda was yellow, cola was brown, orange was orange. We knew everyone in the shop that night except you. But you had vanished."

"So the soda turning red was an omen?"

"Omen is an overused term," Scott corrected. "Let's just say it was a heads up. Red always has been a warning signal, you know, like 'the rivers ran red'. Then the storm blew through and we knew the damage was supposed to expose something. A couple of days later Vivian called and said you'd been to the HARP office with some very specific pottery cup shards you'd dug up."

Penny thought back to that day. "Was she the one with the green robe and pink hair?"

"No, that's Brenda. Lovely woman, but mad as a March hare," Jeff said. "After that, we had a meeting and it was determined you were on to something and we needed to keep an eye on you. Two weeks later we saw you in the street and brought you in."

"Your clock on the wall stopped," Penny said. "Was that another omen?"

"Yes, but by that point we didn't need it. We knew we had to keep you in Icelton and digging."

"I was attacked in the dig by someone who was trying to burn the tooling shop down. Did you have anything to do with that?"

"Heavens no, that was Len's doing. He hired a thug to scare you off. Reno had offered him a big slice of the profits once the property was his. Len had one job, and that was to deliver the foundry, the Icelton Football Club ground, and all the adjoining car parks to Reno. He almost did it, too, until you showed up."

Penny remembered the attack. "There was someone else there that night. Someone pulled the guy off me, who was choking me."

"Yours truly," Scott waved his left hand. "Bloody bugger, broke my wrist."

"I remember," Penny said. "It was in a cast for weeks!"

"It's all been sorted. We tracked him down, delivered him up to friends on the Metropolitan Police," Jeff said with satisfaction. "It turns out he had several warrants out for his arrest and he is now a guest of Her Majesty for eighteen months. But we worried they'd send someone else, someone not as stupid as that yob. You were right to take the torcs to Dylan's house."

Penny gaped in astonishment. "You know about the torcs?"

"We guessed you had found something, and something big. You were as happy as a clam," Jeff said.

"Don't ever play poker," Scott advised. "At that point it was just a matter of waiting for HARP to show up. We thought about speeding that up but then Icelton kept winning, and it was decided we had to see how things were going to play out. It wasn't until Pavarotti fell over and Sue Paulin walked in the door that we made the connection."

"Nasty piece of work, that one," Jeff muttered under his breath. "We weren't sure what would happen if she got a hold of you. Mrs Baker at number eighty-one called this morning and said Sue staked out the corner of Park Road, so we had to scramble to get Gerald and Ken over there before you left Dylan's."

Penny swallowed, her mouth dry. "Thank you. Were those guys really from Immigration?"

"Oh yes," Jeff said. "We do have day jobs, you know."

They were speeding up the A5 and Penny saw they had almost reached Icelton. "Where are we going now?"

"First, back to Elthorne Road to pick up the gold torc."

"Why?"

"You need to wear it at the FA Cup final this evening."

Penny was horrified at the thought. "But it's an antiquity. What if I break it?"

"Trust us on this one," Jeff assured her. "You have to wear it."

"Me wearing a bit of metal around my neck isn't going to change anything."

Scott downshifted and got off the exit. "Let us be the judge of that. We have all the pieces, and they have to come together at the final."

"No one will get hurt, will they?"

"We shouldn't think so. But our task is clear—Reno Tedesco has to be defeated."

Chapter Sixty-Nine

LEN LEFT THE HOUSE on Elthorne Road quickly, brushing past Eddie on the stoop without a word.

"Was that Len?" Eddie asked, bewildered. "Good Lord, I didn't recognize him. Dylan, what are you still doing here? The team's already at Wembley."

"Yes, I know, I've got to get moving," Dylan said. "Mum and Gwen will explain. Look, here's the car I ordered for you. Wish me luck."

"Dylan," Gwen took his arm, "please be careful. Someone was willing to drug you almost to an overdose over that land. Who knows what else they will try."

"I've got this, Gwen," he assured his godmother, and gave her a smacking kiss. "Cheer us on!"

When everyone was safely on their way, Dylan unmuted his mobile phone and was astonished to see a string of text messages from the girls. He scrolled through them quickly, following their rising panic that Penny had not shown up at Mortager Park, where they were waiting for her.

`I'll be right over` he texted back.

"Penny was supposed to be here two hours ago," Chloe said when he came in the door of the clubhouse.

"My neighbor said they saw a van pull up, and she got in," Cassie added, distraught. "They said it was from Immigration."

Terror gripped Dylan's heart. He mentally counted back the months she had been in the United Kingdom, and it was more than the allowed six. Anger welled in him—this was Reno's doing and he had gone too far.

His mobile rang, the number displaying as Ye Olde Kebab Shoppe. "Scott?"

"Look Dylan, I can't explain much now, but we have Penny and she's fine."

Dylan exhaled. "Thank God. Where are you? I'll come and get her."

"Can you hold on for a bit? We'll bringing her to you."

"Scott, unless you've forgotten, I've got a pressing engagement this afternoon—"

Scott laughed. "Yes, but you're going to be getting an important visitor very soon. This is what's going to happen."

Dylan listened to Scott for several moments, his fear evaporating. "Right then," he said when Scott had finished, "you're sure about all this?"

"Completely sure. See you soon. Good luck, mate."

"Girls!" Dylan turned to the nervously waiting team. "We've got a job to do, so listen closely."

Five minutes later Dylan looked out his office window and saw the red Porsche speed down the lane to Mortager Park. Sue parked in the handicapped spot as usual, and he heard the door to the clubhouse slam shut behind her. She found him sitting at his desk, reading through some paperwork.

"Dylan!" Sue panted, out of breath. "Thank God I've found you—"

"Oh, hi Sue," Dylan said without raising his eyes from the letter he was reading. "What's up?"

"It's Penny. She's been taken by Immigration!"

"Really," Dylan nodded, scribbling his signature at the bottom of the paper. "That's terrible."

Sue dropped her voice to a conspiratorial whisper. "I think I know where they might have taken her."

Dylan made a production of casting about his cluttered desk. "I know Alan said he put the club insurance information here somewhere..."

"Dylan, this is serious!" Sue reached over the desk to grab his arm. "C'mon, I'll drive. There's no time to lose!"

"There's no rush, Sue. Penny's a smart girl, I'm sure she'll be able to handle herself." Dylan pointed at the stool opposite his desk. "Take a seat. Let's you and I have a chat."

Dylan stood and closed the office door, and Sue had no choice but to back onto the little seat.

"You don't seem very upset. I thought you liked Penny," she said, confused.

"She's a nice girl," Dylan conceded, leaning back against the door. "Although she's nothing like you."

Dylan's mobile beeped and he paused. "I need to answer this," he apologized. Sue sat stiffly while he read the message and typed a quick reply, then put the phone on the corner of the desk, face down. "Sorry about that. Sue, I've been wondering about something."

Sue was suddenly wary. "What?"

"That tooth powder, and the energy drink you introduced me to. Where did you get them?"

"I don't know what you're talking about."

"Sure you do. A week after we moved into the flat in Chelsea, a jar of energy powder appeared on the kitchen counter. You mixed me up a glass and then drank one yourself. Remember?"

Sue made a dismissive motion with her hands. "Oh, that stuff."

"And the tooth powder you loved so much. You used to make sure I never ran out. Where did it come from?"

"I don't remember. It's been a long time."

Dylan looked on her with pity. "Sue, Len came to the house this morning. He told me and Mum everything."

Sue paled. "What do you mean, everything?"

"He told us about him and Reno," Dylan said, and then made a calculated gamble. "And you. He confessed everything about the plan."

"He doesn't know everything."

"What doesn't he know?"

Sue's mouth snapped shut and she stared at the wall.

"I had the stuff analyzed at a lab. The tooth powder you gave me had a huge amount of cocaine in it. And the energy drink was laced with prescription narcotics." Dylan watched Sue carefully. "What did Reno promise you?"

Sue was obviously struggling with a huge internal dilemma, yet stayed silent.

Dylan decided to try some compassion. "Did he say he'd marry you?"

Sue exhaled a revolted snort. "God, no."

"What, then? You deserve a lot for your loyalty," he said gently, hoping his reasonable tone would dull her common sense. He knew her ego would take it from there.

"You're bloody well right I do. President of Tedesco Media Corporation. The first woman president of the biggest entertainment conglomerate in the United Kingdom," Sue announced with grim satisfaction.

"Very impressive." Dylan whistled through his teeth and repeated the title. "I guess that's kind of fallen through? I mean, now that the Crown is buying everything here. Len told us Reno really wanted the land."

"That was Len's part, and he completely botched it. I did my part."

"But you can still get Reno the FA Cup." Dylan paused and mentally counted to ten. "Do I still have time to forfeit?"

Sue sat bolt upright, fueled by the desperate glimmer of hope Dylan dangled before her. "You're serious?"

Dylan dropped his head and studied the carpet. "I don't fancy the humiliation we're going to face, without Tommy, Tamba, and Ned, for a lousy two million pounds payday."

"Yes! Yes, there's still time! The deal Reno gave you is still on the table, five million pounds." When Dylan seemed to be agonizing over the decision, she added "And I'll make it seven million pounds."

"You're offering me seven million pounds to forfeit the FA Cup?" he said loudly, as if in shock.

"Yes! Right here, right now."

Dylan grimaced and ran his hand through his hair. "I'd want you to apologize to Penny."

Sue nodded enthusiastically. "Absolutely! We'll do a full show on her, how smart she is, how tough she is. And how crazy people are really fine and not a danger to the public at all."

Dylan pretended to consider this. "That would mean a lot to her. But in exchange, I want to know how you did it. Whose idea was it to drug me?"

"Mine," Sue said, "but it was only supposed to be minuscule amounts. Enough to show up on any drug tests you might take as a Premier League player."

"Just enough to get me fired?"

"You were making too much money and could have helped your Dad out financially. Reno wanted to bankrupt you, so you'd have to sell to him. The way he explained it, it was supposed to be for your own good. He was going to pay you a reasonable price for all this, and you'd be set. Len would get his fee, and I'd get to be head of the studio. It was a good deal for everyone."

Dylan nodded, following the story. "So your part was to help that along."

"Yes. But then you quit Kingsbury Town. I thought you'd found out that the tooth powder and drink powder were laced. I panicked and threw you out."

"But even after you threw me out, and I moved back here, the delivery people still found me."

Sue had the decency to look a bit ashamed. "I had put a tracking app on your mobile."

Dylan raised his eyebrows. "And then you kept stringing me along, saying you just needed a little more time. Was that the plan? To bleed me dry with the flat payments and the Porsche lease? So I'd go broke and lose the club and the property?"

"Yes."

"Instead you almost killed me," Dylan fumed.

"You weren't supposed to die, just go broke," Sue reasoned. "And after you moved out, it was out of my control, so it really isn't my fault. I think Reno told those people at the lab to up the concentration, so you'd sell faster. But then it seemed to stop working."

"It stopped working because I stopped taking it. If it wasn't for Penny, I would be dead," Dylan crossed his arms over his chest. "You ruined my career and drugged me. I should go to the police with this."

"You have every right to be angry," Sue tried to calm him. "But be reasonable. No one can touch Reno. Give him what he wants, and the future is yours."

"Was he responsible for me losing Tamba?" Dylan asked grimly.

"That was me," Sue winced. "Sorry. I managed to pull some strings with the producers. I promised them financing and a distribution deal with Tedesco Media that made them jump out of their seats!"

"I guess I should count myself lucky you were just trying to kidnap me," Dylan said ruefully.

Sue stifled a small giggle. "I admit I can be very motivated when I want to be."

"Why shouldn't I go to the police with this?" Dylan asked.

Sue shook her head, her expression pitying. "You have no proof, Dylan. No one will believe you. Forfeit and take the money."

Dylan sighed. "You're right. They won't believe me."

Sue smirked, seeing victory within her grasp. "That's right. So you need to—"

"But they'll believe you."

"Excuse me?"

"They'll believe you," Dylan repeated, "in your own words. That's all the proof I need."

Sue stood slowly, her back straight and her hands on her hips. "It would be your word against mine."

"No. It will be your word against your word."

Sue's eyes narrowed. "Dylan, we had a deal. Now you're just being stupid, again. I really don't have time for this."

"I think you're going to be having a lot of time," he replied, "very soon."

Dylan watched as Sue swung her messenger bag over her shoulder and brushed her hair back from her forehead. "I'm not staying here a minute longer. Go ahead, go lose the FA Cup and make a disgrace of yourself. Get out of my way."

He quickly obeyed her order. With a huff she yanked the office door open and was immediately halted by a phalanx of teenage girls dressed in identical tracksuits, their hair pulled back into pony tails and their arms crossed. They stood shoulder to shoulder, blocking her exit.

Chloe stood at the front, holding her mobile phone before her like a trophy. "Not so fast, Sue."

"Let me through," Sue snapped.

"Did you get all that, girls?" Dylan asked.

Seven heads nodded in unison. "We recorded it all."

"Clear as a bell."

"Every. Last. Word."

Chapter Seventy

Sue slumped backwards until she bumped into the stool and collapsed on it, stunned.

Dylan reached for his phone and tapped a few keys. "Yes, I got it as well."

The door to the water heater room opened and four more girls poured into the office, all holding their mobile phones.

"And just in case they didn't get it, we also recorded every word, you nasty witch," Kenna said.

Cassie moved to stand next to Sue and showed her the screen. "Recognize that white car, Sue? We found pictures of it delivering here in December, while we were training. See, got the plates and all."

"Won't take long for the police to find the driver," Charvi noted. "Look, I can see her face clearly in that picture."

"They probably know you!" Crystal added.

The blood was rapidly draining from Sue's face. "You set me up?" she looked to Dylan in appeal. "After all we've meant to each other?"

Dylan nodded, knowing that no one had ever disgusted him so much in his life. "Exactly because of what I meant to you."

From behind them they heard the doors to the clubhouse open. The girls in the hallway turned around, their faces lighting up. "Penny's here!"

Penny appeared in the doorway, and Dylan knew he had never seen anyone more beautiful. Her hair was down, the tawny ringlets hanging past her shoulders in a glorious mass, and she was wearing the brightly colored rain jacket he had given her. Around her neck was the golden torc, the color glowing warmly in the overhead light.

Dylan pulled her into his arms. "Thank God you're safe."

"Sue just confessed everything, Penny!" the girls crowed. "We helped get it all recorded. You're going to the clink, Sue."

"Nice job, girls," Penny congratulated them.

"Sue was the one responsible for the tooth powder and energy drink being drugged," Dylan said. "And Len confessed he was trying to bankrupt Dad to help Reno get the land."

"Len also sent the man to burn down the tooling shop," Penny added. "And it was Scott that pulled him off me."

"I had nothing to do with that," Sue muttered.

"Don't convince us, convince the prosecutor," Dylan snapped and then turned to the girls. "Is everyone ready to go win the FA Cup?"

"Where's Biscuits?" Penny asked.

"Oh, he's at a cricket match with Thomas Mitchell and his kids," Chloe said.

"But Biscuits wouldn't miss this for the world!" Penny said.

Chloe shrugged. "Cricket's all he talks about anymore. Night and day. Bit of a relief, actually."

As they all headed down the hallway, Penny turned around. "Wait, there's just one thing. Sue?"

Sue glared at Penny from where she crouched on the stool. "What?"

"I'll take the keys to the Porsche."

Chapter Seventy-One

Penny and Dylan sat in the red Porsche in a traffic jam, with Wembley Stadium looming before them. The sun was shining and Penny had insisted on putting the convertible top down.

"We're going to be late," Dylan said nervously from the passenger seat of the Porsche. "Kick off is in an hour and a quarter. Maybe I should just get out and run."

"Relax, I'll get you there in plenty of time," Penny assured him. "Are Jeff and Scott still behind us?"

"Yes," Dylan grunted, unconvinced. "The team has been at the stadium for ages now."

"I wish it wasn't just a mile," Penny said, fondling the stick shift in her left hand. "I bet I could get us to Colchester in under an hour."

The traffic lights changed and the road ahead cleared. "Penny," Dylan yelped, "remember when you make a left-hand turn you go in the other lane—"

"Sorry," she grinned and waved at the driver she narrowly swerved around. "Which way do they want us to go in?"

"Through there—wait, watch that guy on the scooter!—okay, turn right—no, the other right—wait, that sign says One Way—"

"But we're only going one way!" Penny grinned.

"I narrowly avoid being killed by one girlfriend, only to be killed by another..." Dylan growled darkly.

Traffic ground to a halt again and Penny shifted to neutral and revved the car, loving the pulsing purr of the six-cylinder engine. "There is no other car that makes that sound," she confided.

Dylan checked his watch again. "We're not getting anywhere."

"You're right." Penny nudged the car off the road and onto the sidewalk. "Stand up."

"What?"

"Stand up," Penny said. "Stand up so everyone can see you."

"In a moving car? Penny, that's very dangerous," Dylan scolded. "I don't know what they do in America, but here in England you are *most* definitely not allowed to drive on the pavement—"

"I'm being careful. But stand up, it's the only way people are going to get out of our way."

"You're mad."

"I've already gotten that diagnosis!" Penny beamed, the sunlight glinting off the gold torc around her throat. "Now, do you want to get to Wembley or not?"

Dylan made a silent appeal to heaven before moving the seat back as far as it would go and struggling to his feet. He kept one hand gripping the windshield and gave a tentative wave with the other. Penny punctuated this by revving the engine loudly. People spun around and gaped.

"Oi! That's Dylan Rhea!" a woman yelled. "Why ain't ya in the stadium?"

"Trying to get there!" Dylan yelled back.

More people turned around, and the crowd began to part. "Gotta get this man into Wembley!"

Penny followed the path made by the parting crowd as they cheered them on. People pointed up a ramp and to Dylan's horror she followed it. "Penny, you cannot drive down the pedestrian walkway!"

"Dylan, I've got this. It's a lot easier than driving in the street, you know. There's no wrong side of the sidewalk."

"I don't think I'm living through this day," Dylan gulped, knowing the whole procession was being recorded by the thousands of mobile phones that surrounded them.

By the time the main gates were in sight the cheers had grown deafening and the jubilant crowd twenty deep along the pathway they had cleared. A squadron of uniformed guards appeared around a corner and ran towards them.

"Oh thank God, a security escort," Dylan blurted out.

Penny stopped the car and Dylan leaned down to kiss her. "Thanks for the lift."

"Good luck!" she said, but he had already leapt out of the car and run off, escorted by a dozen guards.

Chapter Seventy-Two

THE WEMBLEY SECURITY GUARDS made it clear they were not amused by Penny's decision to drop Dylan directly at the front door. They formed a cordon around her and directed her to a safe spot to park before giving her a stern lecture.

Penny managed what she hoped was a contrite apology, and then followed the crowd through the main entrance towards the crowded stadium mezzanine, where she caught up with Jeff and Scott. "Sorry, love, but we decided not to follow you onto the pavement," Jeff said. "Is that something they do a lot of in America?"

Penny rolled her eyes. "It doesn't look like there's a lot of South Quay Road fans here today," she said as they made their way to the sky box elevator. "I see a lot of Icelton green and grey, and lots of colorful outfits, but not much purple and white."

The usher in charge of the elevator scanned their tickets and they got on. "Hmmmm, yes, it seems there was quite a snafu with the ticketing process," Scott said conversationally. "At the lowest levels, of course. Some programmer messed up a routine maintenance upgrade, and for a few days they were only able to process ticket orders with email addresses that began with the letter 'B.'"

The elevator doors whooshed open, and they stepped inside. Penny glanced between Jeff and Scott, both of whom wore angelic expressions.

"I told you we have day jobs," Jeff grinned. "And don't look so concerned. They fixed the problem quickly and many South Quay Road fans were able to get their tickets."

Icelton had been allotted three sky boxes and Penny visited each of them. The girls' team had taken over one box, and in the next Padma Jain was chatting with Dylan's mother and Gwen.

"Thank goodness you're here!" Gwen said. "The girls were frantic."

"Has Dylan arrived?" Janice asked, looking stricken.

"Yes, I just dropped him off."

Professor Jain smiled at Penny, then her eyes grew wide and her jaw dropped open. "Oh my goodness, is that—" She reached towards Penny's neck with a tentative hand and Penny pushed the collar of her jacket back so the professor could see the torc better.

"It's—it's spectacular," Professor Jain finally was able to say. "Is it heavy?"

"A bit. Do you want to try it on?"

"No," Professor Jain dropped her hand as if she had been scalded and took an involuntary step backwards. "No, thank you. I think you're the only one it's intended for. But please be careful. It hasn't been worn in almost two thousand years."

On the big screen television behind the bar, Joe Lyons was beginning his pre-game show. "Hello, and welcome to the long-awaited FA Cup final between Premier League side South Quay Road and Atlas League Icelton. We are here at Wembley Stadium in north London, where I must say, things just keep getting stranger and stranger."

The show switched to footage of Penny driving the red Porsche through the pedestrian walkway at Wembley with Dylan standing next to her, waving to the crowd.

"Icelton arrived at the stadium almost two hours ago, absent their manager Dylan Rhea. He, however, has just been delivered to the front gate in a red Porsche convertible, driven by Miss Victoria Adams."

The camera cut back to Joe Lyons, whose eyebrows were raised so high they seemed to be touching his scalp. He looked directly at the camera and shook his head. "After this Cup season, I can't believe I'm letting anything surprise me."

He cleared his throat and continued. "Today's FA Cup winner will be taking home almost three million pounds, and the loser about half that. Today's attendance is a sellout 90,000, many of whom are wearing very... well, I guess we could call them *unique* outfits. And while they are not the usual type we see at football matches, the local constabulary are reporting no issues at all."

The footage switched to an interview with a policewoman in a street near the stadium. "Naw, they're lovely. Most peaceful crowd we've had in years. Polite, too. Yeah, they look a bit odd, but we'll take them over the usual yobs any day."

The television camera panned around the stands, which were indeed full of brightly garbed men and women with rather wild hair.

"Delightful day," a man told the camera, "nice outing with the wife. We've never been to a football match before, you know. What, darling? Oh... wait, I've forgotten... oh yes—*Go Icelton*!"

The camera returned to Joe Lyons, who was staring at his monitor with an expression of puzzled disbelief. He quickly regrouped. "Now let's talk football. Late last night it was announced that Reno Tedesco, the owner of South Quay Road, had sacked the team manager and most of his staff. He will be coaching the team himself this evening."

"Icelton, for their part, have fought their way here through eleven matches, helped in some ways by extraordinary luck. But no one can deny they have put in some very solid performances and been brilliantly managed. Unfortunately, Icelton's ranks have been cruelly depleted in the last two weeks. They've seen the departure of striker Tamba Taray, who has been offered a starring role in the next James Bond franchise movie, and midfielder Tommy Peele, who has accepted a contract to play for SQR next season. It is a contract, one should note, that is fully payable regardless of his playing time.

"But perhaps the biggest loss is keeper Ned Winter, who last week suffered a double fracture in his left ankle after a freak training accident. These are devastating blows to the team, and I don't see how they'll overcome these absences so close to the big game."

Penny made her way to the balcony and leaned on the railing to watch the teams below go through their warm-ups. Reno was on the field with his team, blowing his whistle and making wild arm movements that his players seemed to ignore. Dylan stood on the sidelines with Ned Winter, his left foot in an air cast, talking with his replacement, Charlie Moore.

"What's that clicking noise?" Penny asked, hearing a faint rumble, like a train approaching from far away.

Jeff and Scott joined her at the rail, looking over the spectators filling stadium. "What clicking noise?"

"It's coming from the stands," Penny replied. "Like people are making the noise with their mouths, but I can't see anyone's lips moving."

"Fancy that," Jeff said.

On the field, South Quay Road midfielder Toussaint Badeaux was standing in the middle of the pitch, staring wildly at the stands.

"What's the matter with him?" Penny asked.

"Toussaint? He's originally from Haiti," Scott said. "Lots of voodoo there, or so I've heard. And Yaba Owusu, over there on the touchline with the towel wrapped around his head, is from Ghana."

Penny raised a skeptical eyebrow. "Also a hotbed of voodoo superstition?"

"Perhaps," Jeff replied, his focus glued to the South Quay Road end of the pitch where Reno was screaming at Yaba to get on the field.

As suddenly as it had started, the clicking sound stopped.

⸻◆⸻

Penny sat in the seat outside the sky box, noting the absence of the raucous fan songs that usually accompanied play. Instead there was just a buzz of pleasant chatter, and Penny could feel the attention of hundreds of small binoculars on herself. Or rather, the torc around her neck.

The two teams left the field and the opening ceremonies began. It was immediately apparent to Penny that something was off—when both teams walked out together, there was a deafening roar from the crowd. Only it wasn't a roar, it was more of a war cry. Icelton stood with polite respect for the playing of "God Save The Queen", while the South Quay Road players fidgeted. The referee blew the whistle and the match began.

"Play is beginning fast, the style SQR are noted for," Penny could hear Joe Lyons broadcasting, "but I'm immediately seeing their passing game, which has never been a strong point, is very poor today."

"There seems to be a lack of connection between the midfielders, and Badeaux and Owusu, in particular, look frankly overawed by the game. These are big-time players, respected internationals, and yet they are so tentative. Even with Taray and Peele absent, Icelton are comfortable with the ball and they are the ones looking more likely to make a breakthrough.

"Of course, there is a long time to go, but SQR have a big hole on the coaching bench with only Reno Tedesco managing the team. He is gesticulating at his players, shaking his fist, screaming, and I'm not sure if the players understand his instructions."

⸺⟡⸺

In the fortieth minute, Joe Lyons tapped his earphones in the broadcasting booth. "I don't know if you can hear this at home, but a curious humming has begun," he said before putting his hand over the microphone. "Barbara, is it just my earpiece?"

The producer checked the sound board and shook her head no.

"My producer says it's not my earpiece, but instead seems to be coming from the crowd."

The camera panned around the stadium, focusing on the spectators who remained tight-lipped and expressionless, their attention riveted on the South Quay Road players.

"The humming sound is getting louder. I'm looking at the security forces, and they don't seem to know what to do," Joe continued. "From here in my booth, the sound seems to be coming from everywhere."

The low hum continued to grow until it seemed the entire stadium was reverberating. Yaba Owusu stopped suddenly and put his hands to his ears, letting Zaki Dunbar dash past him with the ball. The SQR defense scrambled to slow his run, but they could not stop him passing to Connor Shaw, who ran forward and drove a shot past the diving SQR goalkeeper and into the goal.

As the Icelton players ran to mob the triumphant Connor, the humming stopped, and the crowd erupted in a thunderous war cry. A shiver shot up Penny's spine as she listened to the ferocious sounds coming from what had been, moments before, a mild-mannered crowd.

As the players jogged back to position the humming started again, but this time very quietly. Yaba Owusu stood at midfield, drenched in sweat, while Toussaint Badeaux visibly trembled, his eyes squeezed shut.

Penny turned to Scott and Jeff. "They need to stop humming, it's making those two players mad. They need to stop now."

"Okay," Jeff said, "tell them to stop."

"Me?"

Scott nodded, not taking his eyes off the field. "You."

Penny paused, uncertain, and then stood and made a discreet crossing motion with her hand, like a bidder at an auction. The sound stopped immediately.

On the field Yaba Owusu ripped his jersey off and threw it to the ground, followed by Toussaint Badeaux. The two men stalked towards the sidelines.

Reno galloped into their exit path, waving his arms. "You will bloody well get back on the field!" he thundered loudly enough for the on-field microphones to capture every word.

Without breaking stride, Yaba Owusu put one huge hand on Reno's shoulder and shoved him out of his way. Toussaint Badeaux marched one step behind him, jaw clenched, and both men disappeared towards the players' tunnel. Reno sat on the grass where he had landed, sputtering ineffectually, a broad green stain running across the back of his pristine white shirt.

The referee, caught out by the sudden turn of events, ran toward the touchline brandishing his yellow and red cards at the retreating players.

Reno turned around to look for two substitutes to take his stars' places on the field, but the referee insisted play resume immediately and SQR were forced to play with nine men against Icelton's eleven until halftime.

As the teams left the pitch, Joe Lyons summed up the half. "We have reached halftime and the Icelton miracle continues. In the last five minutes, they scored through Connor Shaw and SQR, we think, had Owusu sent off and Badeaux booked for walking off the pitch, though both may have seen red for pushing over their manager Reno Tedesco. But even before then, Icelton have had far the better of the game.

"Charlie Moore, the teenage goalkeeper replacing Ned Winter, has had very little to do, but when called into action, has done everything with calmness and confidence. Who would have thought? He has barely a dozen first team games in his career and they were in the third step of non-league football, the seventh tier of the English game.

"As for SQR, we may be seventy rows above the dressing rooms but we might be able to hear what Reno Tedesco says—more likely screams—to his players. Frankly, they have been awful and I don't think Signor Tedesco is the right man to get the best out of his team today."

⸺⸺◆⸺⸺

Dylan watched Icelton run back on the field looking relaxed and confident. He'd kept his changing room speech deliberately low-key and positive and had mapped out a straightforward second half game plan. The players had sat quietly, offering some observations and suggestions, but no one wanted to say the obvious out loud. They had a chance of winning.

"Here comes Reno," Ned said. "Why's he wearing sunglasses?"

Dylan looked down the pitch and saw that indeed the flamboyant owner had not only changed his shirt but was sporting a pair of large, mirrored designer frames. He was standing on the touchline, talking with twenty-year-old Istvan Schwartz and nineteen-year-old Ruben Santamaria, the two youngest and least experienced members of his eighteen-man squad.

"I don't know. But I'm not seeing Gavin Keane or Serge Dumas," Dylan said, naming the SQR captain and key midfielder.

"Here they come," Alan nodded to the players' tunnel. "Bloody hell, they're in their street togs. And they've got bandages on their hands!"

"I bet they popped Reno one good in the changing room," Ned whistled. "Look, his cheek looks all puffy like."

A wide grin broke out on Dylan's face. "Reno's subbing in those two lads for his linchpin players?"

⸻◆⸻

Second half play began and South Quay Road were immediately in control. A midfielder moved forward and passed to a striker who shot, but the ball just missed the angle of the post and crossbar.

Janice, sitting next to Penny in the outside seats, sighed. "Now this is more like the Potters we all know. That was a crisp move. SQR is back to hitting on all cylinders."

Penny inched further up her seat after that play. Dylan, still looking calm, was conferring with an assistant coach and pointing to several players. A South Quay Road injury after another attack gave Icelton a pause to catch their breath, but Penny could tell they were looking over-matched.

SQR dominated briefly in the second half but faded quickly. Charlie Moore was inspired, making three great saves, twice from Santamaria and once from Schwartz. Jack Palmer, who had become captain when Tommy Peele signed for South Quay Road, was a superb leader, organizing the defense, making key tackles, and winning headers from badly directed SQR set-pieces.

"We are at the eighty-six minute mark and Icelton has barely been troubled by their Premier League opponents, who of course have played for more than 45 minutes with nine men." Joe Lyons announced. "The score is 1-0, and the Potters—after a strong 20 minutes at the start of the half—seem to have completely given up, or, more likely, run out of steam. Without Owusu and Badeaux, they have lost their shape, and even their set-pieces are shambolic. This team looks uncoached and uncertain what to do.

"Icelton is focused, determined, and frankly not facing much resistance. The Potters' defense is still holding up, but their offense is almost non-existent. This is easily the worst performance SQR have put in all season."

The referee signaled there would be four minutes of added time. Dylan and his assistants prowled the coaches' technical area, yelling for one last effort from the players. The mood in the sky boxes was triumphant, and the spectators had begun a rhythmic clap.

"Penny, Dylan wants you and his mum to get down to the front of the stands by the side of the pitch for the trophy presentation," Scott said. "We're to escort you."

Penny could barely hear him over the din. "Are they really going to win?"

"It's looking that way."

The thrill of victory surged through Penny and she let out a whoop of joy. "Let's go!"

Chapter Seventy-Three

Janice, Scott, Jeff, and Penny followed a team of security through the halls to yet more elevators until they arrived on the field. Around them the walls of the stadium were reverberating with the foot stomping and cheers from the jubilant Icelton supporters.

The last seconds of additional time were ticking down and then the final whistle blew and the fans erupted in ebullient cheers. The Icelton players mobbed their keeper, Charlie Moore, in celebration as the South Quay Road players trudged off the pitch, their manager nowhere to be seen. Dylan shook the assistant coach's hands before being surrounded by his team and lifted on their shoulders in victory.

Order was quickly restored and the team was directed up the stadium stairs to the royal box, where a row of dignitaries shook their hands. Lord Lambton handed Jack Palmer, the captain, the FA Cup, and they all turned towards the field while confetti and streamers showered them. The players took the Cup back to the field, where they were joined by their families for a victory lap.

Penny, her ears ringing, stood for pictures with Janice and answered questions from remarkably respectful reporters.

Only one was brave enough to ask if she thought Boudica was behind Icelton's win.

"No, we have to give this one to the Icelton supporters," Penny answered truthfully and heard Scott and Jeff laugh quietly behind her.

When Dylan returned to the field Penny launched herself into his arms, and their kiss was captured across newspapers worldwide.

"We did it," Dylan whispered in Penny's ear, with a palpable look of relief on his face. "We won."

"We did!"

By the time Dylan and the players finished the post-match press conference and got to the banqueting suite, the party was well underway.

Sir Frank Poleski, owner of Kingsbury Town, shook Dylan's hand heartily. "Congratulations, what an interesting game. I just saw Lord Lambton and he said he's ready for a long holiday in Barbados. What are your plans, Dylan?"

"I don't know," Dylan said. "I honestly haven't thought that far."

"Do you want to keep playing?"

"I don't think so. I'm actually liking this manager business."

"You certainly have a knack for it," Sir Frank agreed. "How about coming back to Kingsbury Town as an assistant manager?"

Dylan looked at Sir Frank in shock.

"Giles's idea, actually," Sir Frank added. "I agree though, most heartily."

The idea of managing at the Premier level staggered Dylan. "Thank you, sir, but I think I'm going to stay with Icelton for now. See if I can't get us out of mid-table in the league next season."

Sir Frank laughed. "I see from the news you're going to need to find a new playing ground. Any chance I can rent St Augustine to you?"

Dylan shuddered, remembering the decaying school in south London. "The pitch is lovely, sir, but that school..."

"Yes," Sir Frank grimaced. "Unfortunately it has been declared a National Heritage site and I'm stuck with it. I can make you a very reasonable offer, though..."

"No sir, Icelton has to stay in Icelton. But Townsend Lane Stadium is only a mile away. Would you consider a ground-share?"

⸺◆⸺

Across the room Penny was saying goodbye to Scott and Jeff.

"Congratulations, love," Scott leaned in for a kiss.

"And sorry about the mix up this morning," Jeff grinned, kissing her cheek.

"What are you two going to do now that Boudica's been found?"

"No more bloody amateur opera, that's for sure," Scott exhaled.

"Whoever decided that cover story should be shot," Jeff agreed. "We're selling the kebab shop and taking a holiday. After that, we'll see where else we're needed."

"Is she at peace now?" Penny asked.

Both men nodded. "She's at peace."

Professor Jain approached with a woman she introduced as Dr Qualley. "Dr Qualley is the Master of St John's College. That's my college at Cambridge."

"Lovely necklace," the Master complimented Penny, unable to keep her eyes off the torc. "Congratulations on your find. I understand from Professor Jain that you plan to go back to the United States to attend college?"

Penny blinked, realizing she had totally forgotten about Indiana University. "That was the plan, yes."

"I would like to offer you a full scholarship to St John's College at Cambridge. You would study under Professor Jain as a scholar."

"You mean, study history at Cambridge?" Penny was dumbstruck by the offer. "Professor Jain says the excavations at Icelton will take years. Probably decades."

The Master nodded in agreement. "At the least. You already have enough research to do three doctorates. "

Penny rubbed her fingers along the torc, the gold warm against her skin. "I appreciate the offer," she began, "but no thank you."

Professor Jain's face fell. "No?"

It took a moment for Penny to put her thoughts into words. "I appreciate the offer, I really do. And I want to stay involved in the dig. But I know you and HARP will do a wonderful job—the people you have working there are dedicated and love what they do."

"But... what are you going to do?"

"I want to study psychiatry. I want to be a doctor, and work with people with schizophrenia." As Penny heard the words come out of her mouth, it became clear to her that this was the future she wanted. "There's a lot of good research being done with drugs, and maybe I can help find a cure. Or at least invent drugs that people can take once a week, or once a month, so they can manage their condition easier. And get their lives back."

The Master listened closely to what Penny said. "That would be important work, and Cambridge would be an excellent place to do it. Let me see what I can do."

Penny carefully removed the torc from around her neck and handed it to Professor Jain. "Here, please take this. I don't think I need it anymore. She's yours to protect now."

⸎

The party was winding down when Chloe pointed at the big screen television. "Oh, my gosh! Look at Reno!"

A news broadcast was showing Reno being led away from a Gulfstream jet in handcuffs. "Media emperor Reno Tedesco has been arrested trying to leave the UK from Luton airport on a private jet this evening," the news anchor intoned. "He is being held at the request of the Italian government on tax fraud charges. There may, however, also be charges brought in London over the events in Icelton in the past year."

Reno glared at the camera following him on the tarmac as he was being led away, "This is a *fabbricazione totale*!" he declared passionately. "I will not go down without a fight!"

Chapter Seventy-Four

THAT NIGHT, PENNY AND Dylan stood at the gates to the Icelton Foundry and waited for the guards to let them in.

"You've been scratching your tattoo all evening," Dylan noted, his arm around Penny's waist while the other held the FA Cup.

"I know. I'm not sure what it means," she said, enjoying the feel of his big body against hers.

"Does it usually mean something?"

"It used to. Whenever it began to itch I knew that something was happening, or going to happen. Sort of a heads up."

Dylan nodded. "Good things, too?"

Penny thought about this a moment. "Yes, I suppose so."

The guard rolled opened the gate, a state-of-the-art upgrade from the old one. "We're just going to step into the tooling shop for a few moments," Dylan said.

The guard nodded. "Not a problem, Mr Rhea. And congratulations on the win today! I say, is that the Cup?"

"It certainly is."

The guard reached out to touch the colorful ribbons on the handle, his hand trembling with awe. "Will those chaps behind you be coming in as well?"

"No, they're letting us take it in privately for a few moments. We'll be right out."

"Right-o."

The guard unlocked the new door to the tooling shop and flicked a dozen switches. Dylan whistled through his teeth as light flooded section after section, and Penny realized it had been weeks since he had been in the building and hadn't seen the transformation. A platform with catwalks had been built over the dirt floor, the entire length of the building was reinforced with a new steel frame, and industrial lighting hung from scaffolds.

"Good Lord," he breathed. "I don't recognize the place."

"Those are state-of-the-art ground sensors," Penny pointed at a group of sophisticated looking monitors connected to hundreds of feet of cables.

"Where did they find her?"

"Over here," Penny led him across the maze of low scaffolding and pointed to an area covered by brightly patterned blankets. Dylan sat down and dangled his feet over the edge, almost touching the ground, and set the FA Cup next to him, and then tugged Penny's hand to sit down next to him. "They've discovered another four bodies that they think are two younger women and two children, there."

"Her daughters?"

"Perhaps. The DNA results will take a while. Scott and Jeff brought the blankets around, they are traditional Celtic patterns her tribe would have used. Professor Jain insisted they be laid over the graves. They also brought along some blankets for us to wear in the parade, if we like."

"The parade?" Dylan shook his head as if to clear it. "Of course, we'll have a victory parade."

"It will be tomorrow. Your mom, Gwen, and Eddie are arranging it right now. It's going to start here, and end up at the cemetery where your dad is buried," Penny squeezed his hand. "You can take him the FA Cup."

Dylan slumped over and buried his face in his hands. "Oh, my God. That's perfect."

Penny wrapped her arms around him, feeling his body heave with sobs. "Sorry," he finally said, brushing his arm over his eyes, "I still can't believe it."

"I think everyone's still in shock," Penny agreed.

"Professor Jain took your torc pretty fast at the party," Dylan laughed.

"She and Dr Qualley took it right back to the British Museum. I'm going to miss it, though. I kind of liked wearing it. I felt like I could conquer anything."

"I think the Wembley police are just as happy you won't be wearing it again, I can tell you that," Dylan said ruefully. "But I've got something else you might want to wear instead."

"Oh yes? What's that?"

Dylan reached in his pocket and took out a small velvet box, and pressed a button. The lid popped open, displaying the diamond ring nestled inside.

"Do you like it?" Dylan asked when words failed Penny.

"I love it," she breathed, the overhead lighting making the facets of the diamond twinkle brilliantly. "It's gorgeous. And the band, it's twisted, like a Celtic knot."

"Chap at Malbrey Jewellers idea. I told him I wanted to ask a wonderful girl to marry me, and that the ring needed to be as unique and beautiful as she is." Dylan took Penny's left hand and held it in his own. "Penny Adams, I love you and want you to stay here with me. I want us to have a wonderful life together, with our friends and family. Will you marry me?"

Penny felt tears spilling down her cheeks. "I love you too, Dylan. I will marry you."

"I also want you to take driving lessons," Dylan added, sliding the ring on Penny's finger.

"Yes, alright," she laughed, admiring the glittering ring. "Do you think she approves?"

At that moment, the lights cut out and the generators went silent, plunging the tooling shop into darkness. From outside they heard the muffled curses of the guards as they scrambled around the foundry yard.

Dylan's lips found Penny's in the darkness. "I know she does."

Epilogue

FROM THE FRONT PAGE of the Princeton, Indiana *Daily Clarion*:

Local Family Wins Millions in English Soccer Bet

Against staggering odds, the Adams family of Patoka, Indiana, has won almost $6,000,000 on a bet that the English soccer club Icelton FC would win the FA Cup. The FA Cup is a knock-out competition that began last August with 748 clubs across England and culminated last Saturday when Icelton Football Club defeated the South Quay Road Potters at Wembley Stadium in London.

Billy Dale, a British bookmaker, has confirmed that the betting slip is legitimate and will make arrangements for the payment, which is legal under US law.

The £100 ($125) wager was placed last November at the astronomical odds of 50,000 to 1. The payout will be £5,000,100 which, adjusting for the current exchange rate, will realize $5,930,000.

Mr and Mrs Adams declined to comment on their win. However their daughters, Ruth and Angela, issued the following statement:

We are very proud of our sister Victoria for her strength and perseverance, and share her gratitude to the doctors and staff at the Alms Park Psychiatric Hospital in Cincinnati, Ohio.

Their sister, Victoria, has gained worldwide fame for discovering the resting place of the English queen, Boudica. Victoria is a graduate of Princeton High School in Princeton, Indiana.

———— ◄O► ————

A notice appeared on the website of Her Majesty's Foreign, Commonwealth & Development Office, London:

EFFECTIVE IMMEDIATELY: Susan T Paulin has accepted the position of Assistant Director of Communications and Media Relations for the British Indian Ocean Territory.

Ms Paulin is the former host of the television show *Fraud War,* which is on permanent hiatus.

She will be stationed at the Office of the Commissioner of the British Forces, which is located on Diego

Garcia Atoll, just south of the equator in the central Indian Ocean. Ms Paulin's duties will include implementing and executing plans developed by the Foreign, Commonwealth & Development office in London, and supporting the 4,000 US and British military and contract civilian personnel stationed on the atoll. The territory is administered by a commissioner of the Foreign and Commonwealth Office in London.

Author's Note

Ever since Philippa Langley discovered the remains of King Richard III of England under a car park in Leicester, England, and the coincidental stratospheric rise of that city's professional football club to the top of the Premier League, I have been itching to write a story along the same lines. It's just too good a tale to pass up.

For those of you unfamiliar with the story;

In 1485, Richard III had been king of England for less than three years. He had seized the throne in 1483 from his nephew, the twelve-year-old Edward V, who along with his younger brother were imprisoned in the Tower of London and never seen again (for an interesting read on this topic, I recommend Alison Weir's *The Princes in the Tower*, Ballantine Books 2011). A distant relative, Henry Tudor, also claimed the throne through his mother, Margaret Beaufort. She was a great-granddaughter of Edward III's son John of Gaunt via a liaison with Katherine Swynford. When John of Gaunt finally married Katherine Swynford their children were legitimized but barred from succession to the throne, so Henry Tudor's claim was very shaky (for a graphical representation of just how much of a hereditary mess England was in circa 1483 I recommend: Shakespeare English History - War of the Roses Family Tree: Unnatural

D   e   a   t   h   s
(https://www.rachaeldickzen.com/blog/2019/11/20/shakesp
eare-english-historywar-of-the-roses-family-tree-unnatur
al-deaths)).

Nevertheless, an exiled Henry Tudor garnered the support of powerful English barons and invaded England. Richard III assembled his army, and the two forces met at the town of Market Bosworth in Leicestershire on August 22nd, 1485.

The battle, in an area later called Bosworth Field, reportedly lasted only ninety minutes (quelle coïncidence, as we shall see). It was dramatized by William Shakespeare in his play *Richard III*, in which the fallen king yells: "A horse! A horse! My kingdom for a horse!" We don't know what Richard III actually said, but contemporary chroniclers tell us that after he was killed, his body was stripped naked, thrown across the back of a horse, and taken to the monastery of the Grey Friars in Leicester. There it was exhibited for three days before the monks hastily buried him under the choir of the church.

Henry Tudor went on to be crowned King Henry VII, and in 1495 had a monument laid over the grave of his predecessor with an epitaph that read "Here lies Richard Plantagenet, sometime King of England". Henry VII ruled England for twenty-five years and was succeeded by his son, King Henry VIII, who in 1536 ordered the disillusion of the monasteries, including the Church of Grey Friars in Leicester.

What happened to Richard III's remains next gets murky. By 1540, the Church of the Grey Friars was abandoned and had fallen into ruin, and a chronicler reported in 1611 that the bones of Richard III had been dug up and thrown into a nearby river. The church property passed through several owners until the 1930s, when Leicester City Council built offices and a car park over the area.

Modern Leicester still retains part of its medieval footprint, including several streets that have been in existence for hundreds of years. Fifteenth century maps clearly show the location of the original Church of Grey Friars directly across from St Martin's Church, which is now Leicester Cathedral. In the early 2000s, the Richard III Society (http://www.richardiii.net), which has been promoting research into the life and times of the king since 1924, began to seriously investigate the idea of the king still being buried there. Their research was so promising that in 2010 they formed the Looking For Richard project, and commenced a successful world-wide fundraising effort.

Philippa Langley, who founded the Scottish branch of the society, visited Leicester in 2005 and went to the car park located directly over the original church choir. She relates in her book, *The Search for Richard III, The King's Grave* (Hachette 2014) "I was aware of a strange sensation. My heart was pounding and my mouth was dry. As I got near the wall, I had to stop, I felt so odd. I had goose-bumps, so much so that even in the sunshine I felt cold to my bones. And I knew in my innermost being that Richard's body lay here. Moreover, I was certain that I was standing right on top of his grave."

The project was granted permission to use Ground Penetrating Radar in the car park, and based on those promising results a limited excavation was undertaken. On August 25th, 2012, bones were found under an area of the car park marked 'R', which turned out to mean 'Reserved' but the coincidence was extraordinary. A remarkably well preserved skeleton, minus the feet, was exhumed, and further digging proved the area was indeed the choir of the original Grey Friars Church. At a press conference on February 3rd, 2013, it was announced that carbon dating established the bones were from the late fifteenth century, and a DNA match between Richard III and a living relative via his sister Anne was confirmed. It really was Richard III. Thunderous applause broke out and excitement spread world-wide.

A court case erupted over where the body of Richard III would be buried, with the city of York making a credible claim that he'd had a strong attachment to the city and that it was his own wish for his final resting place. Her Majesty Queen Elizabeth II, herself a direct descendant of Henry VII, wisely deferred to the courts. In the end they ruled that Richard III had spent the last five hundred years in Leicester, so that's where he would stay.

On March 26th, 2015, 35,000 people gathered to watch the horse-drawn funeral cortege of Richard III process through the streets of Leicester. The funeral oratory at Leicester Cathedral was given by the actor Benedict Cumberbatch, a second cousin of Richard III sixteen times removed. No member of the current royal family attended.

On the same day, Leicester City Football Club was in last place in the Premier League table. They had been promoted to the Premier League from the Championship the year before and had struggled all season. But nine days after the funeral, a miracle occurred. Leicester City FC hosted West Ham United and won, their first League game win since mid-January. Two more wins followed, and then a nail-biting victory over Burnley in April lifted them out of the relegation zone. They finished the season fourteenth in the twenty-team table, concluding with a run of seven wins, one draw and one defeat—to champions in waiting

Chelsea—which meant they avoided relegation by a respectable six points.

No one was impressed however, and at the start of the 2015-16 Premier League season the bookmakers had the odds of Leicester City winning the Premier League championship at 5,000:1. As a comparison, the odds of Elvis being found alive are currently 2,000:1.

But Leicester City FC caught fire and stayed on fire. They began the season with two defeats in twenty-five (out of thirty-eight) matches and were well on their way to capturing the championship, the first in the club's 111-season history. The superstitious and romantic quickly pointed out the coincidences that pointed to Richard III's help from beyond the grave—the new owner, a Thai business man, owned a company called *King* Power; one of the club's most stalwart players was Andy *King*; and a club assistant coach was named Craig *Shakespeare*.

Jaime Vardy, the captain of Leicester City, quickly got tired of answering questions about Richard III's contributions to the team's success. He pointed to the influence of the new manager, Claudio Ranieri, and his team's excellent play. The team was indeed comprised of several hidden gems who suddenly had a burst of confidence, and two of their main competition, Chelsea and Manchester United, had collapsed.

But no one was fooled—the hand of the dead king was obvious—and fans of Leicester City and romantics around the world rejoiced on May 2nd, 2016, when Leicester City won the Premier League. The final convincing nail in the coffin: York City, at the bottom of the League Two table, had been relegated to non-league status.

The story of Richard III and Leicester City Football Club is stranger than fiction, which is right up my alley. This was a tempting plot.

⚬

On a lovely Saturday afternoon in October 2016, I sat in the stands at Silver Jubilee Park in north London, watching my favorite Non-League football team, Hendon, play Tooting & Mitcham United. Silver Jubilee Park is located just west of Hendon and north of the Welsh Harp Reservoir, on the southern edge of the Edgware plain. From my seat I could see the deeply rutted car park (which has since been updated) and wondered… who's buried under there?

The list of missing British monarchs is rather short—Henry I (who died in 1135) is most likely buried somewhere under Reading Cathedral, and no one seems to care where King Harold II, who was defeated at Hastings by William the Conqueror in 1066, is buried (they're not even sure he died at the battle). But there was one British queen, Boudica, who was known to have traveled through Hendon two millennia before on her way to burn London to the ground (and worse; if you must find out for yourself the atrocities committed, I recommend *Boudica: The Life of Britain's Legendary Warrior Queen* by Vanessa Collingridge, Abrams Press 2007).

I knew I had a story. But who was Boudica?

If it wasn't for the work of Tacitus, the Roman historian and politician, we probably wouldn't even know her name, or that she existed at all. Tacitus wrote a biography of his father-in-law Agricola, a Roman general present in Britain during the time of the Boudican Revolt. Agricola seems to have passed along firsthand knowledge of the Roman occupation and the story of the revolt, as well as a picture of the tribes and life in first century AD Britain. While Tacitus is considered a reliable historian who paid careful attention to his sources, he also made no secret of his disdain for the Celtic tribes and their female rulers.

After the Roman Empire fell in 476 AD, rare copies of the works of Tacitus were preserved in Italian monasteries. During the Renaissance they were rediscovered and publicized by the writer Boccaccio and the humanist Vergil, who read them and were fascinated. Boudica was reintroduced to British history in the nineteenth century when Prince Albert championed her, causing a sensation in Victorian England. Prince Albert, who was married to Queen Victoria, pointed out correctly that the two queens shared a common name that translated to 'victory'. He also commissioned Thomas Thornycroft to create the statue of Queen Boudica that now stands in front of Parliament (and Andrew was correct; Prince Albert asked the sculptor to add the spikes, or scythes, to the cart wheels as a Persian touch).

In the second century AD historian Cassius Dio embellished Tacitus with a few gossipy details that point to at least one other source, now lost. With Tacitus and Dio the only primary sources we have for Boudica, it has been left to secondary sources and archeology to fill in the rest of her story. Here's is what we know:

- Julius Caesar does not name the Iceni tribe amongst the tribes he met when he visited Britain in 55 BC, but they were certainly there and based in the Thetford area of Norfolk. They were sophisticated and wealthy, and amongst the most advanced gold and metal workers in the world at that time; their work far outpaced anything produced in the Roman Empire. Excavations have revealed they operated at least three mints, and one of the coins minted between 34–45AD features the name of Boudica's husband, Prasutagus.

- In 43 AD the Roman Emperor Nero Germanicus (Reno is an anagram of 'Nero' and Tedesco is Italian for 'German') knew he had to get Britain under control or abandon it. Wealthy Roman investors, like the stoic philosopher L. Seneca (Len Case is an anagram of his name) were not willing to walk away from the investments they had made in Britain and pushed Nero to send a military governor who could get the unruly tribes under control. Nero chose Suetonius Paulinus (whose name sounds a lot like Sue Paulin, doesn't it?) a seasoned veteran, to head the legions in Britain. (Side note: Roman legions marched under the standard *Senatus Populusque Romanus*, or 'The Senate and the Roman People', which was abbreviated SPQR. South Quay Road Potters FC, the Premier League football club owned by Reno, is a play on this abbreviation.)

- Julius Caesar, in his firsthand account of the Gallic Wars, correctly identified Druids as a very influential group in Gaul and later noted their presence in Britain. Suetonius Paulinus knew his first job had to be getting rid of them, and his defeat of the Druids at the Battle of Mona in Anglesey, a small island sacred to the Druids off the north Wales coast, was by all accounts a bloodbath.

There is a great deal of archeological evidence testifying to the destruction of Colchester by fire in the timeframe of the Boudican Revolt. Excavators only need to dig down a few feet to find a thick layer of ash, and you can still visit the catacombs under the temple to Claudius where the town people hid, waiting for the 9th Legion to save them. London has a thick layer of fire debris from exactly the same timeframe, as well as decapitated skulls.

The missing piece of the Boudican Revolt puzzle continues to be the location of the last battle between Suetonius Paulinus and Boudica's army. Tacitus describes the battle location Suetonius chose:

> *Suetonius had the fourteenth legion with the veterans of the twentieth, and auxiliaries from the neighborhood, to the number of about ten thousand armed men, when he prepared to break off delay and fight a battle. He chose a position approached by a narrow defile, closed in at the rear by a forest, having first ascertained that there was not a soldier of the enemy except in his front, where an open plain extended without any danger from ambuscades. His legions were in close array; round them, the light-armed troops, and the cavalry in dense array on the wings. On the other side, the army of the Britons, with its masses of infantry and cavalry, was confidently exulting, a vaster host than ever had assembled, and so fierce in spirit that they actually brought with them, to witness the victory, their wives riding in wagons,*

which they had placed on the extreme border of the plain.

Many potential last battle sites across Britain have been identified and some excavated, yet as Penny says, none have yielded any conclusive evidence. Steven Kaye, in his excellent 2013 analysis *Boudica: Logistics* (http://www.bandaarcgeophysics.co.uk/arch/boudica_logistics.html) has identified and ranked a potential 110 high-quality site possibilities, whittled down from a previous 263.

Which one was it? I'm afraid I don't know any more than the next person. But the idea of Moat Mount Open Space as the setting of the last battle is just as viable as any other claim and it does fit the topographical description. Roman generals did indeed need a source of fodder for their horses and water for both troops and horses. Dollis Brook and Dean's Brook were considerably larger waterways in 61 AD.

Tacitus tells us that after the battle Boudica took poison and died, and Cassius Dio, writing one hundred years after the battle, tells us she died of her wounds and was given a lavish burial. Which one is correct? I went with Cassius Dio on this one.

What happened to the Iceni after the Boudican Revolt? Even though Suetonius Paulinus had defeated Boudica and wiped out the Druids, the Roman Senate quickly realized he was the wrong person to subdue the rest of Britain and get things back in working order. He was recalled to Rome and given a half-hearted victory parade, then continued his career as a military advisor and general. His fate remains unknown.

It took the new military governor of Britain several years to finalize Roman control. The Iceni were forbidden to mint coins, and they, along with other Britannic tribes, were probably absorbed into the post-Roman populace after the Roman Empire collapsed in 476 AD. We do know that the Iceni never returned to their lands in Thetford.

The British Museum in London is home to the Great Torc of Snettisham, which was probably part of the Iceni royal jewels. It was buried around 70 AD and discovered in 1950 by a farmer plowing a field in Norfolk, near the village of Snettisham. The British Museum also has a good collection of Boudica era coins and other metal jewelry. Across from this display case is the impression of cart wheels from cart burials in Yorkshire. Yorkshire is the only place they have been discovered, but the Iceni were known to be excellent charioteers and if Boudica's grave is ever found it would not be surprising to find evidence of these chariots buried with her.

In crafting this story, I added some fictional touches; Silver Jubilee Park became Mortager Park, a combination of two Latin words, *Mort* for death and *Ager* for field. So a death field is a cemetery. Icelton was another hint, with the Most Reverend IC Elton as the founder of the area, a red herring. The Historical Antiquities Recovery Program (HARP), is a thinly veiled mirror of the Portable Antiquities Scheme, run by the British Museum and the National Museum of Wales. The Roman historian Herodian wrote about the Britons around 200 AD but didn't mention Boudica.

Finally, I gave a lot of consideration to how a young woman from southern Indiana could have shown up in London to dig up a parking lot and make the archeological discovery of the century. There had to be a spark, and a voice in her head (also called an auditory hallucination) was a possibility. Patients experiencing high fevers frequently report them, and research has shown that head injuries and even sinus infections can trigger them. Living with Schizophrenia UK, an organization run by people with direct personal experience with the condition, is an excellent resource for understanding the symptoms, treatments, and the daily challenges of living with the condition. You can visit them at https://livingwithschizophreniauk.org.

In researching this book, I spoke with several recovering patients. They told me of the successful therapies they were using, but that the stigma they lived under, and the crippling loneliness they experienced, were almost worse than the voices in their head. They asked me to handle the malady and its treatment with respect. I hope I was successful.

Acknowledgements

Cup-Tied could not have been made possible without the assistance of family and friends who graciously shared their expert knowledge of the broad range of research topics Penny and Dylan's story required. As always, all errors are my own.

My gratitude to my editor David Ballheimer, whose patience in explaining the intricacies of British football and sorting out the timeline of Cup-Tied knows no bounds. Author Nancee Cain (https://nanceecain.com) provided much needed encouragement and direction in the field of addiction and withdrawal. Writer Angela Bell (https://hashtagretired.com) and Pip Imports and Domestics helped me craft the food and wine sections that should be making your mouth water. Georgina Waldman, PharmD, was instrumental in her support and review of the pharmaceutical details of this book—it was a fine line between having Dylan addicted but not killing him. Leah Miller, PharmD, is the inspiration for Leahzapine and a wonderful sounding board for every story idea I come up with.

Thank you to the Ver River Society (https://www.riverver.co.uk) for their help in researching the waterways around St Albans and the possibility of quays having been present along the Ver River in antiquity. Trying to fit a football club acronym to some variation of SPQR delayed this book by easily a month.

I read with fascination Steven Kaye's 2013 work *Finding the site of Boudica's last battle: Roman logistics empowered the sword* (http://www.bandaarcgeophysics.co.uk/arch/boudica_logistics.html) This is a thorough analysis of the logistics of the Roman Legions in Britain, the topography, and most importantly, the water and forage supply in every area of Britain. I recommend his very readable analysis. I will warn you, though, researching the Boudican Rebellion is a fascinating rabbit hole to fall down.

Most of all, thank you to my friends at Silver Jubilee Park and Hendon Football Club for their friendship and support.

About the Author

Marina Reznor lives with her rugby-player husband and their two Labradors in Birmingham, Alabama. She became interested in English Premier League football (or soccer as she occasionally slips up saying) when American television began broadcasting matches and she realized there were almost no commercials.

Impressed by the players' agility and stamina, Marina began following their exploits off the field. As fiction authors know, the start of a good book often begins with "I wonder what would happen if..." From the first chapters of *Cup-Tied*, the characters formed themselves and wrote their own story. Marina swears she just wrote it down as it happened.

In the course of researching English football, Marina fell in love with Hendon Football Club, a semi-professional club based in West Hendon, in the London Borough of Brent. The Kingsbury Town Football Club series is dedicated to their spirit. Visit Marina at her website, https://marinarezn or.com, and join her on Twitter @MarinaReznor and Instagram at @MarinaReznor.

While you're at her website, keep in touch with Marina by joining her charming, interesting, and very infrequent newsletter. Infrequent as in "My goodness, is the next ice age here already?" She doesn't share and she doesn't spam.